PENGUIN BOOKS

Lord of Misrule

Gareth Jones was born in London in 1951 of Welsh parentage. His family home is in Llanfihangel-y-Creuddyn, Cardiganshire. His father was a foreign correspondent for the BBC, and during his childhood he visited many parts of the world including India and the Middle East. He attended an unorthodox free school in Berlin while the wall was being built, boarded at Westminster School and studied Modern Languages at Cambridge.

After a postgraduate course at the Guildhall School of Music and Drama he became Assistant Director of the Prospect Theatre Company, then worked for several years in regional repertory. In 1978 he became Director of Productions for Theatr yr Ymylon, a Cardiff-based bilingual touring company, then branched out into television with HTV Wales. Next, he adapted *My People* by Caradoc Evans, a Cardiganshire writer, and co-authored *Solidarity* with his wife, Victoria. Both plays he directed for Theatr Clwyd, Mold. *Solidarity* was also on Radio 3 as part of the Radio–Theatre Festival 1981.

Gareth Jones is now a freelance theatre and television director, currently directing the 1930s comedy series *Brass* for Granada Television.

This is Gareth Jones's first novel. It was originally published in the United Kingdom under the title *The Disinherited*.

LORD
OF
MISRULE

Gareth Jones

PENGUIN BOOKS

Penguin Books Ltd, Harmondsworth, Middlesex, England
Penguin Books, 625 Madison Avenue, New York, New York 10022, U.S.A.
Penguin Books Australia Ltd, Ringwood, Victoria, Australia
Penguin Books Canada Ltd, 2801 John Street, Markham, Ontario, Canada L3R 1B4
Penguin Books (N.Z.) Ltd, 182–190 Wairau Road, Auckland 10, New Zealand

First published in the U.S.A. by Farrar, Straus & Giroux, Inc. 1980
Published by Gollancz as *The Disinherited* 1981
Published in Penguin Books 1984

Made and printed in Great Britain by
Richard Clay (The Chaucer Press) Ltd,
Bungay, Suffolk

For Tory, with love

AUTHOR'S NOTE

1745. Cardiganshire, trapped without roads behind the mid-Welsh mountains, was one of the most isolated, forgotten regions of Britain. The Established Church was in decline; half the county's parish churches were unclergied; and the later Methodist Revival was no more than an ardent desire in the lives of a few itinerant evangelists. Ancien Welsh customs and superstitions reasserted themselves, and a respected individual in many communities was the conjurer, who provided charms for the sick—men and animals alike—ensured good weather, and exorcised malignant spirits. There was no middle class, no buffer between the starving, ignorant peasants and the landed gentry, who kept them in subservience through high rents, short leases, evictions, and arbitrary justice. Cardiganshire's one claim to fame, and the basis of its economy, was its cattle-breeding. Not that the farmers who raised these herds ever tasted beef. Twice a year, the herds were bought for a pittance by drovers—the cowboys of Wales— and driven over the mountains to be fattened in the lusher pastures of England. The Roast Beef of Old England was never English at all; it was Welsh.

In this morass of helpless, uncomforted humanity, anyone with a message and the courage to deliver it was bound to make an impact, whether the Calvinist preacher with his vision of a life to come, or the populist agitator with his demands for a better deal in the here-and-now. For some, the Jacobite Rising of 1745, in which Bonnie Prince Charlie claimed the throne for his father, the would-be James III, was the liberation they had been waiting for. But the struggle would be far, far longer.

Welsh pronunciation has its difficulties. A few rules that should help with the names in *The Disinherited*: "dd" is pronounced *th*; "y" can be a long *e* or a short *i* or *u*; "w" as a vowel is a long *oo*. Thus: Gruffydd = Griffith; Ystwyth = Ustwith; Cwmystwyth = Coomustwith; Iolo = Yollo; Hywel = Howel.

I would like to thank my editor, Victoria Petrie-Hay, for the energy, perspicacity and love that she has devoted to this book; my agents, Elaine Markson, Jackie Baldick and Leslie Gardner, for their support and friendship; my parents-in-law, authors Sesyle Joslin and Al Hine, who gave me the courage to be a writer; my beloved grandmother Athene Seyler, who kept the wolf from the door for three lean years; my parents, Jane Ann and Ivor Jones, who gave me my Welsh heritage; and dear friend Jeanne Moorsom, in whose peaceful home I worked.

I would also like to thank the National Library of Wales at Aberystwyth, the Welsh Folk Museum at St Fagan's and the University Library, Cardiff, for their kind co-operation in my research.

10 November 1979   GARETH D. JONES

December 1745

CHAPTER ONE

GRUFFYDD STOOD ON the great rock Grogwynion and stared at his homeland.

Nothing changed, he thought, amazed. He scooped up a handful of earth and rubbed it over his face and arms. Then he lifted his ragged cloak and pissed over the edge, whooping with laughter as the torrent formed a perfect arc and plummeted hundreds of feet to the River Ystwyth. "We used to have competitions," he shouted to his son, "to see who could reach farthest upstream."

Iolo didn't give a tinker's cuss about pissing competitions. He was plaiting some stray wool into string to tie up what remained of his boots. The leftovers he stuffed into a corner that had pinched his little toe since Welshpool.

"I found this stone here, the day we left," said Gruffydd, sitting down beside him. A long narrow pebble with a hole in one end hung on a leather thong around his neck. Iolo remembered playing with it as a baby, riding cross-country in his father's arms. "My father told me that if I wore it, I wouldn't die until I stood here again."

"You said you found it in a castle."

"This was a castle," Gruffydd answered. "Once."

Iolo didn't think much of it. Just a pile of earth with a ditch round it.

"Look!" Gruffydd waved at the wooded hills and valleys hidden in the mist below them. "All this land, as far as you can see and farther, belonged to the Lord Rhys." He unfurled the yellowing parchment strapped round his shoulder under his cloak. "Here at the top"—he pointed with a grimy, calloused forefinger—"is the Lord Rhys, written in his own fair hand. And this cross at the bottom is you—Cadwaladr." This was Iolo's real name. Cadwaladr, Gruffydd had told him, was a Welsh king destined to return one day. But the English could not pronounce it, so he had always been called Iolo. "All this country should be ours," Gruffydd concluded, carefully rolling up the parchment. "And it will be, soon."

Iolo pulled his boots back on. "How much farther now?"

"Just past that bend in the valley." Gruffydd was already half-way down the hill. "But I want to show you something first."

"Miles away still!" Iolo cursed and hobbled after his father, curling his toes to hold up the soles of his boots. He couldn't see why they had come here at all. Gruffydd had been doing very nicely with the travelling circus. At last someone was paying them to be vagrant and they had a roof to sleep under, the first in Iolo's twelve years. The circus people were friendly. The fat man and the bearded lady looked so odd that nobody bothered to bait Iolo because his ears stuck out and his face was skew-whiff where his father had dropped him, aged three, off a horse outside of York. Besides, Iolo liked the circus animals. Then three days ago, in Derby, people ran around shouting that the Scottish were coming. Prince Charles Edward had beaten George II, there was a new King in London and the Highlanders were eating anyone under twenty. Iolo didn't know who this prince was but he wished the man had stayed in Scotland, where he obviously belonged, because Gruffydd had no sooner heard the news than he jumped on Black Jane, who was a performer, not a racehorse—and didn't belong to them anyway—and whipped her as far as Shrewsbury, where she died. From there, Gruffydd had done the same to Iolo on foot. No one had given them food, shelter or a kind word since England and everyone talked Welsh here, which Iolo had only picked up from his father. He didn't believe half of what Gruffydd said about the place. They'd be spending Christmas under God's roof, as usual.

Gruffydd pushed his way through the knotted undergrowth to a deep gully where a stream fell out of the hillside, white as churned milk, into a bowl hollowed out of the rock. "I used to sit for hours here," he said, pulling Iolo down beside him into a shell-shaped cave. "Sit still and listen."

Iolo heard only the water and the trees.

"Can you hear her?"

"Hear what?" Iolo squinted at him, whispering without knowing why.

"The lady singing behind the waterfall. She came out and spoke to me once, when I was very young." Gruffydd closed his eyes tight. "I think she wants to talk to you now."

Holy God! Iolo was suddenly scared. He's not going to leave me to talk to her alone? His back was sticking to the clammy wall of the cave. Beside him, Gruffydd was in a trance. She's turned him to stone with her song, Iolo thought, in a panic. Already Iolo's legs felt icy. With a great lurch, he pulled himself away and plunged into the thicket. At once he was hopelessly entangled. He stumbled over dead wood, carried branches and brambles along with him. The forest was closing in. He turned to fight it off, both fists flying, but a huge old oak stretched out its roots and grabbed him by the ankles. Iolo screamed and fell headlong. He was still flailing when Gruffydd emerged from nowhere, grinning and relaxed, to rescue him. He hoisted Iolo up into his arms.

"Did you hear her? She said we'd find a good fortune here. The new King is going to give all our lands back."

Gruffydd had once met Bonnie Prince Charlie riding out with a hunting party on a road outside of Paris. "When Charles Edward runs with the hounds," Gruffydd had shouted, waving them on with his staff as they cantered past, "the German fox will fear for his crown." The Young Pretender had wheeled about at once and leapt from the saddle—encouraged perhaps to hear a friendly word in his own language—seized Gruffydd by the arm and, suddenly dwarfed by this rugged giant of a man, replied: "With such friends, how can we still have enemies?" Then he pulled the silver brooch from his tartan cape, pinned it through the only solid patch on Gruffydd's threadbare cloak and galloped off as fast as he had stopped. Gruffydd had worn the brooch on his shirt—out of sight—ever since.

With the boy on his massive shoulders he strode along an open heath above the valley. The coarse moorland grass streamed in the wind.

"What's that down there?" Iolo steered Gruffydd's head by his long, knotted hair.

"A hunting lodge—Hafod it's called. It was stolen from my great-great-grandfather, who came back to haunt it. They called in a conjurer once, who chased him from a cat into a goat into a hare and finally trapped him, as a spider, in a bottle. Then he threw the bottle into the pool below that bridge"—Gruffydd pointed to the river where a crumbling arch joined the two rocky banks—"and said he'd banished the ghost to the Red Sea. But I dived in the same night and set him free. He must be there now." Iolo wished the ghost were safely at the bottom of the river.

"Look," said Gruffydd, as they turned the bend in the valley. "There's Cwmystwyth."

Ahead of them, grey stone cottages and farms were scattered over a couple of barren hills which toppled towards each other, smothering the river.

"It's not very big," said the boy, disappointed.

Gruffydd was lost in thoughts of his own. They had chased him as far as here, that day. Him and his father. Friends and neighbours had chased them as far as this very spot, throwing stones and sheep's dung.

"What's that grey patch on the hill there?" Iolo asked.

"Lead mines. You can pick it off the hillside. Sometimes silver too."

Iolo tugged at his father's rampant beard, which grew so long and thick that it sometimes got tangled with his head hair. Gruffydd had sworn to shave it off as soon as he quit his circus act. "You can get rid of this now, can't you? Or else no one'll recognize you here."

"Perhaps that's just as well, for the time being," Gruffydd muttered and took the boy off his shoulders. He didn't want to be known until he chose to be. He refused to be remembered as the shy, gangling boy who had fled from all company and had been ignored in turn. Let them be dazzled, first, by the new man he had become, before he revealed how they all had misjudged him. They would never recognize him—not with his vaulted chest and rolling voice, and his weather-beaten forehead lined with half a lifetime of travel. Let them wait.

Iolo trotted on ahead. He walked over the first cottage in Cwmystwyth without knowing it was there. It was burrowed into the hill like a rabbit warren, the most pitiful hovel he'd set eyes on. "Anyone there?" he shouted. No answer. He dived inside to take a look.

"Want a bite?" he asked, catching up with Gruffydd. "Weasel, I think. Just left by the fire."

Gruffydd accepted. It was their first taste of meat since leaving England, and he was starving.

"Down through the birch copse there," he said, picking at a tiny bone, "lives Dan Rowlands. He was my only friend. He pulled me out of the Ystwyth, when I was five."

"How did you fall in?"

"He dared me to jump, and I couldn't stop myself."

Iolo admired his father, even though he was daft sometimes.

"One Midsummer's Eve when I was fourteen, Dan carried an old cousin of his out from the farm, so drunk she couldn't stand, and put her down under that birch there. Then he threw back her skirts and showed me exactly how you do it. She didn't remember a thing the next day."

"Same as with that nun in Brittany?" asked Iolo, counting all the bushes and walls he'd been made to wait behind.

"No," answered Gruffydd solemnly. "That was holy communion. This was profane."

Ahead was a low farmhouse.

"Dan, Dan Rowlands!" Gruffydd shouted, running to the door. It swung open. Hens scuttled away, squawking. The room was empty and the fire had gone out. A couple of blankets were thrown over a low trestle. The only furniture was a three-legged stool and an upturned pig-trough. "He's fallen on hard times. His parents used to have a bed. Over there it stood, by the hearth."

Iolo went straight for the corner where the hens were roosting. Five, six eggs! He pulled from his sleeve one of his few possessions—a pin he had stolen from a tinker in Crewe—and pierced them in the crown. Then he threw back his snub-nosed head and sucked hard, tossing the empty shells back in the corner together with a full one that had got mixed up with the others as he guzzled.

"They must have gone out in a hurry," said Gruffydd, opening the door to the cattle shed at the other end of the room. A dead cow stared up at him from the floor, its eye sockets empty. The whole carcass was pitifully shrunken, and around the tail was tied a bright red ribbon, such as girls wear in their hair on Sundays.

"Murrain," Gruffydd muttered to Iolo, who was wiping egg-yolk off his chin onto his elbow. "Cattle plague. Like those herds we saw in Carnac."

"Why is that ribbon there?"

"It keeps away witches. This too." A branch of mountain ash was nailed above the stable door. "We had a murrain here before, when I was a boy. They tried all sorts of cures. Nothing worked until they caught the witch who'd done it. Drowned her in the Ystwyth and the cows recovered."

"Who was she?" asked Iolo, feeling uneasy. They were passing more cottages. Still no sign of life.

"Marged was her name. She lived near us, a mile from here, up on the commons. She kept herself to herself, like us, and no one gave her a thought, until the murrain came. Everyone's cows died except hers, so she had to be a witch." Gruffydd hadn't had much sympathy for the old crone until he and his father were accused of souring the milk, a few years later. He stopped abruptly. "We've come the wrong way. There's an old shack I want to have a look at."

"Ours?"

"No. Wait here." He hared up the hill before Iolo could argue. At the top he waved and disappeared. Iolo sat down under a red-berried holly tree and waited.

Could he still make the top in one go? Gruffydd had been eighteen then, and in love. Almost every night he had run this way. Cae Glas Farm sped by on the right, where dogs used to bark at him. Today it was silent. Up through the woods of Penlan, past the turf hut, now deserted, where Luke the Hermit had watched him race by, always with the same quiet smile. To his right the lead mines loomed and fell away. Two more hills, one by the fishpond with the cabin, the other just under the lake. Gruffydd's mind flew ahead of his aching legs. Sure enough. Fishpond with another hill. Straight stretch, and a steep, short sprint to the top of the bank which stopped Llyn Isaf from emptying into the valley.

"Thank God, they've not gone!"

A small wooden shack was propped up against a slab of grey rock at the other end of the lake. Gruffydd sauntered towards it, suddenly shy. How well he knew this water. White pebbles. Waves rippling eastward with the wind. Trees hanging overhead. A rich pasture by the water's edge.

"I'm back!" Gruffydd knocked at the door, then pushed. Inside, the room was just as he'd remembered it. A kettle hung from a hook above the fireplace. On a slate table, pewter vessels were laid out in a row and the cradle that Gruffydd had woven out of rushes from the lakeside dangled beside the hearth. And the box-bed. Always too narrow for the two of them, a hopeless squeeze to fit in it let alone make love as they used to. Gruffydd smiled at the patchwork blanket she had knitted, and pulled it back. Maggots were squirming in the sodden mattress. He stepped back, sickened, and knocked over a milk pail. A rat fled, squeaking. Everything had been left untouched, as in a house struck by plague.

"Halloo!" he called across the lake. Not even an echo answered. He ran behind the shack. In the ground stood two wooden crosses made from slats off the pigsty hammered together with bent nails. Gruffydd stared at them without moving, then turned away, tears streaming down his face and the long ache of guilt in his heart.

Iolo waited under the holly bush. Two ravens flew by and settled on a dead cow. Still no Gruffydd. Iolo was tired and scared. He got up and walked to the ridge where his father had disappeared. Towards the valley stood a small hut on a hillock. Gruffydd must be down there. Iolo set off. But before he reached it, he stopped short.

In the evening mist which hung low over the Ystwyth meadows, a huge gathering, men and women, old and young, stood in silence around a circle. Behind them, cattle without number grazed along the river, a black smudge on the grey landscape. Iolo had never seen such herds. In the middle of the circle stood a man with a long white beard. He wore a skull-cap and a pleated gown. In his hand was a silver staff;

beside him, a burning brazier. He lifted his staff, dashed it to the ground and fell howling on his knees, beating the earth with his fists. Suddenly he lay still, his forehead flat on the ground, then slowly and deliberately he raised his head and looked straight at Iolo. The whole crowd swung round and stared at the boy. A path to the centre of the circle opened up in front of him and the old man, smiling, beckoned gently. His gown was billowing in the wind and his body swayed inside it. Iolo felt the crowd close behind him. Two yards from the old man he stopped. A white circle was painted on the ground.

"Where is my father?" Iolo asked in halting Welsh.

"Come to me, child," whispered the old man, his eyes fixed on Iolo's. "Do not be afraid of them." His voice was low and soothing, offering safety. The others all stared at him as though his face had sprouted horns. "Come here, child," the old man crooned again. Iolo stepped inside the circle.

The crowd roared. Iolo tripped and landed on his face. "Have I caught you, Achitobel?" The conjurer dug his knee into Iolo's back and his fingers closed around the boy's throat. Iolo shrieked. He kicked and bit and scratched like a wild-cat, but the nails dug deeper into his neck until the blood flowed. Finally he lay mute, half throttled.

"See how the demon hides his ugly face! Now you will do my will. Upon your belly you will swallow up your curse. Say after me. God bless . . ." Iolo writhed and screamed again. "Behold! He is harrowed by God's name," cried the conjurer, his mouth frothing. The crowd bayed for more blood. "Say after me: God bless these herds and mend the evil I have wrought. Say it!" Iolo could not have uttered a word, even if his wits had been intact. His mouth was too full of earth. "Witness it! He will not call upon the Lord!" The old man thrust the sharp end of his staff into the brazier.

The red-hot stake was poised above Achitobel's palpitating heart when Lucifer himself descended on the crowd to rescue his lieutenant. His face was black as sin, holly and mistletoe sprouted from his limbs, upon his head were two monstrous horns and in his hands two firebrands from hell. Some saw flames leap from his mouth as he flew down the hillside, scattering all before him.

"Keep away, Satan!" The conjurer quailed inside his charmed circle, waving his staff, like a cross, at the Evil One. One torch set his gown ablaze and the other scorched his beard. He screamed and tried to tear off the gown, and then plunged like a comet into the Ystwyth.

Gruffydd quickly threw off the horns, borrowed from the bleached skeleton of a cow. Impersonating Beelzebub was a dangerous affair and he was a little shaken by his own success. Immediately the frightened crowd took new courage and surged forward, twice as savage for having been tricked. Gruffydd looked for an escape. Pitchforks, dung-rakes, hay-scythes closed in from all sides. In desperation he picked up Iolo, who was cowering, half dead, by the brazier and held the boy out at the advancing horde. "Scream. Make as much noise as you can. And throw your arms about." Iolo hissed and spat and bared his teeth, like the circus monkey when it was baited. The front row wavered and ground to a halt outside the white circle.

"Kill him," bellowed people at the back, and one man lunged at Gruffydd with his pitchfork. But nobody put a foot inside the circle. Then a bull-necked, red-haired labourer pushed his way to the front.

"I'm not afraid of that puny goblin!" He raised his scythe and aimed at Gruffydd's neck. It was the red hair that saved Gruffydd's life.

"Stay where you are, Siôn Edmunds!" A name jumped off the man's face.

Siôn Edmunds nearly dropped where he stood. To be named by a total stranger augured certain death. "Or shall I set Rolo Blacksmith onto you?" Rolo had knocked out Siôn's front teeth in a fist fight fifteen years ago. Some said the Devil had helped him. Siôn Edmunds turned tail and stumbled back through the crowd.

"He must be a demon! How else would he know Siôn's name?" cried a violent old hag with pouches under her bulging eyes.

"And you are a witch, Mali Fishpond. Do you still change into an owl at night?" The woman went pale. A gap opened up around her. "Where's your boss-eyed wife, Thomas Jenkins? Is she catching toads for her potions?" Thomas Jenkins' neighbours squinted at him and shifted to one side. "And what about your hunchback sister, Dewi Cobbler? Perhaps it's she who has bewitched the cattle?" The whole crowd was backing away. Their rage had vanished; only fear remained.

"The conjurer is dead," came a cry from the river. "Drowned in the rapids." A terrible groan swelled through the valley. The womenfolk fell to the ground, weeping. Men knelt round the dead body and tried to coax life back into it.

"Who will help us now?" wailed Mali Fishpond.

"Friends!" A bald elder with hairless, glassy cheeks raised his arms. The crowd fell silent. Morgan the Brewer was known for his wisdom. "If this man here has the power to slay a conjurer, he must be one himself."

No sooner said than believed.

"He can cure them! Let him try and cure the cattle."

"I am no conjurer," protested Gruffydd, but nobody listened or cared. The skull-cap and charred gown were stripped off the corpse and thrust at him.

It's either the Devil, Gruffydd thought, or the deep blue sea. He lifted the skull-cap above his head and solemnly crowned himself. Then he held out his arms for the gown. It was soaking wet and several stitches too small and he looked more like a scarecrow than a shaman, but the mob fell back in awe and waited.

"You will fetch me," he said at last, remembering a cure his grandmother had used for sheep's colic, "a quart of old strong wine and a bucket of hen's dung." Immediately a boy was sent running to the nearest farm for the manure and a posse of men set out for the flour-mill, where there was thought to be some wine under the floor-boards. Simeon the Miller followed them, swearing to God he had no wine anywhere. They soon returned with several gallons, still pursued by Simeon, who was covered from head to foot in flour.

Gruffydd muttered a few words of English, which might pass for an incantation. He measured the hen's dung in the palm of his hand and stirred it into the wine. For each handful, a new prayer. Then he poured the solution down the gullet of the nearest cow. The beast shook convulsively; a thin yellowish fluid gushed from its mouth.

"The demon is leaving her," cried Gruffydd, but the cow rolled over on its side, snorted and was dead.

"He has murdered my Lisbeth!" bawled a black-haired, swarthy cottager, brandishing a meat-cleaver at Iolo.

"The devil in them is strong, but I will wrestle with him." Gruffydd searched frantically for another idea. He had once seen a drunken gipsy in Ireland dancing to bring bad luck on the local innkeeper. He laid aside the gown and skull-cap and strutted about like a prize-fighter. Then, with a great war-cry, he stamped, beat his chest and plunged to the ground in mortal combat with the demon.

"Strong magic, Isaac," mumbled a grizzled old man.

"Ay, power, great power he has."

Gruffydd was in a sweat. All eyes were riveted on him, and there was not a soul who didn't see the fiend incarnate yielding before his onslaught. With a great leap he seized the conjurer's staff and stabbed. The demon snarled in pain, belched fire and flailed with its hideous claws and then breathed its last.

"We cannot rest yet," Gruffydd shouted, not daring to pause for breath. "I need firewood that has never been inside a house." Gathering parties left in all directions. In Brittany he had once seen a ceremony that they called the Need Fire.

"Where can I find herbs here?" he asked a boy with very black eyes who was following him.

"I have some dried rosemary, sir." Gruffydd held out his hand. The boy hesitated.

"Well?"

"May I be your apprentice, sir?"

"By all means," Gruffydd said gravely. "We can teach each other."

Bonfires were built up and down the valley. Gruffydd threw herbs onto the flames, muttering gibberish. Smoke rose in dense canopies and soon the valley was drowning in it.

"Drive your herds through the thickest smoke, then carry a torch up to the other farms."

Pandemonium broke loose as each farmer goaded his bellowing cows into the fumes. They kicked and bolted. One herd stampeded another; their owners cursed and stumbled. Fights broke out as friends and enemies stole one another's cattle in the chaos.

"Iolo!" The boy might be anywhere in that babel. Someone was pulling at Gruffydd's cloak. It was his black-eyed apprentice, glued to his side.

"He's by the river, sir."

Iolo was curled up under a bush, terrified. Gruffydd scooped him up and waded through the river. His disciple stared at them in dismay as they fled up the hillside.

They cut their way through deep forest. Night was falling. A conjurer jumped out at Iolo from behind each tree. Every shadow was a black gown, every patch of light a burning brazier. Soon it was so dark that Gruffydd couldn't see the end of his nose. "No point in going any farther. We'll move on as soon as it's light." So he wrapped Iolo up inside his cloak and hugged the boy flat against his chest, whispering one of his oldest stories. Iolo fell asleep to his father's heartbeat.

They haven't changed, Gruffydd thought, as he dozed off. In twelve years, no change.

CHAPTER TWO

GRUFFYDD BLINKED. ABOVE the trees a white cloud was pinned against an ice-blue sky.

A blouse on the washing line. He was dreaming of the washer-woman in Derby. A face of polished pewter and gargantuan arms wringing the last drop out of him. Gruffydd stretched luxuriously, but her bed somehow felt harder than it used to be. He groaned.

"Holy St Christopher, my back!" He was frozen solid. Field-mice were dancing on his chest and ants marched in purposeful columns up and down his spine. He scratched his back on the ground and snorted. A sea-gull cried high above the trees. Unusual this far inland, he thought, and realized where he was. His heart leapt, but not quite high enough to rouse him.

"Plenty of time," the washerwoman said lazily. "They'll never find us here." He grunted, relishing the chaos he'd left behind. That would show them. Just wait till the Prince gets here.

Gruffydd edged over onto his side, back into the forest night-time, carefully turning inside his cloak so as not to wake Iolo. He yawned and blinked again. A fairy was sitting perfectly still on a toadstool, watching him. Gruffydd sat up. He was surrounded by spirits of the forest.

"I am sorry I startled you," said the strange creature, opening a lid in the toadstool. "But we were loath to disturb your sleep." He held out something in his hand.

Gruffydd focused his bleary eyes. Cheese. He looked again at the toadstool: a knapsack. And the fairy, upon closer inspection, proved to be his would-be apprentice. Gruffydd froze. The bald dome of Morgan the Brewer swam out of the forest.

"Why did you leave in such a hurry?"

"We wished to thank you," stammered an honest, hen-pecked face—Thomas Jenkins.

"And we beg your pardon." Siôn Edmunds' red mane was several shades more sober.

"For the injury done to you, and to your familiar." Morgan threw a

21

sidelong glance at Iolo, fast asleep inside the cloak. "Please accept our excuses and our hospitality. How could we celebrate this miraculous recovery without you?"

Gruffydd rubbed his eyes. Morgan was, indeed, flesh and blood and appeared to have said what Gruffydd had heard. Miraculous recovery? The cattle? Gruffydd's first impulse was to laugh loudly, but he crushed it.

It must be a trick. They'd be murdered as soon as they were back in Cwmystwyth. But Siôn Edmunds would soon have murdered them in their sleep. Holy dread swept through Gruffydd. Who had possessed him to work this miracle? Whom was he serving? Was it an act of God or of the Devil? The impersonation of Beelzebub had surely not summoned him? Gruffydd feared for his soul, but the earnest appeal stamped on Thomas Jenkins' face delivered him. Gruffydd threw back his head and shook with laughter. One by one the villagers joined in bemused.

"Your cruelty stinks in my nostrils," he shouted abruptly. They cowered. The red-hot stake poised above Iolo's heart had flashed through his mind. It was this rabble, crawling to him now, that had hounded his father and they would pay for it later. "I should leave behind a curse to blight your cattle, crops and children!"

They wilted, bowing in submission to whatever penalty he chose.

"However," Gruffydd relented, "since you come on bended knee, I shall have pity on your innocents and forgive you."

Morgan snapped his fingers. Two boys stepped forward with barley bread, cheese and herring.

"There is a feast prepared in the village, if you will come, but we brought this in case you were hungry."

Gruffydd picked at the food with as much indifference as he could manage on a stomach three days empty. Iolo was waking up in a daze with acorns and pine needles in his hair, looking like a hedgehog.

"Just listen and keep your mouth shut," Gruffydd whispered, thrusting a herring into his hand. Iolo had no intention of saying anything. Today was beginning as uncomfortably as yesterday ended. He munched distrustfully, following every movement they made. They, in turn, stared at him, curious to see a demon eating earthly food.

Gruffydd's black-eyed apprentice sat down cross-legged beside them. Gruffydd frowned at this familiarity.

"How did you find us, then?"

The boy was unabashed. "I knew you would be here."

"How?"

He shrugged. "I am lucky. The miners say so."

"What do the miners know about it?"

"They pay me to go down with them. I show them where to dig. I am always right." His mouth curled into an arrogant smile, unshaven black down on his upper lip. Gruffydd was amused.

"What's your name?"

"Mihangel, sir."

"And where do you live?"

"With Mali Fishpond, my foster-mother. She has already taught me a little of your trade."

"I dare say she has. And will you bring *me* luck, too?"

The boy laughed admiringly. "You have it already, sir."

"That is truer than you know," said Gruffydd.

Thomas Jenkins was hovering nearby, waiting to be noticed.

"Welcome, Thomas," Gruffydd beamed. Thomas had always been teased about his stutter, which predisposed Gruffydd to like him. "Sit yourself down with us."

Thomas sat down, pulling threads out of his frayed jerkin.

"Well, what is it, man?"

"Sir, I have never seen you before in my life—and yet you picked me out of a crowd at forty paces." His mouth twitched for an explanation and the whole party waited, hungry for more wonders. Gruffydd watched their faces. The truth certainly wouldn't do.

"Thomas," he said, holding him round the shoulder with one arm and gesturing at the sky with the other. "There are more things in heaven and earth than you dream of." Thomas gazed at the firmament, expecting a revelation. "And tell that wife of yours"—Gruffydd gave him a dig in the ribs—"that unless she stops bullying you, I will turn her into a crow." Thomas looked at him with a mixture of terror and gratitude.

"Shall we go?" Gruffydd got up, and Iolo's heart sank.

"We're not going back there, are we?"

"Why not? There's a feast waiting for us."

"But they tried to kill us!" Iolo scratched the oozing scab on his neck. He was nearly in tears.

"That's all right, we're safe now. Pull yourself together, they're watching."

Two massive labourers hoisted Gruffydd onto their shoulders and the whole party set off down a woodland path. Iolo trotted as close to his father as he could get, but Gruffydd's two porters flinched from him in alarm, like shire horses from a terrier. Mihangel smiled and put an arm round him.

"They think you're a demon."

"But I'm not!" Iolo shrugged him off.

They came to a clearing, furrowed by deep trenches where peat had been cut for fuel. From his vantage point, Gruffydd could see right across the valley.

"That farm by the birch copse. Dan Rowlands lives there." Morgan looked at him curiously.

"No, sir. Your familiar has misled you. Dic Richards works it now. Dan Rowlands used to live there."

"I meant, used to. He died, of course."

"Did he, sir?" wheezed Sam Jones under him. "He was alive when he left here. How did he die?"

"Drowned at sea." Gruffydd lied through his teeth, cursing himself for having spoken at all. Trust Dan to get him into trouble.

"Poor man." Sam clucked as though his tongue were too big for his mouth. "Dan Rowlands had bad luck ever since Viscount Kirkland hedged off the common land around his farm and said it was his."

Gruffydd's mind raced. Kirkland? Never heard of him.

"Dan was left with nowhere to graze his cows," Huw Lloyd said with simple malice. Dan had once walked off with his fancy woman. "They grew so thin the drovers wouldn't buy them. Then he couldn't pay the rent, so John Ffowlke threw him off the farm as well."

"Viscount Kirkland, you mean?"

"That's him. He knows what he's doing, John Ffowlke."

Gruffydd raged inwardly. So they gave him a title! For killing off my family, cheating Dan and betraying his own people, George II made John Ffowlke a viscount. Gruffydd saw Charles Edward and his Highlanders sweep up the valley like the riders of the Apocalypse calling the usurper to judgement. Not long now and all would be put right.

The path turned downhill and they burst from the forest into bright sunshine. Cwmystwyth was transformed. The barren slopes had come alive. The herds grazed peacefully along the hillside and wandered in twos and threes among the smouldering bonfires where they'd been left until the conjurer returned with new orders. A boy ran down the stony track ahead of them shouting, "They're coming! They've found him!" His shrill voice echoed round the valley. People poured out of the farmhouses and cottages and ran laughing and cheering down to the Ystwyth to greet them, the women in their red home-spun shawls, men in flannel shirts white in the pale December sun.

Heaven be praised, it was a miracle indeed! Gruffydd's doubts vanished. It was palpably clear: he had been chosen to save his people, he had been given the power to redeem them. He bowed his head, receiving this burden with humility and sudden apprehension, then he lifted the amulet stone to his lips and offered up thanks. He had come home.

A little girl dashed up to him and held out a packet of cheese and butter. "From Ffynon Farm, sir. My mother asks you to write a charm for our sickly lamb."

"Thank you, my sweet. Your mother shall have her charm soon." He had never held a pen in his life.

A bevy of young women hurried up the track towards him and a bosomy lass with a round, innocent face dangled a strapping baby for him to look at.

"He won't grow, sir. Is he a changeling?"

"No, indeed not," pronounced Gruffydd. "I've seen many and they look far worse than him."

"Thank you, sir! Thank you. Here's a groat for you. It's not much but it's all we have till the drovers come."

Gruffydd tried to press it back into her hand but she was lost in the throng. Sam Jones and Huw Lloyd broke into a trot along the home stretch. The crowd cheered and Gruffydd waved, exuberant.

"Who stole my ribbon last year, sir?"

"The man who wants your maidenhead. He's trying to bewitch you."

"Will I have a husband before Christmas?"

"Only if you kept one of his hairs," yelled Gruffydd over his shoulder. "One of the short and curly ones!"

Sam and Huw, slavering at the finish, charged into the Ystwyth and carried Gruffydd in triumph up the opposite bank. Everyone jostled to get a view of the big man. Mothers held up babies for him to touch, fathers carried sons on their shoulders. Ismael, the blind harpist, was led to the wych-elm by the river. He sat down against its forked trunk, cradled the harp against his chest and sang extempore. He sang of Gruffydd's victory over the false conjurer, of his wrestling with the demon, of the bonfires which had purged their herds. The congregation sat in reverent silence and at last joined Ismael in an old song of welcome. It was the proudest moment of Gruffydd's life.

Iolo was sulking by the river, trying not to listen. He had had a bellyful of these people. Whenever he smiled they scowled; whenever he spoke the women giggled and the men swore. Whenever he minded

25

his own business, which he usually did, they crept up behind him and looked for horns in his hair.

Gruffydd settled down to a second breakfast. Each cottage in Cwmystwyth had brought some contribution, which he accepted with good grace while he parried their requests for potions, charms and talismans as best he could. A little girl like a corn-doll, with fair hair and blue eyes, came forward with a goat on the end of a tether.

"A present from Bryn Twrog," said her father, Dic Richards, a heavy man with huge hands like shovels. "You saved my six cows."

"That was Dan Rowlands' place. How do you keep cows there with no pasture?"

"I drive them right up to the top every morning, past the old commons that John Ffowlke hedged off."

"Why didn't Dan do that?"

"He did, at first. But he gave it up. He didn't have the patience." Dic weighed his words, as one who knew. "Besides," he added pointing to Gruffydd's mug of ale, "he took too much of that."

"He was robbed," said Gruffydd angrily.

"True enough. But a different man would have come through it." His tiny daughter milked the goat into a saucepan and offered the milk to Iolo.

At least someone isn't scared of me, he thought and took it with a smile. Dic watched the girl and smoothed out the creases in his leather breeches.

"Did nobody fight for the common land?" asked Gruffydd scornfully.

"Fight, sir?" Thomas Jenkins was puzzled.

"Did you just let them take it from you?"

"Dan Rowlands punched one of the constables," said Sam Jones, "but they arrested him."

"John Ffowlke had a new law passed," explained Old Isaac, tapping his bent nose, "which said he could take as much of the commons as he wanted."

"That's right, Isaac," said Morgan. "John Ffowlke is in Parliament."

"He won't be much longer," Gruffydd said.

"How is that, sir?"

"My familiar told me." Iolo was appalled. They all stared at him worse than before.

Gruffydd sat up on a fallen tree-trunk so those at the back could hear. "Who made this John Ffowlke a viscount?"

"The King, of course," scoffed Simeon the Miller, who hadn't forgiven Gruffydd for requisitioning his wine.

"Ay, the King," everyone agreed.

"But which king?"

"George II, sir," a young boy called.

"Very good, George II." Gruffydd clapped his hands. The women giggled. "But if a new king came along, perhaps John Ffowlke would no longer be a viscount?" The crowd shifted, straining to catch every word. "I will tell you a story," said Gruffydd, holding out his mug for another quart. "Long ago my ancestor, the Lord Rhys, ruled over all this land." He opened his arms wide and to a man they saw a wise and noble Prince sitting on his throne. "He was much loved by all his subjects, because he was one of them and cared for them. But one day"—Gruffydd pointed eastward—"the soldiers of King Henry came from England. They tore down his castles and enslaved his people. His sons and his sons' sons lived in humble cottages, and for a while their people respected them. But a time came"—Gruffydd's face clouded—"when the Welsh forgot their true princes. A time came," and his deep voice shook with passion, "when Welshmen rose with torches and spears in the night and cast my own father, who was their Prince in all but wealth, out of his last miserable hovel onto the winter hills, where he died." A low moan rose along the valley.

"Who could do this?"

You could, Morgan, thought Gruffydd. You were shouting louder than any that night.

"Where did it happen?" Thomas Jenkins' honest face was ablaze with righteous anger.

"Not so very far from here, in a place a bit like this. And they are slaves to this day."

"Where?"

Gruffydd started on his third quart. "No matter where, because very soon my ancestor will come into his own again. A Prince is coming . . . the scourge of God. With fire and sword he will drive the usurper out of these islands." There were frenzied cheers as Gruffydd jumped onto the tree-trunk and waved his beer mug. "But this Prince is merely a herald for the King who will follow, the King who has been sleeping under the hill and now returns to claim his kingdom—the sacred King Cadwaladr!" With a flourish, Gruffydd pointed at Iolo, whose head was just emerging from the saucepan drenched in milk.

Stunned silence. Isaac fumbled for words.

"But, sir . . . this is your familiar, your spirit."

"No." Gruffydd chopped the air with his hand. "This is my son."

"He's a demon," Simeon shouted.

Gruffydd hoisted the boy onto the trunk beside him.

"This is my son, and I will tell you how I came by him. Be quiet!" He hurled a lump of dead wood at Sam Jones and Llewelyn Tapster, who were arguing noisily. "I buried my father beside a lake. As I was digging his grave a herd of oxen, white as the hoar-frost, rose from the waters to graze on the hillside. They were attended by a maiden fairer than any of you can hope to dream of." Gruffydd paused, dazzled by his own vision. Too many memories were clamouring for too few words. "She approached me where I knelt and wiped away my tears. For a year I lived alone beside the lake and spoke to her daily. When the year was over I married her and went to live with her family below the lake. Her father taught me many things—to see the future, cure the sick and drive out devils. A son was born to us. At his birth it was prophesied that he and his heirs would be great kings. This is he."

Cwmystwyth was struck dumb. The hills leaned forward the better to hear him, and the river stopped dead, waiting for more.

Why? Iolo cried to himself. Why in front of them? In twelve years he had never heard his mother mentioned once, nor would he ever have asked. It was an unspoken rule of friendship between them, though he could not say why, and now this lady with the oxen was graven on his heart for ever. Gruffydd must have his own reasons for telling the rest of the story. It was beyond Iolo. Who wanted to be a King, anyway?

"Sir, will you come quickly, please?" A girl of about seventeen in a red flannel dress, wearing no bonnet or shawl, was pushing her way towards Gruffydd, her dark hair streaming around her naked arms and neck.

"What's the hurry, Madlen?" asked Thomas Jenkins, annoyed at the disturbance. She strode past him, ignoring the cat-calls of the other men, and fell at Gruffydd's feet.

"My sister Rhiannon . . . she's been in labour two days. The midwife says she'll be dead by nightfall." Her young, impulsive face stared up at him pleading. There were tear stains around her tired pearl-grey eyes, which never once flinched from his. Her voice was unusually resonant, compelling, for her age. "Only you can help now."

He knew instantly he couldn't refuse her. A jackdaw cawed in the wych-elm nearby. A good omen.

Gruffydd drained his beer mug and threw it back at Llewelyn Tapster. "I will come with you," he announced, swaying slightly.

He's gone mad, Iolo thought in alarm. He couldn't deliver kittens!

28

Gruffydd took firm hold of Madlen's hand and let her lead the way. She tried to hurry him, while the crowd jostled after.

"Siân Evans, the midwife, says there's a spell on Rhiannon's womb stopping the baby from coming out. Her husband's family are cruel to her because she's his second wife." Madlen's full red lips tightened in anger. "For hours they forbade me to come to you, though they saw she was dying."

"Why did they forbid you?"

"They are Calvinists."

"So?"

Madlen hesitated and then said boldly: "They do not believe in your art. They call it superstition."

"And what do you call it?" He smiled down at her, admiring her lithe, warm body.

"I saw you cure our cattle, sir." She glanced away, suddenly shy, sensing in him a different world. "They did not."

"Then why do they turn to me now?"

"Siân Evans has scared them with talk of this spell. And the master is away." The way she said "master" irked him.

"Who is the master? And why is he away?"

"Hywel Bevan, Rhiannon's husband." Her bosom heaved as they climbed a steep track. She leaned on him, her smooth, cold skin ruffling the hair on his forearm. "He is the leader of the Awakening here. He preaches throughout Ceredigion."

"And what does he preach?"

"I really don't understand," Madlen confessed and they both laughed. "Though Hywel has tried to explain. He is convinced I am damned," she said gaily. Gruffydd liked her irreverence.

"And that he is saved?"

"Of course." She suddenly frowned. "He is hard on Rhiannon. She thinks she will go to hell if she dies now. Three years she's wanted to give him a son."

"She won't die. That's why I am here."

"I believe you." Her face opened to him like a sunflower. He brushed a wisp of long dark hair off her flushed cheek and said: "I believe you do."

Madlen shivered. He seemed to know her already.

They came to a stone farmhouse. It was tidier than most, with a separate wooden shed for the animals and a yard around it. Cows lowed impatiently at the gate, waiting to be milked.

"Were they with the other herds yesterday?"

"No. The plague didn't spread here." Madlen shut the gate on the cows and the crowd. A dog snarled. Gruffydd hauled Iolo over the fence and followed Madlen past a compost heap to the door.

"She has been sleeping." A buckled old woman, her face wrinkled and leathery like black cabbage, met them as they entered.

"This is the conjurer," murmured Madlen.

Siân Evans screwed up her eyes at him. "You'll need strong magic here," she cackled, pointing down the long room. Hywel's family sat around the hearth watching them. An imposing woman with neat grey hair, in a black dress, was treading a spinning wheel, and a girl of about Iolo's age was reading aloud from the Bible.

"Peace be with you," said Gruffydd, his hand on Iolo's bony shoulder. "May my son sit by your fire until I am done?" The girl closed the Bible with a snap.

"If my father were here, you would not be under his roof now."

"Rachel, hold your tongue." The grey-haired woman hurried towards him. "I am Ruth, mother of Hywel, the master of this house." She looked him in the eye. A beautiful woman, though her bold face was deeply lined. "Do you come in God's name?" Gruffydd met her gaze.

"I do."

"My daughter-in-law is in the loft," she said, pointing to a ladder at the far end of the room. "Come with me, child." She took Iolo's hand. "What is your name?"

"Iolo, mistress."

"This is Rachel, my granddaughter. Rachel, go on reading." The girl peevishly opened the Bible.

"'And Moses said unto Pharaoh . . .'"

"What's Pharaoh?"

"A King," Rachel said condescendingly.

Not another. Iolo had had enough kings for one day.

The loft was just under the roof. Gruffydd bent double to reach a low pallet bed, where Rhiannon was lying in a half-sleep. An oyster-shell lamp burnt beside her. Her delicate face was as pale as a death mask; dust clotted in her tangled fair hair. She was a wasted replica of her sister. As Gruffydd sat down beside her she opened her eyes. They were green and scared.

"What is stopping him from coming out?" she breathed, and feebly grasped the stranger's hand. She had almost given up.

"Lady, have no fear. A spell has closed your womb." Gruffydd dipped a cloth into the cauldron of hot water which Madlen had brought. He squeezed it and laid it across Rhiannon's belly. He had seen farmers in Suffolk wrap their sheep in hot towels during a difficult labour.

"Whose spell? I have no enemies. Who wishes to hurt me?" Rhiannon shuddered; the pains had returned.

"I cannot tell you, but he lurks somewhere nearby." Gruffydd pitied her from his heart. Every line on her face bespoke possession. He took the oyster shell and peered into the burning oil. "I will call him up for you." He intoned a low chant. Madlen and Siân Evans watched him anxiously. "Ah . . . I think he is coming." He held the lamp out to Rhiannon. "Search very hard and you will drive him out."

Reluctantly she looked into the light.

"What do you see?"

"Nothing," said Rhiannon. He was dragging something out of her, something that should stay hidden.

"Look harder." Gruffydd held her head and forced her to look. "You must help me." Rhiannon felt him taking control of her; she wanted to yield but couldn't.

"Still nothing," she pleaded. Only the flame throwing strange shadows on the pearly shell. Then something moved beneath the oil.

"I see a face," Rhiannon said, terrified. "Black hair." A vein throbbed on her temple.

"Whose face?" Gruffydd whispered softly in her ear. His beard brushed her neck, as in a dream. Rhiannon shook her head. She wanted to close her eyes and couldn't.

A draught. The face blurred. Two dark shadows leapt under the oil, and as the flame settled, two familiar dark eyes were staring into hers. She screamed. Immediately the contractions returned.

"Hold her shoulders. She'll kill the child if she doesn't stay still." Gruffydd tore a linen cloth into strips and started lashing a flailing ankle to the rafters while the other leg kicked at him wildly. Siân Evans struggled with it until Gruffydd relieved her and Rhiannon was trussed to the roof like a Christmas goose.

Madlen was fighting a losing battle with Rhiannon's shoulders. Pray God he was doing right with her! This wasn't her sister. The fiend was in her. Gruffydd crouched behind Madlen and loosened his heavy belt. He leaned over her tense, coiled body and began to strap Rhiannon to the bed. Madlen trembled as his arms stretched round her, brushing her breasts, and his muscular chest pressed against her back. She could feel his heart pounding against her ribcage and something was leaping in the pit of her stomach. A drop of sweat trickled between her shoulder-blades and down her arched neck into

31

her hair. Then another. Gruffydd's mouth closed around it and his tongue sucked it up, his beard mingling with the short hairs on the nape of her neck. Madlen quivered. Rhiannon's distorted face stared up at her, shrieking like the banshee. Gruffydd tore up another rag and stuffed it into her mouth.

Holy God, he hasn't killed her? thought Iolo, as the screaming stopped. Rachel was explaining what would happen to him in hell, but the noises from the loft sounded far worse. Nobody round the hearth seemed to take any notice.

Gruffydd laid a hot towel over Rhiannon's swollen belly and massaged her. The sporadic convulsions relaxed into rhythmic heaves.

"He's coming," cried the midwife and thrust her pincers into the bleeding gap. Rhiannon gasped. It felt as though her entrails had spilled. One yank with the tongs and a pair of legs appeared.

"He'll be lucky. He's landing on his feet," Gruffydd said. Madlen looked on aghast. Siân Evans tugged, but the baby stubbornly refused to make his entrance. "Her stomach's seized up."

Gruffydd moved the midwife out of the way, braced his foot against the end of the bed and the baby came away in his hands.

"A daughter, lady, congratulations. And born at the full moon. She'll be a wise one." But Rhiannon had fainted. Madlen was puking in the corner. Gruffydd smacked the new child. Not a sound came from it.

"Not stillborn, please," he said in despair and suddenly noticed a thin film of tissue covering the baby from head to foot.

A caul! The luckiest talisman possible, his father had told him, preventing violent death and injury. Gruffydd tore it off and the baby, red in the face, bawled handsomely. He bit through the umbilical cord—it tasted tough and salty, like gristle—then he furtively rolled up the shrunken, rubbery caul and hid it in his pouch. He would look after it until she was old enough to understand its value. Her family would only destroy it for her.

"She makes almost as much noise as her mother!" Gruffydd laughed and handed the caterwauling bundle to an ashen-faced Madlen. She managed to raise a smile as he wiped her face with his cloak.

"Forgive me for doubting you." He smiled at her and said: "Your faith saved her. I didn't."

"A girl. It's a girl!" Siân Evans called to the silent family by the fireside as she hurried to the door.

"He has broken the spell and saved the mother. It's a girl!" The crowd burst in through the gate, yelling and cheering.

"Where is the conjurer?"

"Where is the baby?"

"Show us the child!"

Carried along with them, shoving harder than anyone, was a short, thick-set man of about thirty-five in a travel-stained clerical coat. His close-cropped curly black hair was spattered with mud and his powerful, square face was tired and worried. He elbowed his way angrily to the house, pushed Siân Evans, still gossiping, to the side and bolted the door behind him.

"Thank the Lord you are back," cried Ruth, kissing his muddy forehead. "Your wife has borne you a daughter. She was in labour for two days. Siân Evans had despaired of saving her . . ."

"So my sister Madlen called in a conjurer," said Rachel, not looking up from the Bible. Hywel stared at them in disbelief. "He is in the loft now," she added, "with my mother."

"Please understand, my son," stammered the old woman, clutching his coat. "It was hard with you away. How could I greet you, your wife dead? Siân Evans said this man was our only hope . . ."

Hywel freed himself and strode to the ladder.

Madlen was holding the baby in a blanket. Its tiny hand clasped her finger. "She has a will of her own, that's clear," she said, almost envious of her sister now.

"Ay." Gruffydd raised an eyebrow at her. "She led us a fair old dance." Madlen coloured crimson and rocked the baby as Hywel reached the top rung.

"Is she alive?"

"Very weak, but she will live." Gruffydd was bandaging Rhiannon, still unconscious, to stop the flow of blood. "And you have a fine daughter."

Hywel took the baby from Madlen and watched Gruffydd washing Rhiannon's bloody thighs. "Who are you?" he asked quietly.

"My name is Gruffydd."

"Why are you here?"

"I was called." Hywel glanced at Madlen.

"He's a healer," she blurted.

"What illness did my wife have?"

"A spell had locked the child in the womb," Gruffydd said, tearing a strip of linen between his teeth. "I lifted it."

Hywel gripped his wrist. "If you saved my wife and daughter I thank you, from my heart. But you have brought doubt and superstition into my house, and I must ask you to leave it."

Gruffydd slowly freed his wrist. "Very well." He dropped the bandages and untied his belt from the bed. Rhiannon woke as he moved her arms.

"Thank you," she said, gazing up at him. "I am indebted to you for ever." Hywel winced. Never had he seen her so radiant, never had she looked at him with such gratitude.

"Rhiannon," he groaned. Her face creased with fear at his voice.

"Forgive me." She struggled for words. "I was so afraid. God had deserted me. He was sending me to hell."

"God deserts only those who desert Him," Hywel cried, kneeling beside her. "You were assured of Grace. You had received the pledge of God's love." He hid his face in his hands while she pulled at his sleeve convulsively.

"He would rather she were dead," Gruffydd said, amazed.

"Better she were dead with Faith," blazed Hywel, "than alive with the canker of your heathenism."

"Examine your own heart for the canker." Gruffydd turned to go.

"What do you mean?"

Gruffydd looked at Rhiannon's crumpled face and made to answer but cut himself short for her sake. "I came in peace," he said mildly, "where I was called. You abused me under your own roof."

Hywel was taken aback. "By whose authority do you heal?"

"By whose authority do you preach? Are you ordained?"

"Who ordained the prophets?" exclaimed Hywel. "The Church has abandoned this country. God constrains me to save it." He banged his fist on the rafters. "God speaks to my conscience and my heart."

Gruffydd laughed. "Any poor fiend knows God well enough to imitate His voice. Ask your God his real name the next time he talks to you."

"Leave my house!"

Gruffydd was already at the bottom of the ladder. Iolo came to him, glad to leave.

"Thank you for your kindness to my son." Ruth turned away. Rachel scowled. Gruffydd opened the door and pushed into the crowd, to be hoisted aloft and carried above their heads to an apple tree half-way up the hill, in whose branches they enthroned him for one and all to pay homage.

Hywel paced up and down the room, wrestling with despair. "I travel night and day to bring light into this wilderness. God makes me His servant to awaken hundreds, yet He allows the serpent to defile my home."

Ruth pedalled the spinning wheel faster. "If you had stayed at home and done your duty as a husband perhaps we would not have fallen as easily."

"O woman," he called out in torment, "your name is Frailty. Rhiannon! Rhiannon." He had worked so hard to strengthen her, to crush those doubts which tainted her innocence and tried God's patience.

Upstairs Rhiannon cowered in Madlen's arms and pulled the blanket up to her chin to hide the baby at her breast.

Hywel slid back the window hatch. The crowd was hooting with delight. Mihangel crowned Gruffydd with a wreath of hazel twigs and Dic Richards held up his little daughter to hang a red scarf round Gruffydd's neck.

"I must speak to them," said Hywel, suddenly resolved. Ruth ran to him.

"Don't go, my son."

He held her face in his hands, and said gently: "What is our faith unless we bear witness to it? If I leave them to him now, all our work will be lost."

"Husband, stay with me," screamed Rhiannon from the loft. "It was all for your child. Tell me I will not be damned."

Hywel unbolted the door, walked out into the yard and climbed onto a slatted wheel-cart by the shed. The jubilant villagers on the hillside turned to face him.

"Show us the baby!" a few voices shouted. Hywel held up his hands and they fell silent. He could command an audience here, as elsewhere.

"Neighbours, you know me well, and I you. There are many here now who have prayed with me in my own house." Dewi Cobbler slunk behind a bush. Thomas Jenkins shuffled his feet and Morgan looked around blandly. "You know that I care only for your salvation. Neighbours, in the thirteenth book of Deuteronomy, God's Holy Word, it is written . . ." Hywel's voice hung in the air like a peal of bells. "If a prophet or a dreamer of dreams arise among you, even one who gives you a sign or a miracle"—he raised a warning finger—"and if he then says to you 'Come, let us follow other gods,' do not listen to him." Hywel spat the words out like poison. Then with great deliberation: "For the Lord your God is testing you." He paused to let this thought ferment in their hollow skulls.

"Fine speaker," muttered Old Isaac. "Knows the Bible, beginning to end."

Gruffydd watched them, perturbed.

35

"Now, friends"—Hywel's face softened—"perhaps you are wondering why this chapter and this verse? I will tell you. Just such a false prophet has arisen in our midst! A man who calls himself a healer but comes to destroy. A man who claims to drive out devils but brings them howling in his wake." His voice came crashing down in judgment. "This man is Antichrist!" Hywel's brawny arm shot out rigid at Gruffydd, who sat pinioned in the branches of his apple tree. "He saves your cattle but corrupts your souls. All those who follow him . . ." A lump of cow-dung exploded against the shed behind Hywel. ". . . forfeit eternal life!" Clods of earth, stones and branches hailed around him. Thomas Jenkins, outraged, was hurling everything he could lay his hands on. Siôn Edmunds was happy to throw anything at anyone. Gruffydd lobbed rotten apples indiscriminately and nearly fell out of the tree from laughing.

"The constables!"

Gruffydd heard horses galloping towards them and jumped down from the tree. Someone must have squealed on him already. He grabbed Iolo's arm and they fled up the hill. The crowd scattered in all directions.

A black-robed magistrate, with the sheriff and two armed constables, rode into the yard and trotted through the debris to the wheel-cart where Hywel was kneeling with a hand over his eyes.

"Are you Hywel Bevan?" asked the magistrate, an elegant young man with a ring of black onyx on his little finger.

"I am."

"My name is Thomas Powell. I have a warrant for your arrest." The magistrate flicked aside his lace cuffs and displayed a scroll of paper. "At the suit of John, Viscount Kirkland for breach of the peace and preaching without a licence."

"This rabble has nothing to do with me."

The magistrate's horse stamped nervously as the inquisitive mob crept back. "The warrant is for the disturbances you caused at Rhayader Wednesday last, Tregaron the week before, and Llangurig yesterday. Though I dare say that the judge will take this incident into account as well." One of the constables grabbed Hywel's arm and hauled him up behind the saddle. "In the name of His Majesty King George II," drawled Thomas Powell, "I call on you to disperse and return to your work." The crowd jeered and whistled and Siôn Edmunds waved a pitchfork. The four horses turned tail and cantered away.

A bit rough, thought Iolo, peeping out from behind a rock, to be stoned and then arrested for it. Gruffydd was delighted that John

Ffowlke had taken care of Hywel for him. His insults rankled and Gruffydd had no intention of turning the other cheek. He ambled down the hill, Iolo at his heels.

"You see what happens to anyone who threatens me," he said as they gathered around him again. Iolo couldn't believe his ears. "Do you know who cast the spell on the unborn child?" They were all too terrified to speak. "Sam, can you tell me?" Sam shook his head. "Thomas?" No answer. "Can anyone guess?" Iolo could hear the river splashing far below.

"It was Hywel himself," Gruffydd whispered. "I summoned the spirit who had bewitched the mother of the child, and he came. Her own husband." Gruffydd bowed his head. Even Iolo was awestruck. His father was changed out of all recognition. "Beware of this man! Look at his cattle—it's no accident they alone escaped the plague. I pity your withered lives if ever he should ensnare you."

Gruffydd held out his hand to Iolo and walked grim-faced through the crowd.

"Where are you going?" bleated Thomas Jenkins.

"It's getting late. We must be on our way."

"No, don't go, stay!" They blocked his path.

"Friends, there are others who need me elsewhere."

"But who will protect our herds?"

"Who will save us from Hywel's spells?"

"Stay with us!"

"How can I? I have no home here. No livelihood. I live on the generosity of those I help . . ."

"We will build you a house," said Thomas Jenkins.

"But where, friends? I have no land."

"A one-night house on the commons," suggested Old Isaac.

"What's that?" Gruffydd knew perfectly well. His father's last shack had been a one-night house, until these people had burned it down; but he wanted it spoken.

"There is a law," Isaac declared, "that a man owns common land if he builds his house in one night and lights his hearth-fire before dawn. As far as he can throw an axe-head will be his land forever."

"Well and good, but what am I to live on?"

Rapid deliberations.

"Master," said Isaac as their spokesman, "we have very little, scarcely enough for ourselves, but if you assure us of your good offices we will give you a pig, six cows, and a bushel of barley a month."

"Fair play," they murmured, "very fair." Only a few men in Cwmystwyth owned as much.

Gruffydd stroked his beard, muttering dubiously.

"We're not staying here, are we?" whispered Iolo. It was getting worse and worse. Gruffydd sighed.

"It's a great sacrifice, but I pity you. I will stay."

They all cheered and Thomas Jenkins danced a jig.

Holy God, thought Iolo. To live in this madhouse.

The torchlight procession swept along the hillside. Wind whipped the flames into long, fluttering pennants; glowing ashes sped upwards. Dogged, lined faces were seized for an instant, then thrown back into darkness. Dirty, matted hair clung to angular heads, hollowed with much work and little food. Women held their threadbare shawls at the neck; frayed skirts dragged in the mud, caught on briars. Furtive glances darted into the forest as an owl hooted or a fox fled to its lair. On such nights spirits walked, but the only spectres on the mountain tonight were the villagers of Cwmystwyth, their huge shadows floundering across Black Rock behind them. Far on the other side of the valley, miles above Cwmystwyth, a lonely crofter crossed himself and muttered: "The fair people are dancing tonight."

"Here!" shouted Gruffydd, at the head of the column. He had found the spot he was looking for: a broad, oval meadow with good pasturage, wedged into the mountainside like an emerald in a silver clasp. At the far end Black Rock rose vertical from the floor of the clearing to its jagged summit, a monolith without foothold or vegetation that seemed, on a clear day with clouds scudding over it, to be toppling eternally into the valley without ever moving. Round its two long sides the meadow fell in thickly-wooded, craggy slopes, steep near the top, then curving inwards in a perfect arc to where three yew trees stood in a circle around a rectangular stone. Competitions had been held here when Gruffydd was a boy, but mostly the villagers avoided the place, for it had an eerie stillness of its own which made them feel like intruders.

"This shall be my hearth," Gruffydd declared, climbing onto the stone as the last of the villagers gathered round. "I want as much turf as you can dig," he said to the women, sending them down the hill.

Madlen was lying in the tall bracken out of sight, watching the way Gruffydd had them scurry about like sheep-dogs to the shepherd's whistle. No one had ever brought them to heel like this. Madlen felt a huge pride in having persuaded him—a man of power who only ever gave orders, never took them—to follow her to Rhiannon's bedside. She wondered if she could do it again.

On the edge of the forest they were chopping down four firs. Billhooks flashed as the branches were lopped off. A gang of forty carried the tree-trunks to the yew grove, where Iolo had dug a pit for the centre post next to the hearthstone. The men heaved and groaned at the end of the horsehair rope as they raised the tallest fir. It slipped into Iolo's pit and they lashed it to the hearthstone. With a leg-up from Gruffydd, Iolo and Mihangel shinned up the yews and finally moored it safely.

Madlen saw how Gruffydd's powerful body strained in the torch-light and wondered why he didn't just order a palace to appear on the spot. After all, he was a conjurer. She was struck by the endless possibilities this suggested.

Handbarrow-loads of turf were relayed up the hillside and circular walls, buttressed by the yew trees, rose around the centre pole. As the night wore on, the men threw off their fetid jerkins and the women tucked up their skirts, leaving calf and thigh bare. Sweating faces laughed, swore and flirted, each group vying with the other to build faster. Siôn Edmunds hoisted a giggling red-faced wench into his arms and disappeared with her into the forest. A very drunk Morgan leered at owl-eyed Mali Fishpond, who sat in front of the fire, bony legs splayed open. She flashed him a toothless grin and fondled her foster-son, Mihangel, dozing beside her, while Lissi, her daughter, threw loose glances at Rolo Blacksmith.

In midwinter? Madlen shivered under her shawl as they paired off and dived for cover. She knew this happened on Midsummer's Eve. The Bevans never let her out at night but she heard the women gossip about it the next day. She pretended not to listen. They were coarse, brutish people—but at this moment she desperately wanted to be one of them. They were all so friendly with him and she couldn't bear being left out, she who had more right to be near him than any of them. She shadowed Gruffydd and waited for her chance. It soon came. Gruffydd stood back from the crowd, surveying the work. He was only twenty paces away from Madlen and alone.

Now go, she ordered herself, quaking. Five, four, three . . . She was forcing herself to get up when she heard a hefty rustling sound in the bracken next to her.

"That's it. Harder," came a breathless female whisper, and a voice very like Siôn Edmunds' said "Squeeze" and grunted loudly. Much thrashing and groaning followed. Madlen listened transfixed. Hywel always sent everyone outside when he went to Rhiannon, so Madlen had no idea of the exertions involved. Her knees were shaking. They were coming closer. Any moment they'd roll over onto her. And then, suddenly, a shrill, piercing cry rang out, and a bellowing like Morgan's bull.

Madlen was horrified and hugged the ground. But Gruffydd hadn't noticed. In fact he was starting to walk back towards the others. Before she could stop herself she was running after him.

"It's a lovely house," she gasped, tugging his cloak and trying to catch her breath.

"I didn't know you were here." Gruffydd's face lit up. He'd been looking out for her.

"I'm not," she said, and then laughed abruptly. "I just came to say thank you."

"What for?" Gruffydd smiled as if he'd forgotten.

"For helping Rhiannon, of course." She swallowed and waited, uncertain whether to leave it at that.

"I only did it because you asked me to."

Madlen was overwhelmed. It was what she wanted to hear but she wasn't convinced. "Why for me?" she said dubiously. She wasn't sure now she could handle him at all.

"Because you're the most beautiful girl in Wales." He turned and looked at her with obviously exaggerated approval, which made her cross.

"Only in Wales?" Madlen felt crosser. She didn't want to fish for compliments, nor had she meant to be compared with any other woman. She pulled away. "I must go." The smoke and the sweat in his beard and on his chest scared her. So did the hunger between her legs. "Don't think badly of Hywel," she found herself saying—why? She always thought badly of him herself. "His belief can get the better of his charity."

"You heard what he said about me?"

"Yes."

"And am I the Antichrist?" He held her by the arms and drew her in close to him.

"It wouldn't surprise me." She wriggled and was astonished to feel his mouth pressing hard down onto hers until it almost hurt.

"Now if I were Satan"—Gruffydd's tongue played with her lips—"your mouth would be scorched by now."

"It is," she said, and locked her arms behind his neck without knowing she was doing it. "But I don't believe you're Satan."

"He has nothing between his legs except a tail." Gruffydd unhooked her skirts and put his hand between her thighs. They were warm and moist, like the mossy bed of the forest. "And I have something much better than a tail." He lifted her off the ground and

40

carried her to the forest. His cloak fell from his broad, heavy shoulders as he laid her down gently and parted her legs. Her body glowed amber in the torchlight flickering through the trees and her nipples cast dancing shadows across her belly.

The washerwoman in Derby could not have been further from Gruffydd's mind as he took possession of the richest pasture in his homeland. He felt as though he'd never left, and twelve years' dusty exile were no more than a wrong turn at the signpost half a mile back.

Streaks of red already touched the hilltops when the last sod of earth was pressed into place at the pinnacle of the house.

"Gruffydd! Master!" shouted the anxious crowd. He had not been sighted for two hours.

Gruffydd wandered out of the forest, tying up his belt, to the ribald hoots of his audience.

"The fire is built," said Mihangel. "We were waiting for you to light it." Gruffydd thrust the last torch into the pile of wood and smoke rose from the hole in the roof as the sun fell through the door onto the hearthstone. He hurled Rolo Blacksmith's pickaxe into each corner of the meadow, and his claim was secure.

"Father," said Iolo, as they lay resting in his first home, "where is that lake?"

"What?" Gruffydd grunted, miles away.

"Where is the lake where my mother lives?"

Gruffydd's face tensed. He bit his lower lip and a tear slowly ran down one of the wrinkles around his eye, onto a fleck of grey hair at his temple.

"It is high above the mines on the other side of the valley. Don't ask me about her again."

CHAPTER THREE

I

JOHN FFOWLKE HURLED his periwig into the marble fireplace and roared at his frightened major-domo.

"For two hours? He's been waiting in the kitchen for *two hours*? Well, of course I want to talk to him, damn you!" Reuben bowed obsequiously and fled to the door, but Ffowlke hadn't finished with him. "There's a conspiracy in this house and you're the ringleader."

"Me, sir?" Reuben fingered the gold chain of office round his neck. "No, sir . . ."

"I've been in here all night, awake *all night*, waiting for the first hint of news, and you keep a man who was in England yesterday—yesterday!—flirting with the kitchen girls. Get out!" Reuben needed no more encouragement. "And if it's bad news," Ffowlke shouted down the corridor, "I'll string you up by your own gold chain."

He slammed the door and paced up and down his study. His shirt was filthy from the night's vigil, wine and tobacco stains on the lace front and cuffs.

"They're all out for my blood," he muttered, running his hand over his bald head. "By now everyone in the country knows who is King of England except me." The servants in his house were no more reliable than those other Welsh out there—his tenants in their revolting hovels. Ffowlke was as Welsh as they, but he'd thank no man for reminding him. "What in hell's happening out there?"

He gazed up the Ystwyth towards England, two days' ride away, but the river offered no answers. He turned to refill his glass. The decanter was empty. "More port!" he shouted, and caught a glimpse of himself in the gold-framed mirror above the fire. Grotesque. He looked like a lead miner, not a peer of the Realm of Scotland. Scotland! That still riled him.

"After all I did in Parliament for his damned Germans"—Ffowlke tried to shake the soot out of his wig—"to brush me off with a Scottish title! Kirkland, indeed!" Ffowlke had never even been to Scotland. Didn't know which end of it Kirkland was. "George II doesn't know who his real friends are." He tried to adjust the wig over his bullet head. With his puffy red cheeks, bloated from too much drink and too little sleep, it made him look like an ageing cherub.

"Damn the thing!" He threw it back on the floor. He was a wolf and didn't need sheep's clothing. "Besides, perhaps I'm not even a Scottish peer by now."

John Ffowlke stared at the astral globe standing on its tripod beside the fireplace, painted with all the constellations which governed his fate and that of Kings, and tried forlornly to reassure himself.

The Stuart star rising? Impossible! Cumberland will have sent Charles Edward packing. It was astonishing that the hot-headed Prince should have embarked on this expedition at all, let alone defeated a well-trained British army in Scotland, and then, with staggering impudence, marched into England to claim the throne for his father. The so-called James III didn't even want to be King, not after the fiasco of '15. Only a few mad Highlanders took the idea seriously. Who wanted the Stuarts back anyway? Ffowlke spun the globe. The country had got used to the Georges from Hanover. They were dull but efficient. Business was good. People got rich. And Ffowlke was in the ruling Whig party, whose fortunes were inextricably linked to the German dynasty. "There," he said with satisfaction, as the globe ground to a halt, its rusty frame squeaking. "Capricorn rising." Capricorn was the Hanoverian constellation. Aquarius, the Stuart, was in total eclipse.

A tall, burly peasant was pushed into the room, carrying a cut-glass decanter with "Port" engraved on a silver pendant. Footsteps scurried away. Ffowlke took the decanter and scrutinized the man. He knew the type: face all defiance, eyes all greed, nothing a shilling wouldn't put right. John Ffowlke had lived with it since he was a boy.

"What's your name?" He turned to fill his glass.

"Padrig Jonathan."

"And where are you from?"

"Tregaron." His face was quite impassive, but his narrow eyes followed Ffowlke closely.

"So why were you in England?"

"Droving."

"Ah! It's a fine life!" Ffowlke beamed. They were rogues to a man, the drovers. Ffowlke had sentenced more of them than he could remember for rustling, embezzlement or fraud, but it was no use bullying them. They were indispensable and knew it. You had to offer them something, not necessarily very much.

"I imagine you have the latest news from England, eh?" Ffowlke sprinkled snuff liberally onto the back of his hand. "Listen, I've a proposition to make you." He inhaled noisily, his cavernous nostrils twitched and he sneezed into his cravat. "My tenants are just about ready to sell. I could make sure they sell to you." Padrig Jonathan shifted to his other foot and waited for the deal. "But in return, I want to know everything—*everything*—that you heard in England." Padrig Jonathan smirked and nodded in agreement. "And if you lie to me, you will never drive another cow again, understand?"

Another nod, without the smirk.

"Right." Ffowlke took him to the map draped over his desk by the window. "Where was Charles Edward positioned, the last you heard of him?"

The drover slowly raised his short, stumpy forefinger and brought it down on London.

Ffowlke turned pale. "Don't play the fool with me. How did he get there?"

"Through Derby." Padrig Jonathan ran his finger over the map, looking for Derby.

"Through Derby, fine," Ffowlke spluttered. "But there were two armies between him and London."

"Charles Edward thrashed the Duke of Cumberland by Derby. Then the London army joined him."

Ffowlke sat down and poured another glass. His hand was shaking. The nervous face of Morgan the Brewer, bleary-eyed and hung-over, looked round the door.

"Excuse me for disturbing you, Your Honour, but I've been talking to Reuben . . . and he said that what I told him, about what's happening up the valley . . . being a matter of urgency . . . ought by rights to be told to you . . ." His voice trailed away.

"You expect me to listen to this drivel? Get out, you oaf!" Ffowlke threw a paperweight at him and turned back to the map. "Where exactly . . ."

Thomas Powell, the magistrate, breezily pushed past Morgan. "We caught that fellow, sir, the one who was making trouble with his hellfire rubbish. We put him in with the others last night." He took off his gloves and laid them on the map, displaying very white hands and his black onyx ring. "But after an hour he'd frightened the poor louts so much with his preaching that they begged the constable to take him away."

"Not now, Thomas, not now . . ." Thomas Powell was the son of Ffowlke's principal ally in the county and must be humoured.

"There's far more important news. Why don't you ride over to Nanteos and tell your father to get here as fast as he can?" Ffowlke picked up Thomas's gloves and steered him out.

Talbot Ffowlke, John's younger brother, lounged in the doorway, blocking their path. He was an arrogant man of military bearing and polished manners, a full head higher than John but with the same bulldog frame and more hair. His uniform, the scarlet with gold brocade of a cavalry officer, was immaculate.

"Well, John, what will you do now? Good morning, chuck." He slapped Thomas Powell affectionately on the cheek. Ffowlke pushed Thomas out.

"What do you mean, *do*?"

"Exactly what I say—do! Now that we have a new King."

"How do you know?"

Talbot nodded casually at Padrig Jonathan. "I talked to the drover as soon as he arrived."

John controlled himself with difficulty. Talbot had his finger in every pie and was constantly undermining his brother's influence. John found his presence unsettling. Talbot had been to France with the army and come back with foreign airs. He himself had only left Wales twice, to sit in Parliament.

"Rumours." He attempted to sound flippant. "I don't believe a word he says."

"Really?" Talbot was amused. "He saw Cumberland's defeated army. Has he told you?" Talbot snapped his fingers at Padrig Jonathan, who lumbered across the room and said: "Cumberland's men came running through Shrewsbury shouting that Charles Edward had sold his soul to the Devil and nothing could stop him."

Ffowlke looked at him suspiciously. Damn me if he hasn't learnt it by rote, he thought. Talbot's put him up to it. By God, I'll have his hide for this!

"Deserters, probably," he said, taking more snuff. "Talked big just to save face."

"You think so?" Talbot was surprised at his brother's composure.

"If you think I'll act on this kind of intelligence," Ffowlke said caustically, "you're a bigger fool than you take me for."

The clattering of hoofs and muffled cursing rose from the paved courtyard, and a gaunt gentleman spattered from head to foot with mud staggered in and collapsed into an armchair.

"Oxley!" John Ffowlke cried. "What's the news?"

Oxley, Ffowlke's political agent, was too out of breath to speak. He had ridden from London in three days, spending a fortune on horses.

People were hoarding all they had, prices had doubled overnight, inns were closed and no coaches were running. The last gallop through the rain over the mid-Wales mud-tracks had finished him off. "We've lost," he gasped.

"Get him a drink," John snapped at Talbot, who looked as startled as he did. Oxley downed two glasses of port and wiped his mouth on his mud-stained sleeve.

"Charles Edward beat Cumberland outside of Derby. James landed with the French at Harwich. The Duke of Newcastle, with the London army, has declared for the Pretender. The King and his family—and the Crown Jewels—will be in Holland by now, if the French fleet hasn't caught him on the way."

John Ffowlke poured himself another glass and sat down. So that was that. Wealth, power, title lay shattered at his feet.

"Those cattle, sir," said Padrig Jonathan into the silence. "Those cattle you promised me."

"Not now, blast you. Get out. Don't bother me."

"Come, brother," Talbot said sanctimoniously. "A bargain is a bargain."

"Talk to my steward," Ffowlke said, and with an automatic acquisitive reflex added: "I take fifty per cent commission on your buying price."

Padrig Jonathan ambled towards the door, his heavy boots leaving muddy prints on the Persian carpet.

Outside the door bedlam had broken loose. Everyone was shouting at once. Loud thuds, like a corpse being dragged downstairs, mingled with hammering noises and breaking of glass. John Ffowlke stormed into the hall.

"Have you all gone mad?" Trunks and travelling bags, jewellery cases, wig boxes and a portable commode were piled high by the front door. The harpsichord lay on its side and a four-poster bed was half-way down the stairs, four grooms and the banisters sagging under its weight.

A faintly idiotic head with wisps of grey hair protruding from a night bonnet leaned over the gallery.

"Don't interfere, John, we have little enough time as it is. Watch what you're doing, girl!"

John Ffowlke barged past the four-poster and caught up with his wife in the bedroom, where she was stuffing clothes from a heap on the floor into one small valise.

"Have you taken leave of your senses, ma'am?"

"I will thank you to keep a civil tongue, my good man."

He immediately apologized. Maude was indeed eccentric but she was also the granddaughter of the Earl of Caversham, the favourite of James II, and John Ffowlke, having a high respect for her pedigree if little else, usually treated her with nothing but courtesy.

"Why don't you sit down, ma'am? Come and take some port with us . . ."

"There's no time, John." Maude brushed him aside and took some pictures down from the wall. "I knew this would happen. They should never have got rid of James II, let alone invited that German over. Now James III wants his throne back and he's quite entitled to it. And *you*," she said, thumping her husband's chest with a bed-pan, "are in it *up to here*. Silly man. You should have known the Stuarts would come back. Now come along and help—the ship won't wait for ever."

"What ship, ma'am?" John Ffowlke was utterly bewildered.

"The ship I chartered for you," said Talbot from the door.

"Chartered?"

"To take you to safety. It's waiting in Aberystwyth harbour."

"I will thank you, sir," John exploded, "not to meddle in my affairs, and least of all, in those of my wife."

"Don't be ungrateful, John," Maude said in her singsong. "Talbot has been most thoughtful."

"And where do you propose, ma'am, that we should go? And what shall we live on when we get there?"

"Gold," Maude said. John could be so tiresome.

"Yes indeed, ma'am, and I have none. Why? Because all my gold is out there." John wagged his finger at the Ystwyth valley. "And unfortunately you cannot fit ten thousand acres of Wales into a ship."

"Perhaps you could win some money at game?" Talbot suggested.

"My gambling losses, sir, are no affair of yours, and if you complain of your diminished inheritance, sir, I will remind you that my wife may yet bear me a son who will cut you out of it entirely."

Talbot raised an eyebrow and said mildly: "I pray for your heir night and day."

"Now." John took his wife's arm and led her to the stairs. "We will take some port and consider what best to do."

John Ffowlke stared out of the window at the French gardens laid out by his father with such precision: triangles, squares, diamonds in perfect symmetry, hewn out of the wildest, most uncouth terrain in Britain. And beyond the garden wall, barely thirty yards away down by the river, the country and the people were as barbarous as they had always been. As soon as his back was turned they would swarm up over that wall. Weeds would sprout within weeks and those perfect triangles and squares would be obliterated. Ffowlke was not a sentimental man, but he valued that strip of civilization as he valued the rents and tithes, the tolls and tributes that his stewards squeezed from his cussed peasantry. A ship? What did Talbot take him for?

He looked up at the portrait of his father, who had survived the Revolution of '88; of his grandfather, who fought for Charles I, then backed the regicides and still got promoted to High Sheriff by Charles II; and of the many Ffowlkes of ages past who had played the great Llewelyn against the Normans and got paid for it.

There was only one way: do the same as them. George II had made him a viscount. James III would make him an earl. Ffowlke's mind was made up.

"Oxley," he shouted, striding into the hall, where clients were perched on bits of furniture and bundles of clothes, awaiting his pleasure. Oxley appeared, in a clean shirt. "I want all the members of our party here by nightfall. Anyone with property. Ride to Trawscoed for Lord Lisburne. Fetch all the electors and the wealthiest merchants from Aberystwyth. Take horses and as many men as you need. We're leaving tomorrow to meet the new King." Oxley vanished, indefatigable. Ffowlke was besieged by his impatient clients.

"That commission for my son, sir . . ."

"The letters patent for the shipbuilding yard have arrived, sir . . ."

"About my field, sir . . ."

Ffowlke caught sight of Thomas Powell in the morning room. "Ah, Thomas, where is your father?"

"They were harnessing the carriage when I left, sir," Thomas said, rising to meet him.

"Good, I'll be in my study."

"One minute, sir! What shall we do with this preacher, Hywel Bevan?"

"Put him in the stocks, I suppose." Ffowlke flicked through Oxley's despatches. "Who is he?"

"Just a farmer, but he's been causing trouble preaching. People don't like it."

"Oh?" Ffowlke looked up. "Preaching what?"

"Salvation . . ." Powell coughed, embarrassed. Religious fervour of any kind was in supremely bad taste. "He's been saying the Church is corrupt."

"Like the dissenters?"

"But noisier."

48

"Doesn't like Catholics?"

"Hates them, sir, I imagine."

"Keep him around, then. We'll try him after lunch—for preaching rebellion against His Catholic Majesty James III. A conviction might stand us all in good stead. Good lad." Ffowlke touched the boy's shoulder and went back to his study. Morgan slipped in behind him.

"Well, what is it, Morgan?" Ffowlke was getting bored with this little man. His information was useless and his ale worse.

"Well, maybe it's not very important, Your Honour . . ." Ffowlke waved his hand impatiently. "But there's a man arrived in Cwmystwyth, yesterday, says there's a new King. Lots of folk believe him . . ."

Ffowlke groaned.

II

Madlen could hear the baby sucking at Rhiannon's breast. She opened one eye and saw her sister beside her in bed, her long fair hair falling round the baby and her face lost in wonderment. Madlen closed her eyes and lay still. She wanted as long to herself as possible. If only this blissful waking sleep could go on for ever. In every second of it she relived last night in perfect detail, more intoxicating at every turn, doubly voluptuous in recollection, it swirled and throbbed inside her until she seemed to burst with it. The acrid, musty smell of bracken in her nostrils, smoke in the air, laughter, naked bodies glistening with sweat, Gruffydd's smile as he turned to her: "Now if I were Satan . . ." knowing it was inevitable and no will to stop . . . Sweet abandon. Madlen heaved a sigh and rolled onto her belly. She even forgot that it had hurt, at first.

Nightmare, Rhiannon thought and left her alone. Never wake a dreamer. The soul is out wandering and can easily get lost. It must return to the sleeper in its own time.

Madlen was lying on the forest floor. Gruffydd, a black shadow against the torchlight, towered above her, knelt beside her . . . Madlen woke with a start. It was broad daylight. She could hear Ruth giving instructions to Rachel below. A tin shovel grated on the stone fireplace.

Madlen tried to rescue those last moments. But she was awake. Furtively she felt between her thighs. No difference. She was disappointed. Would her face look different? Would Rhiannon see it from her face? Suddenly a host of doubts swept through her: Did anyone see? Had he told anyone? Madlen sat up and shook her hair.

Rhiannon looked at her curiously and leaned over to kiss her.

"Thank you for fetching him yesterday." She glanced at the baby. "Neither of us would be alive otherwise." Her escape seemed more and more miraculous. The conjurer had descended on Cwmystwyth exactly in the hour of her need, come to her bedside as though it were his real destination, identified the spell at first glance and lifted it with almost godlike despatch . . . He must have been sent. Some divine agency had brought them together. In a shaft of sunlight that filtered through the rafters, Rhiannon saw one of the old gods, descending in a shower of gold to claim his child or the Angel Gabriel appearing to a certain virgin in Galilee—a blasphemy that terrified her as soon as she'd thought it. Her mind kept wandering back to the conjurer; she remembered him only vaguely, like the tantalizing fragments of a dream. It felt as though he'd left something inside her by mistake. She had thought about those dark eyes in the oyster shell. They still scared her, though she didn't know whose they were. The conjurer must know. She would ask him one day.

"Why did you give us so much trouble, then?" She rubbed her nose in the baby's face and offered her to Madlen to admire.

"She's beautiful," Madlen said, half jealous. The baby's face was like a rose, red and wrinkled. She stroked a cheek with her little finger and it dawned on her: perhaps she was with child herself?

"Were you with them last night?" Rhiannon asked secretively. "Building the house?" She had stayed awake until dawn for Madlen to return with news of the conjurer. Madlen hesitated, then nodded. Could she tell her the rest? She usually told Rhiannon everything.

"I'm glad you helped. We owe him so much. But don't tell Ruth." Madlen nodded and handed back the baby. "Dewi Cobbler came by this morning and asked for you."

Dewi was one of many who had courted Madlen, none with any success. It jarred on her even to hear his name now.

"Listen, my love," Madlen said earnestly. "I have something to tell you." But a sudden cloud crossed Rhiannon's face. She hadn't even thought of her poor husband, wherever he might be.

"Hywel will be all right, won't he?"

"He'll be fine." Madlen squeezed Rhiannon's hand.

"Will they let him go?"

"I expect so." Madlen threw a shawl round her shoulders and climbed down from the loft. Rachel, cleaning cinders from the fire, watched her walk to the door. She followed the easy sway of Madlen's hips under her petticoats, the slight tremor of her breasts, and quoted those verses on Potiphar's wife. Never, Rachel swore to herself, whatever the shameful changes taking place in her own body, would she flaunt herself as Madlen did. All those men who came to her poor father's prayer meetings . . . Rachel understood enough to know what they were after.

It was a sullen day. Mist hung in the pine trees on Black Rock. What is he doing now? Madlen wondered, splashing cold water over her face and neck from the rain barrel behind the house. Keeping an eye on the shed and the path up the hill, she lifted her skirts and washed away the blood on her thighs. He did that, she thought, amazed. As the water settled, her face looked up at her from the barrel. She smiled. It was a good face. She turned her head to one side, trying to catch her profile as she teased out the knots in her hair with a comb that she kept hidden under a stone by the barrel. But however much she squinted, the side of her face always eluded her. She had never seen it. Not once. It worried her now. Was she as beautiful from the side?

As she turned to pick up her shawl, she saw Ruth watching her by the shed door, a pile of logs in her arms and with that look of reproach that Madlen hated more than anything in the five years she had lived here.

"Well, help me, child," said the old woman. Madlen took the logs and put them on the pile in the shed. Then she followed Ruth up the hill for more. Another day. Same chores. Same struggle to be grateful to these people, who never laughed, never cried, always prayed.

"Where were you, child?" asked Ruth gently, as they walked side by side. Madlen knew what was coming. Why should she have to lie to them if she went out for half an hour? She was a woman now.

"I was with the others up on Black Rock," she said, and held her breath.

"Good, child. Always tell the truth." Madlen was a difficult girl. Not insensitive to goodness, but stubborn, hard-hearted even. "They nearly killed your father last night."

"Hywel is not my father," Madlen blurted and instantly regretted it. Why did she always fall into that trap? Honesty never paid.

"You live under his roof, child, and eat his food," Ruth said with a wan smile, "and he cares for you like his own." Precious little the girl brought in return.

"I am sorry." Not the moment for a quarrel. She had a quick temper and had learnt to use it to good effect, but the best of instincts were inadequate against the Bevans' implacable righteousness. If they'd taught her anything, it was to lie. "I will always be grateful for Hywel's kindness. I am sorry I joined them last night."

"I know that he forgives you." The girl's will was broken, but she should not get off lightly. "But for your own sake, perhaps you should confess your fault to him yourself?"

And so it always ended. Madlen would go to Hywel, explain her misdeed and ask his forgiveness or, worse still, be made to humble herself in a prayer meeting before the whole family, sometimes even with outsiders there. How could Rhiannon bear to watch? Madlen was more ashamed for her than for herself. But Rhiannon was not her confident big sister any more. She had changed so terribly. One day they were playing hide-and-seek together behind the tombstones while their father gave his sermon to a congregation of six; the next day their father was dead and Rhiannon was betrothed. They had both lived in an open coffin since.

Madlen pretended to look for wood as far from Ruth as possible. Rhiannon couldn't love Hywel—she'd hardly known him before they were married. It made Madlen sad for her sister, but angry too. What call did Rhiannon have to throw herself on Hywel's charity? Their father had left a little money. They could have managed, together, and Madlen wouldn't have minded working for herself. But Rhiannon had said yes that very day.

Madlen was suddenly appalled at herself. How was she any different? She scarcely knew the man up there. A complete stranger. She hadn't even waited for him to ask. It made her feel sick. Not one man in Cwmystwyth had laid a hand on her though plenty had tried, and one or two of them she liked and knew well. She knew nothing about Gruffydd. Couldn't even picture his face, now. Just a beard and two eyes.

"Anyway, he's probably moved on by now," she muttered, trying to disentangle a log from thick brush, "house or no house. With that queer son of his." She was crying. She had no idea why. It wasn't the stranger. If she didn't know him, what matter if she never saw him again? But something was lost. Given once, never to be given again. Squandered! She was surprised at the deep anger that welled up out of her for thinking that. Who else in this country was worthy of her? No other man was fit to hold a candle to him. She had done wisely and no one was to reproach her, not even herself. She was glad of her choice. Proud to have got him. Hers to give and she'd given freely, without conditions and without regrets. And if God had blessed her, she had a young conjurer in her womb today. Her eyes were dry. She could see

Gruffydd clearly now. She remembered why she had wanted him, and she wanted him again.

Rachel was waiting in the shed when Madlen came down the hill with her load.

"My mother wants to talk to you." If only Madlen could say "my father" as Rachel said "my mother" she would have no trouble here, though it was said with as much feeling as "my dog" or "my stick". Rachel could remember her real mother only as someone who had dressed her, fed her and occasionally dangled a ball made of cotton for her to play with. When her father told her one day that Mam was in heaven she accepted it quite naturally. "Heaven," Hywel always said, "is a step away." And then, later, when he said to her, "This is your new mother," she had accepted it with the same obedience. Mothers were not the point. It was her father she worshipped—who was always right and told her she was thrice blessed. Anything that offended him offended her, and recently her mother had offended her a great deal.

Rhiannon was kneeling at the top of the ladder, braiding and unbraiding the same lock of hair. She grasped Madlen's hand. The baby sagged in her arms like a bundle of washing.

"Madlen, my love, run down to Brithgoed and see what John Ffowlke has done with Hywel."

"Shush." Madlen took the baby and changed its soaking linen. "Hywel can look after himself. This one can't." Rhiannon looked on distractedly.

"But I've been so worried for him. What if they send him away somewhere? Oh, please go!"

Madlen knew this anxiety. Scarcely a day when Hywel was away that Rhiannon didn't torture herself with worry. Remorse, making up for not loving him. The baby should have changed all that, but no . . .

"If it makes you feel better, I will go. But you will have to make my peace with Ruth—"

"I will. I will."

"—because there isn't nearly enough wood yet." Madlen handed back the clean baby. "You should be happy," she said, a little sadly.

Rhiannon smiled. "I am." And again, "I am. Now go." She shooed Madlen away.

Madlen needed no prompting. Anything to get away. Brithgoed was a good morning's walk down the Ystwyth. She opened the front door, just a crack. Ruth and Rachel were nowhere. She made a dash for the forest. Behind the first tree she looked back. No one had seen her. Why so secretive? she asked herself. I'm only going for Hywel.

She headed down to the river where the path was smoother. Madlen liked the river. Before her father died she used to play ducks and drakes with the boys in the pool below Hafod. People said it was haunted but Madlen hadn't cared. Spirits held no fear for her.

This isn't the river! She had turned off on the higher path, cluttered with fallen timber. *It'll take forever this way.*

No it won't, said another voice, obstinately lying, inside her. The path was rough, but her heart shouldn't be beating quite so fast.

You can't do that. You promised Rhiannon to go to Brithgoed.

We are going to Brithgoed, the voice lied again, just as her feet turned sharp left and raced up the hillside towards Black Rock. *Just for a minute. He won't be there, anyway.*

She scrambled over the rocks, tearing her skirts on brambles and thorns. Brithgoed was forgotten. He'd better be there, she thought, he'd better be there.

Madlen emerged from the woods just below Black Rock and climbed cautiously up to the meadow. No one about. It was odd to see a house, round like a beehive, where yesterday there were just trees and a standing stone. Branches, turf and ashes were scattered around the meadow and a cauldron lay on its side, milk dripping from it. Madlen leapt from turf to tussock, her torn skirts hitched way above her ankles. She stopped beside the doorway, and then crept inside. He was there, still asleep. She smiled and then saw with a shock how old he was. His bearded face, so strong last night directing the whole village, had deep lines around the eyes and forehead. Of course—why hadn't she thought?—he had a son. Must be thirty at least. Maybe twice her age! Madlen realized with a jolt that Gruffydd was not one of the smooth-faced boys who tried to flirt with her in Cwmystwyth. But if older, it was also a kinder face than she remembered. She shouldn't be here. He should have come to her this time, if he wanted her.

She got up to go.

Why didn't he wake? Madlen was annoyed. She couldn't stay here for ever. She kicked over a log. Still not a stir. Was he dead? She knelt down beside him. Gruffydd was rigid. Where was his son? Had he killed him and run off? Madlen put her ear to Gruffydd's heart. Beating, all right. Pounding in fact. She looked up at his face again. Transformed. His wide eyes were laughing. Every line in his face had sprung alive. He looked like a boy of ten. Roaring with laughter, Gruffydd threw his arms around her and kissed her all over her face and neck. She gasped for breath and struggled away.

"I only came to see if you needed anything," she said, sitting up.

"Just the pleasure of seeing you again." Gruffydd brushed away some dirt that had stuck to her skirts in the scuffle.

Madlen faltered. Wasn't that what she wanted him to say? But she wasn't such easy game. He must have said as much to dozens of women. She wanted more this time. She wanted to see inside of him. She wanted to share his secrets.

"Please don't think that I . . ." Madlen couldn't finish. Who knew what he thought of her?

"You were very brave," he said kindly, watching her tear the bark off a twig by the fire. She had long, slim hands with round half moons at the base of her finger-nails. Clean, agile hands, not made for working. "I hope I didn't hurt you?" He knew he got carried away sometimes.

"No. You were very gentle. Thank you," she said flatly, longing for him to say more. He seemed so remote.

"It was none too soon," Gruffydd said, breaking firewood over his knee. "Most women are mothers at your age."

"Perhaps I will be."

Gruffydd looked at her intently. "Perhaps you will." It was the last thing he needed right now. He laid more wood on the fire and blew the embers into flame. Madlen held out her hands to warm them. She was determined to have an answer.

"What'll I do when I grow big? I can't stay at Hywel's and no man would have me."

Gruffydd had never thought of these things. There had always been a road the next day, leading somewhere else. She was a fine girl, Madlen, but not worth changing a lifetime's habits. And there were other reasons, too.

"Did you see Iolo outside?" Madlen shook her head. She was heartbroken. He wanted none of her. Gruffydd went out and rescued some of the milk from the cauldron.

"Iolo!" he shouted up at the hills. "Iolo!" Perhaps the boy was hunting for their breakfast. "Hope he's not too long," Gruffydd muttered and went back in.

Madlen was hunched over the fire, her head bowed in perfect misery.

"Listen," said Gruffydd, crouching behind her and encircling her with his strong arms, "the best to be said for maidenhood is that you can only lose it once." Madlen tried to shake him off.

"Because afterwards you have nothing else to lose . . ."

"But much to gain," Gruffydd interrupted. "Listen. I knew a woman, once, who inherited a small fortune from her father. She

55

decided to keep it all as a dowry and hid it in her meadow. Men came by her house and never stopped because it looked so poor. No one ever asked her to marry, though she was convinced the right man would come. Finally, when she was seventy, she fell ill and needed the money. By then she couldn't remember where she'd buried it."

Madlen started laughing through her tears. He made her feel better, somehow, though she knew she had been rejected.

Gruffydd wanted her more than ever. She was very rare. All her moods were contagious. He was nearly crying himself. "Silly story, really," he said.

"No, a good story. Where did you get this?" She fingered the long pebble hanging on his chest. "Do you always wear it?"

"Yes. I found it," he said evasively, and lifted her hand to his lips.

Madlen felt a pang of jealousy. Another woman must have given it to him.

"Has Hywel ever told you that line in the Bible?" Gruffydd asked. "Which one?"

"About not burying the talent you've been given." He put his arm around her waist. Her hair smelt of pine needles and last night's love-making.

"Hundreds of times. Practically every day."

"Well, then, you should take his advice." Gruffydd laid her gently on the floor and put his hand on her breast.

No, not so easy, this time. She longed to take him, but more than that she wanted to keep him. She jumped up.

"I should be in Brithgoed by now."

"What have you got to do there?" Gruffydd was irritated.

"I promised Rhiannon to see how Hywel was."

"Do you care?"

"Yes," said Madlen. "I don't like him but he's been good to me. Besides," she added, "there's a man down there wants to marry me. Perhaps it's not too late."

"What man?" Gruffydd tried to sound indifferent.

"Quite wealthy. Good-looking too. A bit old, but then who can help that?" She smiled blandly.

Impudent hussy. Gruffydd was angry with himself for feeling slighted.

Madlen threw her shawl round her shoulders, kissed Gruffydd on the forehead and collided in the doorway with Old Isaac, who had arrived with six calves, one pig, a bushel of barley and a large deputation from the village.

"Always in a hurry, Madlen!" hooted Sam Jones.

"Up early today, Madlen!" Huw Lloyd blew her a kiss through his fleshy lips, while Sam stuck one finger in the air and slapped his thigh continuously.

"It's the early bird catches the worm."

"Quiet, out there!" Gruffydd appeared in the doorway, furious. "The business she came on is beyond you. If you trouble her further, I'll turn you into geese, the lot of you." There was a sudden hush. Sam shifted uneasily, wishing he were elsewhere.

"No offence, Madlen."

Madlen looked at each one in turn, then slowly headed for Brithgoed. I'll get you . . . all of you. And you watch out for yourself, too, Gruffydd Conjurer.

Gruffydd left them outside for half an hour to clear his mind, then called them in. Without knowing why, they all found themselves whispering. This wasn't the house they had built with such festivity last night. Gruffydd had taken possession of it and his uncanny presence stretched from wall to wall. The bare turf breathed his secrets.

Gruffydd knelt by his hearthstone. They all squatted around the fire as he murmured an incantation, his eyes closed. They looked round uncomfortably. It was a lonely place.

"Where's his familiar?" blind Ismael whispered to Simeon.

"Not here." Simeon scoured the shadows. "Running errands for him. Back in hell. How should I know?"

Gruffydd turned to Old Isaac. "The spirits are propitious. Proceed."

"We brought you our gifts." Gruffydd nodded, unimpressed. "And we wish to consult you on an important matter . . . Gwilym, you tell him." Isaac tapped his nose nervously at a swarthy cottager to his right. Gwilym cleared his throat. He expected nothing from the conjurer, having threatened his familiar with a meat-cleaver two days ago when his cow Lisbeth had died from Gruffydd's evil potion, and at this moment Gwilym couldn't think why he'd come at all.

"I have a field. At least . . . well, ay . . . there's the point."

"The field's mine, as everyone well knows." A rotund farmer with greasy chops and drooping blond whiskers dug at his party for support.

"Ay," they chorused loudly.

"Quiet!" Gruffydd rapped with a stick on the hearthstone. This seemed to impress them, so he did it a second time. "You will speak when I tell you. Now you!" He pointed the stick at Gwilym.

"Well, sir." Gwilym plucked up his courage by kneading the black and white sheep-dog crouched beside him. "I've worked the field the last ten years. Then Joshua here rents Cae Glas Farm next door from John Ffowlke and John Ffowlke tells him the field goes with it. But I've always worked it, so by rights it's mine." There were a few muted "Ayes" from his corner.

Gruffydd turned and tapped Joshua on his ample belly with the stick.

"Well now, you see," Joshua began expansively, "I have a paper here and it says the field is mine . . ." Gruffydd took the evidence and perused it attentively, not understanding a word. But it had the Kirkland seal on it.

"What does it say, master?" Isaac's nose twitched like a blood-hound's. Gruffydd gave his judgement.

"It says here that the field belongs to Cae Glas Farm . . ."

"There." Joshua beamed as his friends shook his hand. Gwilym got up to go. Gruffydd stopped him with his stick.

"However, there is an ancient law of Hywel the Good, whereby anyone enjoying undisturbed pasturage for eight years or more may not be deprived of it, not even by the owner. And that includes Lord Kirkland. Cae Glas owns the field, but Gwilym here has sole right of usufruct for as long as he may live. No more argument. This hearing is closed."

"Lord Kirkland would say otherwise," Joshua blustered angrily.

"He may say what he likes. The ruling stands."

"Lord Kirkland will hear of this." Joshua collected his friends and left.

"Much good may it do him," Gruffydd shouted and roared with laughter. The assembly watched him, amazed.

"I thought it was clear for Joshua," blind Ismael whispered, "with John Ffowlke behind him."

"Ay, ay," Isaac nodded wisely to himself, chewing an old straw. Gwilym, lost for words, seized Gruffydd's hand and strode out with his dog.

"What else?" Gruffydd asked, delighted with himself. He had never wielded authority before, but it came naturally and gave him a pleasurable self-respect. He was just beginning to feel at home in his new job when two horses galloped up outside and Samson the Constable appeared in the doorway, saying, "Viscount Kirkland wants you."

"And so, friends," Viscount Kirkland was saying to the Whig electors gathered in his study at Brithgoed, "our only hope lies in going to meet Charles Edward with loyal greetings before his soldiers arrive to wring them from us." Ffowlke squeezed his handkerchief in his fist to demonstrate their likely fate and then wiped away the sweat trickling from under his wig.

A long silence followed his tirade.

"Will James III restore Papism?" asked John Stedman of Strata Florida in total dejection. His ancestors had thrown out the monks during the Reformation. Henry VIII had given them the abbey and its rich lands. And now to be dispossessed by Jesuits . . . Ffowlke attempted to reassure him.

"If we rally to him we have some hope of preventing it. Any more delay will only push him further towards the Pope and the Tories."

"Lewis Pryse and the Tories have gone to join Charles Edward already," said William Powell, Thomas's father, a distinguished county gentleman with grey whiskers on his prominent cheek-bones.

This news alarmed them all. Lewis Pryse, leader of the depleted Tory faction, had been waiting twenty years to throw the Cardigan-shire Whigs out of office.

"I'm for going," declared Evan Pritchard stoutly, his jaw jutting like the prow of one of his ships. Personally he was quite happy. The new King might confiscate land, but not boats. And perhaps the French would re-open the salt trade.

"The Powells will go, of course," said Thomas enthusiastically. Thomas had once been presented to George II at a levée.

"*Where* are you from?" The King had scowled up at him from his commode, badly constipated after an evening of sweetmeats.

"Cardiganshire, sire," Thomas had repeated, blushing as the royal member pissed noisily.

"Ah, Wales," George had rumbled, with a heavy German accent. "Lots of beef." And he'd heaved with laughter. Thomas didn't see the joke, but apparently he'd found favour because the royal bowels had been vacated shortly afterwards as a direct result of the hilarity he'd occasioned. Thomas's refined sensibility had been outraged and he secretly transferred his allegiance to the King over the Water. Charles Edward was in far better taste. Not that Thomas stuck his neck out. The Powells were all Whigs and so was he, especially since Lord Kirkland had made him a magistrate. But he would shed no tears for George II.

"So," Ffowlke said, "that is settled, gentlemen. We leave to-morrow." His guests took their leave of him until the evening banquet.

"What have we here?" Thomas Powell laughed, leading them into the mahogany-panelled hall, now cleared of Maude's luggage. "A cave-dweller?"

A huge countryman was standing impassively in the middle of the floor, dwarfing the spacious room. If he moved, he would bring the chandelier down. One jerk of his wrist and the porcelain on the mantelpiece would shatter. Beside him sat Samson the Constable, like a faithful dog. They crowded round, inspecting him as though he were some rare beast brought back from the Colonies. John Stedman poked him.

"Is he a performing bear?"

"No, sir," shouted Thomas Powell through the laughter. "A Scotch Highlander. For they wear no breeches, you know." The man's sinewy legs were bare below his fantastical plaid cloak.

"You'll be doing homage to the Highlanders soon enough, Thomas Powell," Gruffydd said calmly.

Abrupt silence.

"Dammit, an educated bear! Speaks English." But the others had gone. Jokes about the Scots were more than they could stomach. Powell followed them foolishly into the morning room, leaving John Ffowlke surveying Gruffydd and being scrutinized in turn.

Gruffydd was disappointed. So this was the man who had robbed his family of its inheritance. He'd imagined a man very like himself—the reverse side of his own coin, a worthy adversary. Instead, here was this paunchy little runt bustling round his doll's house with toy courtiers in attendance. He was not worth the spit to roast him on. How did someone like this keep thousands under his thumb? Why should they obey him? Had Gruffydd come all this way to find no better object for his revenge?

"In here," Ffowlke said. The man was staring at him unconscionably. "You speak English, don't you?"

"I do." Gruffydd walked into the study.

"Where did you learn it?"

"In England."

"But you are Welsh?"

"As you are."

Ffowlke tried to lean casually against the fireplace. This man somehow wouldn't be dominated. He sat down at his desk but that felt worse, if anything. "You have travelled a good deal?"

"Only in Europe." Not a trace of irony in his voice. John Ffowlke had never seen the Channel, let alone crossed it.

"I see." He pretended to read a report on Gruffydd. Never let a Welshman past the Severn—he comes back insolent and far too clever. There was something unnatural about him, like a slave who whistles. John Ffowlke knew where he was with his tenants: invariably they wanted something from him. A Welshman who wanted nothing was an aberration. From there it was only one step to equality.

"I hear you made quite a stir in Cwmystwyth," he said affably, settling for politeness.

Gruffydd nodded, accepting the implied compliment. Ffowlke forced a laugh.

"Admit it, though. It was a fluke, wasn't it?"

"If you sentence a man and he hangs, would you call it a fluke?"

Ffowlke smiled wanly. Those eyes were more than just insolent. "So you claim to have magic powers?"

"As the man hangs, so the cows were cured. Your word works one miracle, mine another."

Ffowlke grunted. The man talked in riddles.

"Who taught you your art?" he asked, then cursed himself for being so gullible. With his sophisticated London acquaintance John Ffowlke had played the fashionable cynic, losing heavily at cards with feigned indifference and claiming to be an atheist. It never quite worked. As he tossed his fortune onto the gaming table, Ffowlke was obsessed with the laws of fate which would make him win or lose. Even as he ridiculed the notion of divinity, he feared the thunderbolt that would strike him dead.

"My father was once saved by one of your sort," he said, trying to draw Gruffydd out. "One minute death rattle, next minute downing a bottle of Burgundy. All the fellow did was walk round the bed two or three times muttering something in Latin." Ffowlke stopped and gazed at Gruffydd's face. "He looked a bit like you."

"There are many mysteries in our art," Gruffydd said darkly.

"I dare say. And what is your line?"

"I can see the future."

"Indeed?"

"Most certainly. I can tell you the exact time, place and manner of your death, if you wish."

"No. Not now." Ffowlke backed away. "How did you learn all this?"

"It cannot be learnt. You are born with it."

"Born with it!" Ffowlke laughed incredulously. He had fought for everything in life, even for his mother's milk.

"It is inherited," Gruffydd said, unperturbed. "Like aristocracy."

"And how did you inherit?" Ffowlke was contemptuous and fascinated.

"I will tell you." Gruffydd poured two glasses of port. "Seven generations ago my family were Princes. They ruled this land." He handed John Ffowlke a glass.

"Thank you," Ffowlke said absently. Gruffydd sat opposite him, beside the fire, in Ffowlke's leather-covered armchair.

"One day, my ancestor, the Lord Rhys, went hunting with his kinsmen in his own country. This was the time of the great Glyndŵr's rebellion and they fought for his cause . . ." Ffowlke made a feeble attempt to interrupt. He felt a stranger at his own hearth, but the conjurer's beguiling, liquid voice washed over him, numbing all resistance. " . . . High above the hunters, to their right, an eagle followed them, which they welcomed as a good omen. But they searched fruitlessly all day and found nothing. Not a deer, not a fox. Night was falling when they entered a long, wooded valley. None of them had known it was there, so well was it hidden. Beside a stream a strange creature was grazing, half lion, half lizard. It was a fine prize and they chased it. But just as they were gaining on it, another party rounded the far end of the valley and stole their prey from them and made off with it. From their colours, they were Welsh supporters of King Henry against Glyndŵr. The Lord Rhys pursued them but his horses were exhausted. On the ridge of the hill, as the thieves disappeared, the last rider turned, raised his crossbow and fired one bolt. The eagle fell like lightning from a clear sky. As the Lord Rhys dismounted and knelt beside it, the eagle said to him, 'Eat of my flesh, even to the seventh generation. Though they drag you down, yet shall you soar.'" Gruffydd threw a burning brand back into the fire. "The Lord Rhys did as he was bidden. So did his son and his grandson. In me, the seventh, the prophecy is fulfilled."

Ffowlke woke as from a deep sleep. It was dark outside.

"If you can read the future," he said thoughtfully, "tell me this: who will be King of England tomorrow?"

Ah, Gruffydd thought, at last we have it.

"Tell me. Are we right in riding to meet Charles Edward?"

So that was the plan? Gruffydd was worried. It hadn't occurred to him Ffowlke might make his peace with the new King.

"No," he said abruptly, as though receiving a revelation. "Charles Edward is a comet, nothing more. Tomorrow he will be gone. You and I will see far greater changes." Gruffydd muttered a spell, spun the astral globe beside the fire and left John Ffowlke staring at the swirling zodiac.

"Capricorn rising," Ffowlke said, horrified, as it came to a halt. "The Hanoverian constellation."

But the conjurer was gone.

IV

"Iolo!" Gruffydd shouted desperately. Still no answer. The house was dark, the fire dead. "Iolo!" His voice echoed off Black Rock, mocking him.

"I've lost him," Gruffydd said to himself, scrabbling on all fours for two dry twigs. "He's gone." It was not just that Iolo was his best and only friend, though life would be unbearably empty without him. No. Iolo was Gruffydd's only hope of redemption.

Gruffydd thought of those two crosses by the lakeside. What sense did her suffering make, how could he possibly justify himself to her, if her son had chosen to spend his life as a circus turn? For that must be where Iolo was heading. He had friends there who would welcome him back. It had been cruel to drag him away, but the boy had grown up knowing nothing of his real home and scarcely spoke his own language. For so long Gruffydd had waited for the right moment. If this was not it, it would never come.

"Light, damn you!" His wrists were aching from rubbing the twigs together. A faint glow appeared on the smooth wood. A spark jumped onto the tiny pile of dry grass and caught. Gruffydd breathed on it and gingerly laid the finest sticks on top. They kindled just as the flame was dying. At last the fire was alight and Gruffydd huddled close to it, thrusting his toes into the meagre flames, too cold to move and too hungry to stay still.

And what now? Run after him and bring him back? Wait till Charles Edward arrived? What was the point if he had no heir to pass his land to when he'd recovered it. Or should he stay here as conjurer and marry Madlen? He felt absurdly possessive of her. Could he be in love with her? No, he was too old for that. But he needed her and couldn't wish it away. He could have used her warmth and young resilience now. But marry her? He thought of all those faces, those different bodies and different souls he had known, and relived with each that relief at moving on, as though barely saving an ancient covenant with himself.

Perhaps those crosses by the lake had changed all that. If he had known, he might never have returned. It was for Iolo, mainly, and for Iolo's mother . . . Though there were other reasons. His father had to be avenged. All across Europe that thought had sustained him. Yet now that he was back, the connection between an old man dying in the snow and the ridiculous stooge who had questioned him at Brithgoed seemed hopelessly remote.

And so what?

A noise behind him settled the issue. Gruffydd didn't turn around. He knew it was Iolo.

The boy sat down opposite him. "Any food?"

"No," Gruffydd said curtly, "unless you want to grind that." He gestured to the sack of barley standing by the wall.

"Whose calves are those outside?" Iolo asked. He had stopped to watch them grazing.

"Ours." Gruffydd had completely forgotten about them. The morning seemed far away now. "How many are there?"

"Six." None had strayed.

"They should be all right for tonight. And the pig?"

Iolo shook his head. "Didn't see it."

"It can't be lost, can it?" That was all they needed. Gruffydd was feverish from lack of sleep. He kept nodding off and waking up with a jerk to the hollow feeling in the pit of his stomach. A grunt came from the doorway and a long snout protruded round the side. With much snuffling, the pig pushed past Gruffydd and slumped down beside the fire.

"He knows it's home," said Iolo. "Not likely to get lost again."

Gruffydd reached for his knife. "We could have him for dinner."

"No. Mustn't waste him. I'll catch a rabbit in the morning."

So the boy was staying after all.

"I was arrested today," Gruffydd said.

"Oh?"

"They took me to Brithgoed. John Ffowlke wanted to meet me." He watched Iolo for any sign of interest.

"Well?" Iolo said at last.

"He's scared to death. Wanted to know if the Stuarts would win. I told him no." Gruffydd laughed. "He'll be surprised when they get here."

"And what will happen then?"

"Things will change." Gruffydd held the boy between his legs and they both stretched out their hands to the fire.

"How?" Iolo was glad to be back safe and warm with Gruffydd. It was the longest he'd ever been away from his father and the thoughts that come when one's alone had frightened him.

"Many ways," Gruffydd said in his ear. "Everything will be turned on its head. Ffowlke and the gentry will be thrown out. The poor will be rich and we will get our lands back."

Iolo had thought about this. He couldn't imagine it. Strange things had happened to them since they came here, but that would be stranger still. The poor were always poor. Everyone knew that.

"I told John Ffowlke about the Lord Rhys." Gruffydd pointed suddenly over Iolo's shoulder. "Do you see how that flame is shaped like a sword?" Iolo looked into the fire.

"Yes," he said, seeing nothing.

"That is our family sword. And you must seize it bravely." If only the boy could understand the task that lay before them.

"Father, are your stories true?"

"How do you mean?" Gruffydd sounded uneasy.

"I was up by the lake all day, the one above the lead mines. I waited there till it was dark, but I didn't see anything."

Gruffydd rocked him gently to and fro and the boy closed his eyes.

"Will my mother speak to me?" Iolo asked as he dozed off.

CHAPTER FOUR

I

JOHN FFOWLKE WAS clinging for dear life to the highest chimney of Brithgoed.

I'm going to die, he realized, incredulous.

The Ystwyth had burst its banks, had invaded the house and was now steadily creeping up the gabled roof. Below the water, Ffowlke's French garden resembled a sunken city.

"My ark!" Ffowlke commanded as black clouds rained liquid grape-shot. But there was no ark. "God, why me?" he wailed and the thunder answered: Because you betrayed your King.

"This is absurd!" Ffowlke made a last effort at reason. "Floods don't happen nowadays." But the Ystwyth was tugging at his feet, wrenching him away from that last chimney-pot. Ffowlke shouted and woke up. His night-shirt was soaking.

"Too much port," he mumbled and held back his soaring head. Through the diamond-paned window of his bedroom the sky was clear, the full moon like daylight. He was already asleep again. His head went on falling long after it reached the pillow.

And now he was back at the coronation of George II in Westminster Abbey. But however similar the ceremony, he was uncomfortably aware that this was not the first coronation but a second. Just as the King bowed his head, an eagle flew through the main door straight up the nave, snatched the crown from the Archbishop of Canterbury and disappeared with it into the clerestory. Now Ffowlke had a crossbow in his hand. Without hesitation he aimed it and shot the eagle through the heart. The bird plummeted and desposited the crown beside King George. Ffowlke was a hero. Then the Archbishop of Canterbury turned into the preacher Hywel Bevan who had been so unco-operative at his trial yesterday, and started lecturing Ffowlke about his drinking habits, which irritated him so much that he woke up again.

Eagle? Second coronation? With a pang of anxiety, Ffowlke remembered Gruffydd. He had sat up till two, drinking compulsively to bolster his courage and trying to dismiss the conjurer's prophecy as arrant fantasy, but the more he jeered at it, the more he believed it. He had finally passed out in an orgy of indecision.

"Too late to back out now," he said and forced himself to sleep. But he was awake. There were three hours till dawn and Gruffydd inhabited every minute of them.

Reuben, Lord Kirkland's servant, knocked a second time at the door.

I won't have to shake him, will I? Unhappily he pushed the door ajar.

"Come in, you ass! And get me Dr Madog." John Ffowlke was lying rigid, his face deep purple.

"Don't touch me," he gasped, as Reuben tried to drag him up onto the pillow. "Get the doctor."

Within minutes the household was at his bedside. Maude sat next to him tenderly swathing his forehead in cold compresses that made him shudder. Dr Madog, an ex-Welsh Fusilier whose only medical experience was of holding down wounded men during amputation on the battlefield, clutched Ffowlke's wrist and shook his head.

"Fast, very fast." Ffowlke's guests and neighbours looked worried.

"Bad humour, today, Your Honour," Madog barked, as if on parade. He rolled up the sleeve of his threadbare red coat and pummelled his lordship mercilessly. Ffowlke cried in pain. The spectators winced and turned away.

"Won't be on his feet for a week," muttered William Powell. John Stedman nodded glumly.

"Too much bile and not enough blood in the microcosm, Your Worship," pronounced Madog, tossing Ffowlke onto his stomach and pounding his buttocks. Ever since his colonel had called him a rogue and a coward and cashiered him with ten strokes of the lash and no pension for leading his platoon at Blenheim on a lengthy outflanking movement to the local alehouse, Madog had seized the retributive purpose of medicine and wielded it like a knout against all those in authority. John Ffowlke, for his part, submitted without protest. Madog was the father confessor to an over-indulged stomach.

"Friends," Ffowlke said stoically as he came up for air, looking decidedly worse, "give me half an hour and I will be with you." He threw his legs out of bed to show willing.

"Out of the question, sir." Madog glowered. No one escaped that easily.

"Take care, John," Maude cried.

Another attack set in before Ffowlke was on his feet. Thomas Powell and Evan Pritchard rushed to support him. Anxious faces peered at him through the curtains of the four-poster while Madog wiped a ladle on his coat-tails and fished in his jar for his favourite leech.

"Friends," Ffowlke croaked, "I am in despair. My flesh fails me in the hour of our need." William Powell comforted him.

"Calm yourself. My son will lead your party to England and present your humble apologies to His Majesty."

Thomas bowed. "Delighted to be of assistance."

Talbot was lurking near the door. Not for a moment did he believe this charade, but no news had arrived since yesterday, so why should John back out? He's just got cold feet, he thought. This is my chance.

"Come, Thomas," Talbot said, taking his arm. "We will ride together. Gentlemen?" He ushered them out.

"This is the leech, sir." Madog held it up for Ffowlke's approval. "Zachariah, I call him. The best in Wales."

"Later, Doctor, later," Ffowlke said feebly. "Reuben, give the good doctor some breakfast. Cheese, herring, ale . . . whatever he wishes."

Outside in the courtyard, horses stamped and grooms ran to and fro. Talbot and Thomas Powell were exchanging bawdy jokes.

Ffowlke stood at the window and watched them ride up the Ystwyth towards England. "Safe journey and God be with you." He poured himself a port. Energetic Zachariah had fallen on the floor in his hunt for nourishment. "What a terrible accident." Ffowlke raised his heel from a glob of black pus mixed with blood. "Poor little fellow."

He got back into bed and slept peacefully till noon.

II

The stony-faced warden of the Aberystwyth gaol would admit no visitors.

"Please, sir, he hasn't seen his new daughter yet."

The gaoler shook his head and slammed the door. The baby woke and started bawling.

"Shush," Rhiannon whispered. "What shall we do now?" She instinctively turned to Madlen.

"First sit down," said Madlen patiently. Rhiannon shouldn't have come at all. After a day spent eavesdropping in the kitchens and ante-rooms of Brithgoed for any mention of Hywel, the only news that Madlen had returned with was that he was being held in Aberystwyth gaol—which was worse than no news at all. Rhiannon had wept inconsolably and then towards dawn conceived it as her sacred duty to visit Hywel and comfort him. In such a frame of mind nothing could stop her. If only Gruffydd were with them, he'd have spirited them through any number of closed doors.

Rhiannon sat down on the edge of the town well, in the middle of the market-place. She glanced nervously at the men drinking outside the Sailors Inn and slipped her blouse off one shoulder to feed her baby. Her resolve had withered as Thomas Jenkins' cart clattered and jolted along the rutted tracks into Aberystwyth. She had meant to be so brave but with every mile her fears seemed more real, less imagined. She shivered. Her face was paler than the morning. A numbing wind blew in off the sea and the ten-foot breakers crashing around the ruins of Aberystwyth Castle sent icy spray across the quays and the market-place.

"I told you no visitors," said the warden angrily, having climbed the thirty-two steps from his guardroom with a separate curse for each one.

"I know, sir." Madlen put her foot in the door. "I just thought you might lack for company. We have come so far. Could we not sit by your fire for a while?"

Steffan Turnkey, or Crooked Steffan, as he was known in the town—not for his dishonesty, which was equally proverbial, but for the hunch on his back—had never had guests before. People said that the gaol, buried deep in Aberystwyth Castle, was the gateway to hell and that Steffan made an extra penny by carrying damned souls to Lucifer, which was why his hunch got worse by the year. Not even Leisa, the whore of Little Darkgate Street, could be enticed into his lair, though she boasted to have slept with Satan himself and borne him a son which she had left one January night on Pen Dinas Hill for the father to collect. So a free request for shelter from a woman, and a woman, unlike Leisa, with straight legs and all her teeth intact, was enough to make Steffan stop and think. A smile broke on his face like a rift through granite.

Madlen ran to collect Rhiannon.

"Once he's talking," she whispered, "you look for Hywel."

Steffan looked askance at the baby and led them down a steep and narrow stairway carved out of the rock.

At the bottom they squeezed through a crack in the wall to a tiny hollow chamber lit by a single taper. The straw on the floor was clotted with ordure, animal bones and remains of food. The fetid stench of urine rose from the far corner; the only other sign of human habitation was a blanket and two bottles of ale, one of them half full.

Steffan crouched on the blanket and beckoned to the women to sit down.

Rhiannon looked around, her bowels churning. Dear God—if this was how the warden lived, what were the cells like? Steffan groped around in the corner by his blanket and pulled out an object swathed in a dirty cloth that had once been fine white linen.

"Guess what this is." He leered at them.

"What is it, sir?" Madlen asked.

"Guess."

Madlen nodded to Rhiannon and went over to Steffan to look at it. It was round and shapeless and might contain anything under the wrapping.

"Is it an egg?"

Steffan laughed out loud.

"A piece of coal?"

He shook his head and giggled. The woman was stupid. Rhiannon gathered her skirts and crept up the passageway on tiptoe. By the stairway she looked back. Steffan's face was criss-crossed with a thousand lines of childish amusement and scorn, while Madlen frowned in exaggerated puzzlement.

"God bless and protect her!" Rhiannon felt her way along the damp tunnel. No light at all up ahead. A hand stretched out of the darkness and caught her arm. She strangled a scream and ran back the way she came, and stopped by the taper on the stairway. "Just a crust of bread, for our Lord's sake," came a dull voice behind her. It was only some poor prisoner. She tried to calm her terrified heartbeat. She took the taper and retraced her steps. The haggard old woman who had asked for bread covered her eyes with her hand, whining at the light. There were five or six prisoners to each cell, caged into natural caves behind heavy iron grilles. Some were chained and shrank from her as she passed; others crowded to the bars and tried to touch her, asking for help.

"Carry a message to my mother in Talybont," cried a white-haired cripple who looked older than time.

"What's her name?" Rhiannon asked quickly.

"Beth," said the man. "Say I'm alive."

"How long have you been here?"

"What year is it?"

"Our Lord 1745." Rhiannon shuddered in the long pause that followed.

"Fourteen years," he said at last. "I was twenty when they put me here."

"What had you done?" she asked, imagining some gruesome murder.

70

"I stole a cow, I think. At least, John Ffowlke said so." All he could remember was the name of his judge.

"I will pray for your deliverance," Rhiannon tried to say, but it would not come out. Could this be the world she lived in? Her mind howled as though deranged. She had seen misery before: a child born with no arms or legs, an old man dying of hunger beside a road. This world is harsh, a vale of tears, a trial of our strength and faith. All this she knew well and could accept. Even that human love is pitifully inadequate to our condition. But that this wretchedness could be self-inflicted, actively willed on one man by another—this shook her to the core. What crime—if a man had killed his mother to take the food from her mouth—could justify this? Who remembered these people? Who knew they were here? Did God? She caught that thought on the edge of her mind and flung it back where it belonged.

"Not ours to reason why," she said instinctively. "But if not ours, then whose?" Hywel had taught her not to question the ways of God to Man. "He tempted Job to the uttermost," Hywel had said, "and Job did not lose faith."

"But God did not tempt him with this," Rhiannon answered, as though Hywel were in front of her.

Where could he be? She didn't have much time. She ran along a passage with massive oak doors on either side. Pray God he was not troubled by the same thoughts. She couldn't bear that. For so long his belief had sustained her, sweeping away her doubts like dead wood in the Ystwyth at springtime. What would she say to him if he had lost hope? That she loved him. But if he had given in? Would she have the strength? Would she still love him? Could she do without him, year after year? An abyss opened inside Rhiannon and doubts, long caged like these creatures down here, shook off their chains and crawled out.

She lifted the taper to the barred window of each cell and at each the scarred, battered face of humanity looked out at her in infinite variety of suffering. And yet the same face. She felt a bond of communion with them. Perhaps pain united them. Then she remembered those abject prisoners thrown in together. These ones on their own were luckier: you cannot share pain. It must be hoarded, or you lose even that.

Still no sign of him. Rhiannon was beginning to panic.

"Hywel!" she whispered as loudly as she dared. All along the corridor faces pressed against the bars, staring at her. "Who is there?" came a voice from the far end.

"It's me, your wife. Oh, God, where are you?"

"Here!" She hurried towards him. Surely his face would not be like all these others? Not after two days. But in two years, longer perhaps?

Hywel held his arms through the narrow barred window and threw them around her, pressed her face to his.

"Mind the baby," she said and they both laughed with relief. He was unchanged. His face was bearded and tired but still wore that utter composure and gentle strength.

Rhiannon held the baby up against the bars.

"Bless her," she said, and Hywel made the sign of the cross on her forehead. "You left in a hurry." They laughed again. "You never said what to call her."

"What name have you chosen?"

"I thought perhaps Hannah."

"Then Hannah it shall be."

Rhiannon had never seen him so serene, so calm.

"How are you?" she asked, wanting to know more.

"I am well," he said evenly, "and happy to carry Christ's cross. I hope I am worthy of it."

"You will be home in no time." Rhiannon did her best to sound brave. Hywel looked away. So they hadn't told her. She still thought he was here for preaching without a licence. How could he tell her he stood convicted of treason and would be taken from gaol as soon as the Scots army arrived, and hanged in public as a traitor to King James III? He wouldn't lie to her, but he couldn't tell her the truth either. It would be easier for her if she found out afterwards.

"It may be. Tyranny will always burn itself out. But I am resigned to my fate, whatever becomes of me. I know that God is with me." Rhiannon was helpless. Had he cried and complained, she would have known how to comfort him, she realized that now. But what comfort could she offer that he had not already taken?

"Do they feed you?"

"Enough. No different to what I eat when I travel."

"We miss you," she said, wishing they could cry.

"Please don't." How many hours he had spent fighting off this vision that said life was warm and to be lived! "I must turn my back on you. Not towards death but towards life eternal." His dark eyes took on that glazed look that shut her out more surely than the prison doors, his soul retreating to an inner sanctum she had never penetrated, but which ruled his life and hers. She felt abandoned. Did he love her, inside there?

Stop it, stop it, she told herself. That is beneath contempt. But still it hurt. To have come so far to be locked out.

"I must go."

"How did you get in?" Hywel asked, suddenly concerned. Rhiannon had been so ever-present in his thoughts—and his thoughts like worlds with a life of their own—that he had almost expected to see her. His worst fears were for her. She depended on him, he knew, in every way.

"Thomas Jenkins knows the warden," Rhiannon lied, not wanting to worry him.

"Go, then." Hywel kissed her. "My blessing on you all. Look after our children and my mother."

As so often before, Rhiannon took her leave of him with a heart neither empty nor overflowing, wishing they had both said more and been less brave.

"Is it a secret charm?" Madlen said brightly. She was running out of stupid ideas and was scared of hitting on the right one, but Steffan shook his head happily at each with the same dogmatic grimace.

"A love-spoon from your sweetheart?" She didn't like the way his lips curled upward in a thin smile at this suggestion.

"You'll never get it. Do you want to give up?"

"No," Madlen persisted. Had he really not noticed that Rhiannon was gone? "Is it a precious stone?"

"Ah," he hissed. "Yes and no."

"A diamond?"

"No."

"A ruby?" Madlen was getting nervous. It was clear to both of them that she was now the mouse and he the cat.

"No." Steffan grinned triumphantly. "Shall I show you?"

If he touches me, Madlen thought, I'll brain him with that beer bottle. She shrugged.

Steffan meticulously unwound the filthy cloth, as though undressing a doll. There was a second, cleaner layer underneath, stuck together in a kind of sheath, which he slipped off with furtive rapture. Underneath was a brightly polished pebble, about the length of Madlen's little finger, in the perfect shape of an erect phallus. He held it up for her between his stubby thumb and forefinger.

"It's very small," she said and watched him like a hawk.

"Take it!" Steffan said imperiously. Madlen refused. "Take it." This time she heard the menace in his voice. She stretched out her hand and he squeezed it into her palm.

"I found it in the Ystwyth when I was fifteen and have never shown it to anyone. Have you a lover?"

Madlen was taken aback.

73

"Yes," she said, blushing.

Steffan gloated at her in impotent lust. "If he ever annoys you, rub the stone like this and he will do whatever you say." Rhiannon slipped into the chamber behind him. "It has magical powers. Cannot fail." Madlen quickly tucked it into her bodice—she might need it one day—as Steffan jangled the keys on his belt and led them up the flight of steps to the sunshine.

"Visit me again," he said to Madlen, "if you need me." His narrow lips pouted to blow a kiss after her and the door slammed shut. Rhiannon sank onto the well and cried with anger for Hywel and relief for herself, to be out in the clean air under an open sky.

III

Gruffydd and Iolo had been working since first light.

"We need a door," Gruffydd had said as they woke up. The east wind had kept the fire leaping all night and frost had almost reached the hearthstone. They heated the remaining sour milk in a tin cup over the fire; then Iolo took Gruffydd's knife and a brand from the fire and set out up the hill for some breakfast. He could scent a rabbit warren from a hundred yards upwind. He came upon a fair-sized burrow in the roots of a copper beech, and looked around for the bolt-runs. No point in starting before you've found them all. "That's number one." Iolo blocked a crack hidden under a huge boulder. "And number two," which lay in the bank of a winding gully. "Watering hole," Iolo muttered. "But usually more than one." Sure enough. Another one, identical, just ten yards down, under a honeysuckle. "Leaves three, maybe four." Iolo scoured every rill and hollow within a fifty-yard radius. Next hole was easy. It came straight out onto the best patch of grass on the hill. But Iolo could find only one more, close to the main tunnel. "Smoke-hole," he decided and tapped the copper beech three times for luck. He quickly built a mound of brushwood in the smoke-hole and set it alight with his fire-brand. Then he dashed back to the master tunnel and stretched his rabbit bag—which also served as a cape in bad weather—over the hole. For minutes, nothing. "I must have missed an escape route." His empty stomach would hardly take him as far as the next warren. Then they came. A panic-stricken, half-asphyxiated rabbit ran blindly into the bag. With one stroke Iolo seized the stone beside him and crushed its head. "And another!" He was jubilant. "And a third—a little 'un. One and a half for each of us." Iolo always divided the spoils evenly with Gruffydd.

He enjoyed the hunt. Hunger didn't leave him much time to feel sorry, though he did occasionally. They were such furry, fluffy things, he would rather have played with them, on the whole, but Iolo had never had much time for playing.

Back at the house Gruffydd had plaited together a door of springy evergreen branches, which swung on rudimentary hinges of gnarled roots stuck in the mud walls.

"Not bad," Iolo said as he raced in, waving his three rabbits. "How about these?" He stopped dead. Gruffydd was kneeling on the floor. "What are you doing?"

Gruffydd was silent a moment.

"I was asking for a small favour from the spirits of our hearth."

"Did they speak to you?"

"I believe so."

"Father," Iolo said as they skinned the rabbits, "was there really a demon?"

"Where?"

"The one you fought with?"

Gruffydd scraped a hide clean with a sharp stone and said: "The whole of Cwmystwyth saw it. So many people cannot be wrong."

"They were wrong about me."

"Listen, there are many spirits, good and evil, in this country. If you are kind to them they will help you."

Iolo remembered how the circus people had smiled when Gruffydd talked like this. Friendly smiles, but distant, superior even. They made Iolo a little ashamed for his father. Sometimes they would egg Gruffydd on—and he always took the bait, talking louder and faster while the English whispered about mad Welshmen until Gruffydd would throw something at them and storm out, leaving Iolo wanting half to believe him and half to disown him. So he usually slunk away on his own, because he would never join in any laughter against Gruffydd. It was different here. Everyone believed him.

They roasted the rabbits over the fire on a spit. Gruffydd guessed what was going on inside Iolo.

"This country is yours. You don't know it, but it is yours. Learn to love it and take it as it is. Listen to it. It will teach you more than you can imagine."

"This is not my country," Iolo answered bluntly. "But I'll live with it." At times he had thought of going back to the circus, but he could never desert Gruffydd.

"Your country is where you are needed," Gruffydd said. "Make yourself needed."

The new door squeaked on its precarious hinges and Mihangel walked in carrying a knapsack over his shoulder. He looked pleased with himself. Gruffydd eyed the bundle hopefully.

"What have you brought us?"

"My belongings."

"What for?"

"I've come to live with you," Mihangel said, puzzled.

"You have, have you!"

"Who says?" Iolo didn't want to share Gruffydd with anyone.

"You said I could be your apprentice, didn't you? Well, you're lucky I'm here. Mali Fishpond didn't want me to go. I had to leave when she wasn't looking." Mihangel opened his knapsack and tipped it up. Out fell a blanket containing a saucepan, a knife, a stale hunk of bread, a rush candle, two smooth stones, a tinder and flint pouch and several earthenware jars. He arranged them in a neat row along the wall on Iolo's side of the room and then helped himself to some rabbit. Gruffydd inspected the jars. In some there were herbs, in others evil-smelling, mushy substances of yellow and green that he'd never seen before.

"What's this?"

"Ram's liver. Don't you use it for impotence?"

"Yes, of course." Gruffydd had no idea. "Whose ram was it?"

"Oh, I was given it." Mihangel was obviously not going to reveal his secrets and Gruffydd did not press him. An assistant would be useful in many ways. Perhaps some of the boy's confidence would rub off on Iolo, who was now sulking over the remains of his rabbit. Mihangel could also run errands and bring up the news from Cwmystwyth, since he knew the place so well. Charles Edward should be only a day's march away by now. Perhaps an advance party had already arrived.

"What's happening in the valley?"

"Nothing much. John Ffowlke has just sent his bailiff round with a drover to buy up everyone's cows. The farmers are moaning about it, but there's nothing they can do." Gruffydd put down the jars and reached for his cloak. He remembered this yearly visit well.

"Why didn't you tell me before?"

"Why should I? Why should you be interested?" Mihangel stopped chewing on his rabbit bone but Gruffydd was already out of the door. What cause did a conjurer have to bother about a cattle sale?

Gruffydd strode down the hill with Iolo and Mihangel trotting at his side.

"This drover is only offering a pound a head," Mihangel said. "And that's less than what they paid for them."

"Then why are they selling?"

"Because John Ffowlke says so and if they don't do as he says . . ."

"They get evicted." The villagers spent years minding their cattle, driving them up to pasture in the summer, keeping them in during the winter—cows and men shared the same roof and the same food from November to April—watching the calves grow, breeding them and then a few precious months of milk, until one day John Ffowlke's rent collector came round with some drover or other and years of labour were whisked away in a few minutes. And always the price offered for the cattle was the same as the rent to be paid. Nothing left over. It was a rare family that had any coins under the hearthstone from one winter to the next.

"What are you going to do?" Iolo asked. Gruffydd's mouth curled down at the edges and he stuck his jaw out. He had looked like that at Stafford Fair before he nearly drowned the tapster in his own ale for calling him a liar. How Gruffydd got away with it Iolo never knew. The whole town turned on them, shouting "Welsh thief," and someone knotted a noose which nearly did for Gruffydd. In the nick of time Iolo produced the gunpowder purse he'd picked from a dragoon only an hour earlier, thinking it was money. He dipped it into the blacksmith's fire and flung it into the crowd.

But it was all very well dwelling on past escapes. There was nowhere to escape to here—especially if Gruffydd wanted to stay. And what would happen if anyone recognized him?

"Wouldn't it be better," he suggested, running beside Gruffydd to keep up, "to wait until the new King gets here?"

"Wait?" Gruffydd said, clearly set on a plan of his own. "If the cows leave now, half of Cwmystwyth will be starving by the spring."

A paddock had been thrown up in the Ystwyth meadow. The herds Gruffydd had cured only days ago were strung out along the river, each tended by its anxious owner. Beside the paddock stood two tables made from a tree-trunk sawn down the middle. At one of them sat Padrig Jonathan, the drover, paying whatever he saw fit, and at the next sat John Ffowlke's steward, Mr Wynn, who collected the year's rent and renewed—or declined to renew—the tenant's lease for another twelvemonth. Behind them three constables warmed their hands at a brazier.

Gruffydd walked through the timid, submissive crowd. These were the same people who would have murdered Iolo and they couldn't lift a finger to help themselves. He hated them more than ever, queueing up to be fleeced without a murmur.

Dic Richards was sitting in the damp grass, his hardened face creased like his prized leather breeches. He pointed at the paddock.

"Five years I've raised those beauties. Now they're gone in five minutes."

"How much did he give you?"

"A pound a head."

"Why did you sell, man?"

"I didn't want to. I had just enough cash to pay Ffowlke his rent. But Mr Wynn there wouldn't take it."

"Why not? Why wouldn't he take your money?"

"I don't know," Dic said, bewildered. "He just refused to renew my lease, so I took what the drover was offering." This was how Ffowlke cut down any tenant who became too independent. "I had no choice." Dic caught Gruffydd's cloak. "Ten years of my life I've put into that farm. I can't let him throw me out now."

"Don't worry," Iolo said to Dic's little daughter, who was frightened because her father wouldn't get up off the ground. "Here." He pulled out one of the rabbit skins which he'd been keeping to make into ear flaps. "This'll keep you warm." The girl looked at him wide-eyed, and then held the rabbit fur up to her cheek with her thumb firmly wedged into her mouth.

"Thank you, sir," Dic said with difficulty. He took the girl on his knee. "Since I was her age, I thought that hard work and careful saving could put me on my feet and give her a good husband." Iolo knotted two blades of grass together and listened. "But I've been cheated." Dic's round, cumbersome face shed its innocence like a slough. "I thought, because I lived here so long, the place was mine. It isn't. Never will be."

Iolo felt sorry for Dic. It was like leaving the circus, for him. Although he had never had a home to lose, Iolo began to understand why these people were scared of losing theirs. It must be hard for them.

Padrig Jonathan was inspecting Thomas Jenkins' cows. He prised open their mouths and prodded their hindquarters until the beasts bellowed and shied away. Rolo Blacksmith, pressed into service for the day, was having difficulty in holding them, especially with Thomas's boss-eyed wife darting around like a gadfly, trying to keep the drovers off.

"You can't take these till tomorrow," she said.

"I won't be here tomorrow," Padrig Jonathan replied curtly.

"They're not worth having anyway. I'll give you eighteen shillings a head."

"You swindler!" she shrieked, her voice breaking. "I can't sell now. My husband is away. I can't sell without him."

Mr Wynn, a withered scribe with bloodshot eyes and a broken nose inflicted years ago by Rolo Blacksmith upon refusal of an extension, waved his quill at her impatiently and said with a malicious lisp: "No rent, no lease. Pay today or clear out."

The onlookers were jostling round for a better view.

"Get him, Sioned," shouted Huw Lloyd at the desperate woman and the crowd hooted. Sioned was always good for a laugh.

Gruffydd was sickened by their old, easy choice of scapegoat. They laughed at her chains and could not see their own.

"Bastards, all of you," she yelled helplessly. "My husband is drunk in Aberystwyth and none of you will lift a finger for me."

Gruffydd leaned over Mr Wynn and said quietly in his ear: "Excuse me. I believe it's unlawful for a woman to sell her husband's property." Mr Wynn looked up at him with sagging, myopic eyes.

"What if it is?"

"Well—this woman clearly is not entitled to sell these cows."

Mr Wynn put down his quill and placed his hands flat on the table.

"I have orders from Viscount Kirkland to terminate any lease which is not paid in full today." Gruffydd could feel the crowd pushing him on.

"Has the necessary twenty days' notice been served on the tenants?"

"Who *are* you?" said Mr Wynn irritably.

"The Lord Chancellor," Gruffydd sneered.

"Get away, you buffoon, or I'll have you arrested."

Something about the way Mr Wynn flicked his quill, as if to brush a fly from his sleeve, unlocked Gruffydd's anger. He placed the open palm of his hand on Wynn's oily grey hair and smashed his face down on the smooth, white wood of the table, completing the demolition that Rolo Blacksmith had begun. As the constables leapt towards him, Gruffydd lifted the makeshift table and sent two of them staggering back into the brazier, and the third, Samson, was felled by a backhand sweep between the eyes which the lion-tamer had used to quieten the Queen of Sheba when she got frisky.

Padrig Jonathan and his partner leapt onto their horses and tried to round up their herd. The crowd turned on them. Rolo Blacksmith, who had taken orders all day from the overbearing Padrig Jonathan and was longing for revenge, vaulted over the drover's horse and dragged him off it, holding his head in a vice with one arm and thumping it with the other.

"Now get rid of these cattle, fast," Gruffydd ordered as the constables came at him again. They tore down the paddock and drove the herds back to their farms at a gallop. By the time a detachment of militia arrived to restore order, the Ystwyth meadow was deserted. Not a cow in sight.

IV

Madlen's arse was ridged two inches deep from perching on the rim of Thomas Jenkins' hay cart. Blodwen, his mangy old mare, had pulled them over precipice, through bog and into every delectable meadow in sight, until Madlen was blistered from hauling at the reins and hoarse from swearing. Thomas himself, whom she'd dredged like a sodden vegetable from the Sailors Inn, was spread-eagled in one corner of the cart, his head lolling over the edge, and roaring lewd songs, while Rhiannon was curled up in the other and hadn't stopped weeping since they'd left Aberystwyth.

"Go on!" Madlen yelled, as Blodwen ground to a halt beside the privet hedge at the Nanteos porter's lodge. Blodwen curled back her lips, rolled her eyes and refused to budge.

"Look at this," Madlen said enticingly, holding out an apple which was meant for their lunch. Blodwen took it without thanks and returned to the hedge. "Damned mule." Madlen lost her temper and thrashed at her with fists and feet. Blodwen backed away into the porter's allotment and Thomas Jenkins, finally routed by the change of direction, puked fulsomely into the turnip patch. The gatekeeper of Nanteos came out just in time to see Blodwen trampling on his winter supplies.

"What do you think you're doing?" he howled, red in the face.

"Teaching her how to dance. Well, help me, you idiot." The porter lunged for the reins and Blodwen reared. Madlen dragged Thomas Jenkins out of the cart by his tattered jerkin. "Get up and do something! She's your jade, you deal with her." Thomas couldn't stand, let alone tame a frightened horse. Madlen rounded on Rhiannon.

"It's no use snivelling. It won't get Hywel out of gaol or us back home." Rhiannon looked up startled.

"It's not my fault you can't drive a cart half a mile." Madlen gasped. "And don't you dare speak of Hywel like that. How do you know what he's going through? You've always hated him . . ."

"That's a lie! I've done my best to love him. It's you—you—who hate him deep down."

The turnip patch was forgotten. The Nanteos gatekeeper, who was, at bottom, a decent fellow and used to make soup for the paupers and beggarwomen who trailed along this road into Aberystwyth, left Blodwen to her ravages and tried to appease the women instead.

"Now, it's all right. We'll have Blodwen out in an instant. Don't worry, my love." He turned to Rhiannon. "She means well." His face was a beacon of human sympathy.

The sisters were wavering between tears and further abuse when two constables escorting a prisoner cantered over the hill and stopped beside them.

"What's the problem?" asked Samson, peering through a very swollen black eye. The porter immediately assumed responsibility for the whole business.

"No problem, Samson. We're just getting this cart here out of my turnip patch."

"Need a hand?"

"No thanks." The porter was anxious to avoid a fuss, for Squire William Powell didn't like trouble of any kind. But Samson was determined to have a go and jumped down from the saddle, yanking the rope tighter round the prisoner's neck. Madlen glanced up.

"Good day to you, lady," said Gruffydd with a bow. "I'm sorry to see you're in difficulty."

He looked so proud she couldn't believe he was tied up. He wore his halter like a silk kerchief and seemed to be guarding the two constables, not vice versa. Then Madlen suddenly saw him at the bottom of those steps in Aberystwyth gaol.

"I'm sorry to see *you* are," she said feebly.

"Is there anything we can do?" asked Rhiannon, startled at how similar—yet strangely different—he was to her memory of him. She had relived their first encounter so often that he seemed somehow less real in the flesh than in her mind. His presence vaguely offended her, but it also gave her a chance to verify her suspicions of divine intervention. "I have been meaning to thank you for your help. You see . . ." She watched his face closely as she held up Hannah, who had slept peacefully all morning. "She will be a fine girl." Gruffydd leaned forward in the saddle.

"She is beautiful. You should be proud."

"Her name is Hannah," she said with a hint of appeal, as if the choice was only provisional and required his approval.

"With such a handsome name," Gruffydd said, noticing how

Madlen was getting impatient, "she will grow up as handsome as her mother." Rhiannon glowed for herself and for her daughter. She had always known she was handsome, though no one had told her, least of all Hywel. Not beautiful like Madlen, but handsome.

"Why have they arrested you?" Madlen asked, wishing Rhiannon would stop wasting time.

"A little disagreement about some cattle. Where have you been?"

"To the gaol," Rhiannon cut in, "to see my husband."

"How is he?"

"He trusts in God," Rhiannon answered, and realized that she shouldn't be talking to this man, who didn't believe in Him.

"We shall keep each other company, but not for long. You will have him home soon." He smiled at Madlen, who was aching for him. "Both of us." Did he really believe that? For an instant she caught a terrible uncertainty in his eye, behind the almost frivolous courage. Whatever his powers, he was human, like other men. Her loss only seemed the greater—there was so much she had to learn about him. She loved him, she knew that now for the first time.

Samson was sweating and beginning to lose his temper with Blodwen. He had hoped to give a display of mastery for the women-folk but the horse was making a fool of him.

"By your leave, sir," said Gruffydd respectfully, enjoying Samson's wrath. "There's an old trick from Russia for dealing with frightened horses. I learnt it from a Cossack in the Imperial Army. May I?" The others knew only vaguely of Russia as somewhere near France and "Cossack" might signify anything.

Gruffydd put two fingers of his tied-up hand to his mouth and whistled a long, piercing note higher than they had ever heard. Blodwen raised her head and pricked her ears. Gruffydd blew the same note again, lifting it slightly towards the end like a curlew calling across a marsh. Blodwen suddenly identified its source. She dragged the cart out of the turnip patch, trotted towards Gruffydd, completely relaxed, and nuzzled her head against his knee.

"Damn my eyes!" hollered Thomas Jenkins, who had sobered up sufficiently to take all this in. The story was repeated in Morgan's Inn at Pendre, with suitable embellishments, for many years to come and never lacked an audience. Samson and the porter simply rubbed their eyes.

"I will see you soon," Gruffydd shouted gaily as he rode away, flanked by two admiring constables. Madlen apologized to the porter, who waved until they disappeared over the hill.

*

Blodwen plodded through the short winter afternoon towards Cwymystwyth. Thomas dozed over the reins and the two sisters sat at opposite sides of the cart. Clouds were gathering in the west behind the massive grey tower of Llanfihangel parish church, its crenellations black against a grey sky. Lead miners hurried down from the top, from the mines at Wemyss and Frongoch. Some disappeared into their one-room shacks sprawled around the church while others headed straight for the Old Barn Inn, where they'd spend the better part of the night.

Rhiannon watched their silent, tired faces. They spent their days underground from choice. How could they bear it? No one stopped to greet the women or seemed to notice them. The file parted to let the cart pass and then joined again behind them.

The track climbed steadily out of the coastal valleys onto the high uplands that stretch as far as England. The wind blew fiercer, straight off the sea, with sharp stinging ice in it, and Madlen and Rhiannon huddled together, partly for warmth and partly in unspoken reconciliation.

Madlen knew now how Rhiannon felt. Why had she accused her of not loving Hywel? She wanted to say something comforting about him, but could feel Rhiannon brooding inaccessibly. So she sang instead, a simple song about the spring—so remote now—which Rhiannon had liked when they were small. Gradually the body beside her unbent and relaxed and Rhiannon lay down in her lap with Hannah tucked under her bosom.

They had passed the now-empty mines of Frongoch and were crawling down the precipitous slope towards the Ystwyth below Hafod, when Rhiannon said: "What did he mean about Hywel coming home?"

Madlen had thought she was asleep.

"Who?" she asked, glad they were on speaking terms again.

"You know—Gruffydd."

"Oh!" Madlen had been dreaming of Gruffydd on horseback in Russia. His name sounded odd coming from Rhiannon. "There's going to be a new King and John Ffowlke will be disgraced." She wanted to go on. She longed to talk to someone about Gruffydd.

"He's very kind," Rhiannon said dreamily, looking out of the back of the cart up the hill, at the treetops of Maen Arthur Wood. "I wonder if he and Hywel will meet in that terrible place. Perhaps they'll understand each other better."

"Perhaps they will." Madlen wrapped her shawl round Rhiannon. "I'm sorry I said that about Hywel."

Rhiannon didn't seem to hear this.

"Did Gruffydd tell you about the new King?" she asked.

"Yes."

"When?"

Madlen was trembling. Gruffydd had talked about Charles Edward that first night they lay together in the forest. But where was this Prince and why hadn't he stopped Gruffydd's being arrested?

"When did Gruffydd tell you?" Rhiannon sat up.

"Yesterday, the day before—I can't remember."

"You've seen him often?"

"More than once." What was the point of lying? She'd find out sooner or later. Madlen leaned over and whispered in her ear, "I love him. God knows if he cares for me." Rhiannon laughed teasingly but Madlen put a hand to her mouth. "I may be with child by him."

Rhiannon searched her face in disbelief. It smiled back at her, proud and scared. Dear God, she was a child herself. Rhiannon remembered the little girl with bare legs playing ball against the church wall when Hywel came to propose marriage the day their father died. She had sacrificed everything to bring her sister up in a Christian home. Was this how Madlen repaid her—by fornicating with a stranger, a man twice her age? It was an insult to their father's memory. What would she tell Hywel? Madlen couldn't stay in the house after this. And what did Gruffydd see in her anyway? It was Rhiannon he'd come for and her bed he'd knelt beside holding the oyster-shell lamp and looking at her as no other man had . . . She wasn't jealous of Madlen, was she? Rhiannon was so appalled by the thought that it jarred her into speech.

"My poor love." She hugged Madlen to her. "I'll take care of you. He's not worth your love. Forget him."

Madlen freed herself. "Rhiannon. I love him, as you love Hywel."

The comparison was unforgivable. Rhiannon's love for Hywel had nothing in common with Madlen's immorality.

"But what are you going to do?"

"I don't know." Madlen wished she had kept quiet. "It looks as though my baby will be fatherless, like yours."

"It's not a question of fathers, it's a question of homes. Where are you going to live?"

Madlen shrugged sullenly. She'd live with Gruffydd, with her husband. But Gruffydd was in prison and would he marry her anyway?

"You know what the Bevans would say," Rhiannon said bitterly.

"I don't care what they'd say! Ever since we've lived there I've had to think of what they'd say. Let them throw me out. I don't want them." But the idea frightened her, because there was nowhere else.

"What about the village?" Rhiannon took the thought from her mind. "They'll soon know, if they don't already. If he hasn't been boasting about it . . ."

"He wouldn't! Ever!"

They followed the Ystwyth past Hafod Lodge, which stood dark and decrepit in the clearing between two woods, and crossed the river at Dologau, from where a path leads up through sprawling Pen-y-Graig Farm towards Black Rock.

She could live up there until he returned. But how many now in Aberystwyth gaol were expected to return? Madlen was not convinced about this new King. The Ffowlkes would always be with us.

Rhiannon was also gazing at Black Rock. She had a half-formed picture of Hywel making love to her in the parlour beside her father's coffin, but it wouldn't come clear—it was not something he could ever have done. Then their two bodies blurred into those of Gruffydd and Madlen lying naked together.

"We must find you a husband," she whispered as the cart drew up by the Bevans' farm. "Dewi Cobbler has asked for you many a time."

v

John Ffowlke was getting impatient with Mr Wynn.

"The accused broke my nose, sir," he kept moaning from under his bandages, and Padrig Jonathan the drover did nothing but prod his finger at his blackened, puffy cheeks. The accused had said nothing throughout the trial.

"This isn't a hospital," John Ffowlke snapped from his sickbed. "It is a court of law." He was tired of his own play-acting. Dr Madog had removed the port decanter in retaliation for Zachariah's death and Ffowlke's legs were twitching from this unaccustomed idleness. "Anyway, this man has committed far graver offences than spoiling your face." Ffowlke didn't trust Wynn in any case. "Your face," he declared in his capacity of Chief Justice of the County, "is merely private property and your grievance purely personal. However"— Ffowlke took some snuff, relishing the acuity of his own judgement— "resisting lawful authority, attacking the King's Officers and incitement to riot are crimes of the most public proportions—a public grievance—and therefore punishable in the highest degree."

Beneath his cool, legal manner John Ffowlke was burning with anger. He'd been tricked. Talbot had paid this conjurer fellow to scare him and was now blackening his name to Charles Edward or King James, even. His reputation wouldn't be worth a mess of pottage once Talbot had had his say. Why had he listened to that charlatan? He blushed with embarrassment at his own gullibility and determined to despatch Gruffydd to the depths of Aberystwyth gaol if it was the last thing he did.

"Have you anything to say in your defence before I sentence you?" he asked with exemplary fairness.

"I have." Gruffydd broke his long silence. He had given up Charles Edward for lost and, having nothing more to lose, was about to call on all the devils in hell to avenge him, his father and all his family, when the door opened and John Stedman stumbled in unannounced and without his wig. He stared at Gruffydd as though he had entered the wrong room, and then gradually found his bearings and focused on John Ffowlke in the four-poster. He had rehearsed his jeremiad from the English border to the gates of Brithgoed at a non-stop gallop through the dark and now could not remember a word of it. He had forgotten even where he'd come from and practically who he was.

"We'll all be hanged," he said at last.

"What?"

"We'll be hanged, all right," Stedman said again and sat down. "We found an encampment of Highlanders outside of Radnor . . ."

"Well then, wasn't that what you all expected?"

"Yes," Stedman said. "No . . ."

"Start at the beginning."

Stedman swallowed a glass of water. "At first all went well. Everyone was in high spirits. Then Talbot and Thomas Powell started arguing about who was in command. Talbot called Thomas a young puppy and Thomas rode ahead of us, swearing he'd get to the Scots first and make fools of us all. We found an encampment of Highlanders but Thomas Powell had got there just before us. As soon as he saw them he galloped down towards them shouting 'Long live King James' and 'Charles Edward for ever' and what have you. And we all galloped after him."

"Well?"

"They were prisoners of war, under guard," Stedman said pitifully. "They thought we were a rescue party from their own army. They started fighting as soon as they saw us. Tried to escape. Most of them were killed by the guards, who fired at us too. Evan Pritchard got a bullet in the head. All the others were arrested—Talbot, Thomas, the lot."

John Ffowlke was struck dumb with horror.

"And Charles Edward?" he mouthed at last.

"Never got farther than Derby. Turned back three days ago without a fight."

"What about our information?" Stedman hid his face in his hands. "Where is Oxley?" Ffowlke bellowed and thrashed around for something to strangle. His eyes settled on Padrig Jonathan, who was squirming in his boots next to Mr Wynn. "You. You, yes, you!" Ffowlke had found his first victim. "You lied to me! You've been trying to ruin me."

"I told you what I'd heard," the drover stammered, his swollen face aghast.

"Lies, lies!" Ffowlke howled, climbing out of bed. "I'm surrounded by liars. Take him away, and leave him where I'll never hear of him again."

Samson seized the drover and hauled him off while Carlo, his mate, marched Gruffydd to the door.

"Leave that one. I've more to say to him. And as for you." Ffowlke rounded on the wretched Stedman. "I have never heard of anything so half-witted in my life. If you are incapable of distinguishing prisoners from soldiers it's your own fault. It's no business of mine. I wash my hands of the whole affair. Mr Stedman is under house arrest until the army gets here . . . And send Reuben up with some port," he yelled as an afterthought and slammed the door. "Liars and imbeciles," he muttered and came face to face with Gruffydd. "What do you want?"

"You said for me to stay." Gruffydd's face was impassive.

"Ah, yes." Ffowlke suddenly felt exposed. His night-shirt scarcely covered his privies. It was like childhood nightmares of being naked in a crowd. He got back into bed.

"So you followed my advice?" Gruffydd said condescendingly.

"Advice?"

"I told you Charles Edward was just a comet. You were wise to stay here." Gruffydd had guessed why he had not gone with the others. John Ffowlke felt a little queasy.

"How were you so certain? You must have had information."

"Information, of course. But not through the usual channels."

"How, then?" Ffowlke scoffed. He was not falling for this a second time. Yet, when he thought about it, what had saved him?

"I knew Charles Edward was doomed before he set foot on English soil, before the idea was born in his head." Gruffydd watched this seed germinate in Ffowlke's brain. "What other information could you trust?"

Ffowlke tugged nervously at the bedclothes.

"They all lie to me . . ."

"Don't trust any of your spies."

"Which is the worst of them?" Ffowlke asked excitedly. "Samson? Morgan? . . ."

"Beware of Morgan especially. You have given him everything, and he hates you for it."

"And what do I do now? The army will be arriving at any moment. How do I excuse myself?"

Gruffydd shrugged. "You can say you were powerless to stop them and stayed here to organize resistance."

"Yes," Ffowlke agreed feverishly. "Ride out with the militia tomorrow, to meet Cumberland." Gruffydd kicked himself for giving such good advice. "Then there's that preacher."

"Release him," Gruffydd said, imagining Rhiannon's face on getting her husband back.

"I can't. He knows too much."

"He's far more dangerous in prison than out, mark my words."

"We'll see." Ffowlke looked at Gruffydd suspiciously. The fellow still had a lot to account for. "Why did you attack my steward?"

"I did it for your own good. If your tenants had sold for what that crook was offering, they'd be starving by Easter and you would have had riots up and down the valley."

"Rubbish! Give them too much money, they spit in your face. Keep them hungry and they'll eat from your hand."

Yes, Gruffydd thought. You are indeed the man who destroyed my family; and he said: "It's a poor farmer who starves his own livestock."

"So what would you do?" Ffowlke demanded.

"Let your tenants sell to the highest bidder. The richer they are, the richer you'll be."

"And let in all the trouble-makers?"

Gruffydd smiled wryly. "Plenty of them anyway."

Ffowlke looked out at the river and pondered.

"Can you keep them in order?" he said at last.

"For you?" Gruffydd was disgusted at the idea, but he had no choice. "They'll do what I say."

"Then tell them to sell where they want—but I'll have my rents in a fortnight."

Gruffydd turned to leave.

"I have a charm against nightmare," he said, "if you need it."

John Ffowlke sat down at his bureau and tried to write some letters in his defence but his mind wouldn't stay on the page. Hywel Bevan worried him more than any other evidence against him. The man must be bought off or silenced before Ffowlke's enemies got to him.

"Excuse me, sir," said Reuben at his elbow.

"What is it?" Ffowlke peered at him more suspiciously than ever.

"I beg your pardon, sir, but there's a man from Cwmystwyth been waiting all day. Says it's important."

"Show him in, then. And send Samson for that preacher in Aberystwyth gaol. Don't tell me it's past midnight. I want him here now."

Ffowlke returned to his writing but the words wouldn't come. He stared at the blank page and gradually became aware that someone was standing behind him. He swung round. The rotund, whiskered peasant bowed deeply.

"What do you want? Who are you?"

"Joshua, your tenant, sir."

"Which farm?"

"Cae Glas," Joshua began. "You see—"

"Can't pay the rent, eh?"

Joshua was horrified. "Of course I can, sir."

"Well?"

"It's the middle field, sir," Joshua said persuasively. "You yourself said it belongs to my farm. So I reckon that must be right." He smiled unctuously. "And now—you'll not credit it—this man Gruffydd says it goes with Gwilym's farm next door. Now—"

"What reason did he give?"

"Something about an old Welsh law."

"Then I dare say he's right." Ffowlke cut him dead. "And if you trouble me again, you'll lose the rest as well."

CHAPTER FIVE

I

"How LONG UNTIL you give us some milk, then?" Iolo said to his six calves. "Two years? Three?" They shouldn't have been taken from their mothers yet. One of them was even a little shaky on its legs.

"Shoo," he said half-heartedly. They had taken to following him everywhere. He didn't mind, but it made work difficult. He tugged up a tuft of grass by the forest where he was building his fence, and offered it as a pay-off to the ringleader. "Now take them away, Sali!" Sali—they all had names by now—was jet-black with one white ear, the left one; she was bigger than the rest and kept them in order by butting them ferociously whenever they annoyed her. Iolo was only just getting to know them. His experience of cows to date consisted of slipping into fields at night with a makeshift pail and milking off enough for Gruffydd's supper. Right now, Iolo had chosen the wrong tactic because Sali kept nudging him for more and the others pushed forward for their share.

"If you feed them by hand," Mihangel had warned him, "they'll forget how to graze." Iolo wasn't sure if he liked Mihangel yet. Of course he was clever, but he was also very bossy and tried to supervise Iolo in their work about the house.

"Not like that," he would say with a grin, which irked Iolo most of all. "You make a fence like this." And he deftly plaited two or three springy branches together into a perfect fence. Iolo didn't mind learning but he hated being teased. Not even Gruffydd was allowed to do that. And he never did. He always took Iolo seriously . . . except about his mother. Iolo was getting used to the pang that came with that thought. He had been up to the lake again last night but seen nobody. A year and a day, Gruffydd said he'd sat there. Iolo resigned himself to a long wait. There was a wood cabin at the end of the lake and no one lived there as far as Iolo could see, so he made himself at home when it rained. He had cleared away the maggots in the bed and the occasional rat didn't bother him at all. Sometimes he thought it was more comfortable than the Round House and couldn't drag himself away till very late. Not that anyone cared, for Gruffydd was never back before morning anyway.

"Gruffydd!" Iolo called towards the house. "Get up and do some work." Iolo had been up since dawn, driving stakes into the frozen ground with a rock he could hardly lift, while Gruffydd lazed in front of their fire till the sun was as high as it would get.

"Oh, go away!" Iolo shouted impatiently at his herd and gave Sali a smack on the nose that sent her careering across the meadow. The others followed blindly. Iolo watched them charge into the mist where the sun hadn't reached over the mountain, and returned to his fence.

"Gruffydd," he shouted again, more angrily, two stakes and a stubbed thumb later. Still no move from the house. Iolo threw down the stone and went inside. Gruffydd was just sitting by the fire, doing nothing.

"Why can't you help?"

"Come here, Iolo."

Iolo could tell his father's moods from a single word, from the back of his head. This one sounded very bad—as bad as the time Gruffydd left their last piece of silver under a tree and couldn't find it in the morning. "The fair people have taken it," Gruffydd said but Iolo thought it was just lost. He sat down next to his father.

"What is it?"

"We must leave here."

"Why?" Iolo was taken aback. Yesterday he wouldn't have hesitated. "Can we take the calves with us?"

Gruffydd shook his head silently. He seemed very unhappy.

"But we can't just leave them behind."

"We'll have to give them back."

"But why do we have to leave?"

Gruffydd turned to him.

"Do you want to stay here?"

"Not really," Iolo faltered. "But you do, don't you? And I like the cows. Besides, we can't leave now. The new King will be here soon and we'll get all our lands back."

Gruffydd winced.

"He's not coming."

"Oh." Iolo paused. "Why not?"

"He changed his mind."

"Maybe he'll try another time. It's worth waiting for."

"No." Gruffydd gazed into the fire to avoid Iolo's eyes. "No, he won't come now. This was his last chance. Maybe ours, too." Gruffydd unstrapped the parchment tied around his shoulder and stared at it. "The whole of the Ystwyth valley belonged to Rhys," he said bitterly. "Who knows how we get it back now. It's ours! And the Ffowlkes will hang on to it till the crack of doom."

"Well, we've made a start already. The fence is looking grand."

"One acre," Gruffydd said morosely, "in ten thousand."

Iolo felt deflated. "So what shall we do? The circus won't have us back. Not after you took Black Jane."

"I don't need the circus," Gruffydd said. "There are better places we can go . . ."

"Where?"

"Russia." Gruffydd remembered his Cossack friend. "I could join the Russian army."

"I don't like armies."

"Nor do I. We could go to sea."

Iolo groaned. His one memory of the sea was stowing away in an empty barrel at the bottom of a Channel lugger and puking all the way from Brest to Southampton.

"I don't think you want to leave," he said. "Or else you'd come up with some better ideas." When Gruffydd really wanted to do something, he never bothered to consult Iolo. "Anyway, land isn't everything. It's what people think of you. You said that. They need you here." Iolo didn't know why he sounded so eager. No one needed *him*. Quite the opposite, and they made no attempt to hide the fact. All in all he would rather leave but he hated to let Gruffydd give up. And then there was the lake. Iolo wanted to meet his mother.

"Can you see me as a conjurer?" Gruffydd asked him.

"Well, you are one, aren't you?" Iolo said shyly.

Gruffydd pushed a brand back into the fire with his foot.

"It depends. 'Conjurer' is just a word people use. They don't know what it is to be one. You see, no man can choose to be a conjurer because no man possesses the power in himself. It is given to him without his asking or wanting it and it can be taken away again, for no reason, at any time."

"Who by?" Iolo struggled to follow. "By God?"

"No," Gruffydd said emphatically. "God doesn't give a cuss either way. Wherever he is."

"By the Devil?" Iolo asked in a whisper. He had sometimes suspected his father of secret dealings with the Lord of Darkness. Gruffydd was too lucky too often for mere chance.

"Not by him, either, but you have to tread carefully or else you invite his attention."

"How?" Iolo was fascinated and scared.

Gruffydd hesitated.

"If a conjurer used his powers the wrong way, he could lose both them and himself together. For the moment, I am a conjurer. It's in here." He tapped his chest. "I can feel it. But it may not always be there."

"What does it feel like?"

"It feels like . . ." Gruffydd fell into a long reverie.

Iolo nudged him. "Well?"

"I was thinking about my waterfall. I must ask the lady what we should do."

"What does it feel like?" Iolo said irritably. He didn't like being side-tracked. Gruffydd did it all the time.

"Like the waterfall, I suppose. Like the stream pouring on and on, out of the rock. It could never dry up, I imagine—but it might." Iolo didn't like the idea of that lady singing inside Gruffydd all the time.

"But she told you that we would get our lands. You said so."

"So she did." Gruffydd had forgotten. "I must ask her again."

"Father, if you're a conjurer, why don't you use magic to get our lands back?"

Gruffydd looked at him curiously.

"Would you do that?"

"No, *I* wouldn't," Iolo said hastily. "But maybe that's what the lady meant."

"Maybe."

Iolo stood up.

"Anyway, try being a conjurer and see if you like it. If you don't, we can go somewhere else."

"That might not be so easy," Gruffydd said, half amused and half apprehensive.

A shadow fell across the floor. Madlen was leaning in the doorway. She had heard that Gruffydd had been released and she'd run non-stop from the Bevans' to Black Rock, singing a victory chant for his safe return and wanting only to hold him in her arms.

"You're back!" She couldn't believe it. Had she only imagined meeting him on the Aberystwyth road with a halter round his neck? He must have spirited himself out of gaol. She squealed with joy, ran over to him and hugged him till he lost his balance and rolled onto the floor. Gruffydd laughed and pretended to wrestle with her and then he picked her up and held her at arm's length to make sure nothing was broken. He winked over her shoulder at Iolo, who had recognized the signs and was already on his way out, wondering whether Madlen would be able to keep Gruffydd any longer than all the others had.

"How did you do it? How did you get out of gaol?" Madlen clamped her arms around Gruffydd's neck and stared into his eyes, expecting miracles. He smiled, amused and touched—he couldn't disappoint her.

"Well, I was never in gaol, but I did have a bit of a fight with John Ffowlke." Madlen was alarmed. No one she'd ever heard of had crossed Ffowlke and got away with it.

"Did you win?" she whispered.

"Yes, I think so. I've done him a favour and he's rather scared of me now."

"What sort of favour?"

"I saved his life, more or less." Madlen sat down on a log by the fire. This was far stranger than anything she'd foreseen.

"Why? Why did you help him? He's not worth it." Gruffydd frowned. There must be some reason why it had turned out this way. Nothing happened by accident. Of course he had some influence over Ffowlke now, but he'd wanted to get rid of him, not impress him.

"I know," she said brightly. "You only saved Ffowlke so that he'd listen to you and you could help us. Isn't that it?" Gruffydd's head jerked up.

"No. I want nothing to do with Ffowlke. I'm not interested in what he thinks of me and I certainly won't give him any more advice." Madlen was shocked. He looked as if he might hit her. She let go of his hands and stared miserably into the fire, not daring to move. She didn't understand him. It was unfair to quarrel with her when she was only trying to help. Gruffydd got up and opened the door and gazed out at the valley. She could see patches of light through his tattered cloak. No one could have taken a needle to it for years, or combed his hair for that matter—it hung on his shoulders in a tangled knot. He needed looking after and she might as well start now, so she scraped up the ashes around the fire with two flat pieces of wood and carried them to the door. Gruffydd stepped aside silently to let her pass, but when she came back for another load he caught her arm.

He avoided her eyes—they were too trusting. A thin film of ash had settled on her hair and turned it grey, the colour of her eyes. She looked like a young widow.

"No point in doing that. I'm not staying here."

"What do you mean?"

"The new King has been defeated, so I must move on."

"But what about me? You won't leave me, will you?" She dropped the bits of wood and tried to catch his eye to see if he meant it, but he turned away. "Oh, God, don't tell me now that you don't love me."

"Yes, of course I do, but there are other things . . ."

"What other things? What else matters? What do you care about a new King?"

"I told you. He would have given me my lands back."

"That's what you think. As if a King would ever remember some-one like you." Gruffydd swung round. She was mocking him. There were tears on her face but her lovely mouth was curled in scorn. She wanted to hurt him. She wanted to show him that even a conjurer couldn't intimidate her. "You would never even have got to see Charles Edward, let alone talked him into giving you any land. Or did you have another spell to cast on him?" Madlen was terrified—he might strike her dead or turn her into a spider—but she had nothing to lose. Gruffydd just stared at her. Then without warning he turned away and strode down the hill towards the waterfall.

II

Hywel woke up with a start. He knew that dream. It often caught him off guard, but he had developed a resistance to it that woke him as surely as the cock crowing on the barn roof.

When they had returned him to his cell with John Ffowlke's ulti-matum ringing in his ears, he had determined to spend the night—his last in all probability—in communion with God and his own soul. John Ffowlke had promised to release him and had quashed his conviction for treason outright. "An unfortunate error," Ffowlke had called it and had given him a document to sign which stated in effect that the trial had never taken place and that Hywel had merely been detained overnight for petty misdemeanours. He would never put his name to a lie. After two hours of curses, pleas and promises, Ffowlke had run out of patience and had sworn to have either Hywel's signature or his life in the morning. Hywel didn't doubt him. Aberystwyth gaol had swallowed up plenty of other men before him. For the rest of the night he had prayed, expecting any minute to hear the footsteps of his last visitor, but sometime around dawn, as far as he knew—for day and night were one and the same here—the flesh had got the better of him and he had dozed off, only to have Satan, ever-cunning deceiver, humiliate him with this old familiar dream, the last thing that should be in his head on the eve of eternity.

In his dream, he was walking through a deep forest and came to a clearing. In the middle was a pagan temple carved with strange figures in wood and in front of the temple, leaning against one of the pillars, stood a woman in a white gown with curling dark hair. In one hand she had a small phial. Hywel had never entered the clearing. Without fail, he woke as soon as he reached it, but he knew instinctively what lay inside the temple. And the priestess, though not resembling her physically, was made in the likeness of a loose woman he had frequented in his younger days, before his first marriage, before his conversion, whose memory he had successfully banished from his waking hours.

Hywel dragged himself onto his knees. He was shivering and his limbs were aching. It was so dark that he couldn't be sure if his eyes were open. He slapped his face twice.

"Blessed are those who hunger and thirst after righteousness . . ." He recited the Beatitudes, which never failed to restore peace to his spirit. Then he reviewed his life, moment for moment, from his worst profligacy to the day on which everything had changed so totally, the day on which he had received assurance of God's grace. It was not easily won, that assurance. No thunderbolt from a clear sky, unannounced and unprepared for. He had worked for it. Every step was a hard-won victory. Hywel had consolidated his salvation more methodically than the Romans their empire.

"God forgive me that first, greatest sin. 'Honour thy father,' it is written, and I reviled him." His father had been too old to work the farm himself and had begged him not to leave, but the rumour of a gold find in Dolaucothi had taken Hywel south, and when he returned, empty-handed, his father was dead. That was the start of it. Then came the years of whoring, drinking and cattle thieving until the pangs of guilt set in, scarcely more than a sediment at the bottom of a good bottle at first, or a lashing of Tewkesbury mustard on a beefsteak from a stolen Welsh runt. But gradually the wine turned sour, the mustard sulphurous and Hywel was crying out for anything that would quench the terrible fear in him. He returned home where his mother was broken with drudgery and grief.

Hywel remembered that first Sunday. He had ventured to church for the first time in five years. There were six people in the congregation and the Reverend Tudor Owen, Rhiannon's father, had preached on the need to take the Sacrament often. He had gazed straight at Hywel. "If you are not fit to come to the Lord's table, you are not fit to come to church; you are not fit to live, nor fit to die." Hywel had choked on the wafer and fled, convinced he was damned. But the old clergyman had coaxed and bullied him into fresh hope and dragged him back from the brink of despair. "There is only one sin," he had shouted at this morbid young man, as obstinately proud in abasement as he had been in vanity, "and that is to doubt the power of God's forgiveness and love."

Hywel had submitted and gone under the yoke, obeying Tudor unquestioningly. His education in the ministry became a second life's work for the old man and the valley's only hope of salvation, for half the parish churches in Wales stood empty and Tudor would not be replaced in Cwmystwyth after his death unless he groomed his own successor. But the Bishop had refused to ordain Hywel because he spoke no English.

Then, Whit Sunday. The whole day spent alone in prayer, and three decisions made from which Hywel had never swerved: to pray as soon as he got up in the morning; to read three chapters of the Holy Bible every day; and to keep a diary in which he would confess in minutest detail, and without sparing himself, his lapses from grace and keep a conscious check on the way he used each moment. He also resolved to marry, this being the best protection against his overwhelming fault, and he had settled on the Reverend Owen's serving-girl, Anna, a humble woman, as plain as she was honest and five years his senior, who gave him a fine daughter and twelve years of untroubled wedlock.

"God bless her," Hywel prayed fervently. "I shall be with her soon." He had often missed her quiet, unfailing courage in the five years since she had died.

"June 18th, 1733." Hywel only had to say the date to feel again that great burden of sin lifting. A day in early summer, not especially warm for the time of year. Anna was pregnant with Rachel and had morning sickness. Hywel had got up at dawn and, as usual, turned to his private prayer. The Lord's Prayer, he started with. At the fourth line he could go no further. "Thy Kingdom come," he repeated and a great light welled up inside him, blinding him, dissolving his frail existence in some inconceivably more powerful being. "I felt suddenly my heart melting within me like wax before the fire with love to God my Saviour" were the words that Hywel used in his diary—and to his attentive congregation—to describe his re-birth.

That was only the beginning. There had been lapses—moments of anger, of lust, such as last night's dream—but Hywel had been confident in his covenant with God. Many times he renewed it in the secrecy of prayer, and having once experienced God's grace he could never remain indifferent to the terrible danger in which so many others, deprived of all spiritual care, remained. With Tudor's blessing he began his work, preaching under the sky, for he was not allowed to use a church, first at home and then farther afield.

He knew his mission was unfinished. It was perhaps his one regret. But not for a minute, tonight, had he wavered. John Ffowlke's demands were impossible. How could he further the work of salvation if he perjured himself first?

A key turned in the lock. Hywel recalled his soul to earth and struggled to his feet, fully prepared for whatever was in store for him. A taper-flame appeared in the doorway, blinding him. He squinted through his fingers and saw a long, kindly face with a serene smile.

"Who are you?"

"Sir Lewis Pryse," the gentleman answered. "I am sorry to see you so poorly lodged. I have come to take you out of here."

Hywel leaned against the wall of his cell. "Why?" was all he could think to say. He suddenly felt exhausted. Hunger and thirst burst upon him. His legs sagged. Lewis Pryse seized his arm and gently lowered him to the floor.

"I want food and drink at once," he said to Steffan, who was waiting outside. "This prisoner has been criminally neglected. You shall answer for it."

He squatted beside Hywel, his silk brocade coat sweeping the fetid straw.

"You have been the victim of the most gross injustice, but you will be saved and restored to your family."

"Why? Why?" Hywel repeated, delirious. "I was so close to God. Why call me back? I had reconciled myself to my fate."

"This world is a wilderness," Lewis Pryse said understandingly, "and blessed are those who are rid of it. But you have been recalled, and you must bear your cross gladly."

"Do you know of my work, sir?" Hywel was amazed to hear his duty put so clearly by one so far removed from his own station, and by the leading Tory of the county and a suspected Catholic at that.

"Indeed I do. I have followed your mission with admiration. You are about God's work, and I am ready to testify as much before any court in the land."

Hywel looked more closely at his saviour, as his eyes became used to the light. His features were refined and sensitive, with high cheekbones and a narrow, slightly hooked nose. He was about Hywel's age, perhaps older, but his face was unlined and apparently free of earthly passions. It suggested a familiarity with the spiritual world such as Hywel had seen only in illustrated Bibles, in pictures of Our Lord curing the leper of Galilee or raising Jairus' daughter.

"I shall pray for God to reward you every day of my life," Hywel said and kissed his hand. "When may I leave?"

"Very soon, I hope. Just as soon as your persecutors are brought to justice."

"I desire no revenge, sir." Hywel said. "I forgive them freely. But if I could confront them with their sin, perhaps they would repent more readily." Lewis Pryse shook his head.

"I doubt if they are susceptible to your ministrations, but you must indeed confront them and arm yourself to confound their lies."

"How do you mean, sir?"

Lewis Pryse paused. Steffan came in carrying barley bread and a dried herring.

"I wish that I could take you with me when I leave here," Lewis Pryse said. "At least you are in no danger, now, but Lord Kirkland remains Chief Justice and Lord Lieutenant. I cannot free you without his written pass."

"But he will never grant that!" Lewis Pryse raised his hand and went on.

"Lord Kirkland has abused his trust. Tomorrow there is to be a tribunal to investigate his conduct. Your evidence will be crucial."

"*I* will be called?"

"As a witness. Your testimony will sweep away the corruption of this government and restore to the county a just and healthy authority."

Pryse watched him expectantly. Hywel's face betrayed nothing.

"My business is with heaven," he said, "not with this world . . . What will they do with Lord Kirkland?"

Lewis Pryse pursed his lips. "He has committed many grave offences."

"You are asking me to judge my judges. An eye for an eye . . ."

"You will judge no one. You will merely tell the truth."

"To buy my freedom with that of a man I have forgiven, from my heart, as I am a Christian?"

"That is not your choice," Lewis Pryse said earnestly. "Justice must take its course."

"There *is* no justice in this life! I am the living proof of it."

"And your countrymen? Sold into bondage like Israel into Egypt—"

"The Promised Land," Hywel declared, "is not of the here and now. The worst oppression can only lead us the sooner to our real goal."

"But how will your countrymen find it without you to guide them? There are many who will lead them astray. One man especially has already undone all your good work." Hywel started. The conjurer had never been far from his thoughts, but how did Lewis Pryse know of him?

"It is up to you," Pryse said, in the doorway. "You will be called to testify. I cannot change that even if I wanted to. What you say is between you and your conscience, but the truth is known to me. Anything less will not suffice."

At the top of the stairs, as Steffan was unlocking the prison door, Lewis Pryse pressed a guinea into his palm and said: "The town is now commanded by General Fleming. No messenger from Lord Kirkland is to see the prisoner. Understood?" Steffan nodded. "But if his wife or mother should visit him," Pryse added as an afterthought, "they may stay as long as they wish."

Lewis Pryse galloped through the town gate and turned his horse towards Cwmystwyth.

III

Gruffydd walked down the mountainside chopping off plants with his hunting knife. He was furious with himself, with Charles Edward, with Madlen, with the world. He had come on a wild-goose chase to find no land, no Dan Rowlands, no wife; he was embroiled in responsibilities as a conjurer that he didn't want and wasn't sure he could live up to; and now he was being made fun of by a young termagant half his age who was trying to cross-breed him with John Ffowlke. By far the simplest course would be to cut his losses and clear out. He would never work with John Ffowlke, that was certain, however easy he might be to handle. Gruffydd refused to be anything less than master in his own house and he would never return to Brithgoed except in triumph. And yet something told him he should stay here. He was afraid of not being able to tear himself away and that made him angrier still.

He pushed through the bushes and undergrowth beneath Grogwynion, and as he felt his back slip into the shell-shaped niche that might have been sculpted for it, as the slender birches and gnarled oaks sighed above him and the waterfall splashed into its bowl, the shouting in him fell silent. He was at home. He had all the time in the world. No one would ask him for anything and nothing needed hiding. Gruffydd fixed his eyes on one spot in the waterfall directly opposite him: its outline never changed, but within it the light created infinite patterns, never still, never self-repeating, dazzling and soothing at once. With immense relief, Gruffydd let the old serenity seep up through his limbs and take possession of him. Then he waited.

He saw himself as a young boy shooting arrows that couldn't fly straight at sea-gulls coasting on the wind-swept top. He looked at the bow he was carrying. It was made of yew, yew from one of the trees by the upright stone. Gruffydd was climbing to the highest branches to lop off a spray that was springy enough, then he was fighting with Dan Rowlands for possession of the stone. They were laughing and pushing each other off, toppling over and landing in a heap on the ground. Then a crowd of boys was around them and Dan had a bloody nose. Gruffydd knew their faces. They were suddenly twenty years older, waving pitchforks and holding a red-hot stake above Iolo's chest. Except it wasn't the dead conjurer holding the stake, it was Gruffydd, and they were all shouting at him to strike. He was powerless to resist them. As the stake came crashing down, Iolo turned into John Ffowlke. Gruffydd looked down at the mangled body of his enemy and he loved him. It was Gruffydd's father, an old man with a white beard lying in the snow on a mountainside, saying: "This country has killed me but you shall tame it." And Gruffydd was carrying a bundle of white linen with a heart still beating inside it, running away from a wooden shack, along a lakeside, with a woman shouting after him . . .

Gruffydd shook himself. He was sweating and shivering.

It had not been like this before. The pictures had always been clear, beautiful. He glanced back at the water, but fell into the same sickening dive. "Don't desert me," he cried and closed his eyes. Slowly the long fall stopped and he came to a halt, suspended in mid-air somewhere. The noise of the waterfall reached him from far away and behind it he could hear—faintly but unmistakably—the voice of a woman singing like a girl passing through a distant hayfield on a summer's evening, or brushing her hair by the mirror in an upstairs room.

"Still there," Gruffydd murmured. "I thought I'd lost you." The pictures in his head stayed still now, instead of running away with him. They followed each other in due order, separate verses in the song that the lady was singing. Gruffydd saw Iolo, hungry and footsore on a dusty road near Rheims; then he saw him minding their calves by the Round House and building fences. He saw an angry crowd throwing stones, then a mother giving suck to her baby; a dead shrunken cow and a lush valley with cattle grazing. And finally he looked without flinching at a wooden hut at the lakeside, and by it a woman called Gwenllian, who he knew was dead and never to be placated; and saw beside her another, called Madlen.

"No other wife," he found himself saying. His eyes were open, the song was gone, and in the failing light the waterfall was leaden grey. He could give up the road, he realized. There had been mornings when it was an effort to put one foot in front of the other, when only the thought of returning to Gwenllian, one day, sustained him.

He got up and stretched. He didn't mind staying here. And he could forgive them all. Except Ffowlke. Him, never. The old man lying in the snow came back, but Gruffydd shook it off. "Enough," he said. "Decision made."

And Madlen? Gruffydd tried to ignore the quesion. It wouldn't go away. "No other wife," he said again. Since leaving Cwmystwyth he had stayed with no woman longer than a week, for nothing was to stop him returning when the time was right.

But he had returned and she was dead!

If only as a penance—no other wife. But in truth, he was used to escape routes and Madlen would block them all.

Gruffydd was exhausted as he struggled back up to Black Rock through the dark. He wanted to eat and then sleep for the first whole night since coming home, but as he emerged from the woods he saw flames throwing shadows against Black Rock.

It's not on fire, is it? he thought in alarm, and then: As if mud and turf would burn. Now he heard a scratchy tune being played on a one-string fiddle, a harp with it, laughing and shouting, the pig squealing and Iolo yelling above it all, "Don't disturb the calves." Gruffydd dragged himself up the last slope, ankle-deep in mud where the turf had been cut to make his roof. The meadow was ablaze with bonfires and people were singing and dancing, swathed in every piece of cloth they could lay hands on against the cold night air.

"It's Gruffydd," shouted Thomas Jenkins, who had wandered away from the others to lose one bladderful of beer in preparation for another. "Gruffydd is back!"

Gruffydd laughed despite himself.

"You'd better mind those." Thomas had quite forgotten what he was doing and was tripping over his breeches in his haste to give the news.

"Where is he?" cried Dic Richards into the dark.

"Here, over here," Thomas answered and after a few more paces Gruffydd was surrounded by the crowd.

"Is it true about the drover?" asked Dic Richards frantically.

"What did John Ffowlke say?"

"How did you get round him?" Mali grinned.

"Cast a spell on him, didn't he?" Siân Evans answered for Gruffydd. "Like I've been saying."

"Did they put you in gaol?"

"How did you get out?"

"Did you bewitch old Steffan Turnkey?"

"Tell us. Tell us what happened."

"Friends!" Gruffydd raised his hands and at once they were silent. "I was never in gaol, though I dare say that between your kindness and my own devices I would not have stayed there long." A roar of assent. They liked to hear themselves linked with him. "No," Gruffydd went on, his breath sending great clouds of mist into the night air. "It never came to that. And Lord Kirkland can be heartily glad of it. His drovers won't be coming back here. You can sell your cattle where you like, now."

There was a moment's pause, as if they hadn't heard right, then from a hundred voices at once a thunderous cheer went up, echoing off Black Rock up and down the valley as far as Hafod and the Cwmystwyth mines. Dic Richards seized Gruffydd's hand and wouldn't let go.

"You've saved me. You've saved me," he babbled.

"There's a welcome for you at Pen-y-Graig any day, master," hollered Sam Jones from the back.

"Open house for you every day of the week," Morgan the Brewer said and wondered where he stood with John Ffowlke now.

Above the din came the noise of hammering. Rolo Blacksmith was nailing his best and lucky horseshoe to Gruffydd's front door. Iago One-Leg, who had made his first fiddle from his wooden leg out of sheer boredom, struck up another tune and blind Ismael Harpist joined in. Some started dancing again, but others wanted to hear more and called impatiently for hush.

"How did you do it, master?"

"I threatened to turn John Ffowlke into a heifer and sell him to his own drover," Gruffydd called back above the heads of the crowd. The gratitude and admiration on their faces were a sweet wine and he drank it deep.

"Who'd take him?" hooted Siôn Edmunds. "He's not worth the pound Padrig Jonathan was offering."

"And he'd never make the journey to England," Dic Richards threw in with ponderous wit.

"He'd sink under his own weight."

"Or drown in the Wye!"

"What happened then, sir?"

"Well." Gruffydd donned his most solemn air. "When he saw his feet turning into hoofs and a tail sprouting from his arse, he began to get worried, so he went down on his knees and said he'd do anything if I'd make him a man again."

"Did you change him back?" asked Thomas Jenkins, fascinated.

"Well, of course I did, Thomas! You wouldn't want to swallow a piece of John Ffowlke one day, would you? But"—Gruffydd raised a finger—"he's not the man he used to be." Gruffydd paused, and he felt them push forward to hear better. "You see, when I changed him back into a man I told him we were angry with his lordship for the way he had treated us, but I was so busy talking to him that I got the spell wrong. What happened," Gruffydd said straight-faced, "is that the cow's tail got left behind and his own one was somehow missing in front."

Gruffydd's audience shook with delight.

"What did you do with it?"

"Perhaps the cow's got it!" Rolo suggested.

"No, no," Gruffydd said. "I managed to rescue it and I promised him he could have it back in five years if he doesn't bother us in the meantime. Till then I'll keep it in pickle."

"What about the cow's tail, Gruffydd?" asked Llewelyn.

"I apologized to the cow, but I couldn't very well offer her the replacement." Out of the corner of his eye he saw Madlen sitting in the doorway of the Round House. Her usually pale skin was flushed with the bonfires and the cold air, and she was smiling strangely. Just as he turned to her she disappeared into the house. "So if you ever see a cow without a tail," Gruffydd finished abruptly, "you can say, 'That was once John Ffowlke.'" He pushed through the crowd towards the house and closed the door behind him to a final cheer. Iago and Ismael returned to their tune, Thomas, Huw, Siôn Edmunds and the girls to their dancing, and Morgan, Siân Evans, Mali Fishpond and the other old folk to their beds, going over every detail of the story seven or eight times, with their own additions, as they lurched down the mountain to the Ystwyth.

IV

Madlen was sitting cross-legged by the hearth, her dark hair falling forward across her face and nearly touching her knees. Slowly she brushed it off her cheek with a forefinger and tucked it behind her ear, then she tilted her head to one side and looked up at him. Had he forgiven her? She was sorry for having angered him but she wouldn't admit it until he'd apologized to her. Gruffydd padded over from the door, watching her intently. He knelt beside her and his eyes wandered over her face then he put his hands on her shoulders and kissed her on the side of her long, graceful neck just above the collar of her flannel dress. She shivered and pulled away, but he gripped her more tightly and buried his face in her hair, his lips moving over her ear and the nape of her neck. Madlen wrenched free.

"What have you decided?"

"I'm staying."

"Yes, I heard. And what about me?" Gruffydd shrugged impatiently. Wasn't it obvious? "You want me now, but in a couple of months?" He muttered something under his breath and picked up a rat-trap he'd been making, but he couldn't concentrate. He was too aware of the folds of her dress and the way her calves gleamed white in the firelight as she perched on a sack of barley, waiting.

"What do you want?" he said at last.

"I want to move in here and live with you. I can't stay where I am. Rhiannon wants to marry me off." Gruffydd looked up sharply.

"Who to?"

"Does it matter? Who would you like me to marry?" Gruffydd threw aside the rat-trap and started pacing round the room.

"Look. You can't live here, for many reasons. You'd interfere with my work. And . . . I have a wife already."

Madlen stopped herself from crying out. She could hear from his voice he was telling the truth. Why hadn't she suspected it? The stone around his neck was a pledge from some woman. She gazed inertly at the weave in the barley sack by her knee and the acrid smoke from the fire stung in her eyes. It was pointless talking. She might only weaken and give him what he wanted. She made for the door. "It's not what you think," he said, "I have a wife, but she's dead."

"Dead? Then you're not bound to her."

"More than ever. I did her a great wrong and now I can never make it good."

Did he think he could take her in that easily? Everyone knew that conjurers weren't bound by their vows. Let him bring her back from the dead if he loved her so dearly.

"You listen to me now, Gruffydd Conjurer," she said quietly, standing over him while he crouched beside his hearthstone. "I won't hang around as your fancy woman to be called upon one day and dismissed the next. I let you have me once because I wanted to, but I didn't come here tonight to beg for more. You think I'm an ignorant girl, but at this moment I know more about the future than you do." It was a gamble, but she guessed that he'd heard nothing about her news.

"How?" Gruffydd yawned. She felt like kicking him.

"You think you've saved John Ffowlke's life . . ."

"Don't talk to me about Ffowlke."

"What about Sir Lewis Pryse then?" Gruffydd snorted derisively and went to open a window-hatch and stare at the dancers. "Sir Lewis is out for Ffowlke's blood and if Ffowlke hangs you'll hang with him." Gruffydd closed the hatch and slowly turned. Madlen busied herself with the fire, suddenly in no hurry to continue.

"What do you mean?"

"Sir Lewis told me himself."

"When? What did he say?"

"Pryse came to the Bevans' this afternoon. Ffowlke is going to be tried by a military tribunal tomorrow and Pryse is getting Hywel to testify against him. Pryse has promised to release Hywel, and more. He called you the biggest obstacle to Hywel's work in the valley and if Hywel testifies he'll remove you. Those were his words—remove you."

Gruffydd was alarmed. He had no idea that his reputation had travelled so fast. He had made enemies he didn't even know of.

"That's all," Madlen said briskly and pulled her shawl around her neck.

"Wait. Wait a minute."

"Why?"

"I need you." He was tired of fighting.

"Can I live with you?"

Gruffydd nodded wearily. "As soon as all this blows over." Madlen hugged him and tried to get him to dance to Iago One-Leg's tune which drifted in from outside, but he seemed suddenly sad. Now she was conscience-stricken at having won and wanted to reassure him. She kissed him, but he was indifferent to her, and nothing she could think of pleased him—she had never had any girl-friends to tell her what to do and Rhiannon was far too shy to talk about her love-making with Hywel. So in desperation she stepped away from him and started to unbutton the front of her bodice, amazed at her own forwardness. Gruffydd pretended not to notice, but gradually his eyes turned. Her breasts scarcely moved as she slipped off her dress and her nipples were taut and swollen. She watched him as she unhooked her petticoats and stepped out of them. Her legs were blinding white, perfectly curved from hip to ankle. Tiny blonde hairs glowed in the firelight across the long, firm sweep of her belly, deepening in colour till they curled black as oblivion on the swelling between her thighs. She had a birth-mark under her left breast—the one blemish that made her perfection bearable. Gruffydd fumbled with the clasp on his belt, tore off his cloak and laid it on the floor for her. She stretched luxuriously, head and arms thrown back, agile wrists raising her dark hair, then she lay down on his cloak to let him take her as he wanted.

Outside the singing and dancing were as loud as ever. Madlen watched the smoke spiralling from the fire, swirling in the eaves, trying to find its way out. She knew that happy laughter out there, how easily it turned to mockery.

"She's Gruffydd's old boot," she could hear Siân Evans saying in a week's time, two perhaps. "He wore her out fast enough."

"See her . . . ?" The chorus was never-ending. She would have to move in here soon, before word got around. She must make Gruffydd keep his promise to her, because there was no turning back now. She was too preoccupied to enjoy their love-making, but she did her best to pretend. She was worried for Gruffydd especially—having nearly lost him once to Aberystwyth gaol, she didn't want to risk him a second time. When he ground to a halt on top of her she ran her fingers over his hair and whispered: "Listen to me, my love, please do as I say. You must see John Ffowlke at once and warn him." His body tautened and he tried to move, but she clamped herself to him fiercely, locked her legs around his back and started to massage the knotted muscles of his shoulders. "I beg you. Please do this for me." His head moved against her shoulder in consent and before he could reconsider she rolled him off her, threw his cloak round her shoulders and went to the door.

"Mihangel!" she called into the dark. Mihangel appeared instantly at the crack in the doorway. "The conjurer has a job for you. You're to go to Brithgoed. He wants to speak to John Ffowlke."

"Wait for me outside," came Gruffydd's voice and Mihangel caught a glimpse of him lying naked by the fire, his flushed head thrown back over a log. Mihangel smiled knowingly at Madlen as she pushed the door shut.

Had she done the right thing? If Gruffydd saved Ffowlke, Hywel might be kept in gaol for ever and she had just robbed her sister of a husband.

"Rhiannon knows about us," she said as she put on her clothes. "That's why she wants to marry me off." Gruffydd laughed.

"What would you do with a husband—eat him alive?"

She turned to him by the door and did up the top button of her dress.

"I'll not wait long. Come and get me, or I'll find a decent man."
Then she quietly closed the door behind her and slipped into the
forest unnoticed.

v

John Ffowlke perused the sheaf of parchment scribbled with lines and
arcane figures, Roman numerals and signs of the zodiac. After two
hours he was no nearer deciphering it.

"It'll drive me mad," he muttered, reaching for the burgundy.
Empty. "Reuben, another bottle!" His voice echoed down the corridor and in the deserted kitchens. "Where is everyone?" he shouted,
appalled by the silence. Nothing stirred. Maude was in bed, Talbot in
detention and the servants, sensing an imminent upheaval in the
order of things, had all taken French leave.

"Left me, all of them. No gratitude, these people. They'd dance on
my grave." Even Goronwy, the gnarled, deaf-mute doorkeeper, who
never left his post, night or day—even he was gone. "Anyone could
walk in." Ffowlke hastily locked himself in his study. He would have
felt even more scared if it weren't for the detachment of Fleming's
Grenadiers encamped by the Ystwyth, keeping him under house
arrest until tomorrow's hearing.

He hadn't spoken to a soul since General Fleming had arrived and
he had no idea what they would accuse him of tomorrow. He num-
bered off his likely adversaries. What about Lewis Pryse? With any
luck he would be even worse off than Ffowlke. He had probably
reached the Pretender himself. John Ffowlke's information, un-
reliable at the best of times, was by now several days stale, and
incorrect at that. Then there was that preacher fellow. No, he was safe
in gaol and nobody would hear of him again. He picked up the empty
bottle and poured absent-mindedly. So little intelligence to base his
defence on. What could he say? He threw the bottle into the fireplace,
where the heavy sediment spattered over the cinders and sizzled
noisily. He watched it lethargically, glad of any diversion, and then
returned to his desk to stare yet again at his horoscope where, perhaps, tomorrow's outcome lay buried.

Why couldn't she have had it written in plain English or Welsh?
His mother had had this chart drawn up at his birth by the astrologer
to the French court, but she was dead and so was the astrologer in all
likelihood. The thought that his life was mapped out here before
him, yet completely inaccessible, numbed his brain more than the
burgundy.

Ffowlke must have dozed off. He was dreaming of a clear night sky. Thousands upon thousands of stars looked down at him from the firmament. One, particularly, caught his attention and he felt irresistibly drawn towards it. His feet left the ground. He was dragged up through the air at breath-taking speed, and the nearer he got to the star the more he understood the secret that was eluding him. In a confused way he realized that the star was he himself, Lord Kirkland.

The red velvet curtains behind him fluttered gently. A tapping on glass and the creak of a window opening recalled John Ffowlke's soul to earth with a start.

"Who's there?" he called out, terrified. The curtains swayed and billowed. He staggered from his desk to the door and fumbled with the key. It wouldn't turn. "Who is it?"

In the centre of the bow window where the curtains met there was a flurry of velvet and a boy's head, hair black as jet and eyes to match, looked into the room. John stared. A succubus, he thought instantly.

"Forgive me, Your Honour," said the boy. "My master, Gruffydd, sent me. He wishes to speak with you." Gruffydd's name, spoken by this nocturnal visitor, had a curious effect on Ffowlke, as though his dream—and he was not at all sure of being awake—had been induced in him by the conjurer.

"Why does Gruffydd—your master—wish to speak to me?"

"He said it was vital for your safety." Mihangel gazed round the room in wonder. He had never been in such a place before. Half the things in it—the chandelier, the globe, the cut glass—he had to look at twice to see properly.

Ffowlke eyed the boy suspiciously. "Why didn't he come himself?"

"So as not to give you away to your enemies." Mihangel remembered his brief word for word.

"Where is he?"

"Waiting for you above Brithgoed."

This was, in fact, a lie. At that moment Gruffydd was standing in the French flower-bed beneath the study window, listening intently and thoroughly satisfied.

"You're asking me to go out on a night like this?" Ffowlke blustered. He had heard stories of men who had followed the summons of creatures like this and had never been heard of again.

"It's not far," Mihangel said innocently. "I'll lead the way." Ffowlke hesitated. He was in mortal fear of this boy but if the conjurer had news that touched him so deeply there was no refusing. And the image of that star, pulling him up to some unearthly encounter, lingered in his mind. He swung a cape over his shoulders.

"Keep ten paces ahead of me. Which way?" Mihangel pointed to the window. "Through there?" Ffowlke protested. His dignity as a peer of the Realm of Scotland had taken enough buffets recently. "Well, it makes no odds." By the desk he stopped and with a deft flick rolled up the horoscope and tucked it into his cape.

"You were born on a Friday, weren't you?" Mihangel said suddenly.

"Yes." Ffowlke looked at him askance, his doubts returning. "How did you know?"

"It just came to me," Mihangel said and jumped down into the flower-bed. Gruffydd was already half-way up the hill. He had chosen a sheltered hollow above the Ystwyth surrounded by tall larches that droned in the wind. He and Dan had often hidden there on gusty autumn afternoons. An uncanny place. Dan said murder must have been done there and the creaking tree-trunks were trying to tell them of it. Gruffydd had never been there alone and he shivered slightly to find it again just the same as it used to be.

To work! Gruffydd seized a dead branch and carved a circle into the soft turf. It was a bit squiggly, but near enough. Then he gathered brushwood and kindled a fire inside the circle. What next? A small juniper stood beside one of the larches. He hastily tore off three or four branches and threw them on the fire. As the yellow berries exploded, a sweet intoxicating smell spread round the hollow and the evergreen needles gave off a mysterious smoke. One thing more. Gruffydd cut himself a wand, then sat down by the fire locked in deepest contemplation.

John Ffowlke was lurching up the hill by the longest possible route. Mihangel, as instructed, had led him across the Ystwyth rapids instead of through the ford and his breeches were soaking. The night was alive with animal noises, all of which Ffowlke took to be the fair people come to abduct him. His young guide flitted through the shadows like a will-o'-the-wisp, always twenty paces ahead of him, sometimes disappearing altogether. Ffowlke was afraid of losing him. If he'd known the way back he would have taken it, but he was lost. Ten minutes out of Brithgoed and he was hopelessly lost on his own land.

"This way!" the boy shouted and disappeared over a ridge.

Ffowlke stumbled after him. At the top of the hill he stopped in wonder. Through the greenish haze he could make out Gruffydd's huge shape, in ghostly outline, sitting motionless by the fire. The conjurer was too deep in communion with the Beyond to notice him and Ffowlke waited reverently, not wishing to break the spell. For all he knew, Gruffydd might be intervening for him at that very moment. Then Gruffydd spoke. His voice was deep and cavernous and issued from the earth he was sitting on, not from mortal lungs.

"Advance. Take your place inside the circle." Not without misgivings, John Ffowlke walked down into the hollow.

"Sit." John Ffowlke sat. "Five times I have travelled round the world on your behalf. I have spoken with the powers that rule your life and mine. I have called up the spirits of your ancestors. And I find you are in great danger." John Ffowlke felt a cold sweat break out on the back of his neck.

"What danger?" he asked hoarsely.

"Do not interrupt. Your place is to listen," Gruffydd rebuked him. "Not to question. So listen closely."

CHAPTER SIX

IOLO WAS WEDGED in the highest rafters of the old customs house in Aberystwyth where half the notables of Ceredigion were on trial for their lives. He'd slipped in behind Gruffydd and climbed way above the stalls and benches, past the gallery packed with excited supporters of both the Whig and Tory factions to a narrow ledge just under the roof, where wooden beams fanned out in every direction to make a perfect nest. Iolo had never been in a court of law before, but he'd seen plenty of men hanged or whipped and was curious to know how they came to it. And this was an unusual court because, for once, the gentry were on trial.

Straight ahead of him, at the far end of the musty, smoke-filled building, on a dais constructed from the customs officers' desks sat the judge—a hawk-eyed, tight-lipped soldier in a massive wig that doubled the size of his head. Iolo squeezed even farther out of sight, glad that the man couldn't see him. The customs house was swarming like a beehive. Sacks of cornflour, barrels of salt, herring crates and evil-smelling flayed carcasses had been piled up round the walls and lawyers, officers, witnesses—even the defendants—were milling about the floor. How could anyone know what was happening? It was worse than the Smithfield cattle market. They all looked identical in their silver wigs and Iolo imagined himself a sea-gull coasting over a white-flecked, storm-tossed sea.

Then he saw Gruffydd. He was leaning, unnoticed, in a window embrasure, a dark shadow beside the red and gold velvets and brocades. Outside, the crowd of farmers and peasants started chanting and Gruffydd glanced at them through the window, smiled to himself, then leaned forward to whisper something to a pot-bellied, scared-looking man sitting in front of him on a raised bench. The man stared straight ahead, pretending not to notice Gruffydd, but Iolo could tell from the way his head was cocked to one side that he was listening hard. That must be John Ffowlke. What was Gruffydd doing with him?

In the witness-box a young man with a bruised but handsome, arrogant face was giving his evidence.

"... I acted alone in complete defiance of my companions ..."

It was Thomas Powell. Iolo recognized the magistrate who had arrested Hywel.

"Do you expect us to believe that you attacked a regiment single-handed?" drawled the interrogating officer, and everyone in the gallery laughed.

"I can explain everything." A tall, black-haired man rose from the defendants' bench and the liveried sergeant-at-arms pointed his bauble and said: "The Honorable Talbot Ffowlke."

Iolo wouldn't have wanted to meet him on Black Rock in the dark. He was like an angry bull: no neck at all, straight lines from his jaw to his polished boots.

"My Lord, General Fleming." Talbot bowed to the judge and then told a lengthy story about quarrels between himself and Thomas Powell which Iolo couldn't follow at all. Nor, apparently, could anyone else.

"You wish us to believe," interrupted the officer, playing up to the gallery, "that the original purpose of your expedition was to reaffirm your loyalty to George II?"

"Exactly." Talbot scowled through the stifled laughter. "After I insulted him and refused him a duel, Thomas Powell chose to salve his honour as a gentleman by an impossible, heroic attack on General Fleming's encampment, expecting to find certain death. We arrived too late to dissuade him."

Iolo didn't understand the logic of this. If Thomas wanted revenge he should have killed Talbot, not himself.

"I do not condone Powell's action," Talbot was saying, "but it is understandable and in no way touches his loyalty to the Crown." One by one, the other defendants went up to the witness-box and swore that Talbot was telling the truth. People seemed to believe them. Iolo was amazed. If he'd spun a yarn like that he'd be flogged for disrespect.

But it looked as if they'd get off scot-free, and General Fleming was just dismissing the charges of treason and referring Talbot and Thomas's quarrel to a court of arbitration when Sir Lewis Pryse got to his feet.

"My Lord! I have heard you deceived by more perjurers than I can number. I can hold my peace no longer. I have evidence that all these gentlemen—including Lord Kirkland himself—are guilty of conspiracy against our Royal House."

Iolo saw John Ffowlke rise and make to answer, but Gruffydd's arm shot out and pushed him back into his seat. As Lewis Pryse strode to the witness-box, Morgan the Brewer—stationed at a window in the gallery—shouted the latest news to the people outside over the impassive fur-trimmed caps of Fleming's Grenadiers.

"John Ffowlke to the gallows," they bellowed and from their catcalls swelled the chant, "Ffowlke's lost his balls." Gruffydd grinned and said something to John Ffowlke, who was pink with rage.

Iolo lay flat on his stomach and peered out at the crowded market-place and quayside through a rose window just under his ledge.

Talbot and Thomas Powell had been hanged in effigy from the spar of a fishing ketch, while Lord Kirkland—represented by a sack of potatoes, a pumpkin and two peat shovels—was receiving the same summary justice.

"And do you admit," Thomas Jenkins roared drunkenly, wagging his finger at the pumpkin, "that you have been a very naughty boy?"

"I do not," came an angry falsetto from Huw Lloyd "I only admit to having a cow's tail and no cock." His voice was drowned by laughter. John Ffowlke was drawn and quartered and his pumpkin head kicked up and down the quayside until it spattered open against a bollard.

Inside the hall, Lewis Pryse was reaching a perfectly-timed climax. ". . . And so, my Lord Fleming, the whole expedition was set on treason from the first and the moving spirit behind it was none other than Lord Kirkland himself."

A tense silence in the customs house. The crowd outside tossed cobble-stones at the door.

"Captain Mulholland," Fleming called down the hall. "Disperse that rabble."

Iolo saw the Grenadiers raise their rifles and fire in the air. One of the bullets whistled past the rose window. Iolo ducked and crawled away. There was a momentary lull outside.

"Now," Fleming said drily and turned to Lewis Pryse. "These are very grave accusations, Sir Lewis. Have you any witnesses?"

"I have, my Lord," Pryse said, his long, refined face a mask of composure. "My first witness is well placed to know the truth. He is Lord Kirkland's major-domo."

"Traitor!" shouted John Ffowlke, jumping up before Gruffydd could stop him.

"Traitor!" echoed the gallery, laughing.

"Now, Reuben," Lewis Pryse said kindly. "How long have you served Lord Kirkland?"

"Twenty-seven years, sir," Reuben said. Iolo watched his fingers twisting and turning the gold chain hanging round his neck.

"You must be acquainted with your master's affairs?" A loud guffaw from the stalls.

"I don't pry, sir," Reuben simpered. "But you can't help overhearing . . ."

"Quite so. Now tell me: what made you feel duty-bound, as a subject of His Majesty, to break your loyalty to Lord Kirkland?"

Iolo's attention was distracted by a new cry outside and he edged back to the window. Far on the other side of the quay, by the castle, a party was leaving the prison. Iolo pressed his snub nose even flatter to the dusty glass. Hywel Bevan, chained by the wrist to a sullen-looking man with a hunchback, was being brought to the customs house by the two constables who had arrested Gruffydd. The mob was running towards him, pushing and shoving to get to him first, but Hywel hardly seemed to notice them. Half-way across the market-place the crowd milling round him parted with a flurry to let someone through. It was Rhiannon. She threw herself at Hywel's feet and clasped his ankles. Hywel tried to lift her but she wouldn't move. With a hollow feeling inside him, Iolo understood that she was weeping uncontrollably—her back was bent at an odd angle and she kept throwing her head from side to side. Hywel knelt down beside her and she grabbed his head in both hands and refused to let go until the constables tore him away, and Madlen, looking as ashen as her sister, carried her to the Sailors Inn with the help of Thomas Jenkins.

Poor lady, Iolo thought. What was she asking him? Whatever it was, Hywel must have refused it, judging from the way his face closed up and his black stubbly jaw clamped tight. But there was pain in his eyes, too, as he gazed up at the sky straight past Iolo.

". . . And as they rode off," Reuben finished his lengthy and damning tale, "I heard Master Thomas Powell say that King George was a German sausage grinder and it was more meet that Charles Edward should rule."

Muted laughter in the gallery.

"He might at least credit me with a better wit," Thomas Powell remarked audibly.

"Lord Kirkland," General Fleming said. "You may either reply now or wait to answer to your peers in Parliament."

"Now," Iolo saw Gruffydd's lips say, and John Ffowlke leapt into action like the clockwork soldier at Toulouse Fair.

"*Reply?*" he sneered. "Reply to *that?*" Reuben flinched. "Twenty-seven years in my service. I raised him from the scullery to be head of my household and look how he repays me! Would *you* trust such a man?"

A snigger ran round the Whig bench as Pryse's next witness was led up the aisle.

"Where did you dredge him up from, Sir Lewis?" scoffed John Ffowlke.

"From Aberystwyth gaol, where you left him," Pryse retorted.

"Are we to take this seriously?"

"My Lord." Pryse turned to the bench, where General Fleming was scrutinizing Hywel with apparent distaste. "This man is the victim of the treachery and corruption of the Chief Justice of Cardiganshire." Ffowlke raised an eyebrow. "Five days ago, Lord Kirkland sentenced him to perpetual imprisonment as a rebel and traitor . . . As a traitor," Pryse repeated with heavy irony, "to His Majesty King James III, because he hoped to buy favour with the Pretender with this man's life."

General Fleming turned to John Ffowlke. "Did you sentence him?"

"To a few days' imprisonment for trouble-making, nothing more." Ffowlke seemed quite unruffled.

"That is a lie," Pryse stated. Furious arguments broke out across the floor of the courtroom and immediately below Iolo, in the gallery, a venerable clergyman who had muttered something against Lewis Pryse was seized by his long grey beard and made to eat it. A hefty Tory farmer was thrown out onto the quay from the upper-floor window while Dr Madog dropped a leech down the bodice of an irate Tory lady.

"Arrest them all, Mulholland!" roared Fleming, and the unfortunate clergyman was marched out between two Grenadiers.

"Now," Fleming resumed, as the uproar died away. "Instead of exchanging abuse, let us proceed to question the witness."

Hywel had been staring stone-faced at the court. They had forgotten he was there. Iolo watched him closely. He knew what Hywel was thinking: They're worse in here than outside.

"Well, Bevan," Lewis Pryse said. "Will you please tell the court what took place at your trial?"

The gallery strained to hear, but Hywel said nothing. Pryse rephrased his question.

"Is it true that you were sentenced for preaching obedience to King George?"

Still no answer.

"You are keeping the court waiting."

"Are you deaf, man?" Fleming asked, and a voice in the gallery answered: "He can't hear you."

"Is he mad?" Fleming roared. "Is everyone in this place mad?"

Very nearly everyone, Iolo thought and shifted onto his other elbow.

Pryse raged at Hywel, who looked back at him more in sadness than anger. "Please, for God's sake, speak!" The whole customs house fell into embarrassed silence. Iolo saw Gruffydd tap John Ffowlke on the shoulder and Ffowlke rose calmly to his feet. "My Lord, Sir Lewis has descended to the lowest strategems to blacken me. How much did you offer him, Sir Lewis, when you visited him in gaol yesterday? Well," Ffowlke said knowingly, "how much? Was it money? Was it freedom? He will not take it from you at the price of perjury. I salute him." Ffowlke raised his arm towards Hywel and the whole Whig bench applauded. "I confess now that I misjudged him. He is an honest man. I give him his freedom gladly."

"My Lord . . ." Pryse turned to General Fleming.

"Sir Lewis," Fleming said coldly, "you have exercised your right of speech to the full. I am disappointed. I had thought you a man of honour." He rolled up his notes and announced to a delirious house: "The charges are not proven. The Honourable Talbot Ffowlke and Thomas Powell, Esquire, are bound over to keep the peace for five years. Hywel Bevan, farmer: ten strokes of the lash for contempt of court." The crowd in the hall was breaking up in confusion when at last Hywel spoke.

"Falsehood!" he shouted, and the witness-box was suddenly a pulpit. "Falsehood!" he shouted again into the stunned silence. "This court is the work of Lucifer. I was unjustly condemned at my trial and am now unjustly punished at another. There is no justice in this world. You who so falsely administer it are damned and all those who look for it deluded. Leave your vicious ways and turn towards God." Half a dozen constables pounced upon him and Hywel was dragged away screaming.

Iolo started to climb down. On the lowest rafter, just above the judges' bench, he overheard General Fleming talking to his adjutant.

"Kirkland? No. The government needs him here. Besides, the minister has good reason to avoid a witch-hunt." Iolo didn't understand what Fleming meant but the words stuck in his head, and he remembered them years later.

He pushed his way through the crowd, looking for Gruffydd. From his crow's-nest under the roof he had seen him quite clearly, but as soon as he was on the courtroom floor, Iolo was lost. Nobody would let him pass—he was too small for anyone to notice, except when he got in the way and they cuffed him aside. He found Gruffydd in a quiet corner just as Ffowlke was taking leave of him. "Name your reward and you shall have it," Iolo overheard Ffowlke saying, but as soon as his back was turned, Gruffydd spat on the floor where he had been standing. Then he picked Iolo up without a word and barged his way to the door, cursing at everyone in his path. Madlen was waiting outside.

"You did well," she said to Gruffydd and tried to kiss him, but he pushed her roughly away.

"I should have let Ffowlke hang," he muttered through his teeth. "I should never have listened to you." Madlen tried to catch his sleeve, pleading with him, but he brushed her off and when she followed him he swung round and shouted at her, "You've got what you wanted from me. Much good may it do you. Now leave me in peace—I've had enough of you." And he walked straight across the market-place into the Sailors Inn.

CHAPTER SEVEN

I

GRUFFYDD ROLLED OVER into a pool of stale beer.

High seas, he thought and rolled back again. In his dream, John Ffowlke and Lewis Pryse were hanging by the neck from the yard-arm of his lurching ship. Gruffydd clung to the wheel and tried to keep an even keel, only to be thrown across the deck against the bulwark, where he woke up. His bladder was bursting.

He groaned and struggled onto one elbow. His head was floundering and his mouth felt like crumbling parchment. In the murky first light of a mid-December day, the old customs house lay in ruins about him. Nothing inside its great hulk was intact. Crates were torn open, benches smashed, stalls chopped up for firewood. Cinders were scattered across the floor with the charred remnants of roasted carcasses. The witness-box was on its side, laden with beer barrels, one of them dripping monotonously over the inert face of Thomas Jenkins. Bodies sprawled over each other, contorted like corpses in the charnel-house.

Gruffydd tried to stand up and fell back against a woman lying next to him. Her broken teeth leered in her open mouth and she was breathing heavily, dead to the world. A flaccid bosom spilt out of her bodice. Her skirts were rucked up around her waist, legs wide open, yawning.

"Thank God I was too drunk." Gruffydd covered her with an empty potato sack. Last night was rushing back. He leaned over a barrel and puked heartily. The trial, the sheer loathing of these people who governed his country, Ffowlke's acquittal, Madlen's complacent smile, beer in the Sailors Inn, General Fleming's instant withdrawal to the frantic jeering of the crowd, looting the quayside, sacking the customs house, drunken carousal and limp dalliance with this jade beside him—all of it came heaving up out of him.

"That's better," he said. His head was clearing and he surveyed the havoc with pride. Had he done all this? A court of law they had called it. It looked better now. A whore their justice, and a whore-house their court. Gruffydd picked his way through the debris, kicked the sagging door off its last hinge and walked onto the quay. The judge's bench lay on the beach abandoned by the tide, where Gruffydd had ordered it to be thrown. He emptied his bladder over it and swore a solemn oath: "From now on, the justice of the Ystwyth shall be our justice. We shall make the laws and you shall obey them."

The quay was deserted. The redcoats had left without trace. A warm wind blew in off the sea, shearing away the white, tufted clouds off the hillside like fleece from a sheep's back. The Powells were in disgrace and John Ffowlke would do what he was told.

"This is mine," Gruffydd said, looking out over the sea, the castle and the hills behind. "And I shall be master in my own house." He dropped his cloak and ran down the beach into the icy grey waves without stopping to catch his breath. The muscles on his legs and stomach tautened as the water leapt around him. When he could run no farther, he threw himself under the next breaker. He felt it crash above him. The ground swell dragged him back, his chest grazed the sandy bottom. For as long as his breath held, Gruffydd twisted and turned beneath the surface, held himself down, looked up at the sky—the salt and the cold biting in his eyes—and then he explored a colony of mussels on a jagged rock.

Of course she had been right. He'd got Ffowlke where he wanted him. But she couldn't push him around. No woman looked at him like that. Gruffydd's lungs were bursting. With one kick he shot up half his own height above the waves and swam back.

The sea streamed out of his beard and shaggy hair as he walked up the beach, the salt crisp in the lines around his eyes and forehead, flushing out last night's hangover. Iolo was curled up on the quayside watching him, head on his knees, arms hugging his legs. He looked like a wandering spirit who has heard the cock crow but forgotten the way home.

"Where were you?" Gruffyyd asked, wringing out his hair. Iolo nodded to an upturned fishing boat. His teeth were chattering.

"Why didn't you come inside? We had a fire in there."

"Too smelly," Iolo said. He hated these roaring, drinking people. "They're like pigs. Sleeping in their own dung."

"At least it's theirs. It's all most of them have."

Iolo pointed to the customs house. "Why did you make them do that?"

"Listen," Gruffydd said, wrapping himself in his cloak. "If you find a rat's nest, what do you do?"

"Smoke it out."

"Exactly. And we were smoking out the judges and politicians of this world—the rats."

"But they'd left already."

Gruffydd was irritated sometimes by his son's literal turn of mind. "If you disinfect the place," he explained, "they don't come back."

"Smells worse now, if you ask me."

"That may be. But it's *our* smell."

"Not mine." Iolo shut his mouth tight. Gruffydd looked at the boy and felt a pang of guilt for their friendship of so many years.

"Let's go home, shall we?" he said gently and lifted Iolo onto his shoulders. "No one will bother us now." Iolo slipped his fingers into his father's wet knotted hair and nearly dozed off with his even, rhythmic stride.

"Father," he said sleepily as they walked beside the Ystwyth estuary, "will they really whip him?"

"Who?"

"Hywel Bevan."

"I expect so." Gruffydd had forgotten about Hywel. He was watching a flock of lapwings circling above the estuary on the freshwater margin, the loud throb of their wings mixed with intermittent, shrill singing.

"It's unfair," Iolo said. "All he did was tell them they were liars."

"All?"

"You think so too, don't you? You just said they were rats."

"They are."

"And everyone hates him for it. Did you hear them shouting when he was taken to prison?"

Gruffydd nodded.

"They called him a coward because he didn't accuse John Ffowlke."

"Do you think he was right?" Gruffydd needed Iolo's approval. The boy sometimes saw more clearly than he did.

Iolo hesitated. "I don't know. But at least he says what he believes. And doesn't care if they hate him."

"But it doesn't help anybody—not even himself."

Iolo didn't argue. He couldn't explain why he liked Hywel, but he knew how it felt to have people shout and throw things at you because you are the way you are.

"Do you think I am wrong?" Gruffydd asked, sensing what was on his mind. "I didn't accuse Ffowlke either, though I could have done."

"No, no," Iolo said hastily. That thought had never occurred to him. "No, you're different."

"Different?"

"You can do what you like, can't you . . ." Iolo dried up. He couldn't say what he meant.

II

"I've got what you wanted."

Madlen went on scrubbing her petticoats on the smooth stone by the rain-barrel and didn't look up.

"I've got it," Mihangel repeated nervously. She was cross with him and he was anxious for his reward.

"What took you so long?" Madlen remorselessly pummelled the coarse linen. All night she had sat up waiting, Gruffydd's ingratitude gnawing at her like a cancer. The brutal indifference with which he brushed her off when she'd served her purpose! All night she'd waited, till she thought Mihangel had broken his promise. But the boy would do anything for her.

"I couldn't get it while he was awake." Mihangel lowered his voice, as though Gruffydd might somehow be listening. Their conspiracy scared him. There was no knowing what Gruffydd would do if he found out, but it brought Madlen a step closer. She had seemed so unobtainable. Only three years older than he, yet grown-up already. Mihangel was in a hurry to grow up himself and the secret lay somewhere in the confident swaying of Madlen's skirts, in the way she left her bodice unbuttoned at the top.

"Show me," she said abruptly, dropping the petticoats in the rain-barrel and drying her hands on her black hair as she pushed it out of her face. Mihangel furtively drew out a piece of old leather, tightly knotted with threads of hemp from a hawser on the quay. Madlen's hair brushed his cheek as she leaned over to watch, and her bosom pressed against his shoulder. Slowly he untied the thread, relishing her rapt attention.

"There," he said proudly as the leather fell open. At first Madlen could see nothing, then, very delicately, she scraped together something with her fingers and held it up to the light.

"Not very much of it," she said frowning. She mustn't encourage him. He'd get over-confident. Mihangel's devotion flattered her. He was useful and easy to keep at arm's length, but he was just a boy and it annoyed her when he tried to be a man. "I suppose this will do," she said grudgingly. But her heart was pounding with relief, like a gambler whose bet has paid off. Between her thumb and forefinger, Madlen had three hairs off Gruffydd's head and that was enough to catch any man—even a conjurer. Without another thought for Mihangel she made for the back door.

"What about my reward?" he called after her.

"What reward?" Madlen remembered her side of the bargain perfectly but was in no hurry to keep it. Mihangel blushed scarlet. The withering curve of those red lips scared him now. How could he dare come near them?

"You said I could have a kiss," he stammered, wishing he'd never spoken.

"Shame on you," Madlen mocked. "I never did such a thing. You're far too young."

"I've had more than a kiss from Lissi Fishpond," Mihangel said, his pride hurt. Lissi had once lifted her skirts for him, but more as a tease than an invitation.

"Have you indeed?" Madlen didn't like the idea of Mihangel dallying elsewhere. "Then you should be whipped for it. She's a coarse girl anyway."

"Well, what about you and Gruffydd, then?" Mihangel blurted, remembering Madlen half-wrapped in a blanket, her eyes strangely bright and one thigh bare, while Gruffydd's naked body lay distended by the fire. He knew what had passed between them and it made him hot and jealous.

Madlen swung round on him. Her voice was steely. "What do you mean by that?"

"Everyone knows . . ."

"Oh, do they?"

"Yes, they do. And what's more they're laughing at you now."

"Let them laugh," Madlen said contemptuously and thought, How can I show my face again? "Why are they laughing?"

"Because Gruffydd was tumbling Leisa from Little Darkgate Street on the floor of the customs house last night."

He hadn't meant to say it. He was mortified for Madlen and ashamed for Gruffydd, because he worshipped them both. He wanted to share what they had, but if Gruffydd had tired of Madlen it was his turn. She shouldn't have broken her promise. Now she knew what it felt like.

"You're lying," Madlen said. "You snake. You're just saying it."

"He was drunk. That's how I managed to get his hairs." Mihangel would never get his kiss now.

"To hell with his hairs," Madlen screamed. "I wish I'd never seen him." She dragged her soaking petticoats out of the rain-barrel and whipped him round the ears with them. Mihangel turned round at a safe distance and shouted: "All I did was tell you the truth." Then he disappeared into the forest, as miserable as any Judas.

Madlen ran up the ladder to the loft gripping Gruffydd's three hairs. She climbed onto the dresser and fished behind the rafters.

First she found Steffan's stone in its filthy linen sheath, but she'd tried that three nights running and it was clearly useless. The gaoler must have been lying. Then she pulled out a clay figurine about three inches long. It consisted of two round cakes of mud—one for the body, one for the head—held together with rushes that stuck out at the top like hair standing on end. A nose and a mouth and two startled eyes were carved in the face. Spindly legs, one of them broken, were wedged into the body. No arms at all. "Now, Lord Gruffydd, I will teach you not to play me false." Her hands were perfectly steady as she tied Gruffydd's three hairs in a knot around the figurine, then took a pin from her shawl and stabbed, slowly and deliberately. "I hope this kills you." She turned the pin in the clay. "You took me, used me and then threw me away. May you die in torment and rot in hell."

Madlen clasped both hands around the pin.

"I hate you," she sang in a low monotone, swaying back and forward on her haunches, faster and wilder, boring a hole in the heart of the figurine. "I hate you. I hate you." She lunged forward and stabbed, working herself into a frenzy. The pin was bent in two and had pierced a hole in the palm of her hand. A fine trickle of blood ran down it and dropped onto Gruffydd's three mangled hairs. Madlen stared at it terrified, and for an instant saw Gruffydd's torn corpse lying before her. "Oh, God," she cried aloud, "what have I done?" The figurine and the three hairs had been to get him back, not to kill him with. "Pray God it hasn't worked! But why another woman? Why Leisa the whore, of all women?" It made her feel sick to think of him inside Leisa's scrofulous, pox-ridden body when he could have had her, without asking. Madlen sucked the wound in her hand and cried bitterly. Never in her life had she felt so forsaken, so despised.

"My love, what is it? What happened?" Madlen was lying on the floor unconscious. Rhiannon dragged her to the bed.

"Where is he?" Madlen asked as her eyes opened.

"Where is who?" Rhiannon was frightened. Madlen had screamed as though possessed. It was surely not the conjurer trying to hold on to her?

"Gruffydd. He was here."

"No one was here, my love. The house was empty."

Madlen moaned as she saw the remains of the figurine. "Oh, God, help me, Rhiannon." She hid her face in her sister's lap.

Rhiannon rocked her gently. "Don't be afraid. He can't hurt you."

"No," Madlen whispered and then suddenly sat up. "Send someone to find him! Please! He may be dying. Please find him."

Rhiannon made her lie down and covered her with a blanket. "Be quiet now," she said gently. "He is no concern of yours. You must forget him."

"Yes," Madlen said absently.

"You are getting a fine husband. Dewi will look after you."

"Yes," Madlen said again. Her mind was miles away on her one-time lover, never to be seen again. She saw him thrown from a horse, lying at the bottom of a ravine. She heard the horse neigh and stamp and Gruffydd shout. She came to with a start.

"It's him," Rhiannon said, looking through a chink in the roof.

Madlen sat up, her heart racing.

"It can't be." She pushed Rhiannon out of the way. Gruffydd was trotting round the yard on a fine black mare with Iolo clinging on behind the saddle.

"Anyone at home?" he shouted, reining and spurring the horse at once to make it dance. Pigs, cows and chickens stared at him from behind the barn where they'd taken refuge.

"I must talk to him." Madlen made for the ladder, thanking heaven to see him alive. Rhiannon caught her arm.

"You can't."

"Why not?"

"Because of what he's done to you," Rhiannon said indignantly.

"Of course." Madlen remembered Leisa. How dared he show his face here? What did he take her for? "Tell him," she said with all the scorn she could muster, "that I never want to see him again and that I'm to be married to Dewi Cobbler. And tell him," she called after Rhiannon, as she climbed down the ladder, "that I never loved him. He suited me for a while. But I've worn him out. Like an old boot."

Gruffydd was standing in the doorway.

"If you wish to see my sister . . ." Rhiannon began.

"I don't," he interrupted. "I came to see you."

"Me?" Rhiannon stammered, her heart fluttering. "Why me?" Gruffydd watched her face light up, smiled into her naïve green eyes and slowly put his hand out under her chin. Rhiannon stared at him, fascinated.

"It was just to say that your husband will be home today. Without a whipping. I had a word with John Ffowlke and it was all arranged."

He leaned forward and kissed her under her ear lobe. Rhiannon was too stunned to resist. Gruffydd vaulted onto his new mare—a token of gratitude and esteem from John Ffowlke—jumped the fence and was gone.

"What did he say?" Madlen shook her sister by the shoulders.

"You're quite safe from him," Rhiannon said with a faraway smile. "Oh, and Hywel's coming home."

III

Hywel ran the last few hundred yards down the woodland path and burst into the clearing above his farm.

It was just as he'd left it. The yard was as clean as ever—cleaner, because the rubbish they had hurled at him that day was cleared away. Smoke rose from the chimney and Rachel was driving the cows down from pasture for the night. Hywel counted them, recognizing each one.

"Thanks be to God! Lucky is the man who has womenfolk like mine." He was glad of his release now, glad that the cup had been taken from him, that he had not been called to drink it to the dregs, that God's will had been done. Life had never seemed so desirable and he was returning to it with a clear conscience. "And I will use it," he promised, renewing his old covenant, "to further Your work."

Rachel noticed a shadow on the edge of the forest and stopped by the gate. She had hurried to get the herd in before dark but now she stood stock still and watched.

"Father is home!" she shouted. She left the cows bellowing to be milked and raced up the path. The dark figure ran out of the forest and swept her up in his strong arms.

"Rachel, God bless you, child!" Hywel carried her down the hill towards his mother, who was dashing up as fast as her legs could carry her. Rhiannon met Hywel by the gate.

"Welcome home," she said and he kissed her forehead. What could she tell him? So much had happened. Madlen and the conjurer? Impossible. He'd never allow her marriage to Dewi. Rhiannon felt she would never be as innocent with Hywel as before. He was almost a stranger. Why was it easier to love him while he was away?

"From now on," Hywel was saying to her, "I shall remain here with you. We have enough work on our doorstep without looking in the next valley for sinners."

If you had never gone, Rhiannon thought, nothing would have

changed. She threw her arms around his neck, crying, "Do stay with us. Please stay with us always." Hywel freed himself.

"I said I will stay." Perhaps all was not as well as it seemed.

Iolo stood at the edge of the clearing. He had seen Hywel running down the hill towards his family and had suddenly felt terribly alone, robbed of the mother, sisters, grandparents he had never had. He admired and loved his father more than anything but being treated as an equal was not always easy. Iolo sometimes longed to be treated like a child for once. He wanted to be part of the homecoming, which was all his doing if only they knew. Gruffydd had less and less time for him, with people from Cwmystwyth flocking to the Round House at all hours of the day, and the Bevans were the only people here who were friendly with him. He suspected himself of gross disloyalty towards Gruffydd in wanting to be with them, but what choice did he have? If he was going to stay here, he had to make friends. He couldn't always be at the lake. It's my life, anyway, Iolo thought, screwing up his courage. He wandered down the path to the farm and skulked around the yard, trying to catch their attention. Rhiannon noticed him first.

"Go away," she called. "The master has only just come home. He is busy."

"Don't send him away," Hywel protested. "He may be in need."

"No, no," Rhiannon insisted. "Better let him go." Ruth shifted awkwardly and Rachel stared with open hostility.

"Who is he?" Hywel asked.

"The conjurer's son," Ruth said. "He comes here, sometimes."

"And don't you take him in? Encourage him?" Hywel was bewildered. No visitor ever left his house without refreshment, physical or spiritual. "I have time. One so young can do us no harm."

Rhiannon watched through the hatch-window, as Hywel walked to the fence.

"Will he give us away?" she whispered to Madlen.

Iolo was lounging under the barn eaves. Hywel leaned over the fence. "How can I help you?"

"Why did she tell me to go away? I only wanted to say that I am glad you are out of prison and safely home."

"Thank you," said Hywel, with an abrupt laugh. He wasn't used to condescension from children.

"I think what you did at the trial was quite right," Iolo added, kicking a clump of mud off the barn wall.

"Do you?" Hywel said, interested. "You're the only person who does."

"Of course. Why should you say anything to those beasts?"

"Everyone wanted me to."

"They were wrong. People always want what's wrong for you. You have to decide for yourself. Don't you?"

"Yes," said Hywel. "Though I'd put it differently." Iolo felt the approval in his voice and sat on the fence next to him. "Well, what can I do for you?" Hywel asked, wanting to go in.

"Don't be hard on my father. Why can't you be friends?"

Hywel was torn. It went against the grain to teach anything but obedience to a father, but the boy's soul must come first.

"Your father does not believe in God. He is leading a great many people to hell. You among them, if you are not careful . . . I'll show you where it's written in the Bible."

"I can't read," Iolo said truculently. Hell and salvation didn't mean much to him.

"I'll read it for you."

"Why are you so unkind to him? After all, Gruffydd's helped you, hasn't he?"

"How?"

"He stopped them from whipping you, didn't he?"

Hywel stared at him. "Why?" he said at last.

"Because I asked him to." Iolo was tired of giving Gruffydd all the credit. "And because Rhiannon was scared for you." He didn't understand why Hywel's face was downcast. "Aren't you glad?"

"Yes . . . yes," Hywel said. "It was a kind thought. Thank you." He put his hand on the boy's shoulder. "Did Rhiannon know?"

"Of course," Iolo said. "We came to tell her today."

So the conjurer had returned to Hywel's house in his absence and spoken to his wife. What else had passed between them? And would Rhiannon have told him? Even Hywel was tainted, even his safe return was due as much to the conjurer as to his own honesty. Gruffydd's influence had spread like a pestilence, and yet this son of his appeared to be free from it. Hywel decided to carry the fight into Satan's own camp.

"Come in with me, I'll give you a good meal," he said, taking Iolo by the hand. "And if you like I'll teach you how to read the Bible for yourself."

CHAPTER EIGHT

MADLEN OPENED HER fingers and peered out at the bowed heads of Hywel's tiny congregation. Wouldn't he ever call a halt? Her knees were frozen. It was nearly midnight and they'd been at it since sunset, but Hywel showed no signs of finishing his silent prayer and no one would dare raise their heads before he did.

Madlen wondered what they were all thinking about. Hywel probably wished he was back in prison. Rhiannon, too, if she would only admit it. Life hadn't been easy since Hywel's release. He hadn't slept with her once. What had they done to him in there? Rhiannon looked like the Virgin at the Annunciation: hands crossed over her bosom, fair hair gathered at the nape of her neck, skirts falling in a pool at her knees. And what about Dewi Cobbler, then? He was imagining what he'd do with her in bed tomorrow night. If he had the strength for half of it. Dewi's calloused hands were clapsed in heavenly rapture, his eyes closed on a pudgy moon face. The crown of his head was bald, like a tonsured monk. Madlen shifted and coughed. Were they all asleep or dead? As dead as the bones of St Padarn, lying in their glass case. The minutes expired without a murmur. In the erratic flame of the rush taper on the wall, the bent, motionless bodies seemed doubly inert, frozen in stone like the knight mourning on his dead lady's tomb in St David's Cathedral. Madlen was surprised to remember it. Her father had taken her there on his one visit to the Bishop. She had been only five or six. Why did he die? He would never have let her go through with this. She felt scared. They were all in mourning, in mourning for her wedding. Very soon they would lay her with Dewi in a coffin and bury her. And they wouldn't hear her screaming or know that she was still alive.

"Dearly beloved," Hywel's voice rang out like the last trump, "I believe that our prayers for our brother Dewi and our sister Madlen have been heard." Hywel's hand grasped hers and Madlen stared into the glassy eyes of Dewi Cobbler. "Do you plight this woman your troth?"

"I do," Dewi answered.

"And you, Madlen, are you satisfied, before your conscience and before God, that you come here pure in heart and honest in soul to make this man a loving and obedient wife?" Rhiannon smiled at her, a mother proud to give away such a fine daughter. Dewi's family were all smiling too.

Hypocrites, she thought, and said: "I am satisfied."

There was a constancy in her voice Hywel had never heard before, which perhaps betokened a change of heart. "You are a happy man, Dewi." He took their hands, placed them together and said: "Tomorrow on the day we celebrate the birth of Our Lord you will be made man and wife in your father's church. May his spirit guide you."

As Dewi's fingers, blackened by his own shoe hammer, insinuated themselves between hers and he leaned forward to kiss her chastely on the cheek, Madlen realized for the first time how far Gruffydd had brought her. Every night for a week she had slept with his hair under her pillow, every day she had sent Mihangel with a new message, but there was not a word from him. Gruffydd had abandoned her. Not even this mockery of a marriage could stir his pride or fan his jealousy one jot. She wiped Dewi's spittle off her cheek with the back of her hand. She had lost and this was her forfeit. She would have to go through with it. There was no backing out now, not on her own. To throw over Dewi, with no alternative, was suicide. No man—or woman—would look at her again.

Why didn't she just leave? Anything would be better than this. But where to? Out into the mountains in midwinter, with snow in the air and people too hungry to give her a meal even if she paid with her body? And how long would her smooth skin and fine thighs survive the wild uplands, or the drudgery of some farm? Impossible. There was no escaping from here. But I will make your life hell, Dewi Cobbler. I have not lost Gruffydd yet.

Dewi's relatives embraced her, saying, "Welcome, sister," and "Dearest daughter," and Madlen turned to them with a gracious smile.

"Thank you all, for your kindness, I am proud to be one of you, and shall love you all as my own."

"Handsomely said, girl," cried Dewi's father.

"Fine words," agreed Madlen's future mother-in-law, who was determined to bring her down a peg or two. "I suppose you've been taught how to weave?"

"I believe I can weave as fast as another."

"You'll have enough chance to," Dewi's harelipped sister threw in.

A beautiful sister-in-law in the house squashed her last hope of ever finding a husband.

"And Maddi can help me with my boots," Dewi exclaimed. "Can't you, Maddi?"

Nobody had ever called her Maddi and as far as she could remember it was the first thing Dewi had said to her. His voice was an effeminate banter, like the tapping of his cobbler's hammer.

"Mending boots." Dewi nodded with a foolish grin and jerked an invisible hammer up and down in his right hand. "You see? Mending boots!"

"Of course," Madlen said tactfully. The man was a half-wit. Pray God she was already pregnant.

Hywel raised his hands. "Brethren! We must all prepare for tomorrow, but before you go, a mug of hot milk and nutmeg to warm you on your way."

"Fill it to the brim, Morgan," Gruffydd said, and Morgan reluctantly tipped the ale-barrel even steeper over the huge wassail-bowl brought out for the Christmastide. Morgan had no idea why Gruffydd, who had slandered Ffowlke only days ago, should be in such favour with him now. But Morgan's own fortunes were at a low ebb and Gruffydd alone had John Ffowlke's ear, so he poured out the last drop and, as the bowl was still not full, sent Llewelyn Tapster to carry up another barrel from the cellar.

Eighteen hands grabbed the eighteen handles of the wassail-bowl and hoisted it shoulder high. No one could remember where it came from, who had made it or to whom it belonged. It had always been there, stored for the year in the inn at Pendre and brought out once at Christmas and once on the first day of spring. Gruffydd remembered catching a glimpse of it when he was small: a vast red earthenware basin with flowers and animals and zig-zag patterns moulded on the lid, painted in white and yellow. Some of them were chipped and one handle had been broken off, but it was the finest thing he had ever seen.

"First stop is Garmon's barn," he called as they went out into the crisp night air. "I'll meet you there." He spurred his new mare and was away into the night. Over his shoulder he could see their torches leaping down the hill behind him. "Come on then," he shouted back, reluctantly reining in. He wanted to keep moving.

"What's the hurry?" Thomas Jenkins asked breathlessly. "You vanished like the Mari Lwyd."

Mari Lwyd! Gruffydd had completely forgotten her—the hobby-horse, the old grey mare of Christmas, that they used to make and carry round the farms, terrifying everyone.

"Thomas," he said laughing irresistibly. "Do you remember the time they poked the Mari Lwyd through the upstairs window where Mairwen, Simeon's wife, was in bed with Samson Constable?" Thomas nodded and grinned.

"And she was so scared she got cramp from screaming too hard. We had to throw them into the mill-pond to unlock them and Samson was threatening to arrest us all. The pond was near freezing too." Thomas laughed with him and then asked, a little puzzled: "How do you know that, master? Were you there?"

"What?" Gruffydd jumped back to the present. "No, of course not. It suddenly came to me, that's all." And he cantered away just as the others caught up. He was furious with himself. He would have to be more careful. There were things he would never be able to share with them.

The wassail party arrived at Garmon's barn bad-tempered and out of breath. There was no sign of Gruffydd.

"He's probably already by the fire," said Siôn Edmunds. But the house was dark.

"Anyone awake?" called Thomas Jenkins, while the others crept round the back.

"Who's out on a night like this?" asked a suspicious voice from inside.

"The ghost of the old year," Thomas wailed, and they all groaned and whined and beat their fists on the hatch-windows.

"Then we must lay you to rest," came the time-honoured reply. The whole family burst from the house with a yelling and whooping to match their haunters and a mock battle was fought, which the old year duly lost. The wassail-bowl was passed round and the wassailers were about to go in to eat barley bread and turnip soup when Sam Jones stopped dead.

"What's that?" he said. On the other side of the moonlit meadow, the high door of Garmon's barn creaked on its hinges and swung open. They all stared uneasily.

"Just the dog," Garmon said, "or a fox. They often rummage in there."

"A fox? Moving a barn door like that?" said Dic Richards dubiously.

"Maybe just the wind. Let's go in." But before they could stir, a ghostly neighing sound rose in the air and a white, pointed head with glaring eyes and no body to it peered round the barn door.

"Holy St David," whispered Old Isaac.

"It's the Water Horse!" said Siân Evans, her eyes gleaming in her black face, "and he's come for someone."

"Where's the conjurer?" asked Will Garmon. "Can't he talk to it?"

"Oh, God! It's something he's sent to punish us!" howled Mali.

"What for?" snapped Siân Evans. "More likely one of yours, you old witch. You speak to it."

"No!" Mali screamed as they pushed her towards the apparition.

"Speak to it!" they said, holding her fast, and the terrified woman bleated: "What do you want with us?"

"I need a rider," came a high wail, half horse, half human. The spectre floated across the meadow towards them. They backed away in terror.

"It's only a clergyman can ride the Water Horse. All others she drowns in her pool under the earth," said Old Isaac.

"Ask her who she wants," they ordered Mali, and she whined: "Which of us must ride you?"

There was a long silence in which each of them savoured the last minutes of life, and then the answer came back low and fierce: "I want the man called Morgan, who brews your ale."

They seized Morgan, limp and too frightened to resist, and led him to the middle of the meadow. Morgan sank to his knees as the Water Horse advanced on him and he felt its wings envelop him and flap around his head.

"Morgan," came the neighing voice again. The crowd trembled. The apparition seemed to swallow up its victim. "You are guilty of gross crimes against your fellow men. Now you will pay the price."

"I knew he'd find a bad end," whispered Isaac to Siân Evans, who was holding on to his coat.

"Ay. They say he murdered his mother for the brewery."

The Water Horse shook and groaned, working itself into a fury of revenge.

"I sentence you to drink your own ale until you die," it bellowed. "It is cat's piss and may your bladder rot."

They couldn't believe their ears. For seconds they stared in sheer wonder, and gradually the dreaded Water Horse took on a more familiar shape.

"Never heard of the Water Horse drinking ale," grunted Rolo Blacksmith. Cautiously they edged towards it in a solid phalanx.

"Why doesn't it move?" Huw Lloyd asked.

"Too drunk," Llewelyn Tapster said, and they all giggled. Ten yards from the monster they stopped and stared again.

"That's no Water Horse!" shouted Rolo. Laughter and relief swept through them. The terrible horns were a pair of Will Garmon's harvesting gloves on the end of a pitchfork, with a horsehair sheet thrown over it; the glaring eyes were his lucky horseshoes . . .

"Mari Lwyd," neighed the spectre, and the pitchfork leapt into the air to reveal a triumphant Gruffydd and Morgan in a dead faint beside him. "Water Horse indeed! The old grey mare took you for a fine ride this Christmas."

Siân Evans poured ale from the wassail-bowl over Morgan's face to bring him round and Isaac conferred in a huddle with the older men. They were still not convinced that there was no magic behind it.

"This was not what we saw," he said emphatically, dismissing the pitchfork with a contemptuous flick of the wrist. "We saw the Water Horse, then Gruffydd came and beat it off. How would Morgan be alive, otherwise?"

Gruffydd accepted this curious logic without argument and it was commonly accepted from then on throughout the Ystwyth valley. Isaac swore to it on his deathbed, and many times Morgan thanked Gruffydd for his timely rescue.

Gruffydd disappeared under the sheet and immediately the grey mare came alive. "Whoa there," he shouted as she bucked and reared, "hold still, will you?" But she ran riot, sniffing round the women's ankles, tossing up their skirts, trying to trip them up.

"Get away, bad old horse," screamed Lissi Fishpond as a pair of hands stretched out from the sheet and dragged her under it by her ample rump.

"That's no mare," said Huw Lloyd. "Stallion, more like."

"Ay," Siân Evans agreed. "I'll be delivering foals from Lissi in nine months."

They stood around and applauded as the grey mare kicked and lurched and then collapsed in a writhing puddle on the ground. Legs and arms protruded from under the sheet, and the head turned round to watch in amazement. Lissi escaped with her skirts up round her waist and her bodice undone.

"Where next?" said Rolo. Their blood was up.

"Back to the inn for more ale," Thomas Jenkins suggested. The wassail-cup was empty.

"None left," Morgan protested feebly. "You've drunk me dry." Thomas turned to the grey mare.

"Hey, Mari Lwyd, where are you taking us next?"

"I need a rider," neighed the Mari Lwyd.

"I'll ride you," said Siân Evans, but the hobby-horse reared and refused to let anyone mount.

"Only a clergyman can ride the Mari Lwyd."

"Clergyman?" Thomas said. "There's none around here."

"There's one who would like to be," retorted the old grey mare, jerking her head.

"Hywel Bevan!" said Huw Lloyd, "The preacher. We owe him a visit after what he did at the trial."

Thomas was disappointed. "But we'll get no ale from him. Nothing but praying."

Rolo stooped and whispered in the Mari Lwyd's leathery ear. "It's Hywel Bevan, then?"

The Mari Lwyd nodded vigorously, her brassy eyes shining wildly in the moonlight. "Pay our respects to the bride and groom." She was away in one bound, prancing down the hill towards the river and up the other side. The rest ran after her excitedly, a pack of hounds on the scent of a fox. Thomas Jenkins followed on Gruffydd's horse and felt like a king.

The wedding party stood listening to Hywel's homily on the married state as they sipped their hot milk and nutmeg. Dewi was blowing on his to cool it, his fleshy lips curled outwards displaying his pink gums. The Cobblers shifted restlessly, wanting to go, but Hywel droned on. "The blessed union which brings us closer to God . . ." Dewi had blown some milk on the floor but no one was awake enough to care. His mother's face wore the disgruntled patience of an ox and her husband snored on his feet by the fire. ". . . invisible bond of love . . a lifelong vigil against sin . . ." Madlen felt her eyelids closing.

Through the rustle of the forest and the even, scarcely noticeable splashing of the Ystwyth far beneath them, voices shouted. Just a scrap blown on the wind, then gone. Madlen strained to catch more. As Hywel paused for breath she heard it again. Singing this time. Only a few notes, but Madlen recognized it. A bawdy song. Rhiannon glanced at her nervously. She had heard it too. People were coming up the path. The words were audible now:

> *The dowry she brought him*
> *. . . another man's son . . .*

Dewi stopped blowing and listened, his mouth open. Mistress Cobbler kicked her husband in the shins and he woke with a startled grunt. Rhiannon touched Hywel's arm but he shook her off impatiently. His voice rose to a climax. ". . . live in happiness and peace till God takes you to His bosom." He stood in silent contemplation while the others waited in alarm. The rush taper flickered and only the sound of the trees and the river wafted in from outside. "Now let us go our separate ways until tomorrow," Hywel said, and Dewi kissed Madlen again under Hywel's censorious eye.

"Until tomorrow, daughter," said Mistress Cobbler with a smile like curdled milk and took her husband firmly by the arm. "Don't waste time, Dewi!"

Three deliberate knocks at the door. Hywel opened it. Outside stood Thomas Jenkins, hat in hand and a beatific look on his face.

"What is it, Thomas?"

"I beg your pardon for this late visit, sir," he said shyly, fingering his hat, "but a few of us wanted to call in to pay our respects and to wish every happiness to the bride and groom."

"It is very late, Thomas," said Rhiannon firmly. "Perhaps in the morning . . ."

"Men of goodwill we never turn away," Hywel said. "Come in, and all your friends with you."

One by one they filed in, bowed politely to the family and stood round the walls. Soon the room was full and there were three men on the ladder and more outside with no hope of getting in.

"Now, Thomas, who is to speak for you?"

"She's at the back, sir," Thomas said. A gangway was made and down it, head demurely lowered and on her best behaviour, came the Mari Lwyd.

"All honour to the bride and groom," she neighed in a high falsetto and the whole room echoed her. "All honour to the bride and groom."

Dewi grinned foolishly and Hywel looked furious. The Mari Lwyd continued in her singsong.

"Do you, Dewi Cobbler, know of any impediment to this marriage?"

"I do not," he stammered.

"I do not," mocked the grey mare and a titter ran round the room. "Do you, Mistress Bevan, know of any impediment?"

"No," said Rhiannon ferociously and the Mari Lwyd neighed in mock terror.

"*He* certainly doesn't," said the Mari Lwyd, turning away from Hywel, "or else he wouldn't allow it. But what about you?" The grey mare cocked her head on one side and looked inquisitively at Madlen.

"I will not answer to you, or to any man," she said disdainfully.

"Not even to your husband?"

Madlen looked at the brazen eyes. The voice was lower, the falsetto not so assured.

"Is this scarecrow your husband, Madlen? Is this the one to lie in bed with you? Breed your children? Or raise another man's?"

She knew it was he.

"You'd do better with the old grey mare," the voice lilted. "You belong to her."

"What has she to offer me?"

"A life of dreams instead of tapping nails into mouldy leather. Long rides through the night sky instead of cold embraces in a hard bed. A throne instead of a kitchen stool. Fire instead of ashes."

"And what if she throws me?"

"You must learn to ride her."

"She is a hard mount."

"But gentle to those who know her." Very slowly the Mari Lwyd turned. Again, a path opened before her. Madlen felt Rhiannon's eyes boring into her. Hywel's hand was raised in exorcism as though to ward off the evil spirits besetting her, and beside her, Dewi's mouth was open again. Madlen took one step forward and the spell was broken.

"Don't listen to him!" Rhiannon threw her arms around Madlen and tried to hold her, while Dewi screamed hysterically and Hywel thundered, "This is the work of the Devil. Anyone who aids it is surely damned."

The Mari Lwyd was suddenly transformed. Pitchfork, sheet, harvest gloves fell to the floor. Gruffydd rose to his full height, dashed to the hearth and grasped Madlen by the wrist. Hywel seized a billhook.

"Keep back. This maid is betrothed—"

"Maid? Who told you she was a maid?" Someone sniggered. Hywel lunged with the billhook. Gruffydd parried easily with his forearm and pushed him off balance into the crowd. "If she's a maid, how did she come to be carrying my seed?" Hywel struggled to his feet. "Perhaps the wind carried it there?" They were all laughing at him now. Hywel flushed scarlet and turned to Rhiannon, who stammered and looked away. So it was true. She had deceived him. While he'd been in gaol she'd turned Satan's whore-monger and used his home as a brothel, and now that he was back, she'd gulled him into marrying off the conjurer's slut to an honest Christian as an unsullied virgin bride. Hywel broke into a cold sweat and stared at his wife's terrified face. Rhiannon backed away, gripping Madlen's hand.

"In the name of Christ tell him it's not true. The conjurer's lying. You've never been near him, have you?"

Madlen reached out to Gruffydd and he swept her up in his arms and carried her through the delirious crowd.

In the suddenly empty farmhouse Hywel sat on a cheese-press and gazed ahead of him like a man who has just seen his own funeral pass, while Rhiannon cowered among the cinders too scared even to weep. A fiddle started playing. Up in the loft two villagers were raucously making love. Without uttering a word Hywel took his Bible and his stick and left by the back door.

Outside in the farmyard Gruffydd lifted Madlen above his head like an offering. The people of Cwmystwyth went wild, cheering and swirling in a frenzied dance. Then he hoisted her into the saddle, jumped up behind her and they disappeared into the forest together.

September – November 1752

CHAPTER NINE

I

"HOLD!" IOLO CALLED in a piercing falsetto. The two-year-old black and white, shaggy mongrel bitch sat as if caught in one of Gruffydd's spells. Just as well, because Iolo's herd was nervous and restive today and a wrong move from an over-enthusiastic novice might send them plunging over the edge of Black Rock like the Gadarene swine. But Iolo knew his runts and he knew his dog. He wouldn't have risked her on them if she weren't ready for it.

"Out," he growled fiercely and she started with infinite stealth on the outflanking movement Iolo had taught her: legs bent double, belly grazing the ground, neck absurdly extended and her eyes, just above grass-level, fixed on the herd for any sign of a break. More like a snake than a quadruped, she had slipped between the cattle and the cliff down to the Round House before they knew she was there.

"Drive!" Without a snarl or a bark, the dog advanced on the startled herd in rapid zigzag. The left flank gave at once and trotted away toward Iolo. The lazier ones in the lush grass near the cliff were soon dislodged by sudden charges at their fetlocks.

"Good dog," Iolo said ebulliently, as she came up to him with a wolfish grin, tongue dangling to her knees, and asking for the usual cuff as her reward. "Good Cadwal," he said, patting her head till her teeth clicked. Cadwal, short for Cadwaladr, was the seventh of her name—the third generation of herding dogs that Iolo had bred and trained in the six years he had lived on Rhiannon Bevan's farm. The first of them was in retirement, loafing round the new barns Iolo had built for Rhiannon, making half-hearted lunges at the local rat. This present Cadwal, now on her trial outing, was his granddaughter. The name seemed to fit bitch and stud equally well.

"Good Cadwal," Iolo repeated, wondering why he called all his dogs by his own name. Not out of vanity. No one in Cwmystwyth knew he was really called Cadwaladr. Except his father, whom he had scarcely seen these six years.

Iolo stared down at the wisp of grey smoke rising idly from the

Round House in the early morning sunshine. Gruffydd would be glad they were all called Cadwal, if he knew. If he took any interest in his son. When Iolo had found Gruffydd brooding by his waterfall the morning after one of their quarrels and had said, "I'm going to stay with the Bevans for a week or two. You'll be better with me out of the way," Gruffydd had smiled—more in sorrow and remorse than in anger—lifted him off the ground in a huge embrace and answered simply: "Remember the Lord Rhys." Iolo hadn't given it much thought at the time, but as the week or two stretched into months and years and they continued to avoid each other as if by mutual consent, those parting words fermented in Iolo's mind. Gruffydd must have known it was the end. Perhaps Iolo had known it too, really. Their inseparable friendship of twelve years' travelling had fallen apart within twelve months of settling in Cwmystwyth. Gruffydd had wanted Iolo to play along with the villagers' notion of him as the conjurer's familiar and expected him to take over, one day, as his successor. Iolo had pleaded that he couldn't pretend to himself or anyone else, but this only seemed to infuriate Gruffydd and drove him still further towards his eager apprentice, Mihangel, whom he treated as a favourite son, largely out of revenge, Iolo sometimes felt. Mihangel had stepped into Iolo's shoes with the greatest of ease. He worshipped Gruffydd openly and understood the magic power of herbs in a way Iolo couldn't begin to follow In the end Iolo had given up trying to compete with him. He wasn cut out to be a conjurer's son, and there was no point in half measures.

Iolo tried to catch a glimpse of Gruffydd in the crush of men and cattle in the Round House paddocks, but there was no sign of him. Mihangel—now a handsome, lithe young man—appeared to be in charge and was examining each of Gruffydd's runts in turn. Iolo could have put up with Mihangel and the conjuring if only Gruffydd had levelled with him about his mother. For a year and a day Iolo had made the pilgrimage up the long paths past Cae Glas Farm, to sit in the empty wooden shack and watch the slate-grey surface of Llyn Isaf for any unusual movement. At first he'd been convinced that his mother would rise from the icy waters to speak to him. Surely she must, if he waited patiently; but he never saw a soul there. Gruffydd had always side-tracked when Iolo pestered him for more of the story, until that final day, the three hundred and sixty-sixth, when Iolo had dragged himself back to the Round House through the dark and said: "You've been lying, haven't you?" Gruffydd had nearly killed him. What was worse, having doubted his father once, Iolo came to doubt him on principle. They became an embarrassment to each other.

Gruffydd had gone from strength to strength, the undisputed master of the Ystwyth valley, while Iolo worked for his keep as a farm-hand in the poorest, most ridiculed household of that valley. He tried not to regret that choice, though he missed his father like an orphan and sometimes felt he had thrown away the greatest opportunity of his life. But he had to do something of his own. Hadn't Gruffydd himself said: "Make yourself needed"? He didn't need Iolo. No one here needed him except Rhiannon, with Hywel away. But as soon as Iolo decided he was entirely in the right to have left, that Gruffydd had treated him shamefully and was much to blame, *Remember the Lord Rhys* came ringing in his ears like a muffled peal from the sunken bells of Aberdovey and Iolo sensed he had failed his father in some task he had never even grasped.

"Good Cadwal," Iolo said again. The name was all that tied him to Gruffydd now and he gave it to his dogs as a reminder. "All right, girl." Iolo's herd was ambling on its own down the hill. Cadwal tugged frantically at his breeches.

Iolo was suddenly ashamed of his trivial private grievances when he thought of what Gruffydd had done for the valley with all his conjuring. People were starving when they had come here and now they had more than they could eat. The Round House itself was no longer a turf cottage. The men of Cwmystwyth had hacked huge chunks of stone out of Black Rock and rebuilt it slab by slab. Hayricks and sheds filled the meadow where Iolo had built his fence to keep in their first pig and six calves, and he had contributed nothing at all.

Gruffydd's hired men opened the paddocks and drove his cattle down the widened pathway through the woods below Black Rock. Every herd in Cwmystwyth was on the move today. From far across the valley came an unbroken roar of startled, anxious cattle being driven from their usual pasture down to the Ystwyth meadows, ready for the trip to Tregaron market. Gruffydd had brought the valley undreamt-of wealth and security with his annual drove to Tregaron, where every drover in Ceredigion bid for the Ystwyth's herds.

He should be going with them, Iolo admitted. He had a part to play. He could manage a herd far better than they did. He was nineteen, a grown man, with nothing to show for it, except a couple of barns thrown up on someone else's land. He'd achieved nothing by leaving Gruffydd except further isolation. But it was pointless even asking Rhiannon about Tregaron, for she would never allow her cows to go on Gruffydd's drove. She would think it was disloyal to Hywel. Iolo knew how Rhiannon felt about his father.

"They destroyed my life that night, Gruffydd and Madlen between them," she'd said once in a brittle voice that threatened to break at Gruffydd's name. Iolo had never mentioned it since. He didn't fully understand what had happened, but he'd learnt from Rachel's occasional, rancorous outbursts that Hywel had left the same night Madlen had run away with Gruffydd, on the eve of her wedding to Dewi Cobbler, and hadn't been seen in Cwmystwyth since. Rhiannon kept saying that he would be back. She had been more faithful to him in his seven years' absence than most Cwmystwyth women were under their husbands' noses. Iolo didn't like to ask more. He'd loved Rhiannon as a mother from the day she'd taken him in and he did what he could to make her life easier: all the heavy work—tending the animals, digging peat, ploughing and sowing—and he even found time to mind young Hannah. It was Iolo who had hammered together a coffin for Ruth Bevan and dragged it across the valley on a makeshift sled to the abandoned churchyard at Pendre where Rhiannon's father had preached.

How he'd love to be going with them! Gruffydd's serving-girls trooped past behind the herds, laughing and flirting with the herdsmen. Not a woman in Cwmystwyth would look at him and Iolo was fed up with waiting. He was tired of being taken for a demon and mocked because his face was more angular than most. All the time and trouble he'd wasted on Dic Richards' pretty young daughter Rhonwen—carving love-spoons, catching birds for her—to be told to his face last August, the day she turned fourteen, that she'd stayed out among the wheat-sheaves with Rolo Blacksmith one night. It was like taking a six-month heifer to a grizzled old bull.

"Waste myself on you?" Rhonwen had laughed, a high peal of trills. Ever since, Iolo had considered his virginity a preposterous indignity. But how to be rid of it? Gruffydd had started when he was thirteen—as in so many other things, Iolo found him impossible to live up to—and he hadn't stopped since. Iolo didn't know how Madlen stood it.

"Ow!" he shouted. Cadwal had bitten him. With good reason. His herd had disappeared over the hill and would soon be lost in all the others, bound for Tregaron.

"Get 'em, girl," he cried. Cadwal bounded away with lank, almost airborne strides, and Iolo strolled behind.

The Round House was silent as he made his way down from Black Rock and the paddocks were deserted. As usual, Madlen was nowhere to be seen. Perhaps she really was pregnant at last, as people said. For all Iolo knew, he might have a brother or a sister by now.

Gruffydd listened by the door till the last shout and the last heavy thud of hoofs died away in the forest.

"There, they've gone." Madlen smiled up at him from the pristine pillows of their bed, her face flushed the colour of the velvet counterpane. "Happy now?" He nodded slowly, thinking of something else, and went round the room a second time. He poured more oil into the round beaker lamps carved into the stone walls, checked the utensils laid out on the sheepskin before the fire, pausing to stare at the iron forceps, then abruptly emptied the whole herb tray into the fire and knelt beside his upright hearthstone.

Madlen knew better than to disturb him. He seemed to draw his strength from that stone, his massive body trembling like a child's as if some overwhelming power were flowing from the stone into his limbs and shaking him to the core. At other times his hunched shoulders would suddenly tense, muscles coiled as if to lift some terrible burden. He could kneel there for hours, and when he finished, his face would be grey, drained of blood, his body exhausted.

As he wrestled with the stone, groaning occasionally, she wondered what his spirits looked like. Madlen had discovered none of the secrets of Gruffydd's power as a conjurer since moving in with him on that stormy night seven years ago. As a man, she believed she knew his every thought and his most hidden desire even before he was aware of them himself, but as a conjurer he was more remote than ever. "What does it feel like?" she used to ask him constantly, fascinated by this extra faculty which set him apart from other men. Gruffydd would only shrug and mutter about inherited gifts. If she persisted, he would lose his temper, so she'd long since given up trying to penetrate his mystery. She didn't mind him concealing it from her, at heart. The picture she had of those murky depths inside him whetted their love-making.

He's taking no chances, she thought, as his lips moved in silent conversation with the spirits of his hearth. She was moved that he should concentrate himself so utterly on a service he performed for other women without second thought, between curing toothache and lancing a boil. Her pregnancy had brought them together again, renewing the old love of their early days when they couldn't leave each other for weeks on end, before Gruffydd started getting impatient for an heir and the violent quarrelling set in. He never went out after dark now, never raised his voice above the gentlest murmur when he spoke to her. Sometimes she wished she could stay pregnant for ever just to keep this hold on him.

Gruffydd's forehead was damp and feverish against the cold, rough stone. He was shivering, his heart was racing. He was sick with anxiety. Any minute his stomach might erupt. Why was he so nervous about delivering a baby? He'd never made a mistake before. Was it likely he'd fail now, when it was his own heir being born? Reasons did nothing to encourage him. Fear was lodged in his belly like a growth that can only be cut out, not cured, and it had been there for months, years maybe. He hadn't slept well for as long as he could remember. Practically every night he'd wake a few hours after dozing off and struggle out of bed to finish some task he'd forgotten about, only to find it done. By then it was too late to sleep again, so he'd light the fire and pace around the house in the dark, going over and over the next day's work in his mind . . . orders to give, speeches to make. His resources were over-stretched in every way. So many building projects in the valley going at once and he insisted on managing them all. Cash was running short. Ffowlke's rents were due. The drove to Tregaron had to make money this year. He was just worried about that, he reassured himself. Things would ease up once they'd sold the cattle. All this was true—but even added together it didn't explain the way he was feeling.

His luck had held for too long and the likelihood of disaster was becoming unbearable. He sometimes caught himself longing for some slight mishap only to avert a far greater one. The longer his brilliant success continued, the more drastic would be its levelling. His spirits only confused him now when he knelt by his hearthstone. What would go wrong? What would give first? They never advised him any more. Sometimes they muttered like old women behind their hands and he couldn't hear them clearly. As he walked through the woods above Cwmystwyth, Gruffydd found himself looking over his shoulder when he knew perfectly well he was alone. On a cloudless day he would ask Mihangel twice for a weather forecast. He was becoming over-cautious. It was fatal, because his people expected excitement from him, not safe, predictable progress. Even his speeches were rehearsed now Often he detected a restlessness in his audience. They expected an inspired extempore as regularly as their daily bread. Gruffydd knew it, but couldn't stop himself from learning the next speech even more thoroughly.

He ought to talk to someone but he knew there was no one. Madlen had no idea of what went on inside him. She believed in him utterly and her belief was more vital to him than her understanding. Iolo, the one person who might have helped, had betrayed him—and his own birthright—by associating with the Calvinists. And Mihangel . . .

perhaps Mihangel would understand. He knew him better than anyone. They worked so closely together, Mihangel managing all the medicine, so that Gruffydd could get on with his building and the day-to-day business of the valley. Perhaps he should ask Mihangel.

Gruffydd raised his head abruptly. There was a reddish dent just above his eyes from a lump in the stone.

"I'm going to send for Siân Evans."

"Why?" Madlen asked, surprised. "Why do I need that old hag when I have a conjurer for a husband?" She used the word deliberately. They'd been married in no church, for Gruffydd couldn't abide priests and still sometimes spoke of his wife who had died and his vow never to remarry, though he would never say who this wife was or where she had lived. Madlen didn't insist. He'd feel more bound to her without the ceremony, but very occasionally she would call him husband just to remind him. This was one of those moments. She took his hand and shifted over on the bed so he could sit beside her. "You gave me this . . ." She laid his fingers on her swollen belly. "Now you can take it out."

How long she had waited for this child! She had tried every cure for infertility that witch had ever whispered in woman's ear. She had drunk every potion Mihangel had prepared for her—cockerel's blood, ground skull in sea water, goat's bile—till she spewed them up and then pestered him for more. It was so unfair that she should need potions to conceive while others were taking them to abort. Gruffydd would turn none of them away if they came to him. "No one can make them want the child," he would say. "And would you want to be unwanted?" And worst of all she had endured the gossip of Cwmystwyth women behind her back—"a barren woman" they called her, "a blight on the land"—and watched Gruffydd wench wherever he pleased, not daring to rebuke him for fear he might say, "Give me an heir, and then I'll be faithful." Now, after seven years, that heir was arriving. Gruffydd would share her labour pains, like it or not. She'd never let him forget what she'd been through for him. She put her arms around his neck and drew him gently down to her. He kissed her taut pink nipple. Her breasts had filled out beautifully. They glowed unearthly white, like crystal, with a hint of blue tracery on the underside.

"Hey, enough of that," Madlen said indignantly. "You're stealing it from the baby."

"Tastes awful, anyway. I don't know how they can drink it."

"Not poisoned, is it?" Mihangel had boasted to her once he could poison any mother's milk if he wanted to.

"I hope not, for my sake." Gruffydd smiled despite himself. Long cavernous lines spread across his cheek-bones into a sea of turbulent, white-flecked beard. She loved to make his face light up like this.

"What's the matter, cariad?" she said. The smile was gone. He looked scared.

"I can feel him kicking to come out."

"You're not worried, are you?" Madlen asked, suddenly worried herself. "It won't be as difficult as with Rhiannon."

"Of course not." He loved her too much to weaken her confidence in him, now or ever. How could he explain that saving Rhiannon's child had been a miracle, and that not even conjurers can rely on daily miracles or guarantee the absence of catastrophe? With Rhiannon it had been so different. He'd had no time to think.

Madlen gasped through clenched teeth and squeezed his hand. Gruffydd felt her stomach muscles tense in a spasm of pain and slowly relax. Her contractions had started.

"Aren't you going to give me any hot towels?" she said breathlessly.

"Of course." Gruffydd got up in a dream and slipped thankfully into the routine he had used since that first success with Rhiannon. Clean white flannel towels folded in a pile on the hearth-stool. Dip them into the warm water in the cauldron hanging over the fire by a chain which disappeared to the pinnacle of the roof. Wring out the towels above the cauldron. Madlen watched how he bent his arms double to squeeze them dry with one firm twist. She pushed back the bedcover and the white linen sheet and unfastened her shift.

He knelt beside her and laid the warm towels over her stomach. She opened to him as to a lover. He saw her lying on the forest floor—not thirty yards away—on the night this house was built. How long it had taken that seed to ripen. He was all the more nervous of crushing it now. Surely nothing could happen? She was so healthy. He gently rubbed her belly with his supple fingers and she put her hands on his forearms and dug her nails into him, tugging at the sleek, fine hair. The even rhythm of her contractions spread up through his fingertips, carrying him along. He knew her body so well in all its moods and felt one with it now. He'd seen so many children into the world, never without a certain envy of this mystery from which a man was eternally excluded. If men gave birth themselves, perhaps they wouldn't be so bent on destruction. It had been a seven-year struggle to stop the men of Cwmystwyth from burning and tearing down and to get them to build instead. Many of them had bucked under his yoke, but he'd whipped them all into line.

"He's coming," Madlen said in a hoarse whisper.

"You've got a while yet." Gruffydd massaged Madlen's heaving belly.

It always took longer than this.

Madlen shook her head excitedly. "I can feel him coming already." Gruffydd touched her thighs—they were quivering, but not at all tense. As delicately as he could, he put a finger into her distended passage.

"You're right," he said, shocked. "His head's already here."

What should he do now? He was completely off balance. Madlen heaved violently, then a scream burst from her such as Gruffydd had only ever heard in the most frantic moments of their love-making and a new face stared out into the world.

Gruffydd dashed for the instruments. "No," Madlen yelled. "I don't need them. I'm going to finish this alone." She gave two more pushes and the baby was born. Gruffydd stared at his new child, alive and bawling in his hands.

"A boy," he said.

"Yes, a boy." Madlen sighed with satisfaction and fell back into the pillows. She gazed with measureless pride at her son and Gruffydd fell on his knees at her side, tears of relief pouring down his face. He'd escaped again.

"I'll sacrifice a goat, now," he said, half to Madlen, half to the spirits of the hearth. A son was worth a whole herd of goats. A son to inherit his work and his lands, and replace that other son whom Gruffydd sorely missed.

III

Iolo yelled angrily at his runts and Cadwal barked in full support, adding to the din. They had bellowed non-stop all the way from Black Rock, trying to bolt down the valley at every bend in the road to join the other herds bound for Tregaron. Iolo had taken them round the long way and was exhausted. "There's nothing I'd like better than to take you to Tregaron. But I can't. Rhiannon wouldn't allow it. We're staying here."

Hannah was waiting for them at the gatepost, hollowing a new milk-pail out of a forked clump of oak they'd found in the woods after last night's gale. Iolo remembered guiltily that he was going to help her carve it. She didn't look up as he came down the path, just went on stabbing at the oak clump with a pair of shears of all things.

"What's the matter?" Hannah stabbed again and a huge chip flew off, frightening a cow. "You're going to break those shears." Iolo restrained himself as she brought them crashing down once more. They stuck on the log with a loud twang. Hannah had Hywel's black hair and imposing, thick eyebrows under a brooding forehead. But her green eyes were Rhiannon's. So was her delicate, finely-traced mouth.

"Rachel has been quarrelling with Mam again."

"I might have guessed." Rhiannon and Rachel were always at each other's throats.

"My father would come home if it weren't for you," Iolo had overheard Rachel saying once. "Get a husband if you don't want to stay here," Rhiannon had snapped back. Iolo was bored with it by now. Women did nothing but fight.

"Never mind," he said half-heartedly. Hannah only looked more hurt. "What was it about?"

"Father, as usual. It's so stupid. He's not coming back." Hannah was the only one of them who would admit this. Hywel was just a name to her. She'd heard passing travellers talk about him while Rhiannon fed them with all they could eat to get them to stay longer; but the saintly preacher who walked from village to village giving sermons and saving souls was as remote to her as God.

"If he's been to every village in Wales," Hannah had asked over breakfast one day, "why can't he come here?" Rhiannon had turned pale and Rachel had scolded: "You must love your father." Hannah puzzled over this for days. It made her unhappy. In what way was she meant to love someone she'd never seen? Iolo felt sorry for Hannah. It couldn't be right for Hywel to stay away like this but Iolo remembered him as a brave, kind man, so there must be a good reason.

"You've got a father," Hannah said abruptly, fixing Iolo with one of those looks he couldn't answer. "Why did you leave him?"

"Because of my mother," Iolo said sadly and walked away up to the edge of the forest, to a den he'd made himself in a beech tree with a good view of the valley—a useful refuge when women started fighting.

Hannah wondered what Gruffydd was really like as she climbed onto the first rung of the gate to slip the latch and let the herd in. Her mother talked of him only in a hurried, frightened way as though he might suddenly come through the door. Iolo looked unhappy whenever he was mentioned and Rachel told scary stories about him in bed at night, about the day Hannah was born—on condition she didn't tell Mam. He must be an ogre, Hannah concluded, seeing someone with very long fingernails who boiled babies for breakfast. She knew where he lived because Iolo had taken her through the forest to a dark, round tower with black smoke coming from the pointed roof. Poor Iolo. He'd had a lucky escape.

"Don't you think you should be helping Hannah?" said a voice at the bottom of the beech tree just as Iolo was settling down to dream about the girls of Tregaron. "She's very small. You shouldn't leave it all to her." Rachel smiled up at him—that painful, crooked smile that split her face in two and said, "Forgive me for being right."

Iolo took the straw out of his mouth. Bossy cow. The trouble was that Rachel was always right. Hannah was bravely struggling with the milking which Iolo had taught her only last month.

"And my mother wants to talk to you," Rachel added just as she turned to go. So like her, Rachel would never admit she'd come all the way up the hill on an errand for Rhiannon. Iolo didn't budge.

"What about?"

"How should I know? She'll tell you herself." Then a furtive, defiant look crossed her face. She sidled back towards him, joined the palms of her hands under her pointed chin and whispered fiercely, as though she were confessing her first love affair: "You won't see me again for a long, long time. I can't bear it here any longer. My mother doesn't believe in God. She's an atheist, though she tries to hide it."

"Where are you going?" Iolo was perplexed. Rachel never shared any of her secrets and had always treated him as a half-wit.

"To Edward Richards' Grammar School in Ystrad Meurig." Rachel threw back her head with great self-importance, watching Iolo's reaction. "I am to teach reading, writing and scripture."

"Really?" Iolo said, with exactly the admiring expression Rachel wanted.

"I was recommended," she said enigmatically.

"Who by?"

"Can't you guess?" She glanced back at the farmhouse. A smile of triumph pinched her lips. "My father. He takes care of those he loves." Iolo was shocked. So Hywel *was* in touch, after all.

"Is he coming home?" Rachel shrugged her bony shoulders, then held up a hand to him.

"Goodbye, Iolo," she said earnestly. "Remember everything I've taught you. Pray, like a good Christian. God is watching you."

She walked back to the cottage as straight as a ship mast off Llanrhystud Head. Her skirts didn't move like other women's. They might be stuck to her. Iolo couldn't imagine her without them. Rhiannon he often saw in only a shift and Hannah frequently in nothing at all, but Rachel only ever showed her hands and her head.

The rest was a mystery. Iolo admired her, in a way, because of it. He envied her new life away from Cwmystwyth. She would make a good teacher. She had taught him all the book-learning he knew; he'd learnt as much from her as from Gruffydd, in a very different way.

He realized suddenly that he would miss her. His reading was good enough to manage the Bible himself now, but he'd miss the stern, censorious tones in which she read out Old Testament stories of Kings and patriarchs and bearded prophets, who had filled many a dreary winter evening with wild fantasies of far-away times and places. Iolo had never been to Palestine but he peopled Rachel's stories with faces and events he remembered from childhood journeys. Noah's Ark was the wretched Channel lugger in which he'd stowed away, the Tower of Babel was a certain lighthouse off Marseilles which collapsed in a storm one night and the Ark of the Covenant resembled a carved wooden chest in which the circus had transported its effects. Iolo never told Rachel, of course. She would have been appalled.

He slid down from his den and went to find Rhiannon. He hated getting involved in women's feuds.

"You don't have to knock, Iolo." A weary voice came from the end of the room as he pushed the door open nervously and blinked in the dark. "This is your home. You come and go as you please." Rhiannon was sitting in the high-backed chair by the hearth where last night's cinders lay unswept. Iolo perched uncomfortably on the stool by the Bible-stand and waited.

Rhiannon stared absently at a patch of sky through the hatch-window, a wisp of neglected, bleached hair that had once been golden trailing across her cheek—such a change since the day she'd found him sleeping in her hay-loft, laughed at the straw sticking up out of his hair and said: "You can stay with us, if you want." Her delicate face looked too delicate now—her cheek-bones showed beneath the pallid skin and her upper lip was wrinkled slightly, like a much older woman's. But she was still beautiful. Hardship hadn't broken her. If anything it made the spirit behind those wan features more startling, more radiant, but today she looked tired and her quick green eyes were vacant, dead.

"Iolo, how long have you lived with us?" Rhiannon's voice was detached, like a sleep-talker's.

"Six years, mam." She was not one to mislay a single day. There were notches on the back door divided into weeks, months, years. Iolo could guess when they dated from.

"Do you miss your father?" she asked abruptly. Iolo was taken aback. Gruffydd had always been the butt of her conversation when she mentioned him at all, and she never asked Iolo how he felt.

"Yes, mam, perhaps," he said hesitantly.

"I think Rachel misses hers, don't you? I think . . ." Rhiannon searched for words, smoothing out the links of her loose-knit grey shawl over the arm of her chair. "I think I've been wrong in keeping you from your father."

"You haven't . . ."

"I have," she said, not wanting to be contradicted. "On purpose. He wasn't good for you. Not a good father for a young boy."

Was it revenge? Her mind drifted again. Was she keeping Iolo away from Gruffydd in return for losing Hywel? She could never forgive Gruffydd for the contempt with which he'd trampled on her life that night seven years ago, driving Hywel away in ridicule and betraying the trust of their first meeting. It seemed he gave with one hand only to take away with the other. Rhiannon had tried to put him out of her mind, but his cruelty oppressed her—she kept returning to it and each time it hurt her more. Sometimes she would realize in alarm that she'd been thinking about him for hours without knowing it and feared she might have been possessed by him ever since he delivered Hannah. At such moments Iolo reassured her. The boy was a hostage and would protect her against Gruffydd's malevolence, but she loved him, too, as a son. He had many of his father's good qualities, with none of the arrogance. If only Gruffydd were more like him . . .

"I've kept you to myself, Iolo. You've been good to me. I don't know how I'd have got by without you."

"You took me in," he mumbled, embarrassed at the way she thanked him. It seemed to be directed not at him, Iolo, her foster-son, but at somebody else beyond him.

"I took you in, for sure." She suddenly leaned forward to seize his face with both hands, tears in her eyes. "You've a heart of gold, cariad. Don't let people use it. You're easily swayed."

"Why are you saying this?" Iolo was bewildered, disturbed. Rhiannon was different. Her measured, dignified restraint was gone, scattered by the strange emotions he couldn't follow.

"You need a change. I want you to take our cattle with the others to Tregaron."

What had come over her? Iolo stared at the floor. He longed to go. He wanted to travel again, even if only to the next valley. He wanted to try out Cadwal on rougher ground, over a longer course. And he had to get away from the women here.

"What will Hywel say?" Rhiannon gazed into the cinders.

"Do you think he'll come back?" There was mockery mixed with her sadness. With Rachel working in Ystrad Meurig, Hywel would have no need to come home to see his favourite daughter. He had obviously washed his hands of his wife completely.

"Of course. You know he will."

"Yes," she said more brightly. "But I've two daughters to feed and I need the money. Besides, the bullocks are ready to sell now, and Catto and Betsi are too old to give us any more milk." She stopped in the doorway and smiled at him—he looked so bemused. "You'd better get ready. I've prepared some food for you. You can take the guinea we've saved too, in case you need money."

"We're off, Cadwal," Iolo whooped, running out into the bright sunshine to find his dog.

IV

Thomas Jenkins ordered the two boys waiting beside the brazier to light the torches, then he inspected his bonfire yet again. He hollowed out the ventilation flues, scraped together a few stray twigs, cut off a branch that stuck out too far.

"Perhaps it would burn better with you on it, Thomas," suggested Huw Lloyd and the crowd laughed.

"Move on there!" Thomas shooed away a group of gossiping old women who were blocking the gangway. "It took my men five hours to build this."

"If you talked less, they'd do it faster," said Huw.

Thomas was unruffled. Gruffydd had appointed him steward of the autumn festival for the fifth successive year, and, having resisted all attempts to get him drunk at Morgan's Inn last night, he was not going to fall for cheap jibes in his moment of glory.

"Now," he said roundly. The two lads thrust torches into Thomas's bonfire. It went up faster than sinners in hell.

"Hooray!" yelled the crowd, staring up at the hillside below Black Rock.

"Can you see them?" Mali Fishpond asked big Siôn Edmunds.

"Ay, they're just above Hywel Bevan's farm." Siôn hoisted the old crone onto his shoulders, where she screwed up her eyes against the bright autumn sun. Everyone jostled for a good position near the river. The autumn festival, when the herds left for Tregaron, was one of the few occasions they all saw the conjurer. Of course, anyone could go to the Round House with a request, but the place had such an eerie mood to it—the dark stone tower and the lowering, wooded cliff— that few of them ventured there unless it was urgent. Even then, they were more likely to see Mihangel than the conjurer himself.

"You can start now." Thomas Jenkins turned to blind Ismael Harpist, who was leaning against the wych-elm tree, while Iago One-Leg, beside him, tuned the one string on his latest fiddle. Ismael started with the song he'd improvised on the day of Gruffydd's arrival to celebrate the curing of the murrain. The crowd joined in. They all knew the words by now, and their singing easily drowned the lowing of the cattle in the crowded paddocks up and down the Ystwyth meadows.

"Cows were dying, children starving . . ."

"A fine fire, Master Thomas!" shouted Joshua Cae Glas above the song.

"It is," Thomas agreed. When the conjurer had appointed him steward, Madlen had taken Thomas aside and suggested he use the festival to celebrate Gruffydd's coming to Cwmystwyth. "A bonfire," Thomas had said eagerly, "like the ones that cured the cattle." Madlen was delighted. "Only don't tell him we planned it," she had said. "Just surprise him on the day." Gruffydd had been deeply moved. Thomas prided himself on contributing some new invention to please him each year, but today Madlen had sent word to scrap the hobby-horse race because she had a surprise of her own which she wanted kept secret. Thomas was worried it might hold things up but no one ever refused Madlen anything, let alone went to Gruffydd behind her back.

"Smoke that choked them, purged them, cured them . . ." went the song.

"There they are!" Mali screamed. Thomas dashed away to the river. On the opposite bank the conjurer emerged from the woods, as seven years ago, on the shoulders of the two brawniest men of the village, who had taken over from Huw and Sam, now too old to take Gruffydd's weight.

It might have been that very day again. The conjurer was unchanged. He wore the same cloak as then—threadbare, ever newly-patched and darned. Nothing about him suggested the greatest man of the Ystwyth after Lord Kirkland. They took it as a pledge that he was one of them. On the far side of the river, the conjurer tapped his two bearers on the shoulder and they let him down to walk the rest of the way through the people.

"Have you a cure for my ear-ache, master?" cried a woman, pushing forward. He smiled serenely and raised his right hand as if to say, "All in good time." They liked him like this. A greater wisdom mingled with the power of his features. His greying beard and deeply lined forehead showed the care he carried for them and his unhurried, steady gaze reassured them that he was equal to the burden. While he watched over them they could sleep in peace. In the middle of the stone bridge which Madlen had had built to commemorate this moment, he stopped and received their acclaim silently, with no sign of emotion, looking at them one by one so each felt especially favoured. They were good faces. The same people but different faces. The same people who would have killed him and each other seven years ago had been transformed by as many years of security and prosperity. That was miracle enough. He raised the stone amulet to his lips and gave thanks to the spirits of the place—and to his ancestors—for making him their instrument to achieve all this.

The lady of the waterfall had been right when she promised him good fortune on the day he returned. He had his lands back. He looked into the grateful faces of his people and knew that he was loved.

And why should he not be? he asked himself, as Thomas Jenkins led him on the agreed tour of the valley. Six good harvests he'd brought them. The upland ploughing had paid off. The village had more than doubled its grain crop and open-sided ricks had been thrown up along the valley from the mines to Haford.

"More tightly stacked here," Gruffydd said quietly, inspecting the latest pile of wheat-sheaves to be brought in.

"Yes, sir." Sam Jones, in charge of stores, rearranged them at once with his crew of young lads, some of them barely old enough to remember a time when Gruffydd hadn't been there.

"The tannery next," Thomas murmured. Gruffydd strode off downstream towards Hafod. The tannery was especially dear to him. He'd seen how Cwmystwyth women went out in bands each day to strip the bark off forest oaks and sell it as a curative to the Rhayader tannery for a pitiful groat a bushel, and how the farmers sold their cowhides for a pittance to travelling dealers only to buy them back at double the price as boots, jerkins, leggings. He'd grown impatient at the waste. They had the materials and they could do it themselves. He'd bribed a tanner from Rhayader called Meredydd to come and build a tannery for Cwmystwyth.

"Where's the hide from Dic Richards' old bull?" Meredydd showed him a fine dark-brown leather stretched out on the curriers' bench. "When will it be ready?"

"A few days now, sir," said the tanner, his face stained purple with the dye of a thousand vats.

"Send it to Dewi Cobbler. I want new boots made for Garmon's widow and children." This was the best of Gruffydd's work. They'd have gone barefoot a few years ago.

Gruffydd strolled round the lime pits in which raw hides were soaking before being unhaired and fleshed, the mastering pits where calf leather was softened up in Ystwyth water mixed with pigeon dung and past the drying racks and dubbin vats and rows of fleshing knives . . . Yet some of them still didn't believe it paid to work together. Many of the farmers had held out for years, tilling their own narrow plot, refusing to join in the harvest round. But Gruffydd's co-operative had got richer, until they were begging to be allowed to join. One day's work in three he asked of them, and shared round the produce as it was needed. He stopped beside a cavernous stone mortar where a diligent apprentice was crushing oak bark into fine powder for the making of curatives. What did that remind him of? A sweet, musky scent rose from it, the smell of the forest floor in the early morning . . .

The Black Forest! He suddenly saw himself walking up one July day on the side of a hill in Germany overlooking a whitewashed, onion-domed chapel, with Iolo, very young, beside him. It seemed a lifetime ago. Gruffydd's worries and doubts suddenly crowded in on him unbearably. Sometimes he was tempted to leave, without telling anyone—just walk away, with no more than he could carry and not one responsibility. Then he'd remind himself: Isn't this the dream that kept you going in exile and that finally brought you back here? Can you abandon it now? . . . Of course he couldn't. But how much easier it had been to carry a vision in his mind than to see it made flesh, with all the strains and shortcomings of the real world. Watching his creation take on a life of its own, Gruffydd often felt jealous, dispossessed, fearing that his own inspiration was dying as his child grew, a perfect cast emerging from a shattered mould. He'd be seized with a violent desire to destroy all his work and start again on a grandiose model that could never possibly be achieved.

"Master," Thomas Jenkins said gently. The conjurer was leaning against the dubbin vat, hand over his eyes, deep in contemplation.

"Yes, Thomas, we must go." It was time for his tribunal. The plaintiffs were waiting.

They walked back along the pebbly reaches of the Ystwyth towards the low dais Thomas had built among the cattle paddocks. "Give me a clear sight and a just mind," Gruffydd whispered to his spirits. Every year he found the discerning of right from wrong more taxing. In earlier days a judgement would leap to mind with overwhelming, self-evident clarity, immediately acceptable to plaintiff and accused alike. But gradually he'd made mistakes: a stray cow awarded to a widow who'd been lying; paternity set down to a lad who knew how many men the girl had been with but refused to shame her in public; then a theft charged to an old crone who couldn't possibly have done it, but was supposed a witch—Gruffydd was happy at the time to save her from worse treatment by reprimanding her. She'd been so mortified that she'd left her shack in midwinter and hadn't been heard of since. Gruffydd had refused to eat for days, knowing he'd sent her to the same death his own father met in those barren hills.

Sometimes he feared his spirits might be deserting him altogether, and sat for hours by the waterfall for advice. Always the same:

"They are fed and clothed," the lady sang. "No blood has been shed." Above all that: two years ago a Scot named MacInver had passed through Cwmystwyth and told Gruffydd of his country's fate since Bonnie Prince Charlie's rebellion. Thousands had been put to the sword by Cumberland. Whole clans had been butchered or fled to America. The language was outlawed, the tartans proscribed. "My country shall never be the same again," MacInver had said, and in the silence that followed, Gruffydd had sworn that such a thing would never happen in Wales. For the last five years no man had killed his neighbour, no houses had been burned, no witches drowned. For this Gruffydd was prepared to live with his own conscience.

Joshua Cae Glas drivelled and digressed, trying to assess the conjurer's mood. "Master, all through the harvest my cows were ailing. I was too busy. I have too much land of my own. I can't manage it all . . ."

"Then share it out to those who can. Instead of a third of your work, we permit you to donate a third of your crop. Next." Gruffydd's heavy oak staff came down on the dais with a dull thud.

". . . And that proves conclusively"—Morgan rounded off a well-documented case—"that Simeon sold half of last month's communal grain to Geraint Bowen, the Aberystwyth corn-dealer, for his own profit."

"Morgan wants Simeon's mill-pond for his brewery," whispered an amused, caressing voice in Gruffydd's ear.

"How do you know?"

"I just do." This was always the answer. Gruffydd had no idea where Mihangel got his information—out of his own head, it seemed—but it was always reliable. Gruffydd accepted his recommendations without second thought.

Morgan ran a hand over his wrinkled, bald pate. "So I suggest that Simeon, to make amends, donates his pond for the common good." A murmur of assent. Morgan affected to quieten his supporters and sat down.

I'll teach you to bring your feuding to me, Gruffydd thought. Neither Simeon nor Morgan ever lifted a finger for the village. Organizing the poor cottagers was no problem, for they had nothing to lose. It was these men of substance, as they thought themselves, who held out longest.

"Morgan," Gruffydd announced gravely. "We all thank you for your vigilance. Simeon shall henceforth grind our common grain without payment, and as a special token of our gratitude you, Morgan, shall take seventy gallons from Simeon's mill-pond each year and brew it for everyone's enjoyment on this day." The staff came crashing down again to loud applause, while bewildered Morgan was congratulated by all.

"Someone's stolen my hanging cradle," wailed a young mother.

Gruffydd had an infallible way of dealing with petty theft. Examining the crowd, as though he were about to single out the culprit, he thundered: "I will give you one chance. Return the cradle by tomorrow morning or else your own baby will be forfeit to the fair people." At the back of the assembly a woman carrying a child in a sling around her neck slipped away unnoticed. The plaintiff would find the cradle exactly where she left it when she got home. There was little theft in the valley. With the conjurer watching, no one imagined they could get away with it.

The next plaintiff was Dilys Edmunds, whom Gruffydd had married to red-haired Siôn only a year ago and who now wanted a divorce with reparations. Siôn's infidelities appeared to be endless and common knowledge—half the women in the valley were implicated— but Gruffydd was reluctant to cast the first stone in case it was thrown back at him. Suddenly his audience peeled away and started rushing towards the river. Dilys stared over Gruffydd's shoulder, tongue-tied, and then raced after the others, leaving him to preside over the cows and Iago One-Leg, who couldn't move without help. Gruffydd was furious, but it was beneath his dignity to turn round and see who was responsible for the disturbance, so he just kept staring ahead of him. They were coming back now, anyway. He could hear them shouting someone's name in acclamation. He didn't like it. Gruffydd was the only name people respected around here.

On a pallet covered with brightly-patterned blankets, carried along by four strong cowherds and with young girls dressed in red skirts and white blouses in attendance, lay Madlen, propped up on an embroidered cushion and holding up Gruffydd's baby son.

"Owain!" the crowd shouted. "Owain!" Gruffydd had chosen the name after the great Glyndŵr.

"I thought I'd surprise you," Madlen said with an arch smile. "Aren't you pleased to see us?"

"Yes," Gruffydd said grudgingly. "You certainly picked your moment." The villagers were scrambling round for a closer look. Gruffydd decided to turn the event to his advantage. "A new conjurer for Cwmystwyth!" he roared, holding the linen-swathed baby above his head.

"A new conjurer!" the crowd roared back.

Madlen lay back well satisfied. That was settled. Other women in Cwmystwyth might have claimed the same honour for their sons, but not now. The succession was clear.

Above the shouting of the crowd a pounding of hoofs resounded from the hillside and fifty head of cattle, clearly out of control, plummeted out of the woods and charged towards the crowd. They scattered in all directions leaving Madlen, Gruffydd and his heir stranded on the dais. Gruffydd leapt forward to head them off, yelling and waving his arms, but they squeezed over the stone bridge and bore down on the dais, where Madlen was screaming for someone to rescue her baby. Then a lone figure ran from the woods. He gave out a cry of inhuman shrillness, and from nowhere appeared a black and white mongrel, flying faster than the Water Horse—indeed Old Isaac maintained to his dying day that it was the Water Horse in canine form, summoned by the conjurer to avert disaster. Two more calls from the hillside followed and the mongrel cut out in front of the raging animals, who shied away from her—and from the dais—as from the sulphurous pit. The herd was brought to a standstill, having come full circle, by the river; and down from the hillside, unperturbed, walked the conjurer's elder, ill-faced son, or his familiar as was commonly reasserted after this incident.

Gruffydd was wild with anger. Iolo had engineered the whole event to show him up. It was part of a plan to discredit him. He shuddered that such an ill omen should cloud Owain's first day on earth.

"It's your herd, not mine," Iolo said, undaunted. "They'd broken out of your paddock. Mine are just coming." A dozen or so runts ambled out of the woods towards them, gently encouraged by Cadwal, who had gone back to fetch them. Gruffydd glanced at the runaway herd: his two-year-old bullocks. The villagers were watching him for their lead. Owain was still asleep. Madlen smiled at Iolo with open gratitude.

Gruffydd decided to dismiss it. He slapped Iolo on the shoulder, threw back his head and laughed. One by one the villagers joined in.

"Are you coming with us?" asked Gruffydd.

"Yes."

"Good." Gruffydd was impressed. Iolo had grown up. His lopsided face had a craggy, manly look to it now, helped by an unruly moustache that curled around his upper lip. The puny, elfin frame had filled out and the slight whine in the voice was gone. "You seem to be thriving on Calvinism." Gruffydd held out his hand. "Come up here and join us." Iolo clambered up beside them on the dais and Thomas Jenkins, anxious to restore the mood of festivity after this brush with disaster, bustled round trying to organize the next event, the annual Ystwyth blackball match. The village heavyweights split into two teams of more or less a score each and one group trotted off behind Rolo Blacksmith to the grey scar of the Glog mines—the starting line—while the other gathered round Siôn Edmunds near the dais to discuss tactics. Morgan was under the wych-elm offering to take bets, and Mihangel spread out his earthenware jars on the ground nearby and did a brisk trade in soothing unguents which would be needed after the match.

"Ointments for your bruises, charms for your cattle." A long queue of womenfolk rapidly assembled. "Black toad-skin for your warts. Pine spirit for your rheumatism."

Iolo watched the long, slim fingers move deftly from jar to jar, taking a pinch of this, a drop of that. Mihangel had a word of advice or warning for everyone. He was approachable, obviously popular. The villagers treated him as one of their own, which Gruffydd could never be.

"Up Rolo!" shouted one faction.

"Bring him down, Siôn!" yelled the other. The sweaty blacksmith pounded across the field towards them, pig's bladder firmly wedged under one arm, his team knocking down any defender within reach.

"All together, boys," yelled Siôn Edmunds and a dozen of his bruisers made a stand around the dais. Punches, kicks and the occasional knee to the groin were exchanged. Llewelyn Tapster howled as his teeth spattered onto the ground and he staggered away, bloody mouth gaping empty.

"One way to cure toothache," Iolo said, appalled.

"Better to get it over with before the trip starts," Gruffydd said. "No one feels like a fight for another year after this." Iolo grimaced, exactly the same wrinkling of the nose as when Gruffydd had delayed some long-promised departure because of a new woman.

I've missed him, Gruffydd realized, smiling to himself. Perhaps I could talk to him after all. The drove might be a good time.

Rolo's team was down, but he was swiping away all comers with his one free hand. Siôn jumped on him and pummelled his face with both fists. Sam Jones and Gwilym grabbed a leg each. Rolo staggered on, dragging them all with him, roaring like a bull, and deposited the pig's bladder loyally at Gruffydd's feet.

"Rolo wins." The conjurer held up the bladder for all to see. The victor, for the third successive year, of the Ystwyth blackball match was senseless and had to be carried away together with the beer-barrel he'd won.

"Good for Rolo!" Rhonwen Richards cried ecstatically.

"She's mad," Iolo muttered. He preferred Rachel's Bible-reading to this kind of savagery.

Madlen was staring intently at Gruffydd, who sat hunched forward on his tripod throne, deaf to the clamour around him. An expectant hush spread around the meadow. Gruffydd rose to his feet. Silently he stepped down off the dais into the circle left open by the crowd and dropped his cloak to the ground. His alert, tensed body wore only a short tunic. His eyes radiated a fanatical concentration that spread to every face in the crowd as they stared at him spellbound. Iolo felt their absorption creep over him too, exactly as Rachel described one of her father's prayer meetings—the way people's souls were dragged out of them against their will. In the centre of the circle Gruffydd lifted his staff above his head. Then with a terrible groan he brought it crashing to the ground.

It was the same dance, step for step, that Gruffydd had performed the day of their arrival. The conjurer stabbed with his staff. The crowd roared with relief and thanksgiving. Madlen turned to Iolo with a happy smile and said: "The herds are safe for another year. He's laid the demon." Could Gruffydd really believe that? He'd copied the dance from an Irish gipsy. Did he really think it cured the cattle? Rachel's dogmatic rejection of what she called superstition had nearly convinced Iolo that his father was a fraud, an idolatrous prophet of Baal whose altars would soon be overthrown. "Only God performs miracles," Rachel had said. "Would He perform one for a man who doesn't believe in Him?" But among this frenzied crowd, saturated with unquestioning belief and a common purpose, Iolo could well believe that Gruffydd had spirits at his command. They were a tangible presence in the air.

Gruffydd finished the dance and casually wiped the sweat off his beard as though nothing had happened. The farmers rounded up their cattle by the stone bridge across the Ystwyth, ready to leave. It was getting late and they'd have to hurry to make any headway before nightfall. Gruffydd flung on his cloak and noticed a rider galloping towards them along the river bank—probably a messenger from Brithgoed.. He cursed under his breath, kissed Madlen and his son and briskly mounted the horse which Mihangel was holding ready for him. Samson Constable drew up beside them with a smart salute.

"Lucky I caught you. Lord Kirkland's ill. He wants you at once."

"Tell him I'll be back in four days."

"No. Go now, please," Madlen said.

"The drovers won't wait."

"Nor will Ffowlke," Madlen flared. "The man's sick."

"He's always sick."

"Please wait." Madlen stretched up from her pallet to catch his arm. "What if he dies?" Gruffydd was already away, spurring on the herdsmen, moving up and down the column, rounding up stragglers, exchanging jokes.

"You're impossible!" she shouted after him furiously. He shouldn't be going to Tregaron at all. Would he never understand that he couldn't mix with them? They wanted his protection, not his friendship. It embarrassed them and it weakened him. Madlen had used every ploy she knew to keep him aloof in the Round House, but every few months he'd escape on some trivial flirtation or spend a whole night drinking in Morgan's Inn, spinning yarns to an open-mouthed, ale-sodden audience, as if the dignity of his calling meant nothing to him. He was too lenient with them. Not all of them loved him. When she talked of their enemies he'd wince like a boy with splinters in his thumb and refuse to listen. Madlen hadn't told him she had spies up and down the valley. He'd be shocked and say: "They love me. I must trust them."

What if Ffowlke died? Madlen watched the column of cattle crawl over the hill like a black caterpillar. It was her constant nightmare. Sometimes she'd wake at night believing Lord Kirkland was dead. Everything Gruffydd had done here was by the grace of John Ffowlke: lower rents, tithes left uncollected, security of tenure . . . But Gruffydd couldn't see this.

"I'm responsible to myself alone," he'd say and neglect John Ffowlke for months on end, as though he were some repulsive insect. Ffowlke doted on him, thank God, but behind John stood Talbot, waiting for the inheritance and ready to crush them all at a blow.

"Hush, little baby," Madlen sang to her son. An old lullaby. It soothed her more than it did him. "One day," she whispered fiercely, as the column disappeared behind the hill, "you will be a great conjurer too. Gruffydd will hand all this on to you, intact. I'll make sure of that."

CHAPTER TEN

I

IOLO STROKED CATTO behind the ears to keep her calm.

Something had gone wrong. They had been here for eight hours and there was no sign of a drover. The whole herd was dangerously restive. Two days on the move with scarcely a halt and now packed so tight they couldn't budge—nine hundred of them sweltering in unseasonable fierce sunshine, tethered row after row, rump to rump, the length of the River Teifi by Tregaron. Another ripple of stamping and kicking ran down the line. All it needed was one horse-fly too many and these beauties would head for home.

"They'll be here soon," Gruffydd said yet again, pacing up and down the ranks. "They're just testing our nerve, Huw."

"Ay," said Huw Lloyd turning away.

Iolo watched his father's hand tugging at a wisp of beard. Gruffydd was worried and he couldn't hide it from them. His high spirits had held them all together during the journey, but here in Tregaron, miles from home, the conjurer's power had dwindled. Each farmer back to his own cattle. No more banter. No more sharing. Just hopelessly resigned, drawn faces.

"Scurvy lot," Gruffydd said grimly as he stalked by. "Two days away and they're mewling for their wives and mothers."

"But where are the buyers?"

"Let's go and find out." Gruffydd hesitated a second, pretending to inspect one of Iolo's cows, then strode off alone towards the town.

He wants me to go with him, Iolo suddenly realized, delighted. Gruffydd had scarcely spoken to him on the journey. He'd been too busy encouraging the others and whenever they came face to face someone else would butt in. Perhaps they could talk now. Iolo dashed after him. Gruffydd smiled as he came abreast but didn't change pace for him.

Tregaron seemed to be busy enough. Farmers were driving their pigs and geese to market, evidently expecting a good sale. Others were already making their way home, well refreshed and boasting about how much they'd made. The narrow bridge over the Berwyn into town was packed. A cart laden with milk churns nearly squeezed Iolo into the river, but he hurried on behind Gruffydd through the dingy churchyard where a whining drunkard in the stocks was being pelted with cow-dung by an equally drunken gang of droving hands, and down into the open, mud-churned market place. A dozen drovers in their leather leggings and broad-rimmed hats were lounging around the town well, drinking ale out of pewter tankards and lobbing the occasional cobble-stone at two crippled eight-year-old runts whose frantic owner, hoping for a bid by the end of the day, was taking the cobbles against his own body rather than let them damage his stock. There wasn't another runt in sight.

"Why the Devil don't they come to us?" Gruffydd said, baffled.

"They think they own the place."

"They do own it . . . How's business?" he asked a passing farmer.

"No good for us, man. The Cwmystwyth boys are down by the river, taking all the trade. No one else bothers when they're here."

One of the drovers crossed the square. "I'll give you a guinea for each of them," he said to the cobble-battered peasant, loud enough for Gruffydd and Iolo to hear. "We can do with more fine beasts like them. Especially when there's nothing else on offer." He swaggered back to his laughing partners, the glassy-eyed runts hobbling after him. Gruffydd headed for the Lock and Key, where the drovers left their money for safe keeping.

"Let's ask their banker. He'll tell us." From the end of the dark, low-beamed room, which smelt of ale and urine, a jovial voice said: "Master Gruffydd! Have you all come to celebrate?"

"No," Gruffydd said curtly, as a bulky white-aproned man eased his way down the ladder from the loft.

"Why's that now?" the publican asked, tipping up a barrel over a clay mug.

Gruffydd refused the ale. "Why aren't they buying?"

"Oh, no luck, eh? Not much cash around, you know . . ."

"You've enough to buy us out five times."

"Have I?" He smiled apologetically and turned back to the ladder. Before he reached the second rung his arms were twisted through one gap in the ladder, his head firmly stuck through another and Gruffydd was leaning on him hard enough to block his windpipe. The publican's face turned purple and he kicked feebly. "Now," Gruffydd said. "What's going on?"

"If you'd let me speak I'd tell you," he gasped. Gruffydd eased his grip. "You see, you've been giving my drovers a hard time these last few years. You Cwmystwyth people have forced the price up, holding out together. So they've decided to bring it down again. They've signed an agreement, every one of them. They won't buy from you except at their own price." Outside, horses neighed and clattered away at a gallop.

"It's the drovers. They're heading for the meadow," Iolo said from the doorway.

"Let's go. We'll take the back way." They both sprinted across the market-place, leaving the publican howling to be let down. As they waded through the icy river, they heard the head drover shouting: "Twelve shillings a head or nothing. Make your mind up now."

"They mustn't sell for twelve," Gruffydd said. "That won't pay Ffowlke, let alone feed and clothe them."

The villagers reluctantly held up their hands to slap palms on the deal with the horsemen. Gruffydd charged up the bank. "Whoever sells, I'll feed him to the Water Horse!" he roared.

"Have you a better offer to make, Gruffydd?" mocked the drovers' leader.

It was Padrig Jonathan. Gruffydd recognized him from seven years ago. He had a scar above his left eye where Rolo had thrashed him.

"We're the only drovers for fifty miles. Our price is twelve shillings. Think it over. We'll be back in the morning." With a flick of their spurs they were away. The farmers watched them canter into the dusky haze over Tregaron, then one by one they returned to their herds to set up camp for another night, eke out their scanty provisions to make another meal.

Iolo was desperately worried. What would he tell Rhiannon? He couldn't just drive her cattle home again and he couldn't sell either. She was expecting double that price. And what would Gruffydd do now? They'd throw him out, skin him alive if he couldn't sell. Iolo knew these people by now. Short memories for a favour, long ones for a grudge.

Gruffydd paced slowly up and down along the Teifi, a solitary shadow against the last greyish-blue glimmer of light at the seaward end of the valley, head sunken on his chest, then suddenly thrown back to stare up at the thousands of stars in the night that had settled over England only a hundred miles to the east, but as inaccessible behind those mountains as across an ocean.

Iolo followed his father's gaze. Each one of those stars was a drover taunting them. He shivered. Frost tonight. The heat of the afternoon had vanished as soon as the sun went down.

Always build a fire. Iolo remembered this from countless times

167

caught by nightfall half-way up a mountain or blundering through a forest—stop worrying and build a fire. The instincts of his nomadic childhood welled up in him fiercely, a forgotten spring choked by seven years' vegetation. Within minutes he found the driest firewood for miles and returned with an armful of brushwood and logs. His fingers found the clasp of his iron, waterproof tinder-box in the dark and fished out a few strands of oil-soaked wool as if he had used the box every day for months instead of rescuing it from a dusty corner of Rhiannon's barn as an unlikely afterthought. He recognized the sharp outline of his favourite flint at the bottom of the leather pouch and set the tinder alight with one sharp, accurate stroke of the flint against the metal rim of the tinder-box. In the light of his blazing fire, Iolo settled down on a dry patch of grass and stared with delight at the box—once his most treasured possession—which he had cut from the belt of an Asiatic sailor in the Marseilles brothel where Gruffydd was spending the night. Then Barnabas, the circus animal-trainer, had stolen it and when Iolo found it in his lion-skin he swore the monkey must have taken it. Iolo laughed to himself as he saw wart-faced Barnabas, horrified at being suspected, pat him on the head and say, "Never tell lies, my boy." Iolo dozed off into a blissful half-sleep, in which the adventures of his childhood, long forgotten in the drudgery of Rhiannon's farm, trooped past. Long night rides, stormy crossings, drowsy lifts in a hay cart across the summer countryside, always summer, always moving, faces lingering attractively without losing their mystery, then flitting on. People he'd feared, respected or adored all raced past, leaving a vague regret only to be quenched with yet more movement, more faces . . . Without fully waking, Iolo realized he and his runts were not alone around their fire. From a wary distance tired, familiar faces crowded round him, holding their hands up to the flames which caught them with unnatural brightness. They looked like hunted animals huddled together. Iolo beckoned to them to come closer. None of them budged. Poor fools. Still scared of him after all this time. He drifted away again. This time he dreamt of Exodus, his favourite book, which Rachel had been reading to him only four days ago. He saw the plague of locusts settling over Egypt—except they weren't locusts, they were a herd of cattle swarming across the land, devouring every growing thing in their path. He saw Pharaoh, a scowling taciturn man in leather leggings riding a horse, saying, "Twelve shillings only," and then, with a great surge of love and admiration, he saw Moses exhorting the Children of Israel to leave Egypt.

"A land flowing with milk and honey," Moses said. "The streets are paved with gold, ale runs free in the gutter." Was Moses auctioning the golden calf? Iolo sat up to reprimand him and found Gruffydd hunched up beside him, his back to the fire.

"I saw it in a vision, as clearly as you see me now," he was saying. "We were driving our herds down from barren mountains into a plain where the grass grew golden. Gold leaf sprang from the trees and you could pick nuggets the size of an Ystwyth boulder out of the fields . . . In the market-place was a pair of scales the height of Grogwynion. Into one side we drove our cattle, and into the other they tipped their gold until it brushed the ground. Then in my vision we returned to Cwmystwyth. The whole of the valley was flowering in midwinter. Wheat and barley and potatoes were growing, unsown and untended, on the top of Black Rock where never a crop grew before. On the hillside grazed tenfold the cattle we had taken with us." Gruffydd looked at them, one by one. "The meaning of my vision is this. Across those mountains lies a fortune that will be ours, but only if we have the courage to fetch it. We must drive the cattle to England ourselves."

There was an interminable silence. Iolo watched the clouds of mist rising from the serried herds, their breathing a constant whisper in the night, broken only by the occasional snort as one of them shifted and disturbed its neighbour.

"How do we do that, master?" asked Thomas Jenkins.

"Same way we drove them to Tregaron. It's just a bit farther."

"Ay, but we're not drovers."

"That's right, Gwilym," muttered Dic Richards, rubbing his blisters.

"We got them this far," Gruffydd argued. "Why not to England?"

"Look, master," Joshua Cae Glas explained with a grim smile, "there are strange things between here and England. Only a drover knows how to deal with them."

"What things?"

"You should know, master."

"There's the dragon of Towy Forest, for one," said Siôn Edmunds. "And the Water Horse lives in the Wye, by Erwood. Everyone knows that."

"Ay, and they say there's a pack of demons, half man, half wolf, on the top above Abergwesyn."

"Who says?"

"Why, the drovers."

"The drovers of course, and do you know why?. To frighten you from trying to make the trip yourselves. Not one of those stories is true. I've travelled that way many a time. Even if they were, don't you trust me to keep you safe from demons?" There were heated whisperings to and fro and Thomas Jenkins was pushed forward to speak for them all.

"They say that in Cwmystwyth you can charm any spirit or demon, but no one knows what lies in those mountains. They don't believe," Thomas stammered with intense apology, "that your power stretches that far." He sat down abruptly. Iolo watched Gruffydd's face, poised between fury and further argument. Suddenly it sagged. Perhaps no one else noticed it with the fire behind him, but to Iolo it was clear. His strength was gone. No longer a conjurer, he was merely one mortal among many. He had lost them. They would go no farther. Gruffydd knew it too. Slowly he got to his feet and looked down at them with deep shame, for himself and for them.

"It takes three days for an English soldier to cross those mountains and fasten your chains. Will it be centuries before you dare to take the battle to his own home?" They parted to let him pass, without a word and without meeting his eye. Iolo watched his father stalk down to the river, until his huge frame merged with the trees and the hills. One by one the farmers slouched away to their own cattle.

Cowards! Slaves! Gruffydd paced up and down beside the river. Demons, half man, half wolf? He laughed out loud. All Iolo and he had found in those hills were a few starving fieldmice. He stopped.

If one demon, why not others? Had he ever doubted the demon of the cattle plague, which he slew again each autumn?

But they all saw it!

So? answered the mocking, elusive spirit he was coming to recognize. *Wouldn't they see demons in those mountains, too?*

Then I would lay them, too. Am I not a conjurer?

Are you?

Yes. They believe in me.

They believe in demons you know do not exist, demons they don't believe you could master.

But I could!

How? You don't believe in them.

Gruffydd roared with frustration and plunged head-first into the Teifi to drown his doubts in the icy water.

I'm still here, said the voice as he came up for air and waded upstream through the shallows.

I've known for ages you were there. Go on. I'm listening.

You've been lucky . . .

No such thing as luck, Gruffydd fought back. I was chosen.

By whom?

By the spirits of my ancestors and of my lands.

What if they desert you?

They won't! Gruffydd thrashed about wildly, scattering a school of peaceable trout and sending shivers through the men of Cwmystwyth. They were convinced he was conjuring up the Water Horse to devour them all.

"I have one question to ask you," Gruffydd said to the beech copse by the river. "Haven't I brought prosperity to my people? What matter the means?" The voice was silent. "Tell me that!"

There was silence. The dying leaves of the beech copse rustled in a passing breeze, a discreet titter of old women. He'd won, but it was a hollow victory. The voice would be back, he knew. Gruffydd staggered to the copse, where he threw himself down in his soaking cloak and fell asleep at once. He was awakened much later by the muffled lowing of cattle and whispered voices. Gruffydd sat up. The half moon had risen above the eastern mountains and thick clouds had blown in off the sea. It wasn't just the wind rustling through the grass. Something was coming towards him across the meadow. Vague shapes shifted in the dark. A hoof struck a pebble with a metallic click. The herds were on the move! The first runts trotted gently past the copse, silver-rimmed shadows in the faint moonlight, while a nimble figure urged them along with swishing noises from a leafy branch.

They're heading for home, was Gruffydd's first thought—but they were going in the wrong direction, and anyway no Cwmystwyth man would risk his cattle, or himself, on a night journey.

It was the drovers! The drovers had stolen the lot and were making for England. Gruffydd stared at the man approaching the beech copse, behind the first herd. Padrig Jonathan. He knew him from his loping, bow-legged gait. Gruffydd crept up behind the outermost tree of the copse and waited till his man came up abreast, then he pounced. The thief went down without a yelp, but then a foot appeared from nowhere and kicked Gruffydd in the groin. The drover made a dash for it.

"Not so fast," Gruffydd said, winded, catching his heel. The thief fell back upon him, pummelling his face, scratching and kicking. Gruffydd couldn't get hold of him. He hugged him flat against his chest, then rolled over on top of him and finally got his hands to his throat.

"It's me, you idiot," croaked the thief.

"Who?"

"Me. Iolo." Gruffydd got off him, astounded. Iolo sat up rubbing his neck.

"Where were you taking them?" Gruffydd asked suspiciously.

"To Arabia, of course. Where do you think? To blasted England! That's what you want, isn't it?"

"You can't manage nine hundred head of cattle!"

Iolo was exasperated. "Do you think I'm mad? I'm just taking my lot." Gruffydd looked round. No more coming. It was true.

"But why didn't you tell me?"

"Because you'd stop me, wouldn't you? You never did think much of me. You don't even think I can mix herbs . . ." Iolo subsided into a brooding silence, broken only by the occasional command whistled into the darkness after Cadwal to keep the cows waiting.

Gruffydd remembered how ashamed he'd been of Iolo's incompetence, next to Mihangel. He had underestimated him.

"You needn't have . . ." he said tentatively, wondering what Iolo's real motives were.

"Of course I need. You're in trouble, aren't you? What are you going to do with all that livestock?"

What indeed? Gruffydd was lost for ideas. So Iolo was doing it for him, in part at least.

"Take them back to Cwmystwyth," he said slowly. There was no other way.

"Then what?" Gruffydd studied that determined, unapologetic face, faintly ghoulish in the moonlight. Could he trust Iolo? Had he a chance of getting through? The dangers were enormous. Then Gruffydd remembered the stampede, how Iolo had controlled it. He had saved their lives then and now he was putting his own at stake. How could Gruffydd not trust him?

"Then what?" Iolo repeated.

"Wait for you to get back. I can't come with you," Gruffydd said rapidly, his mind made up. "When the herds get home the whole valley will be in an uproar. John Ffowlke will be bellowing for his rents. You go on to England. Once you've sold your cattle"—he paused, both of them aware Iolo might not make it at all—"get a dozen good men and bring them back here to fetch the rest."

"What if the farmers won't let their cattle go?"

"They'll have to," Gruffydd said grimly. "They'll need the money. What do you think? Can you do it?"

Iolo hadn't been prepared for such a responsibility. He was merely sick of Cwmystwyth. Driving his herd to England was something he had to do for himself, as well as to prove Gruffydd right and to get

Rhiannon a fair price. But wasn't responsibility what he'd always wanted from Gruffydd? At last he was being taken seriously. He was needed.

"I'll do it."

"Good." Gruffydd grinned in the dark. He suddenly saw how Iolo had been shaping up to this from their earliest days. "Take some of mine as well. Can you manage them? Try just a dozen."

"That makes twenty-two," Iolo said dubiously. He'd reckoned on less than half that. "I may lose some, but I'll try."

"Good," Gruffydd said again. "If you get there with most of them you'll make a fortune." They padded back along the river in silence and detached Gruffydd's bullocks from the head of the column without waking the camp. Then Gruffydd followed his son to where Cadwal was patiently guarding the others. Together they skirted the outlying farms of Tregaron and set off up the Berwyn valley.

"It's nearly dawn," Gruffydd said after a mile or so. "I must get back to the others before they sell their livelihood for a sixpence." The two men stopped and faced each other.

"There are things I wanted to talk to you about," Gruffydd said awkwardly, "but it's too late now. They'll keep."

"Thanks for the cattle." Iolo wished they could have said more.

"You're worth it." Gruffydd pulled the stone amulet from his neck and placed it round Iolo's. "Take this. You know what it means?" Iolo lifted the stone to his lips. They smiled, embraced and went their separate ways.

II

"You need a black cockerel."

"How can I find one?"

"I'll send you one. The next time your daughter has a falling fit, tie her to the bed, cut the cock's throat and sprinkle his blood in a full circle around her . . ."

Madlen lay back on her velvet-covered couch, listening to Mihangel dispensing his wisdom to an old woman in the next room. Her new bedchamber panelled in dark, soothing walnut and hung with tapestries from Brithgoed gave her the privacy she needed from inquisitive, ill-smelling visitors. It also allowed her to hear every word spoken in the Round House unseen. She pulled back the heavy, brightly-woven curtain which hung across the door, just enough to see Sioned Jenkins, Thomas's wife, pull a halfpenny from the sole of her shoe and press it furtively into Mihangel's palm.

Thank God he had the sense to make them pay. Gruffydd always refused gifts for his services, though Madlen constantly told him that they'd think it was of no value if it was free. She needed the money. Madlen added up the debts she'd accumulated over the last few months on clothes, decorations for the Round House, special presents for services rendered . . . Gruffydd fumed at her extravagance. He didn't understand how vital appearances were, but she hadn't linked her fate to a conjurer just to look like a fishwife. Where was he? He should have been back by now. Rhodri the Tailor was sitting on the kitchen table cutting her a dress like the one Lady Kirkland wore before she was bedridden and Madlen needed the money from Tregaron to pay him. She would just have to give him more work. Maybe a tunic for Owain. Apart from worries about John Ffowlke, who was sending messages for Gruffydd twice daily, Madlen was quite glad to be left on her own. She could tidy up their affairs without fear of disturbance. Three taps at the outside door announced the first of her visitors.

"Come in, Lissi," Madlen called in a weary singsong. She'd left a red shawl on the line last night. Lissi never missed it. "Well, what have you discovered for me?" Lissi stood at the foot of the bed tugging at the knots in her lank straw-coloured hair.

"I was listening to the menfolk in Morgan's Inn last night," she said with a slack-jawed grin.

"And?"

"They were saying how much money Gruffydd would bring back from Tregaron."

"How much did they think it would be?" Madlen said with exaggerated interest. She'd learnt to encourage Lissi's childlike self-importance. Occasionally Lissi would prattle something useful without knowing it.

"Llewelyn Tapster said two guineas a head. The others laughed and said eighteen shillings." Madlen yawned. "Then Morgan called them all fools. He said Gruffydd wouldn't come back with any." Madlen's yawn died abruptly.

"Why does he think that?"

"Mihangel told him," Lissi repeated faithfully, copying the way Morgan narrowed his eyes when he was pontificating.

Madlen shivered slightly. Mihangel's predictions always came true. But how could he know? Had he heard something from Tregaron? Had he seen something? Mihangel could often tell Madlen more than all her spies together, but why should he talk to Morgan, who hated them all? Morgan must have been boasting—or was Lissi lying? Surely she was too much of a simpleton to invent anything! Madlen trusted none of her informers. They were all driven by petty jealousy, family feuds or simple greed. Each of them was detailed to keep watch on another; every allegation was confirmed or refuted by a second report from a different source, usually an enemy of the first. Between them all, they could be relied upon to give a balanced view, commenting on each other in the process. The testimony of imagined friends could be revealing, too. Of course many of Madlen's agents were widely recognized but her net was cast so wide that any report could be as interesting for what it didn't say as what it did. None of the spies individually understood how his thread appeared on her loom, now bright, now hidden by other colours. Only Madlen, from her velvet-covered bed in the Round House, could weave the colours into a truthful picture of the valley—a picture as intricate and subtle as the tapestries of hunting parties that hung on her bedroom wall. Over the last few years she'd found a way of feeding all this information to Gruffydd. During a meal, or lying in bed with him after making love, she would let slip some vital warning disguised as idle chatter. He never missed it. Her own words were repeated in the advice Gruffydd gave to his visitors the next day and they always left alarmed at how much he knew about them. Not that Gruffydd needed Madlen to inform him. As a conjurer he had his own sources . . . But she was gratified at how he listened to her and used her hints, without admitting he'd even heard them. This made her feel a part of him—as though, despite his strength, she were protecting him.

"Morgan called Gruffydd a thief because of the mill-pond . . ." Lissi rattled off the usual list of people who had abused Gruffydd or, more often, Madlen. One or two new names, nothing very alarming. "Siân Evans said that Gruffydd was under your thumb and losing his strength. She said you bleed him every night while he's asleep."

Madlen hated the low gossip Siân Evans spread about her. Not that she cared about the villagers' malice, but anything she did seemed to reflect badly on Gruffydd.

"All right, you can go." Lissi smiled, a teasing, open-mouthed smile, shy and insolent. "Well?"

"Young Mifanwy, Rolo's daughter, is pregnant."

"Is she?" Madlen stared at her coldly, one eyebrow raised. Lissi fell silent, frightened. Her own five-year-old son was the very image of Gruffydd but she'd stopped talking about it since her shack was set on fire one night. "That's very interesting. And now you may go." Lissi slammed the door behind her. Owain started to cry.

"Hush," Madlen said absently, lifting him out of the rocking cradle

175

Gruffydd had built for him. It had a dragon carved in the wood at each corner to protect him from evil spirits. Madlen admired Gruffydd's skill and she knew he had devoted himself to the cradle out of love for herself and the child to come, but it exasperated her that with so many tangible enemies out to get them—Morgan, Simeon, Talbot Ffowlke: she could scarcely sleep for worrying about them all—Gruffydd had wasted days perfecting a talisman against invisible agencies who were surely, given Gruffydd's calling, benevolent towards Owain anyway.

"Hush," Madlen said again, too worried to notice that Owain was choking on her nipple. A sudden stab in her left breast brought her back to the present. Mihangel was standing in the doorway watching her.

"You have a visitor." His black eyes were fixed on the swell of her bosom where Owain was feeding. He scared her sometimes. He'd scarcely changed, outwardly, since she first knew him. His cheeks were smooth, hairless still, and he hadn't lost his boyish earnestness, but now it somehow disguised more than it revealed.

"How long have you been there?" Madlen asked sharply. More than once she'd looked over her shoulder to find him staring at her. Mihangel shrugged his shoulders innocently.

"I've just come in."

"Any news from Tregaron?" Madlen searched his face for any sign of surprise or guilt.

"Not that I've heard. Should there be?" Their eyes met for a second, Mihangel's wide, unblinking.

Madlen had known him for ten years and she had no idea what he thought, felt, did even. Yet he never refused anything she asked. Countless favours she'd demanded of him since he had stolen three hairs from Gruffydd's head for her, seven years ago. He never asked for any reward. "Everyone else pays you," Madlen would say, wishing she weren't indebted to him. "Why shouldn't I?" Mihangel looked as if she'd insulted him. His devotion was becoming oppressive, his acquiescence suffocated her. He had risked too much for her, done too much of her dirty work. He knew too many of her secrets.

"Mihangel," she said with a hint of reproof, as if she knew for certain what she could only guess. "Can I trust you?" For an instant, no more, he seemed off-balance. Madlen wasn't even sure she'd seen it. Then he was kneeling beside her, taking her hand with unexpected fervour.

"But I worship you! What are you afraid of? What have I done?"

"Do you hide things from me?"

"No." He was appalled. His naïve black eyes searched her face, trying to understand. "What things?"

Madlen smiled suddenly. He was still a boy. He'd had no experience of the world. Why should he think of harming them? How could he? She gently stroked his smooth cheek with the back of her forefinger.

"Nothing," she reassured him. "I'm just worried about Tregaron." Mihangel trembled and drew away.

"Don't worry. Please don't—" Mihangel was about to say more when he cut himself off in mid-sentence, bringing an axe down on whatever was stirring inside him. "There's a miner here," he said briskly, pulling back the curtain across the door. "They've found no lead on Graig Fawr for weeks. If they don't strike a new vein soon, they'll starve or riot."

Into Madlen's bedroom lumbered an ageing, wild-eyed miner with a white beard stuck on his chin like a half moon. He introduced himself touching his battered sou'wester with his forefinger.

"Captain Meurig, my lady. You see, my lady," he began uncertainly, not accustomed to using more than a few words at once. "We've picked all the lead off the surface. It's just scree, rubble, what's left on top. Now, we could sink a shaft but that'd take months and we've nothing to live on. There's only one way to get to that lead fast . . ." Captain Meurig was warming up. He sat beside Madlen on the bed and tapped his knuckles on her knee. "*Water.* If we poured enough water down that slope, it'd wash away all the top soil and leave the lead uncovered."

Madlen was amused by his enthusiasm. "How would you carry enough water up there?"

"We wouldn't carry it," he said, deadly serious. "Couldn't if we tried. It's there already—Llyn Isaf—right above the mines. Just a little gunpowder in the bank that holds it in, and whoosh!" He spread his fingers and made hissing noises through his teeth. "Llyn Isaf ends up at the bottom of the hill, in the Ystwyth."

"Does anyone live up there?"

"No one. A friend of mine used to live in a hut up there with his daughter. They died years ago of the plague. I buried them myself."

"It's quite safe," Mihangel said. "It's often done. Hushing, they call it."

"Arrange it." Madlen was tired of waiting for Gruffydd to make the decisions. Llyn Isaf was of no use to anyone. Few people knew it was there.

Captain Meurig kissed her hand and took himself off well pleased.

"Mihangel," she said, "I hear Mifanwy Blacksmith is having a baby?"

"Yes." His look told her all she wanted to know.

"Stillborn," she muttered fiercely. Mihangel nodded and returned to his book.

Strange, Madlen thought. The last she knew, he couldn't read.

CHAPTER ELEVEN

I

"HOLD 'EM HERE, Cadwal," Iolo called breathlessly as they reached the top of the ridge. "It's a steep climb down. I'll come forward and help you." He'd kept the herd packed head to tail all day and wasn't having the leaders run away with him now. "Good going," he said, half to himself and half to his dog. "Four miles, maybe five even." It was more than Gruffydd had managed in two days on the trip to Tregaron.

Iolo looked back at the Berwyn valley with satisfaction. Far in the distance, rising out of the squat cottages and beech groves, he could see the grey stone tower of Tregaron church, where the poor drunkard was probably still in the stocks. He was glad to be rid of the place. With each step towards the mountain he'd breathed more freely and seven years of lonely oppression in an alien land washed off him in the cool breeze. He felt like the Cwmystwyth miners coming up for air, and he saw vividly the upturned, grimy faces of those mole-men being cranked up the shaft in a rickety wicker basket. He knew how they felt when they saw the sky again.

There, just outside Tregaron, was the ford where they had crossed the Berwyn, and above it were the earthworks he'd noticed. He pointed for Cadwal's benefit. He could see them better from here—three rows of circular ditches cut into the hillside, dominating the valley. Fortifications, probably, like Grogwynion. Who could have built them? How long ago? And whom were they fighting? Iolo had no idea but he felt vaguely that they were watching him. He remembered standing with Gruffydd on top of Grogwynion the day they arrived. Those hills and valleys had meant nothing to him then and the Lord Rhys still less. Now, just as he was about to leave this cursed place, he discovered it mattered to him after all. Iolo shook off an unwelcome twinge of homesickness—for his father and for Rhiannon, for Rachel even.

His eye reached the empty paddocks of Cwmberwyn where the valley floor started rising between vertical cliffs. It had scared the cows so much they tried to turn back. "That was the tricky bit, but we kept them going, didn't we, Cadwal?" Iolo cuffed her, seeing himself as a veteran drover already. "Now let's find somewhere for the night."

Iolo turned his back on the Berwyn, on Cwmystwyth and the last seven years, strode to the front of his herd and led them slowly down the rocky gully into the next valley. "That's it, Catto." If the leader came, the rest were sure to follow. White-nosed Catto picked her way from stone to stone as sure-footed as a mountain goat, water from the stream splashing onto her dappled belly. Born and bred for the drove, the black Welsh runt. They would soon be there: the water was flowing towards England already. Iolo didn't really know where he was going. He had no idea of the way or of where he'd end up, but England was to the east. If he headed into the sun he was bound to get there.

At the bottom of the gully Iolo led his herd into a grassy hollow, surrounded by gorse and elder bushes, near the new eastbound stream. Plenty of water, plenty of grass. None of them would stray before morning—they were too tired. Iolo made himself a fire skinned the rabbit he'd caught in Cwmberwyn with Gruffydd's old hunting knife and stuck it on a wooden spit propped up over the flame on two makeshift tripods. Then he put his feet up and dozed off until the wooden spit burned through, the tripods collapsed and he was left with a meal that was charred on top and raw inside. Still, it tasted good enough. Iolo washed it down with several draughts from the stream and thought of Rachel as he cupped his hands like Gideon's chosen soldiers, instead of lying flat on his belly—though the evening was so peaceful there was no call for any great vigilance.

He lay back and stretched his stiff legs and wondered what Rachel was doing now. He enjoyed the stories Rachel read to him, but it was better to be living them for himself, relying on his own wits in open country where anything might happen. When Iolo imagined all the adventures he would have they were dangerous, of course, and sometimes he came very close to disaster, but at the last moment there was always some miraculous trumpet to blow for Jericho to come crashing down at his feet. Rachel was so cold. Iolo's mind turned dreamily to English women and English cities, both of which he remembered as being better built than the Welsh.

"Have at you, sir," he said to a periwigged gentleman in an English alehouse who was molesting the landlord's daughter. Iolo finished his beef-steak and downed his tankard in one gulp. Then he drew his hunting knife, beat off the gentleman in a fair duel and proceeded most pleasantly to molest the lady himself. "Shall we disrobe?" he said gallantly. A feather bed appeared from nowhere, and he was unhooking her stays with infinite dexterity when the soft tread of horses' hoofs woke him.

"Where are you taking them?" said a dark rider, silhouetted miles above him against the darkening sky. Iolo looked at the metal-shod hoof beside his head.

"England."

"Think again," said the other horseman in a warm, caressing voice. "Turn back tomorrow. It's safer."

"Why?" Iolo wondered if he should challenge them to a duel. He ditched the idea at once.

"Trouble up ahead," said the first voice, not unkindly. "We don't want them to hurt you." The other laughed quietly and they both rode on into the night. For an age Iolo lay quite still. Then he sat up. Nothing stirring anywhere up or down the valley.

"Did two horsemen just ride by?" he asked Cadwal. She wagged her tail sleepily. "If they did, why didn't you warn me?" Cadwal yawned, turned over and dozed off again.

It must have been a dream. Iolo tried to recapture the feather bed and the stays. Who could take seriously two horsemen who drifted by like that? They weren't spirits, were they? Iolo sat up again. It was all very well for Rachel to ridicule the idea of demons from the safety of a warm fire and a not-too-leaky roof, but on your own, at night, in the mountains . . . Was it a warning from Gruffydd? Perhaps he should turn back . . . Iolo didn't sleep much that night, but when a dull grey light at last picked out the barren, narrow contours of the valley, the whole thing seemed absurd.

"We must go on," he said to Cadwal as they shared the remnants of blackened, gristly rabbit. "Gruffydd's depending on us." Cadwal agreed whole-heartedly, so together they roused the lazy cattle.

"Heiptroo ho!" Iolo bellowed at them in his fine baritone. It was the cry he had always heard the drovers use—two notes, more sung than shouted, the second five strings higher than the first on blind Ismael's harp and sometimes lifted into a falsetto whip-crack right at the end. "Heiptroo ho-o!" Iolo cried over and over, delighted at how well he could do it. It went to a runt's legs faster than a reel to courting dancers. They were like six-week lambs as they trotted diagonally up the hill. At the top they headed naturally along a shallow trough of flattened grass that ran along the upland ridge for as far as Iolo could see.

How convenient! He was a little disappointed at how easy it all was. The trough was too wide for a track or a path. It was more like a river bed hollowed out of the rock, but there was no water up here and it certainly wouldn't run straight like this. Watching his cattle shuffle peaceably along, he realized with awe that it was their work. This causeway had been cut for them by thousand upon thousand of their kind who had come this way for centuries before them, and they in turn were keeping it clear for the thousands who would follow. Iolo was proud to think he was treading in the steps of drovers long dead and forgotten who had kept the lonely fastnesses of Wales alive with their annual pilgrimage to England, the only travellers between the two countries. It gave him a new respect for his calling. He belonged on this ridge. It was his.

Well, at least I'm going the right way, he thought cheerfully. But it wouldn't be very exciting if this road went all the way to England. It didn't. It ran for scarcely two miles, after which the ridge ended abruptly with a perilous descent into a river gorge, beyond which rose thickly wooded, menacing hills. Iolo remembered the drovers' tales and knew at once where he was: it was the Towy Forest.

There were about a dozen possible ways down, little more than vertical goat-tracks, most of them. Iolo glanced upstream—steeper if anything—so it had to be here. He couldn't risk them all at once. If one fell it would take the rest with him. Iolo herded them gently away from the edge and separated Catto from the others. "Come on, girl," he whispered. She wouldn't budge. He needed a halter and cursed himself for not bringing one. He undid the hemp that stretched four times round his waist, left his tattered knee-length breeches at the top and dragged the nervous cow down after him. Twice she lost her footing and he thought she'd fall on him, but they reached the river intact.

Twenty-one more. Pedr stared at him dolefully from the top, the white patches around his eyes exaggerating his alarm. Iolo clambered back up the cliff, his naked buttocks gleaming against the grey stone. He was half-way up, when he heard horses' hoofs again. Not walking this time: galloping. Cadwal started barking and the cattle roared anxiously. Men were shouting "Heiptroo ho" twice as loud as Iolo ever did. He scrambled to the top of the cliff in time to see his herd scattering in all directions while one of two horsemen laughed and waved Iolo's breeches at him.

"What will they think of you in England?" he shouted, dangling the breeches on the end of his whip. Iolo lunged. The horse reared. The rider flicked the breeches into his other hand and brought his cattle-whip lashing round against Iolo's buttocks. "Go back to your mother," he yelled, and they both turned and galloped away up-stream.

Iolo sank to his knees beside the cliff, crying with rage and shame. He knew who they were, now, his nocturnal horsemen. He knew their faces. They were drovers. They'd been with the others in Tregaron.

For the first time it struck him. They were not his cattle—they were Rhiannon's. What would she do without them? Yesterday he'd only thought of the challenge, and of helping Gruffydd. Now Rhiannon's livelihood was lost in these hills—and Gruffydd was expecting him home in triumph. He couldn't go back empty-handed.

"Why the hell should I give up because of you?" he muttered at the empty hills. "You bastards! Get out of my way!" How dare they stop him driving his cattle wherever he please, as if only a drover had right of passage in this country? Anyway, he *was* a drover. He refused to be excluded. "What are you hiding?" he yelled. "It must be worth having if you're afraid of a poor trouserless sod like me." Iolo calmed down. Cadwal was licking blood off the deep weal in his leg. He was suddenly aware that it hurt, but that only goaded him on. He marched off downstream, where most of his herd had fled, determined to reach England even with only one cow. It was getting dark. One hour of daylight, maybe two if the clouds lifted. Iolo scoured the hills to the west and picked up a couple of stragglers. Most of them had probably headed back along the causeway and were miles away by now. He was exhausted. His feet were blistered, his legs blood-stained and scratched from the mountain brambles. He would have to give up till tomorrow.

He limped through a cluster of birches back to the river and found a perfectly smooth path down the hill only a mile from his ravine. They should have come this way, but it wouldn't have made any difference. As he turned the last bend in the path Iolo's heart stopped. Nestling against the hillside on a narrow strip of pasture, grazing unhurt and unperturbed, were a dozen, maybe fifteen of his herd, Betsi among them.

"Clever girl!" He rested his head against her neck, and his tears ran down her warm black hide. "Did you lead them here? I'll never try and take you down a cliff again." Iolo gently got them moving and their hoofs splashed through the shallow, pebbly river between steep banks so thickly wooded they made a tunnel in some places.

There was no sign of Catto as they passed the ravine. She must be farther along. She wouldn't have climbed back up on her own. Slowly they trudged on. There was barely enough light to see by when Iolo made out a faint black cluster farther on.

"Stay here, Cadwal." Iolo pressed on alone. He found the others, nearly all of them, Catto as well, gathered around Twm, one of the oldest bullocks, who was floundering in pain. He must have fallen over the edge of the cliff. His limbs were hopelessly twisted and one of his leg bones stuck out through the hock. Iolo sent his companions off to rejoin the herd, then lifted the biggest stone he could find and brought it down on Twm's head, just above the eye. He died without a murmur. Iolo covered him with rocks and branches as best he could, then waded back grim-faced to his herd.

One dead. One other lost—one of Gruffydd's. Before he lay down to rest, he cut himself a six-foot staff of solid oak with a knot at the top and wove together a sling out of creepers, such as shepherds use to shoot pebbles at buzzards during the lambing season.

The next morning was cold and overcast and a light drizzle hung in the air. Iolo's naked haunches were freezing. He sharpened his hunting knife on a rock and tried to rouse Cadwal, but she yawned and licked her chops and seemed quite uninterested in finding any breakfast. Iolo suddenly realized that she must have been at the corpse upriver. Why hadn't it occurred to him that Twm would make the best meal he was likely to get between here and England? What was he driving his herd there for, if not to be eaten? He didn't much like thinking of his companions as roast beef, but Twm was already dead, so there was no point in going hungry. Iolo carved a thick rump-steak from a part of the carcass unchewed by Cadwal and various other nocturnal visitors, built himself a roaring fire and didn't get moving until well past noon, by which time he felt ready to face a dozen drovers. He practised shooting stones at tree-trunks all the way up through the forest, but kept the sharpest flints that he could find in his shirt pocket. The drovers were bound to be back. Hours passed. The forest closed in more tightly round the narrow path and there was still no sign of the drovers. Perhaps they thought he had turned back. He was just beginning to breathe freely when the two riders appeared at the end of a long straight stretch in the track. Iolo stopped. He ordered Cadwal to wait and walked on alone to meet them. For seconds they didn't move, just watched him approach. Then, at maybe a hundred paces, they broke into a gallop and thundered towards him.

Iolo reached to his shirt pocket. The top stone was jagged between his thumb and forefinger. Quite slowly he took it out, placed it in the cup of his sling and aimed at the knitted eyebrows of the first rider. They were black and bushy and met in the middle of his forehead in a bristling frown. Then Iolo fired. The man fell like lead. Iolo stepped to one side to let the riderless horse career past, then he gripped the thin end of his staff in both hands and swung the knout straight into the face of the second horseman. The drover screamed and toppled. His foot got caught in the stirrups and his mount bolted, dragging him for yards down the path. He worked himself free, kicking and swearing, then he slowly got up and turned back to Iolo. Blood was streaming from a gash in his cheek and ran in rivulets into his mouth. He picked up his whip, drew a short skinning knife and spat onto the ground.

Iolo knew he was going to be killed. An animal's eyes stared at him in utterly blind rage and he was paralysed. He did nothing as the man bore down on him. He couldn't run. Couldn't strike. Couldn't think.

The drover wiped his cheek with the back of his hand, a smile on his unshaven, blood-stained face. Then he swung back his elbow to raise the whip.

"Drive!" Iolo screamed in his highest pitch. Cadwal barked and the drover glanced over his shoulder. Iolo lunged with the staff at his chest. The man doubled up. Iolo drew his hunting knife and thrust it in just below the belt.

Like cheese. He was startled when blood spurted all over him as he drew the knife out. For a moment they stared at each other, equally horrified. The drover tried to say something, but blood came out of his mouth instead. With a vomiting noise, he collapsed at Iolo's feet.

"I've killed him." Iolo lifted the man's head. As grey as Cwmystwyth slate. "Serves you right!" Iolo shouted desperately. "Why did you attack my cattle?" Suddenly he remembered the other rider and raced back. The body was already cold. Iolo's flint was lodged three inches deep, point first, in his forehead just where the bushy eyebrows met and his lips were curled back over his teeth in a silent howl.

Iolo laughed till his stomach hurt. He could have been looking like them. He was too glad to be alive. The very idea of not being dead seemed absurd and sent him wild with hysterical relief, yet he hated them more dead because they'd made him kill them. "You won't need these now, will you?" he said brazenly, dragging the drover's breeches off him. "They just about fit me. And I'll have the leggings too, if you don't mind."

In an orgy of revenge Iolo hacked off the naked drover's privates and flung them as far as he could into the forest.

"You'll look funny in England, too." He sneered at the white, wolf-grinning face. "Why couldn't you leave me in peace? Why have you done this to me?" Iolo knew he'd never forget those eyebrows and the thin curling lips. Already victory tasted bitter. But for now he had to relish it to the full, or else it would choke him.

"You've made a drover out of me," he crowed. He exchanged his leaky boots for a fine polished pair and swaggered over the corpses, wearing a wide-brimmed hat and cracking a whip above his head. "A drover in more ways than one." As the terrible fear of retribution crept up on him, he fell silent, his head cocked to one side, listening to the forest. Then he rapidly dumped the bodies in a ditch, under a holly bush, ran back to his innocent, cud-churning cattle and drove them on frantically towards England.

II

Madlen lay on her bed giving Owain his midday feed. He was a quiet baby. He hardly ever cried and he sucked her milk in the most genteel manner. There was none of the slurping and gurgling she remembered with Hannah. Sometimes she wondered if he was swallowing it at all. She wiped away the milk running down his chin and switched him over. Her left breast hurt again as he touched it, a dull stab. It hadn't let up since yesterday. This was just one of her worries—there were so many that she had made a mental list of them which she checked every day.

Why did Mihangel have all those books? She had searched his corner of the Round House last night while he was out—she didn't know where—and discovered a stack of books, in a language she couldn't understand, hidden in a niche in the wall. Latin, she was sure. One of the titles was *De Profundis*, which she recognized from the Papist psalter her father had shown her. But Mihangel couldn't know any Latin. Nobody could have taught him. Next on her list was John Ffowlke—his bloated, drink-sodden face leapt out at her, looking dangerously ill. Thank God she had gone to see him. He'd have gone mad left alone any longer. She'd managed to soothe him a little, convince him Gruffydd was still watching over him, even from Tregaron. Ffowlke was in need of female care. She'd found him easier to handle than she'd expected. But his news—however exaggerated by drink and his persecution mania—was worrying. Talbot was trying to strip him of the Kirkland title and throw him out of Brithgoed. "My dear brother will try everything," Ffowlke had said morosely. "He'll say I'm a bastard. He'll say I'm a rebel. He'll certify me bankrupt or insane. Anything will do." Backed by a coalition of disaffected Whigs and Lewis Pryse's Tories, who were a force to be reckoned with since their leader's return from his self-imposed exile,

Talbot might succeed on any of these counts. Ffowlke had asked her over and over again about his rents. He needed the money from Tregaron to buy back a few friends.

Where was Gruffydd? He was a day late. And why did he waste his time on cattle?

As if in protest, a distant lowing came up the wind, moaning through the cracks in her hatch-window.

A stray? Or had someone kept their cattle behind? The noise came again. A whole herd. At least two dozen. Before the bellowing came closer, Madlen felt a strange vibration in the bed as though the earth was moving beneath her. She put her ear to the floor. It was quite distinct: the thud of hoofs, hundreds of them. Cattle on the move. She could even hear the herdsmen shouting.

"Dear God!" She turned as cold as the stone flags. "They're ours. They've come back."

The Ystwyth meadows were chaos come again. The cattle jostled each other to get across the stone bridge, and some were pushed into the river. The horrified farmers who had been left behind ran about like headless chickens, trying to get an explanation out of the footsore and bad-tempered herdsmen, and in the middle of this uproar stood Gruffydd.

"Why did you bring them back?"

"What can we feed them on?"

"John Ffowlke has called for his rents. How do we pay him?"

The women were shouting loudest. The old men stood aside, huddled around the wych-elm, and muttered darkly. Nothing like this had happened here before. There'd be trouble for Gruffydd now. It was just as Mihangel had predicted.

"How do I feed my brats?" Lissi Fishpond said angrily, and swiped aside the eldest, who was tugging at her skirts.

"Why didn't you sell?" Dilys Edmunds shouted. "Go back and sell them." The crowd picked it up.

"Back, back," they chanted, waving their arms toward Tregaron, and the men who'd been there chanted loudest of all.

Whatever your reasons, Gruffydd, thought Madlen, watching from the woods, they'd better be good.

"Quiet!" Gruffydd's voice was lost in the din. Slowly he raised his right arm. The shouting stopped.

"You disgust me," he said. "You're not fit to call yourselves Welshmen. I've finished with you." He pushed his way through the silent crowd and started up the path to the Round House. Thomas

Jenkins dashed after him, begging him to explain, and gradually the rest followed. Gruffydd strode on without a word as they milled around him, and they finally got so scared at what they'd done that they lifted him off the ground and carried him forcibly back to the meadow. Then they waited in respectful silence for him to speak.

"Dilys, how much does your husband pay John Ffowlke in rent?"

"Three guineas," she said, embarrassed to be singled out.

"How many cows does he own?"

"Three."

"So how much does he need for each cow to pay John Ffowlke?" Dilys's lips moved slowly, her face creased in puzzlement, as she counted on her fingers.

"One guinea," she said, pleased with herself.

"Good. One guinea. So would you take twelve shillings?" Dilys shook her head firmly. "I want all of you to work it out. Twelve shillings is all we were offered in Tregaron—your brave husbands will tell you why. Now will anyone say I was wrong to refuse?"

"But we still have to pay John Ffowlke," Morgan said shiftily.

"We have to feed the animals."

"And ourselves."

"All right. Leave John Ffowlke to me. He'll wait for his rents."

Ffowlke wouldn't wait another day and Madlen knew it. He needed every penny he could get.

". . . Perhaps he'll even agree to go without them." There were murmurs of excitement.

Madlen could have killed him. He was mad. He couldn't pull it off.

"As for our herds"—Gruffydd raised his forefinger and shook his long hair—"we've finished with thieving, cheating drovers. What use are they? Are they the only ones who can manage cattle?"

"No!" half of them shouted back, unthinking.

"In the future we'll do the job ourselves. At this very moment, my son Iolo is approaching England with my cattle, and when he returns and brings me a fortune ask your husbands why they were too scared to go with him. Perhaps if you ask him nicely he may take yours as well next time."

They weren't convinced. Iolo was an odd, solitary boy, whom no one had seen much of. It was rumoured that he was soft in the head and that was why the conjurer had thrown him over. Morgan cracked a joke about Iolo's face and a chorus of derision spread through the crowd.

"Don't you believe your own eyes? Didn't he break the stampede the day we left? He has a power over animals which none of you dream of . . . and above all he's my son. I've invested him with my power."

Madlen could scarcely believe her ears. To place all their hopes on an untried boy! Iolo might hate them after the way Gruffydd had treated him. How could they trust him? They hadn't helped him, so why should he help them?

"In the meantime, what have we to fear? Our own foresight has provided enough grain for ourselves and our herds for months. This is the time to use it."

They were warming to him now and Gruffydd began to breathe more freely. He had dreaded this reckoning every inch of the way from Tregaron. For the moment he was safe, but he had to keep them busy till Iolo's return. "Friends." He spread his arms as if to embrace them. "Together we are strong—but only together. We have a choice either to be slaves or to be masters of our own fate. If we seize this moment and work for ourselves and each other, we can build a nation, here on the Ystwyth, firmer and more united than anything our forefathers achieved. And from this heart"—he put his hand to his chest and his imposing eyes moved prophetically from the ragged horde at his feet to the surrounding hills—"our nation will grow in strength of purpose until it encompasses the whole of Wales." They cheered wildly. Gruffydd was their conjurer and no one could match the power of his words. He spoke not just for one man but for them all. He shook them to the soul, shook even the earth on which they walked and which they knew was theirs.

"Tomorrow our work will go on," Gruffydd announced. Once he had them in this mood, he could slip in the practical details almost unnoticed. "We will all meet here in the morning. From now on we will work in common every day of the week and share the fruits of our common labour. We have a wool-factory to build. The Ystwyth needs a dam for a new mill to grind our extra grain. We need winter stables for the herds . . ."

Later that evening, Madlen and Gruffydd sat alone together by the hearth of the Round House. The flames cast long shadows over their gloomy faces. A meagre supper lay half-eaten in the ashes.

Madlen had stormed at Gruffydd about giving their cattle to Iolo, neglecting Ffowlke, wasting his time on the villagers . . . all the old complaints; and now she'd lapsed into a brooding silence. He'd never seen her more beautiful or more remote. He stared into her infuriating pearl-grey eyes.

"Do you understand what I'm trying to do? Because I need you, if I'm to succeed."

"I understand." Madlen smiled with much love and even more sadness. "I understand. You are a dreamer, dreaming the most beautiful dream in the world and it is so beautiful you can't believe you're asleep."

Why were her feelings for him always so split? She loved the dreamer in him and admired his dedication, in fact she'd have loved him less if he'd been any different, but his vision of the future was so unlike anything she believed could come about—even given his power over men and spirits—that it made her impatient when he talked about it. She wanted to shake him out of his trance and show him the world as it really was . . . but then he might never get over it, and she didn't want him to change. Sometimes when he was deeply moved, he convinced her that she was wrong after all and that he must have some higher knowledge of their destiny which she was incapable of grasping.

"It's not a dream," Gruffydd said impatiently. Of course he had misgivings about forcing the pace of his work in the valley just when things looked difficult, but it would encourage the waverers, deter any backsliding. Maybe also it would lay that nagging sardonic spirit which rarely left him now. "It's no dream. It's flesh and blood, already."

"But where are the bones?" Madlen opened her eyes wide at him. "The bones are in John Ffowlke's decrepit old body. You will see him, won't you?" She leaned forward and kissed him lightly on the side of his mouth. He smiled, resigned. She hadn't told him of her own visit to Brithgoed. Better kept secret. It might put him off going there himself.

"I'll go tonight. Just to please you."

"I'll come too," Madlen said triumphantly, throwing her arms around his neck. Over his shoulder she saw Rhiannon standing in the doorway.

"I didn't mean to intrude. The door was open. Where's Iolo? I thought he must be with you."

When she'd first heard the muted thunder of hoofs approaching from behind Black Rock, Rhiannon had been in the new barn stacking bales of hay for the milch cows she would buy with the proceeds of the Tregaron sale. She guessed at once what the noise meant. Her cattle were returning, unsold. She had almost been expecting a setback—it was a judgement on her for having let them go in the first place. She should have been satisfied with a modest sale to some passing drover, instead of going with Gruffydd for higher prices. She left the bales strewn around the floor of the barn, opened the farmyard gate for Iolo and went to cook him a meal. He would be hungry, for she had sent him away with only three days' food. It was a wasted journey for him and all her fault. She had no idea what could have gone wrong in Tregaron but she thanked God that she needn't depend on a good sale, because Hywel owned their smallholding and she had no rent to pay, unlike others.

The potatoes boiled to pulp and then turned cold and finally Rhiannon was so anxious that she slipped out to the Cwmystwyth meadows where the valley's herds were gathered. She saw the conjurer talking to a large crowd but couldn't hear what he said for the lowing of cattle. There was no sign of her cattle anywhere. She asked one or two people, but they were too busy to answer or didn't seem to know. She went home and put Hannah to bed. Iolo must have driven her cattle up to Black Rock to graze for the night. She sat up by the fire expecting to hear him any minute and tried to knit a shawl for Hannah. He must be with his father at the Round House. But surely he'd at least come home to greet her? Or had Gruffydd taken control of him? And then another fear seized her: Iolo had had an accident, he was hurt and no one had told her. She would go to the Round House and ask. But she'd sworn never to speak to Gruffydd or Madlen again—when they met by chance she avoided them—and she'd never left Hannah alone at night before because the house wasn't safe and anyone might come in. In the end she couldn't bear the waiting. She checked that Hannah was sound asleep and raced up the long stony path to Black Rock.

Madlen rose to greet her with a welcoming smile as if they'd seen each other only yesterday, kissed her on both cheeks and held her hand, thanking her for coming.

Rhiannon had no idea what Madlen was saying or how she replied. She was looking past her into the shadows around the side of the room. Iolo wasn't there. Gruffydd sat alone beside the hearth, a vague outline against the fire, half turned away from her.

"Please tell me. Where is Iolo? Is he all right?"

Madlen looked at Gruffydd uneasily but he said nothing.

"Iolo is doing some very important work." Madlen was talking as if to a child.

"But where is he?"

"He's gone to England."

Rhiannon caught her breath. "Why?"

"To sell the cattle."

For an instant Rhiannon couldn't believe she had heard right and asked Madlen to repeat it. Then she realized Iolo had absconded with her cattle. Her livelihood was gone. She'd lost everything and would never survive the winter. She felt Madlen's arm under her shoulder and let herself be sat down on a stool beside the fire. Gruffydd looked round at her and smiled—she couldn't think why.

"You should be proud of Iolo. He's a fine man. I want to thank you for raising him."

He was trying to apologize to her. She could hear the uneasiness in his voice. So he had agreed to Iolo's going, perhaps he had even suggested it. Suddenly she understood it all. Gruffydd hadn't had any luck in Tregaron so he was sending his own son and her only means of existence to England to save himself. God knows what would become of poor Iolo. She pushed aside the cup of hot milk that Madlen offered her.

"You've robbed me," she said fiercely. "You've robbed me of my son."

"It was his choice."

"But you encouraged him. You had no right. He's a boy, not a drover!" Gruffydd tried to take her hand but she pulled it away.

"Do you know how much your kine will fetch in England? Iolo will make you a wealthy woman."

"I don't want wealth. I've learnt to do without it. I want Iolo back again. How could you send your own son into such danger?" Gruffydd ran his fingers across his forehead. Of course the journey was dangerous but it was worth the risk.

"Iolo can look after himself. Have you seen the way he handles cattle?"

"What do you know about Iolo?" She found it hard to believe that someone familiar with the secrets of this world and the next could be so ignorant about his own son. "You think he'll be safe just because he offered to go. Don't you understand? Iolo would do anything for you, just to win a word of praise, just to think that you take an interest in him." Gruffydd picked up a stick by the fire and started carving it with his hunting knife. He felt shaken. He could hear his own conscience speaking through Rhiannon and he didn't care to listen, especially not with Madlen watching them. He wanted to ask Rhiannon about his son, about the way he'd grown up, what he talked about, how he spent his time . . . but it would be taken as a sign of weakness by both women, as if he wasn't as sure of Iolo as he made out.

"Please! I know him better than you think."

Rhiannon paused and stared into his enigmatic, distant eyes, praying that he was right now as he had been when he delivered

Hannah. He couldn't be all evil, however much he might have harmed her by humiliating Hywel that night. There was gentleness in him which she remembered from their first meeting, and a pleading almost, as if he wished he could say more but was permanently constrained to silence. She would have liked to help him but she didn't know where to begin.

"Why did you neglect Iolo all this time?" she said helplessly. "He missed you more than you'll ever know."

Gruffydd tossed the stick onto the fire and rose to his feet. She was stirring old pains in him that he couldn't afford to dwell on. He had too many worries already. He started rearranging some herb jars on the smoke-stained dresser by the wall, but she ignored this invitation to leave.

"I didn't neglect him. I never wanted him to leave here in the first place."

"Then why didn't you visit him ever?" Her logic maddened him.

"Why didn't he come here?"

"Because he felt unwanted. You never made this into a home for him—either of you." Madlen put her hand lightly on Rhiannon's shoulder as a warning. She could tell that Gruffydd wouldn't take much more of this and she didn't want a new quarrel.

"That's not fair. It was Iolo's own decision to live with you and we wouldn't have dreamed of stopping him."

"Of course not," Rhiannon said drily. "He was in your way, wasn't he?"

Gruffydd threw one of the jars at the wall and it shattered in all directions.

"I'll tell you why Iolo never came back here. Because you poisoned his mind against me with your Calvinist bigotry. I'll have you drowned, you witch. Get out of here. Get out!" Rhiannon was already half-way to the door. Madlen sat down wearily on the stool. She could have predicted this would happen. But as Rhiannon opened the door, Gruffydd suddenly changed his tone, reluctant to let her leave in anger.

"Don't worry about Iolo, you won't suffer. I'll see you get your cattle."

"Do you think it's the cattle I care about? I wouldn't take charity from you if I was starving." She left the door open just as she had found it.

CHAPTER TWELVE

I

IOLO HADN'T SEEN a soul since he despatched the two drovers to their maker. The forest went on forever. Two nights he had spent in it, more than a lifetime, and he couldn't find any way out. His legs were past exhaustion now, they moved independently of him, detached from his weightless body. His head floated high in the branches, a log drifting gently down some lazy river. At first the cattle had strayed and refused to move on, scavenging for grass where there was none. Now they too were resigned and slipped along noiselessly, in a dream, without any encouragement from him, their hoof-fall deadened by the soft, leaf-strewn floor, the occasional hungry complaint stifled without echo in the undergrowth. Iolo had ceased to direct them. The path led them on, a subtle, irresistible current. If they came to a fork, the cattle chose which way to go. Hour after hour of narrow, winding path, always the same path, the same trees gliding past. Iolo knew them all—they were the gnarled faces of hanged men, gargoyles spouting blood. No trace of sky, besides the occasional chink in the leafy ceiling. An eternal half-light, neither day nor night. He'd lost all sense of time. Sometimes he'd hear the sound of hoof-beats and turn, expecting two ghostly riders. Or far away someone was shouting to him, he couldn't make out what.

He was in hell he thought. Locked in hell with their dead spirits tormenting him. Perhaps he had gone mad the moment he plunged his knife into human flesh and his mind would circle around that spot for ever. He was not surprised to see a certain patch of light appear at the end of a long straight stretch and to discover a rust-coloured stain in the middle of the path, his sling lying beside it.

Perhaps he had only imagined that he had killed them. Iolo hoped he was indeed mad. But in that case—he glanced at the broken undergrowth—he would now imagine that there were two corpses under a holly bush in there. But if there were no corpses . . . ? Iolo pushed his way through the foliage and found his holly bush at once. He lifted the branches. There in a shallow ditch lay the two drovers, already decomposed, one of them badly gnawed at. Iolo puked. Nothing came up, but it cleared his head.

"We've come full circle," he said to Cadwal. The sound of his own voice jolted him back to life. "If we don't pull ourselves together we'll rot with them." The drovers were dead and not to be brought back to life. Guilty or not, he couldn't change that. Time enough for judgement later. Iolo covered them with a few branches and scraped some earth into the ditch. Then he spread leaves over the blood stain on the path, picked up his sling—which was useful anyway—and wearily started on his journey again, this time turning right where the runts had chosen left before.

The half-light was fading. Iolo despaired of surviving another night without food. Only the fear of death, of lying under a holly bush for rats and wild-cats to feed on kept him going. If he stopped now, he'd never get up again. In his dazed, hollow-bellied distraction he heard Rachel reading to him from Exodus. Never any doubt that the Israelites would reach the Promised Land. It was ordained. Jehovah was with them, however much they sinned against him. Iolo stared at the dead leaves passing beneath his feet. They would never turn to manna, not if he wandered through his own Sinai to eternity.

He was utterly alone and had a terrible fear of the nothingness into which he was about to pass. Exodus had been just a good story, and Jehovah no more than an actor in it, like Moses. He had never believed, because he'd never needed to. Now he was to die without God, and there were two drovers snapping at his heels down the path to hell. Iolo could see hell—it was the fiery furnace—but he had no picture of heaven. He wished he could pray, but had no idea of God to pray to. "Thou shalt not kill," Rachel's voice rang brazen in his ears.

"Why didn't you teach me properly?" he cried out to her. "You talked of God but you never showed Him to me."

Around nightfall, Iolo and his cattle came to an upland clearing above the valley. Below him was a village with an inn by a river. Only a few cottages, but it was enough. He'd been delivered.

"Thanks be to God!" Iolo cried. It was the first time he'd ever addressed himself to God and he wasn't yet certain what he meant, but somebody needed thanking. Somebody or something had saved him, twice. "Holy God!" he said less reverently, glancing at the surrounding countryside.

From the north, south, and west, cattle in their hundreds were pouring down the mountains from three separate valleys and converging on this one village, like souls at the Last Judgement. The first arrivals were herded into meadows around the village, their drovers bargaining with local farmers and swearing at each other when their herds got mixed. Gradually the grazing land was filled and late-comers had to be content with higher ground. Iolo, scared of being recognized by Tregaron drovers, settled down in his clearing above them all where his runts could glean a meagre supper. After many misfires, he finally caught a couple of crows with his sling. His fingers shook as he tore them apart and thrust them into a fire and his mouth watered uncontrollably at the smell of roasting meat. Tired of waiting for them to cook, he gnawed them off the bone half raw. Then he fell into a deep sleep.

He was woken a few hours later by raucous singing and laughter from the inn, where oil lamps burned brightly in the windows, spreading a welcoming glow onto the surrounding grey heavy-stoned cottages. He longed to join them, but doubted whether he could ever be readmitted into the human fold. The only men he'd seen for days he had killed. Surely anyone could read it off his face. He raised his hand to his forehead. It was burning. He carried the mark of Cain for sure. He lay for hours listening to the happy voices below, till he seemed to know each of them, had put faces to them all. Finally he could bear the loneliness no longer. Even if they set on him and stoned him, it would be better than this exclusion from all human fellowship.

The creaking sign above the lintel told him, in clear blue letters, that this was the Drovers' Rest, Abergwesyn. Round the edges some clever hand had painted a string of cattle in such a way they seemed to be arriving for the night around the word "Rest" while in the other corner a sickle moon smiled down on them benevolently. Underneath the painting was scrawled: "Bed 6d. Bench 4d. Clean straw and all you can drink 3d." Iolo summoned his courage, pushed the door open and stood blinking in the smoke-filled room.

"Shut that blamed door!" shouted a bearded drover two feet away. Iolo did and the drover turned away. No one looked at him oddly. He couldn't see any of the Tregaron men.

"You with Dai's mob?" asked the landlord, a sallow-faced man with whiskers, from behind an oak counter loaded with dripping barrels.

"Yes," said Iolo, scared of drawing attention to himself.

"Take this, then." Iolo found a jug of ale in his hand. "You'd better get on with it if you want your share." Iolo took a deep draught and stood staring at a full-breasted fair-haired woman in red taffeta petticoats that barely reached her knees. She was dancing on a trestle table. Eight or ten drovers sat around her beating their fists on the table in time to a scratchy old fiddle which drove the rhythm on faster as she swirled round and round. She danced beautifully. Her thighs were slim and strong and gleamed white in the pale lamplight when the skirt spun around her waist. She had a long narrow nose which she turned up contemptuously at the men crowding at her feet, shook back her long curling hair and raised her arms till they touched the rafter. She twirled her wrists round and round, like a candle flame, and all the time her sleek hips were rolling, skirt tossing like a fishing ketch in heavy seas.

"Faster," shouted the men, eyes gleaming. All talk had finished and every eye in the room was fixed on the dancer. Even the women were clapping. Men at the back climbed onto the tables and window sills for a better view, kicking over beer mugs, smashing oil lamps.

"Faster, Eluned!" they roared.

Eluned. Iolo mouthed the name. He liked it.

"Heiptroo ho!" she sang with a final stamp and stood stock still, head back, finger thrust skyward. The drovers cheered and rattled their beer mugs. Those closest to her made grabs at her quivering legs.

The landlord pushed his way to the trestle and clambered up beside her, wheezing, while the drovers whistled.

"Gentlemen," he said pompously. "Most of you know the honours of my modest establishment, but tonight I have a special attraction." He preened his whiskers, leering smugly, relishing their attention. "Gentlemen, you have seen her dance." He thrust her by the elbow towards his audience. "One of you tonight will find out how she swives. Who will be the lucky one? Have I any offers?" There was a tense silence. "Who will start the bidding?"

"Penny farthing," said a gruff voice by the window. Someone laughed.

"Shame!"

"I'll give you five shilling," said a tall man with sunken eyes. "There's handsome." He was capped at once.

"Five and six."

"Three florins."

"Half a guinea."

Iolo watched their alert, fox-like faces. There was nothing like an auction to get a drover going. They'd give more for a cow.

"Twelve shillings."

"Thirteen and six."

"Three crowns." The bidding was down to a paunchy old dwarf

with a lecherous grin—obviously a wealthy master-drover—and a lowering, black-stubbled ogre who scowled more terribly with each offer.

"Sixteen shillings."

"Seventeen."

Iolo was disgusted. It couldn't be one of those two. Eluned had turned away from the whole transaction and refused to look at either of them.

"Nineteen shillings," spat the ogre.

"One pound!" sang the dwarf.

"Come on, sir," said the landlord to black-beard. "You can do better than that." He gripped the girl's head with both hands and presented it to them as if on a silver charger. Black-beard was out of the race and ran cursing to the door. "I have one pound. Any more offers?" The girl looked at the dwarf with loathing. She glanced desperately round the room. For an instant her eyes met Iolo's.

"One guinea," he said. It nearly choked him. The whole assembly stared at him in derisive silence.

"What was that?"

"One guinea," Iolo said loudly.

"Who have we here?" drawled the landlord. His customers hooted.

"He looks like my runt Bronwen," said a drunken oaf with a cleft chin, creasing with laughter.

"You look like the back end of her," Iolo retorted. Abrupt silence. The drover reached for his knife. Iolo already had his hand on his.

"Now, now, gentlemen," said the landlord, anxiously. "I'm sure you'll retract that, won't you? Mr Mordecai here . . ."

"One guinea," Iolo snapped. "If he wants her more he can bid more." The dwarf smiled wanly and waved his hand. Iolo shoved his way to the trestle and tossed Rhiannon's golden guinea at the landlord, who bit it and held it up to the light. Iolo took Eluned in both arms and carried her to the door. The bearded drover at the door was standing in his way.

"Are you a friend of Abel Johnstown?"

"No. Who is he, anyway?"

"You should know," the drover growled. "You're wearing his leggings." Iolo looked down. He'd not noticed before. The letters *A.J.* were tooled into the leather in deep red tan. "You're one of his outfit, aren't you?"

"Please," interrupted the landlord, not wanting his inn torn apart by yet another brawl. "The man's paid his money. He'll come back to haunt me if you kill him before he's had his due." Iolo slammed the door shut and raced along the river bank, Eluned over his shoulder. He put her down under a protective willow by the water.

"You're in a hurry," she said.

"I just wanted to get you away from there," Iolo panted, thankful to have rescued her. "That ugly toad."

"Oh, him! He did that last night. He just enjoys bargaining. He's a eunuch anyway." Iolo looked at her, startled.

"Do you know him?"

"Of course." She unlaced her stays. "They all come through once or twice a year."

"Once or twice a year," Iolo repeated, watching her ripe breasts tremble in the moonlight reflected by the river. "And . . . does he always treat you like that?"

"Who?"

"The landlord."

She laughed merrily and pulled up her scarlet petticoats to her waist. "That's my father. He always does that. It gets them excited." She opened her legs wide, took his hand and placed it between them. "Come on." She squirmed playfully. "What are you waiting for?" Iolo took off the dead man's breeches and lay on top of her. She stroked him and fondled him, saying, "Don't you like me, then?" And finally took him in her mouth, which he'd never heard of anyone doing. He felt not a thing. His heart was as heavy as lead and his pizzle was as flabby as a punctured wineskin. He stared up at the sky as her ministrations became more frantic, thinking of Rhiannon's guinea, of Rachel reading the Seventh Commandment, of all the women known to Abel Johnstown, whose privates had occupied the same breeches as his and now lay rotting in Towy Forest, where he had hurled them.

"What's the matter?" Eluned said, a coarse, foreign voice in the dark. Iolo picked up Abel Johnstown's breeches and walked away without a word, Eluned shouting after him in a taunting singsong: "Are all men eunuchs nowadays?"

II

"Open, blast you!" John Ffowlke growled at the recalcitrant Burgundy bottle. He shoved harder. The bent corkscrew slipped on the glass rim and gashed his left hand. Ffowlke was vaguely aware of pain somewhere and looked down from a great height at the red blotch on his skin. "This'll do, then." He sucked at it, laughing at his own joke.

"Won't anyone open a bottle for me?" Ffowlke shouted with histrionic self-pity. He knew perfectly well there was nobody there, except for the cook and Goronwy, the deaf-mute doorkeeper who wouldn't hear him and certainly couldn't answer. Ffowlke had dismissed his servants months ago. They were spies and traitors, every one of them.

"Then damn you all!" Ffowlke broke the neck off against the marble mantelpiece. Wine spattered against the blue brocade wallpaper. Some landed in ancient cobwebs and clotted. A few drops reached the already hazy mirror.

"You just try some of this," Ffowlke burbled to Jacquies, his canary, who was perched on a stand by his desk. He cut his finger drawing wine out of the bottle into a teat given him by Dr Madog, then he forced Jacquies' beak open and squeezed the Burgundy down his gullet. "How's that?" He sat back to wait. Jacquies squawked and preened himself, but did not fall down dead. After half an hour Ffowlke felt confident enough to drink the wine himself. It tasted warm, which only served to remind him he was cold.

"Logs. No damn logs." He pushed one of the legs of his astral globe into the pale embers and blew. Ash rose in fine clouds and settled on his bald and wrinkled crown. What use was the secret of the universe with no conjurer to read it? He was as bad as the rest. He had deserted him . . . refused to come when he was most needed . . . Ffowlke laid his head against the fender and snivelled till he dozed off.

There was a knock at the door. Ffowlke woke up in terror.

"Who's there?"

"Your friend Gruffydd."

"How do I know you're not a spirit, or Talbot?"

"Moon in the first quarter, Saturn in eclipse, Venus in fifth . . ." Ffowlke listened to his entire horoscope—an agreed signal, only Gruffydd could know it—before pushing back the oak chest he kept in front of the door.

"My friend! Why have you abandoned me? I've been calling for you." A shadowy figure moved into the doorway behind Gruffydd. Ffowlke backed away, scared again.

"It's only my companion. She is here to see to your needs." Madlen quickly put a finger to her lips. She had made Ffowlke promise to tell Gruffydd nothing of her visit. Ffowlke squinted at her in the candlelight. Ah yes, it was the young woman of two days ago who appeared to know Gruffydd so well. He liked her—she was clever and pretty— and he found it amusing that they shared a secret to keep from the conjurer. He took Gruffydd by the arm and scurried to his desk.

"Come here. Look. I have proof now. I have proof positive." He took an inlaid wooden box out of the top drawer and lifted the lid for Gruffydd, gazing up at him with fierce expectation. A dead canary lay inside. "Last Monday. Half-empty bottle of port. With my own eyes I saw Talbot drop white powder into it."

"How did you see him?"

"Through the keyhole," Ffowlke said without a trace of embarrassment.

"I'll renew the spell to protect you. You have nothing to fear from Talbot." Gruffydd sprinkled a fine powder around the room. Ffowlke babbled with gratitude, but Gruffydd was perturbed. Surely Talbot couldn't really be trying to poison him? Gruffydd had invented it. Every fear, every natural mistrust of Ffowlke's, he had subtly fed and played upon, scaring him away from any remaining friends, encouraging his lifelong hatred of Talbot, driving him to the bounds of sanity in order to keep him in abject, cringing dependence on Gruffydd's good offices. If Brithgoed was haunted, Gruffydd would exorcise it. If the servants were treacherous, Gruffydd could expose and confound them. If Ffowlke's glass was empty, Gruffydd would fill it . . . and uncork another bottle. No member of Lord Kirkland's class attempted to contact him any more. His family and the Whig Party had ostracized him for his treachery over Bonnie Prince Charlie's rebellion, and his subsequent disintegration confirmed the contempt they felt for him. The only beacon of hope in John Ffowlke's solitary inferno was Gruffydd, his friend and protector. For a long while Gruffydd had fostered his collapse with a cool, long-drawn relish, merely amused by his gratitude. Lord Kirkland was paying a hundred times over for his crimes against Gruffydd's family and people. No punishment could be more hideous than this creeping madness and constant terror of the unknown. But as the years went by, Ffowlke's dementia became grotesque. It spread. His degradation was contagious. It stuck to Gruffydd and wouldn't wash off. Eventually Gruffydd was sickened by the very sight of him. What if Talbot did kill him? He'd be doing Gruffydd a favour. But Gruffydd knew this was untrue, for however hard he tried to shrug off Ffowlke, his fortunes were tied to this empty shell of a man whom he'd destroyed. John Ffowlke was his bedfellow and if he stank, Gruffydd had only himself to blame.

"I've just got back from Tregaron," Gruffydd said, steering him into his leather armchair where he would listen. "We had a lot of trouble with the drovers there." Gruffydd's mind was wandering. "My son Iolo will sell the cattle in England," he heard himself saying and Rhiannon's voice shouted in his ear, "He's a boy, not a drover. He hasn't a chance on his own without food or friends. How could you send your own son into such danger?"

Rhiannon's reproaches had cut him to the quick. If anything happened to Iolo, the blame would be his. Gruffydd was tormented with new doubts, but it was too late to reconsider. He'd staked everything on Iolo and now he had to sweat it out.

". . . So as soon as the rest of the cattle have been taken to England, the rents will be paid in full. With interest for the delay." Gruffydd stopped speaking. He had no idea what he'd said. Ffowlke was watching him closely, a humorous glint in his sunken, beady eyes.

"You old rogue!" Ffowlke leaned forward to slap Gruffydd on the knee. "Now you're trying to do me out of my rents. I won't have it, my friend. I can't allow it." Somewhere beneath his drink-sodden bonhomie his business instinct stirred.

"Only for a month or two."

"In a month or two I shall be bankrupt and Talbot will have me in prison or the madhouse. What do you expect? I have enemies and I have to buy them off. I have no power any more. Talbot has cheated me at every step." Ffowlke threw the Burgundy bottle into the fireplace. "Who's Member of Parliament for the county? Talbot Ffowlke! Who is Lord Lieutenant? Sir Lewis Pryse, by the grace of Talbot Ffowlke. Who is Chief Justice? . . . He's turned them all against me. Betrayed his own house." Ffowlke choked on his own spittle. His face turned purple and a reddish liquid ran down his chin.

"One thing he'll never be," Madlen said comfortingly, patting his back, "is Lord Kirkland."

"Why do you think he's poisoning me?" Ffowlke spluttered. "He wants the inheritance as well. He can't bear to wait."

Madlen bustled around and cleaned his face. "But you may yet father an heir." Neither of the men noticed how she was steering the conversation.

"With a bedridden hag who's never brought anything into the world alive?"

"I was barren for seven years before Gruffydd cured me. He could do the same for Lady Kirkland."

Gruffydd tensed. They both turned to him, Madlen with a confident smile, Ffowlke with a new fascination.

"Could you do this, my friend?" Ffowlke asked. Behind his leather chair Madlen nodded her head.

"I . . ." Gruffydd's mind was blank. He desperately needed an excuse, a way out. Why couldn't he think? His invention had never deserted him before. "I believe I can do it." An abyss opened at his feet.

Ffowlke was ecstatic. "Get me an heir and I'll waive the rents of the whole valley for a year." He seized a candlestick in his trembling hand and led them into the hall. The staircase creaked beneath its carpet as they went up, with Madlen supporting Ffowlke discreetly under one arm, and their voices sounded unnaturally loud in the empty house. Madlen shivered. The place smelt of neglect. Nobody had looked after it for years. On the landing Ffowlke opened a door and stood aside with a gouty bow to let Madlen pass. A stale, damp draught met her as she walked in. The drapes around Maude's bed fluttered slightly and there was a flurry by the curtains which covered a door on the other side of the room. There was someone else in the house. Was someone really trying to get rid of the Kirklands? Maude was propped up on a pile of dirty pillows, asleep. She was breathing heavily, her wrinkled lips open on blackened, ravaged teeth. She couldn't be many years past forty, but she looked a hundred.

"Perhaps I should come here to nurse her ladyship?" Madlen suggested.

"You should stay with Owain," Gruffydd said, while Ffowlke eagerly accepted.

"We'll get a wet-nurse."

The last thing Madlen wanted was to be away from Owain, in this dank sepulchre of a place, just as she was beginning to enjoy being a mother. But she'd do it, for Gruffydd's sake. He needed more protecting than his son.

CHAPTER THIRTEEN

As soon as the first glimmer of light beckoned him on towards England, Iolo silently drove his herd down from their hideout, past the Drovers' Rest, which was at last living up to its name, and forded the Gwesyn River. Nothing stirred.

He had got rid of the leather leggings. They might be recognized again, and if the Tregaron boys didn't get him, then their enemies would. He'd have thrown off the breeches too, if he could. They stuck to his legs, clammy like his conscience. Ahead of him the drovers' causeway ran smoothly up the opposite hill, but he took a long detour through marsh and scrubland to avoid it. "Better keep out of their way," he explained to Cadwal. "We can do without company." Once he reached the top the going was easier—mile after mile of rolling upland moors, wind-swept grass almost white in the scudding patches of sunlight, like foam on the crest of a wave. But the warm breeze and the sight of an earthly kingdom stretching on all sides at his feet gave him no peace. On a mound to his right Iolo passed beneath a pile of giant stones, heaped one on top of the other till they grazed the clouds. Who had put them there? There was no other rock anywhere. They might have dropped from the sky. God's footstool. Iolo saw Moses astride it with the tablets in his arm.

"Thou shalt not kill." He heard a voice rustling in the grass, howling in the wind. "Thou shalt not . . ." He blocked it out and hurried on past the cairn, eyes lowered. Rhiannon's mild, loving face had reproached him all night. He hadn't slept for a minute.

"For a common whore," he muttered fiercely, over and over, as he tossed and turned on the hard earth. "For a moment of glory in a drovers' brothel you threw away Rhiannon's savings, all she possessed. An honest woman betrayed for a harlot. Your own mother . . ." He would never be able to look Rhiannon in the face again unless he made up that guinea with a good sale in England.

For two days this kept him going and he drove his cattle on faster than was good for them. On the third day the land began to drop again. He found himself in a lush, broad valley far richer than anything in Ceredigion. The farms were better kept, the fields were enclosed and there was far more ploughed land than in Cwmystwyth. Even the cattle were bigger here. For the first time he noticed that his own were not in good shape. They had a shrunken look around the neck, ribs dangerously near the skin. Pedr was lame on his near foreleg and his white-patched eyes were more disgruntled than ever. Pray God they would make it. He slowed them down to a snail's pace, but at this rate they'd never get to England at all. When he tried to pick up speed again, the endless hedgerows made it hard to see where he was going and each time he stopped to open a gate his herd would wander off to graze with the locals and Cadwal could scarcely separate them again.

Towards the end of the day he came to a broad driveway, which passed between two stone pillars with "Garth House" carved on them. The drive ran straight across a broad stretch of parkland, past a mansion with a portico of brilliant white columns, right to the far end of the valley. He would save hours by using it. Iolo stared across the estate. There was no one about. He decided to risk it. In the coach-house opposite the mansion a liveried porter was polishing a black and red carriage.

"Who lives here?" Iolo asked. The porter looked at him curiously.

"An English gentleman, Sir George Cobham."

"And how does an Englishman come to own Welsh land?" The porter shrugged.

"Same as them all, man. He married the Lady Gwendolen, the heiress. This is only the second time they've been here in the last twenty years."

Iolo pushed his herd on. He had almost reached the end of the driveway when a choleric snub-nosed gentleman galloped up on him, flanked by two red-coated bailiffs, and started shouting in English.

"You drovers have been warned! Get off my land or I'll have your cattle impounded and you flogged."

"Get along there!" yelled the bailiffs. Iolo's herd bellowed in fright and bolted along the valley.

"Stop them, Cadwal!" Iolo cried, racing after them. They were out of sight already. "'My land'," he fumed angrily. "'My land'! Who let you come here and call this 'my land'?" He found his cattle beside a broad road. "One man owns as much land as he can lie in, as I will prove to you one day."

The idea of owning huge chunks of earth was absurd to Iolo. A man is owned by the ground he works, not vice versa. Ownership is slavery. Only a man who can move around is free. Iolo remembered that first lesson of his childhood. To restrict that freedom is a crime. God made no provisions for fences in his six-day creation. Everything Gruffydd had said about land made a little more sense to him. When Gruffydd spoke of getting his lands back he didn't mean to throw anyone off them, to steal it from the people who lived on it. He was talking of a love unknown to these people with their bailiffs and their rent-collectors, their uniformed servants like circus monkeys. Land was an obligation to Gruffydd, which he fulfilled for the good of all. To Sir George Cobham and all his ilk it was a thumb-screw on the knuckles of the poor.

Iolo and his herd struggled on along the high road, the first paved road he had seen in Wales.

"You must be a wealthy drover to use the turnpike," said an officious, dapper individual in a tall glazed black hat, white apron and corduroy breeches, leaning on a gate across the road.

"I'm not. Will you let me pass?"

"Twenty cows at sixpence a head," the man reckoned, flicking coloured beads across his counting-frame, "ten shillings."

"Who says?"

"The Turnpike Trust says." The toll-collector pointed to the charges written up on the side of his whitewashed octagonal gate-house.

"Who is the Turnpike Trust?"

"At this moment, where you are standing," the toll-collector said with elaborate sarcasm, "the Turnpike Trust is Sir George Cobham, because he owns the road."

"Did he build it?"

"No."

"Then why should I pay him?"

The toll-collector scrutinized Iolo with growing suspicion.

"Show me your licence," he suddenly demanded.

"What do you mean?"

"Your droving licence."

"To hell with your licence and your road," Iolo exploded, driving his herd off the highway and heading up the hill.

"Iestyn! It's one of those cattle thieves. Fetch Sir George's bailiffs, quick."

What cattle thieves? Iolo decided not to stay and find out. If they caught him they were not going to ask whose cows they were.

"Faster," he yelled, hitting Catto on the rump with his staff. She galloped to the top, dragging the others with her, and Cadwal, barking with delight, last of all. The men were coming after him already, with pitchforks and dung-rakes, shouting, "String him up!"

Holy God! They were gaining on him fast. Perhaps it would be safest just to run for it—but he couldn't abandon the cattle, not having come this far. He'd never live with it. He frantically goaded them on, yelling like a Bedlamite, praying to God that night would come in time to save him.

"If You get me out of this one," he said, "I really will believe in You. I'll never sin again." As if in answer, a deafening clap of thunder burst above his head, forked lightning struck the village of Garth and the whole country was enveloped within seconds by the thickest, blackest, wettest clouds that Iolo had ever seen. He looked back at his pursuers, barely a hundred yards away, in time to see them scatter back the way they'd come.

"And the Lord overthrew the Egyptians in the midst of the sea," he roared as the cloud engulfed them like the waters closing behind the Children of Israel. "I hope it drowns you," he added for good measure. But Iolo was caught in it, too. Not a hope of making any ground. He couldn't see from one end of his herd to the other. He bunched them up against a rocky escarpment which held off the worst rain and there they stood for the better part of the night. Then Iolo heard horses' hoofs, not loud but quite close.

"They said he was hereabouts," said a voice above him, practically in his ear. "Can't have gone far."

Don't move, Iolo silently begged his cattle. Don't even breathe. Clouds of mist were rising from their nostrils into the low cloud. One of the horses stamped. A stone flew over the edge and clipped Catto round the ear. She looked at it in mild surprise and said nothing.

"Your wife's expecting again, isn't she?" said one of the riders.

"Ay, worse luck . . ." Iolo shivered with fear and cold and tried to stop his teeth chattering. He couldn't ask for two thunderbolts.

"Well, we've been out long enough."

"Ay, he probably had an accomplice waiting, anyway." They turned to go. Iolo was just daring to breathe again when Betsi grunted. "Hrrumph." Not loud. Not much like a cow. Just a low, almost human grunt.

"What was that?" said one of the riders sharply.

Long pause.

"Don't know."

"Hrrumph," went Betsi again.

"I don't like it. I've heard stories about things up here . . ." They swung round and trotted away as fast as anyone might dare on such a night.

"Good girl," Iolo said, laughing. "They thought you were the Water Horse."

"Hrrumph," Betsi answered scornfully. Iolo nudged her to one side and wedged himself between her and Catto to try and keep warm, with Cadwal slumped over his feet. The cud was gently churning in Besti's belly as he fell into a fitful waking sleep, still on his feet and numb from cold.

"For God's sake stand still," Iolo groaned about an hour later. Catto was dreaming of the Ystwyth meadows and wouldn't stop fidgeting. It was still drizzling. Iolo turned over and rubbed his soaking jerkin against Betsi's flank. She was awake and restive. Iolo forgot his aching back and sat up. Black as the Cwmystwyth lead mines. No moon. Clouds too thick. Upwind: only a faint splash of water from some stream. Downwind: might be anything. Too much of a gale to tell. But the cows had definitely heard something.

Holy God! Iolo gripped his staff. They've sent a party out for us. A thin flame was coming down the escarpment towards him. Then a worse dread seized him. "Spirits of my forefathers, protect me," he muttered, lifting the stone amulet to his lips. Noiselessly the disembodied flame advanced. Iolo's cattle started moving towards it. Was it a spirit come to tempt them over the cliff? A hollow whistle came up the wind. The flame started leaping like a soul in torment.

He hadn't come all this way to be robbed by a demon. Iolo squeezed out his last drop of courage and charged forward.

"In the name of the Holy Ghost let my cows be!" he shrieked, doubting whether any demon would shift for Father, Son or Holy Ghost. When he finally dared to open his eyes, he was looking into the sacred face of a young woman carrying a candle-lamp.

"What kind of a madman are you to be out on a night like this?" she said breathlessly.

"What creature are you?" Iolo whispered.

"Flesh and blood." They peered at each other through the dark, equally suspicious. "Are you the cattle thief?"

"No, I'm not. I'm a cattle drover," Iolo said indignantly.

"Then why did you run away?"

"Well, what would you have done?"

She considered this, then smiled suddenly.

"You don't look like a cattle thief. More like a drowned rat."

Iolo blew a strand of wet, knotted hair out of his mouth. "What are you doing here, anyway?"

"I live over there." She pointed into the dark.

"And that's why you're here in the pouring rain?"

"My aunt was dying in Garth. I went to see her. She was already dead so now I'm going home." Iolo didn't believe a word of it. "Well, you can't stay here, can you? They'll catch you in the morning."

Iolo backed away from her. "Can't move an inch in this."

"I'll go first." She took Betsi's ear. The whole herd followed her before Iolo could open his mouth.

He was terrified. She was one of the fair people, exactly as in Gruffydd's stories. They came out of the night, pretending to be human, and they vanished back into the night, stealing men and cattle to serve them in their kingdom under the earth. They had secret paths of their own all over the uplands that they knew blindfolded. Their captives obeyed them unquestioningly. Iolo's herd was beyond his control, lurching blindly through puddle and bog after this strange woman. He had no will left to resist either. He grasped hold of Pedr's tail, closed his eyes and resigned himself. Wasn't his mother one of the fair people? Gruffydd had said so. She had a herd of her own, and perhaps she'd sent this girl to guide him home. Would he see her at last? Iolo's exhausted soul thankfully shed all the anguish of guilt and responsibility and drifted into a healing fantasy of subterranean maternal embraces as his feet carried him obediently onwards.

"Not far now," he vaguely heard his guardian spirit say to him.

"Where to?" Iolo's voice was waterlogged. Rain poured through his moustache into his mouth.

"We can leave them in here," she said soon after and he heard her opening a door, but he couldn't see a thing.

"What's this?"

"Cow shed." Betsi led Iolo's troop in single file through the door, their hoof-fall suddenly muffled on thick straw.

"Well, don't stand in the rain," the woman said briskly.

"Whose is this place?" Iolo asked, bewildered. He could hear her strewing more hay for the cows to eat.

"My husband's." Iolo's heart sank. He was still among mortals.

"I'll not enter a man's house without his say-so," he said feebly.

"Then you'll wait outside till Christmas." A hand grabbed his wrist and yanked him across the threshold before he could refuse. "Now, first some food. Are you hungry?"

"Yes." Iolo remembered. He was starving. She led him into the next room. The boy seemed unable to leave his cows.

"They'll be fine," she said soothingly. "You sit here . . ." She steered him through the dark and pushed him gently back into a chair. "I'll get the fire going." Iolo heard her scraping ashes off the hearth. Then a faint, reddish glow appeared and he could see the outline of her face blowing onto the still-live embers.

"It's never gone out once," she said with pride, looking up at him. She had a funny, pointed nose, which turned up at the end, and the wicked smile on her mouth: it had a full, sensual lower lip and a quizzical, short upper one. She had chestnut hair, maybe it was just the light from the peat-fire. She was pretty, in a way.

"Have you gone to sleep?"

"No." He'd been staring at her.

"Then draw yourself some ale. I'll have some too." Iolo looked round the room. Next to the hearth was a box-bed with blue curtains drawn across it. A dresser stood against the wall opposite the door, wooden plates, mugs, food and a beer barrel stacked on it higgledy-piggledy.

"Giff!" she shouted through the door. Two seconds later an off-white, bedraggled mongrel raced in, followed by Cadwal, who had made a friend. "Up you go." She lifted Giff into an enclosed wooden tread-wheel above the hearth. Then she took down a leg of mutton hanging on a hook from the rafters and stuck it on the turnspit above the flames.

"Chase it, then." She tossed a bone into the tread-wheel. Giff chased frantically. The tread-wheel spun round, whirring. At the end of a taut rope the spit smoothly rotated, roasting the joint to perfection. With fearsome dexterity she washed and sliced eight potatoes, arranged them with a half dozen cutlets, carrots, bay leaves, rosemary, butter and a drop of milk in a baking pot which she nestled into the embers at the edge of the fire, lifted a cauldron of water onto the crane in the chimney place, then turned to Iolo, who was nodding over his mug of ale, and said, "Haven't you taken your jerkin off yet?"

Iolo was euphoric. If this was indeed the fairy kingdom, he didn't mind staying. A roof over his head. More food than he'd seen for years. A jar of decent beer . . .

"What's your name?" she asked, pulling off his soaking, muddy jerkin. "I'm Mari."

"Cadwaladr. But everyone calls me Iolo."

"Why's that, now?" She smiled.

"My father . . ." It was too complicated. "Why are you so kind?" he asked. Mari laughed, evidently pleased.

"It comes easier than being unkind. Besides, I hate the whole village of Garth, my aunt included. She was a mean old woman and my husband's a drover, so I know how people treat you." Iolo shifted in his chair, glanced at the door. "Don't worry, he's miles away. Anyway, you could blow him over."

"But I don't like to . . ."

"I hardly ever see him. He's a wild man. He goes his own way. It's nice to have company, especially a lad like you." Iolo blushed scarlet. She made him feel like a child, though she was certainly no older than he. She was so sure of herself. He watched her supple, lithe movements as she lifted the baking pot out of the fire. Yet she was nothing like Rachel. There was nothing strident about her. He felt comfortable and secure with her, as if he had known her all his life.

"You frightened me to death," Mari said, gnawing at the cutlet, her elbows planted on the low table between them. Her teeth were very white in the firelight and pointed, which made her smile even more wicked. "Running at me like that, shrieking like a lunatic."

"You scared me too," Iolo confessed. They both laughed at the thought of being terrified by each other. "I thought you were a spirit. Maybe one of my father's."

"Your father's?" She looked at him curiously. Iolo hesitated. For years he'd wanted to talk to someone about Gruffydd. In Cwmystwyth it would be a betrayal, but this was far enough away. Maybe she would understand. Iolo took a deep breath and started in the middle.

"My father's a conjurer."

Mari's eyes opened wide. "Then what are you doing driving cows?"

"I'm not really a drover . . ."

Mari giggled. "Anyone can tell that. Driving a herd along the turnpike right up to a toll-house!" Iolo protested, his vanity outraged. "Though you handle them beautifully," Mari tried to reassure him. The boy had clamped up. She watched him, amused, while they ate in silence, Iolo lowering at her across the table. The ale had put some life back in his face. He didn't look quite so like a death's head. In fact it didn't matter that his face was a bit crooked. It made him pleasantly scaring, more manly than his years, but at the same time vulnerable because it magnified every emotion tenfold. Transparent, like water. He could never hide anything from anyone. It made her want to protect him, exactly as on that first glimpse of him up on the hills. She'd have run from any other man, but this one you had to help. It must give him a charmed life. How many other women had looked at him the same way?

"You know, Iolo," she said, "you're a handsome man." Iolo

winced. He felt absurd in every way. He glanced at her cautiously. She wasn't laughing at him. He managed to raise a smile.

"At home they take me for a goblin."

"Then they haven't looked straight." Iolo felt a surge of warmth and pride.

"If my father hadn't dropped me off a horse when I was three . . ."

"He can't be much of a conjurer," Mari butted in and immediately cursed her quick tongue. Iolo had seized up again. "Well," she said, when the last bone had been tossed sizzling into the fire. "You'll need some sleep." She threw a pile of clothes out of a battered tin tub in the corner, put it in front of the fire and hoisted down the cauldron of near-boiling water.

"What's that for?"

"You'll not be getting into bed with all that mud on you, will you?"

"Bed?" He looked round. There was only one bed. "Oh, it's all right, I'll just sleep here by the fire."

"When there's a bed big enough for two with clean sheets and a feather bolster?" Iolo headed for the door.

"I must look to my cows."

"They can look to themselves." Mari stripped the shirt off his back at a stroke.

"But I'll be filthy again in half an hour tomorrow." Iolo saw his breeches tumble to his feet and stood there naked as the day God made him. Mari fetched a scrubbing brush.

"That's no reason to be filthy now. Well, get in, man."

"It's too hot."

Iolo was mortified. She was making an ass of him. She poured in a jug of cold water, and Iolo reluctantly eased himself in, his thighs and buttocks turning as pink as an Aberystwyth lobster.

"Hair first." Iolo gulped as she pushed his head under and started lathering his scalp. Soap flew everywhere—into his mouth, his nose, one of his eyes. He spluttered and tried to brush it away, but she tilted back his head and laid it firmly on her bosom. "Well, open your eye, then, or how can I get the soap out?" Iolo opened both eyes and looked up into her intent, concerned face, scarcely a hand's breadth from his. Her hair fell onto his chest. It was indeed chestnut. "There," she said, "better?" Iolo nodded, wishing he had soap in the other eye too. Mari combed the knots out of his hair and swept it back off his forehead. Then she surveyed him, like a wood-carver his latest work. "How long since you shaved?" Iolo shrugged. She used the lethal-looking razor so finely it felt more like velvet than steel. "That's better," she said with huge satisfaction, holding his head in both hands. "You look nearly human. Now get up and I'll soap you down." Iolo didn't budge. "What's the matter, bach?" she asked gently. "Don't you like me?" Iolo nodded vigorously but still refused to stand up. The truth was that below the soapy water his pizzle was as hard and long as the oaken staff with which he'd fought the drover, and he'd die of shame if he disgraced himself before his kind hostess.

"You're an odd lad, Iolo," Mari said, not unkindly, kneeling beside the tub. "Most men would lie back and enjoy it. Don't your sisters or your mother wash you at home?" Iolo tried to sound relaxed.

"I have no sisters. Nor a mother."

"Your sweetheart, then?" No answer, Iolo coughed with embarrassment. How could he possibly admit it?

"Oh, my poor boy," Mari said slowly, not daring to believe that there was a mother's son who didn't rut from the age of fourteen. "I'm sorry, truly I am. If I'd only known. I wouldn't have been so coarse with you." She put her arm round his neck, the palm of her hand caressing his ear. "It takes a bit of learning, like droving, but if you let me I'll teach you both." She kissed him lightly on the mouth and was surprised to find his powerful arms wrapped one and a half times around her and his tongue deep inside her. "You're making up for lost time," she said, coming up for air. "You'll make a grand pupil." She unhooked her dark red gown and slipped it off her shoulders, smiling at his wide grey-blue eyes riveted on her. She started to unbutton her linen shift, then knelt down to him. "You do it, Iolo." His hands were unsteady. She didn't hurry him. Her breasts were small, round, firm. They scarcely trembled as he instinctively put his mouth to one of them and felt the nipple swell beneath his tongue. "Good," she murmured, running her fingers through his hair, pulling him closer. Iolo fumbled with the laces of her skirts. She moved away for a second and stepped out of them. A revelation for Iolo. He'd never imagined anything so beautiful, never realized that a woman's hips were so broad and welcoming. Chestnut hair, redder than her head hair and bunched in thousands of tiny curls. Her skin was darker than his, with a myriad freckles over her shoulders and thighs. Mari stood for a moment, watching him, then she helped him out of the tub, wiped the water off his hair with a towel and pulled him towards the bed. Her skin was smooth and slippery against his. She writhed playfully on top of him, while his hands touched her with awe.

"Remember this moment, Iolo bach, when you're old and grey," she said, holding him, bursting with desire, between her fingers. Gently she lowered herself onto him. Iolo was astounded to feel himself inside her. She seemed to float on top of him, a mermaid, then she hugged his chest tightly and rolled over underneath him.

"Sleep now," Mari said to him, kissing the tips of his fingers. They lay next to each other in bed, half buried in the sheep's-wool mattress. Iolo's tiredness was gone. He'd only just started. He wanted to learn more. For the rest of that night Mari showed him what pleased her. More than once her body shook and quaked beneath him, while a total eclipse passed across her face. It filled him with wonder and great tenderness.

Twelve hours later they were still nestling side by side in bed. They had made love endlessly and then eaten, slept for a while and now Mari was trying to coax new life into him yet again. The sun was sinking already. He had told her about his mission, which he had to complete however much he wanted to stay with her, about his encounter with the two drovers and with the whore Eluned—they had both laughed at that—and for the first time he had talked to someone about Gruffydd.

"Whether he's a conjurer or not," she said, "be your own man, Iolo. You don't need him. There are far better places than Cwmystwyth. You don't belong there. You said so yourself." Iolo had to agree. Cwmystwyth seemed far away now. He never wanted to see the place again.

"But what about Rhiannon's cattle? I have a duty . . ."

"She'll look after herself. Women always do. And, Iolo bach, don't you let people go stuffing your ears full with words like 'duty' and 'adultery'. Life is for those who love the most. Don't take it so hard."

Iolo forgot Moses sitting on his pile of stones. He forgot Rachel's droning voice. He very nearly forgot Rhiannon and Gruffydd too.

"I must leave tomorrow," he said, not believing it, "but I'll be back."

"Iolo." Mari took a playful bite at his nose. "You'll never make a drover. A drover doesn't get out of bed till he has to. Secondly, he knows when his herd can't walk another inch. Go and have a look at your cattle." Iolo leapt out of bed and into the cow shed without bothering about clothes. They were all lying in the straw rested and well fed.

"Look at their hoofs," Mari called to him, "then come back to bed." Iolo lifted Catto's hind leg. The hoof was black and mushy. Iolo prodded it gently. Catto grunted and pulled it away.

"They've got hoof-rot. Now they've stopped you'll never get them moving again till it's cleared up."

"Why didn't you tell me?" Iolo shouted angrily. Mari came into the shed and put a hand on his shoulder. "Iolo bach, what difference would that have made last night? You'd never have reached England with unshod cattle."

"Unshod?"

"They need shoeing, like horses, simpleton. That's the first thing a drover learns. They'll have to recover for a fortnight or so, then you can have them shod by the smith in Erwood."

Iolo spent the rest of the day brooding by the fire. He scarcely noticed that Mari was looking more and more troubled too. After dusk she came and put a mug of ale in his hands and sat beside him.

"Did you ever discover the names of the two drovers who attacked you?" Iolo was miles away.

"One was called Abel Johnstown, I think. Why?" She gave no answer. Eventually he looked round and saw that tears were streaming down her face.

"You're not to blame," she said, taking his hand. "He was a wild man and got what was coming to him." Then, after a long pause: "You were wearing his boots."

CHAPTER FOURTEEN

I

GRUFFYDD STRODE DOWN to the new clearing in the woods below the Round House and surveyed his latest project with satisfaction. The clearing was littered with slender larch trees stripped of bark and branches and glistening silvery yellow in the late October sun. A team of foresters were hard at work chopping down another trunk.

"How's it going, Huw?"

"This is the last one." Huw gave the tottering tree-trunk two more swift, lethally accurate blows with his four-foot axe. It landed at Gruffydd's feet with a dull thump. Huw's crew cheered and set to fleecing it at once. "They just need cutting to size, then you can have them."

"I'll send up for them this afternoon. The new mill's just about ready for a roof." Huw wiped the sweat off the back of his neck.

"I hope we have grain left to grind in it when it's finished."

"Don't worry." Gruffydd punched him playfully on the arm. The grain supply was running a bit low, but he wasn't worried. "Iolo will be back any day now. He's on the home run. I can feel it in the air. Any day now." Gruffydd waved to a cluster of women who were broadcasting corn seed into the rich soil of last week's clearing. "Iolo will make us all rich—if he doesn't run off with the cash!" Gruffydd laughed. He'd agonized for nights over Rhiannon's gloomy predictions and finally thrown them out as hysteria, a blatant, malicious attempt to undermine his confidence. She'd been waiting for years to get back at him. Why should she know Iolo better than he did himself? After all, he had brought him up. The boy had guts. Gruffydd remembered their parting outside Tregaron. He'd felt closer to Iolo than ever before. He was his son, and he could be trusted. Gruffydd had no regrets about Tregaron. It had drawn the valley together. Without this crisis he would never have dragged his fractious people out of their derelict hovels and forced them to work for the survival of all.

This time there were no malingerers. Who had thought Morgan

would ever shift his arse for anyone else? Or Simeon help build another mill to compete with his own? They had to swim with the others, or sink on their own. There were just two conditions for continued success: the rations Gruffydd dispensed each week had to last and Ffowlke's rent-collectors had to be kept at bay. That shouldn't be too difficult for another month. Iolo would be back within a day or two, then they'd only need another three weeks to get the rest of the herds to England. Madlen was working wonders with John Ffowlke. The old man obeyed her like a child. He was down to one bottle of Burgundy a day now and looked nearly human. Madlen had installed a new cook who served Ffowlke his food personally to avoid any chance of its being tampered with. Gruffydd was thankful to have Ffowlke off his hands, especially now that Owain was feeding properly. They'd engaged a wet-nurse, a young niece of Thomas Jenkins called Sera, who had just lost her own baby. Thomas had recommended her highly. She seemed reliable.

Gruffydd emerged from the woods above the new mill and saw the building crew sitting in a huddle beside the empty stone shell listening to Mihangel. Gruffydd waded through the shallows towards them and they scattered back to their work.

"What were they talking about?" he asked Mihangel, who was left alone packing his lucky charms unhurriedly into their colourful painted box.

"How long the weather would last," his apprentice said casually, glancing up at the cloudless sky.

"Is that why they ran as soon as they saw me coming?"

"You caught them red-handed," Mihangel laughed, admitting he'd been trying to excuse them. "They were only taking a short break."

"Really?" Gruffydd gave Mihangel a free rein and liked him to use it but occasionally the boy overstepped the mark. Mihangel was an invaluable partner. Gruffydd shared almost all his worries with him, followed his advice more often than not, loved him as a son. Gruffydd's jest, that first day they'd met, had come true: "And will you bring me luck too?" They'd learnt and developed together, Gruffydd ostensibly as master, Mihangel as pupil. Often the relationship was reversed. Mihangel had long since outstripped Gruffydd in herbal medicine and divination. His predictions were invariably accurate. Gruffydd no longer competed in some fields, glad of extra time for his own concerns. Sometimes though, like now, he felt out of touch with Mihangel. Perhaps they didn't see enough of each other.

"I didn't want to worry you." Mihangel might have read

Gruffydd's mind. The dismissive banter was gone. He looked earnest, worried almost—Mihangel had a gift for accommodating Gruffydd's moods. "Someone has been putting it about that Iolo isn't coming back. They were scared to ask you, so they came to me. I told them they can sleep easy." Gruffydd put his arm round Mihangel's shoulder and they strolled along the river to the new cattle sheds, their heads almost touching as they talked.

"You mustn't protect me. I have to know what's on their minds."

"I'm sorry. I shouldn't have—"

"Don't worry about it." Gruffydd dismissed it with a slap on the back. "What's your impression? How are things going?"

"Fine," Mihangel said warmly. "Anyone can see how much we've achieved. You've achieved." Gruffydd smiled, flattered. Mihangel always made him feel good.

"There may come a time when you want to strike out on your own. Will you tell me in good time? I don't want to stand in your way." Mihangel blushed deeply, the first time Gruffydd had seen any colour on his pallid skin.

"I'll never leave you," he said. "I wanted to tell the men back there but I thought I should let you know first. I've had . . . news from Iolo." Gruffydd looked at him sharply. Whatever spirits communicated with Mihangel, they never lied.

"Well?"

"Iolo's on his way home with a fortune. He'll be back here on All Souls' Eve." Gruffydd leapt into the air, hollering and hallooing.

"You must let everyone know," he said excitedly. "We'll build a bonfire to welcome him home."

Mihangel caught his sleeve, suddenly bashful.

"It'd sound better coming from you. After all, you're his father." Gruffydd accepted gladly. Mihangel often left the announcements to him.

Madlen was waiting for them with a meal back at the Round House.

"Maude's three weeks overdue," she announced proudly. "John can't stop prodding her stomach."

It was odd to hear him called John, Gruffydd thought and congratulated Madlen on her nursing. "Perhaps Maude could do with some bryony, Mihangel?"

"Compound of ash gum and hawthorn would do better." Mihangel took out his stone mortar and crushed the ingredients to a fine pulp, watching the older couple embrace out of the corner of his eye.

Iolo roared at the two cows labouring under the yoke. His makeshift plough had got stuck again. It was only a scythe strapped onto a hand-rake, so he didn't expect much of it, but it would serve to get some potatoes planted for Mari before the winter. Catto and Betsi had recovered far faster than the others, so they might as well be put to some use. "Besides," he never stopped saying to himself as he cut a new slate for Mari's roof, dug barrow-loads of peat on the top, harvested the wild moorland grass for hay or sweated behind the plough, "it's the least I can do for her." She'd have no more money coming in and no one to help her through the long winter. Iolo had robbed her of a husband and was determined to make up for it. He'd slipped effortlessly into Abel's life—his duties, pleasures, possessions, clothes—without realizing it was happening. Mari had called him Abel once, by mistake. After a thunderous silence they'd ended up laughing. It was terrible, but true. Iolo was proud of bedding Abel's wife. She was his by right of conquest. Sometimes he imagined it was only to possess Mari that he'd killed Abel Johnstown.

"You'll break the scythe," Mari called to him from the meagre patch of sunlight in the open doorway, her white linen shift glowing brightly against the chilly shadows inside. "Pull it out and start again." She was sewing, taking in one of Abel Johnstown's coats. Iolo would need it for the rest of his journey.

"Oh, the devil!" His plough had come apart.

"You stubborn old mule!" Mari tilted back on her three-legged chair. "Why don't you ever listen?" Iolo picked up the pieces and wandered disconsolately back to the farmhouse.

"It'll take the rest of the day to fix." He reached behind the door for some more rope while Mari, needle between her lips, measured the coat across his shoulders.

"It's ready."

"Oh?"

"You can set out tomorrow." She watched Iolo laboriously bind the scythe back onto the rake-handle.

"Leave that," she said quietly, touching his hand. "You've ploughed quite enough. I can do the rest myself." Iolo paid no attention.

"There's so much still to be done. Anyway, the cows aren't rested yet."

"Look at them. If they eat any more they won't be able to move." Iolo's herd was grazing peacefully in the meadow below them. They looked healthier than the day they started.

"Give them another day or two." Iolo tied a knot in the rope. For three weeks he'd been dreading this moment, at first because Mari might try to stop him, then because he really didn't want to leave, though he wouldn't admit it. He was happy here. He was learning from Mari. He felt at home with himself and with her because nobody had ever loved him, approved of him the way she did. The farm was his own in a way Rhiannon's had never been. His work was for himself and for Mari, for both of them. He wanted to make something of the place. Two nights ago he had dreamed of Rhiannon, seven lean kine standing by her. He forgot it the moment he woke.

"You're making excuses, Iolo," Mari sighed, pushing her heavy chestnut hair out of her freckled face. "But it has to come. They can't stay here all winter and if you wait any longer you'll miss the market." Iolo flicked a coil out of the rope. "With what you'll get for those beauties, we can build this into the finest farm in Wales." Iolo dropped his scythe and seized her round the waist.

"All right, I'll go." He kissed her fiercely, then put both hands on her temples as if to stamp some message on her mind. "But I'll be back as soon as they're sold. Wait here for me."

They set out at dawn after a sleepless night of love-making, planning and promises. Iolo left Pedr behind because he was still lame. Mari led the cows down a lush, winding valley, avoiding well-trodden tracks to spare their hoofs, until Iolo caught a glimpse of a river crossing their path, wider than any he'd come to yet. It was the Wye and the thriving village which sprawled over its hilly, thickly wooded banks was Erwood, where almost every drover from South Wales and Ceredigion came to use the ford and save many tedious days' march upstream.

"The river may be flooded with all the rain we've had," Mari said. "It's late in the year to be trying to ford it. You may have to take the ferry."

"How do I pay?"

"Don't worry. I know the ferryman."

Iolo couldn't help resenting Mari's control. She made everything too simple. How did she know the ferryman, anyway?

Their first stop in Erwood was the magistrate's house, an impressive building with large glass windows and steps leading up to the door. Mari let herself in as if she lived there and came out a few minutes later with a scroll of paper, which she handed to Iolo.

"Here. You won't have any trouble now." It was a drover's licence. Iolo checked the name at the top.

"It says Abel Johnstown." He was horrified.

"Well, what do you expect? I couldn't say to him. 'Your Honour, my husband's dead, but please renew his licence for my fancy man.' Anyway . . ." Her voice softened and her eyes narrowed slightly. "You *are* my husband, aren't you, Iolo?" She threw her arms round his neck and kissed him deep. The herd drifted past them. When Iolo stood back, Gruffydd's stone amulet was dangling from her hand.

"I'll keep it safe for you," she said, laughing wildly as he chased her in and out of the startled cattle.

"Give it to me," Iolo yelled angrily. He hadn't forgotten Gruffydd after all.

"You are coming back to me, aren't you?" Mari pleaded when he caught her and snatched it away. Iolo hesitated. How could she trust him if he refused to leave any pledge of his return? He could always give it back to Gruffydd later. Slowly Iolo pushed the string over her head and tucked the stone between her breasts.

"Who's your friend, Mari?" grinned the tousled-headed, brawny blacksmith of the prosperous village of Erwood.

"You get on with your job, Iwan," Mari said, pushing him away. Iolo saw the leer in the fellow's eye. He didn't like it. Nor did he like the way Iwan and his mate handled the cows, though they knew their business. Always the same routine: Iwan grips the horns, mate seizes a foreleg, bends at the knee; Iwan twists the horns and the helpless beast keels over on its side; mate trusses up the back legs, hoists them in the air on a forked pole, while Iwan does the same at the front; mate trims away the rot and Iwan hammers two narrow iron plates onto each hoof with a few nails. They'd have finished the lot within an hour if Betsi hadn't panicked and dragged them both into the river.

Serves them right, Iolo thought, reassured at the way Mari sneered as Iwan staggered out of the Wye holding Betsi by the tail.

"You'll have to keep one of the cows in payment," Iolo said to Iwan. "I've no cash."

"Don't worry. What's a morning's work between friends?" Iwan slapped him on the back. "Mari takes care of that."

"Please," Iolo said through his teeth, "you can keep the youngest bullock, there." They drove the herd down to the Erwood ford in silence, Iolo tormented by sudden doubts. The Wye was impassable.

"You'll have to take the ferry," Mari said.

"And will you take care of the ferryman as well?" Iolo snapped.

"There was no harm in it," Mari said lightly. "Abel was away for months at a time. Anyway, they mean nothing to me."

As Iolo herded his cows out of the flat-bottomed boat onto the opposite bank, he saw the bearded ferryman put an arm round her and lead her to his cabin.

CHAPTER FIFTEEN

NOVEMBER 1ST. THE Winter Kalends. The end of summer, the culmination of a fine year's harvest and the turning of the old year towards the new. It was also the day of Iolo's predicted return. Gruffydd turned the whole day over to celebration. That afternoon the villagers followed him up the winding track below Black Rock, past the Round House, to one of the new fields hacked out of the forest only a year ago—which had yielded its first crop—where the last wheat-sheaf of the harvest awaited its ceremonial reaping.

Old Isaac pointed to a single clump of uncut wheat standing alone, sadly naked, amidst a wilderness of prickly stubble. "There she is, master. The old hag of the harvest." The friendly, motherly spirit of fertility resided in this last untouched crop. All through the summer she had fled before the farmers' scythes and this sheaf was her last resting place. The reaping of her was a sacred occasion, conducted with every possible respect to ensure her goodwill for the next year. Gruffydd kneeled before her, after custom immemorial. He divided the sheaf into three parts, then plaited them tightly together. Just below the ears he tied a string, drawing the sheaf into a neck from which the tuft stood up scraggy and unkempt like the grizzled head of an old woman. Then he stepped back ten paces and was joined in a circle around the harvest-hag by the twelve foremen of Cwmystwyth, Morgan, Simeon, Thomas Jenkins among them, his fellow reapers.

Iolo should have been here to take his place with them. Gruffydd had hoped he'd be back in time to join the ceremony, dispelling the prevailing tension. There was time before sunset. He'd be here yet.

One by one the reapers threw their sickles at the wheatsheaf, making them glide horizontally just above the ground to strike at its base. If the old hag could be cut down from a distance no one would carry the blame. Whoever finally severed her from the ground would carry her home in triumph, where she'd be kept till the next harvest. But they missed, without exception, or struck her awkwardly with glancing blows.

"Bad sign," Old Isaac muttered. It was left to Gruffydd, the least vulnerable of them all, to venture forward and gently cleave her from the earth. Thomas Jenkins raced down the hill to warn Madlen, for the harvest-hag must not be allowed to enter any house without a struggle. The womenfolk had to resist her, prevent her at all costs from reaching the kitchen table dry and unmolested, or she'd bring bad luck with her. Madlen and her maidservants bolted the doors, secured the hatch-windows.

The procession arrived noisily from the commons. Fists beat on every door and window simultaneously. No telling which of the attackers carried the old hag under his coat or in a potato sack. The girls emptied buckets of water over them indiscriminately from under the eaves. A churnful of milk splattered over Gruffydd as he clambered in through a neglected window assailed by brooms, ladles and rolling-pins, roaring with mock fury while the girls giggled uproariously.

"Who has her?" Gruffydd cried, his hair white with milk-froth, letting in the other assailants. "Where's the harvest-hag?"

"Here!" They swung round to see Mihangel and the wheat-sheaf, both bone-dry, sitting side by side on the kitchen table. No one ever discovered how Mihangel had got in without so much as a sprinkling. In the harvest-feast that followed he was given the place of honour, as tradition required, beneath the old hag, who now dangled by her neck from the rafters of the Round House. But the brief revelry had subsided. The mood had turned sour again. They ate their mashed vegetables in milk, scraped together out of scanty rations, in silence. Madlen tried to make conversation. It stuck on the same thought which plagued them all: where was Iolo? This was the day Gruffydd had promised them his return. The sun was sinking fast. Thomas Jenkins' splendid bonfire of gorse and thorn-wood waited beside the Ystwyth in the gathering dusk for the taper that would send it blazing skyward.

"Now, master?" Thomas had asked half a dozen times in the last half hour. Gruffydd shook his head without a word, gazing up at Black Rock for that solitary rider who must surely arrive within minutes. Black Rock merged slowly with the moonless sky behind it. The assembled crowd grew restless, murmuring nervously. This was All Souls Eve when the spirits of the dead rose from their shallow graves at Pendre and mingled with the living. On this night no mortal was safe after dark without fire to protect him. Gruffydd held Thomas back until the whisperings had swollen to a howl of fear. With a hollow foreboding in the pit of his stomach he finally gave in. The winter had arrived, the dark, malign season had set in, when man had most to fear from agencies beyond his grasp. Iolo was still not home.

A cheer went up as Thomas's bonfire erupted, and the powers of evil were scattered by the light. Hand in hand they danced around the fire to a frantic tune from Iago One-Leg's fiddle. The younger men leapt through the flames, singeing their hair and clothes, partly as a dare, partly in the unspoken belief that the ordeal would purge and protect them from bad spirits in the months ahead. Huw Lloyd slipped and had to be doused in the Ystwyth to save him from being roasted alive. Some of the villagers—especially the older ones and the ailing—threw white stones scratched with their special mark into the hottest embers, murmuring a prayer. Tomorrow morning at first light they'd rake out the charred cinders to find those stones. If the pebble was still there, intact, the owner would survive to see next year's Hallow Fire; if it was missing or cracked, he could expect an early death. Gruffydd knew he should be there, by the bonfire, encouraging them, helping to brighten their prospects for the coming twelve months, but he had no heart for it. Nor could he join in the merry-making and prance round with a blackened face in women's costume like the other men. He sat by the river under a holly tree, gazing at the flames reflected in even wilder shapes by the rushing water. Events were slipping out of his control. He found it ever harder to put a brave face on the danger that threatened him night and day. He had staked so much on his prediction for Iolo's return, forgetting entirely that Mihangel had put the idea in his head. How could he come up with an explanation? For now the villagers were absorbed in the festivities which must follow their traditional course regardless of worry and disappointment. But what about tomorrow? What would he tell them?

Why *was* he late? Surely nothing had happened to him? He would never forgive himself.

"No sign of Iolo?" asked a quiet female voice beside him.

"No," Gruffydd said absently.

"What are you going to do?"

"No idea." She laughed softly, mocking. Gruffydd tore his eyes away from the river. Not Madlen. He'd thought it was, their voices were so alike.

"Aren't you beginning to believe me?" Rhiannon's face shone with vindicated despair in the firelight. She wasn't accusing him. She was too full of sadness.

"No," Gruffydd growled. "If Iolo's not here tonight, then he'll be here tomorrow." Rhiannon heard the doubt in his voice. He no longer rejected her out of hand. Something in his manner made her stay.

"You don't believe that," she said.

"How can you tell what I believe or don't believe?" Again a surface hostility, but underneath it a willingness to listen. Rhiannon sensed that her accusations of four weeks ago had sunk in. She'd made her mark.

"Because you're listening to me."

Gruffydd snorted impatiently but he didn't contradict her. He wanted to hear more about Iolo. Nothing she could say was likely to reassure him, but he had to hear it. His doubts could only be relieved by more doubts. Rhiannon was his devil's advocate. She was welcome.

"So what do you think has become of Iolo?"

She had no idea. How could she tell? She only knew that Gruffydd was talking to her at last and she wanted to keep him talking. She longed to hear anything about Iolo, even if she knew it already. It exhausted her to keep saying, "He'll be back soon" every time Hannah asked, and there was no one else she could confide in. She would have been glad of even Rachel's company now. Surely Gruffydd must share her anxieties?

"I think he must be in some kind of trouble. Perhaps the cattle are ill." Gruffydd nodded. He'd thought of that. It was possible. "What would he do then?"

"Rest up and find a cattle-doctor, if he's got any sense."

"Thank God he's got money, then."

"You gave him some?" He'd stayed awake at night wondering if Iolo had enough.

"Yes, a little." She was too proud to admit she'd given him all she had.

"Thank you. That was thoughtful of you."

She was surprised to feel his hand close around hers and squeeze it tightly, then move away again.

He laughed quietly with a terrible sadness that she well understood. She couldn't blame him now. He was suffering exactly as she was. How futile the feuding of these last years had been. She was suddenly ashamed of the way she had turned and walked away whenever she saw him coming, the way she refused to join in any of his work around the valley though it was sensible enough and had helped many of her neighbours; and she felt guilty, too, for it was true that she had prejudiced Iolo against him. "I meant it when I thanked you for looking after Iolo," Gruffydd said.

"Yes, I know. Please—it doesn't matter."

"And if I didn't come to see him, it was in part because I wasn't sure I'd be welcome." He could have told her more of his trouble with Iolo, but it involved facts about himself and his position in Cwmystwyth which he could never admit to anyone here. One thing he was sure of, though: Iolo had never discussed him in any detail with Rhiannon, for she knew almost nothing about him. Iolo had stayed loyal to him all this time. He had misjudged his son and all his mistrust had been unfounded.

Rhiannon got up and walked along the river bank away from the bonfire. He watched her for a moment, a ghostly figure in the lattice of shadows cast by the firelight through the leafless trees. Occasionally a patch of light would touch her fair hair and her head lit up like a glow-worm, then moved on into darkness. She was quite unlike any other woman he'd known—proud, long-suffering, intensely private. He didn't understand her, but he felt a great respect for her. She wasn't impressed with the easy charm he used with most women. She seemed to expect something different and better from him. He wasn't sure what it was or whether he could provide it, but she intrigued him. He got up and followed her.

"You shouldn't have felt unwelcome at our farm," she said as if he'd been beside her all the time. "We would have been glad to see you, if you had come."

"How was I to know that? You never spoke to me."

"No, I'm sorry. But can you be surprised?" Gruffydd shrugged and she sensed him withdrawing. He wouldn't be forced into an apology. "Has Madlen told you what happened before that night?"

"Yes. Not in detail."

"When Hywel came back from prison I didn't tell him about you and Madlen. I thought I could protect her, but I should have known better. So you see, when you arrived with all of them"—she flicked her head contemptuously towards the dancers stamping and reeling round the bonfires—"Hywel discovered that I'd been lying to him. He's never forgiven me."

"Is that why he has been away all this while?"

"Yes, of course. What else did you think?" Gruffydd hadn't given it a great deal of thought. He had merely accepted with relief that Hywel had gone and he was rid of a formidable enemy. But he had obviously hurt her more than he'd ever realized and was anxious to make it up in any way he could. He didn't know why, but it was suddenly vital to him that this strange woman should think well of him.

"I never intended to harm you, please believe that."

"I do. Anyway, it's all over now. Iolo is far more important."

"I'm sure he'll be back soon."

"I'm sure he will." Rhiannon smiled. He could see the flames of the bonfire reflected in her eyes, then she took his hand and held it for a moment. "I never thanked you properly at the time, but Hannah and I owe you our lives."

"I did nothing."

"Of course you did. Thank you again." She shook his hand firmly then suddenly ran back along the bank to the stone bridge. He didn't try to follow her.

As the bonfire died, the villagers fled home to escape the spirits closing in on them through the lowering darkness.

"The tailless black sow take the hindmost," they shouted, racing up the hillside till they reached their shacks and slammed the doors behind them.

The hindmost was Gruffydd, who didn't stir. He stayed for an hour beside the fading embers, throwing into them a white pebble, carefully marked, for each member of his family. When he returned in the morning, together with many of the villagers, the pebbles were all intact bar one, which he couldn't find. One of the two pebbles that he'd marked for his sons.

I'll not see Iolo again, he thought, grief-stricken.

"Yes, they're all fine," Gruffydd beamed, when Old Isaac asked him.

"So's mine!" Isaac flashed him a toothless grin.

CHAPTER SIXTEEN

IT WAS NEARLY dawn. Iolo's herd plodded the last few miles along the old Roman road into Hereford. He had followed Mari's advice and travelled at night whenever there was a moon, avoiding the English toll-gates and English farmers. "The border people hate Welsh drovers," Mari had warned him. "They say we ruin their pasture and steal their cattle." Iolo had kept as far from human habitation as he could, waiting for nightfall in woods on the uplands. He felt like an outlaw, convinced that the Tregaron drovers were tailing him to take revenge for their dead comrades, that the bailiffs from Garth had alerted the whole countryside to a strange-faced cattle thief. Iolo knew he was unmistakable. Everyone he passed seemed to suspect him. As the dawn came, another terror seized him: trooping ahead of him along the road were many more than his own cows. He had picked up another half dozen along the way, six prize longhorns by the look of them, confidently leading his own herd into town.

"Shoo!" Iolo shouted as loud as he dare, without waking the roadside cottages. The longhorns scattered. Round the next bend they were quietly waiting, ready to fall into line again. Iolo desperately tried to get rid of them. No wonder drovers were taken for cattle thieves. A farmer riding into market gave him a curious look. He mustn't draw attention to himself. He would just have to hold on to them.

A wooden creak made him start. Two crook-necked corpses swayed limply out of the darkness from the town gallows on a grassy knoll ahead of him. Iolo's knees sagged. "Oh, God," he said aloud, "why did I leave Mari?" How often he'd thought that in the last week. She seemed so distant now. He had difficulty in picturing her face. The warmth of her presence was just a memory, hard to recapture. Could he trust her? Was she consoling herself with the ferryman or the smith? Should he even be thinking of her? Wasn't it infamous to fornicate with the wife of a man he had killed? Didn't it worry her? Abel had been her husband. Would she do the same with Iolo's murderer? Fear and jealousy and mistrust haunted him all the way from Erwood.

The armed gatekeeper looked Iolo up and down. "Your licence," he said. Silently Iolo handed over the scroll of paper.

The gatekeeper stared from the licence into Iolo's face and back again. "You Abel Johnstown?"

"Yes," Iolo managed to say. The man sneered at him. Iolo panicked. They all knew Abel here. They'd know Iolo wasn't him. Maybe his body had been found and they knew he was dead. They'd think Iolo took the licence off him. Oh, God, how could he have been so stupid? Mari had known this would happen. She had sent him into this trap on purpose, to get rid of him, to avenge Abel. She had been planning this all along . . .

"Move on, Welsh imbecile," the gatekeeper shouted at him.

"Heiptroo ho!" Iolo cried without thinking.

His cattle walked on along the narrow cobbled streets. The black-beamed houses all had two or three stories and leaned in towards each other. A toothless old woman emptied a bucket of slops over one of the longhorns from an upstairs window and a gentleman in a carriage yelled at him as he tried to drive past. The early-morning crowd laughed as Iolo's herd, terrified by the noise and the tall buildings, bolted in each direction down a maze of back streets.

"Fetch 'em, Cadwal!" he yelled. Cadwal disappeared to the right, taking a short cut through a butcher's shop. Iolo raced along a winding alley to the left, oblivious to grinning faces, jibes about the Welsh, and the blood-spattered butcher who was standing in his doorway waving a meat-cleaver and shouting obscenities.

"Another two minutes and we'd have had the hide off their backs," said a friendly voice. The six longhorns had followed Catto into a tanner's yard and were quietly drinking from a poisonous-looking trough. "Nice cows. Are they yours?"

"Yes," Iolo said uncertainly. The leather-aproned tanner wiped his inky forearms on an inkier rag.

"I don't think much of the black one." Iolo felt insulted for Catto. "But the other six will do. My brother deals in meat as a sideline and the skins'll make good saddles. I'll give you five guineas apiece, thirty for the lot."

Iolo didn't have the presence of mind to bargain. He slapped the brawny hand held out to him and incredulously took the thirty guineas without counting them. The tanner wished he'd offered less.

"Thirty guineas!" Iolo said over and over again as he led Catto back to the main road. "Thirty guineas and the cows weren't even mine!" Six gone and nineteen more to sell. He was triumphant. He'd done it. He'd arrived.

At the crossroads Cadwal had returned with the other vagrants. She was barking furiously at the butcher, who was walking through the nervous herd prodding, pummelling and measuring.

"Four guineas each for these three," he growled as soon as he saw Iolo return.

"You'd be lucky . . . Hey, you!" Iolo grandly tossed a guinea to a lanky urchin whose eyes opened wider than his mouth. "Lead me to the market-place."

"Yes sir." The onlookers stood aside respectfully to let them pass.

The market was already crowded. The pens were packed with cattle of every size and colour, bellowing continuously, their heads raised anxiously above the hindquarters of their neighbours, eyes rolling backwards in their sockets. Drovers waded ankle-deep in week-old manure, quelling any uneasiness with merciless cudgel blows that frequently drew blood or crippled a hind leg. The runts' well-being was of no consequence now they'd reached England. The stench was terrible. Iolo looked on aghast.

"We're not taking them in there," he said to the boy. They drove the herd into the courtyard of the King George, a respectable three-storied gabled inn set back from the market-place, where there was a clean water-trough and a hay-rack for horses. Catto and Betsi helped themselves and the innkeeper came bustling out and tried to shoo them away.

"You can't leave them here. Take them off at once!"

"I'll leave them where I choose." Iolo scowled, making his face as ugly as he could. "And if you value my custom you'll thank me for it!" An empty threat. Iolo handed him a guinea to back it up. The landlord suddenly relented and fell over himself to be polite.

"Will you be spending the night, sir?"

"If your beds are clean."

"Of course, sir!"

"Then keep the best one." Iolo walked out into the market. He was amazed at himself. Nothing was beyond his grasp now.

Bidding in the market was low and the drovers were settling at two or three pounds a head. Iolo realized that they were scared of not being able to sell. Many of them seemed ill at ease and their natural swagger had gone. Vanished was the arrogance with which they bullied their own people back home. They bargained obsequiously in awkward sign-language and garbled Anglo-Welsh. Iolo despised them. Most of their kine looked worn and shrunken, the bloom on their hides spoilt by a month of hard droving and mishandling. They'd need fattening in Herefordshire pastures before they were of use to anyone. Iolo's cattle were well rested from Mari's. He could outsell this lot easily. He made his way back to the King George without talking to any of the buyers.

"What's your name?" he asked his helper.

"Michael, sir."

"Have you got many friends?"

"Plenty." Iolo put his hand on Michael's shoulder. The boy's mouth opened, expecting new wonders.

"I want you to find half a dozen of your friends. When you've got them, go round the market separately and tell each dealer that a special drove of newly fattened runts has just arrived at the King George. They're selling very cheaply. If it works, I'll pay you all well." Michael disappeared like a shaft from a Welsh longbow. "Landlord! I want some hay for my cattle down here. And send three or four grooms to wash them down."

In half an hour Iolo's cattle were shining glossily in the sunlight, browsing on the clean hay strewn out in the courtyard. The first dealer arrived out of breath and the second was close behind. Iolo watched from the taproom window, mug in hand, as fifteen or twenty buyers arrived within as many minutes.

"Don't push, gentlemen," he said, coming downstairs. "There's plenty for everyone."

"I'll give you three guineas each for these two."

Iolo shook his head apologetically. "I'm sorry. They're already promised at four."

"Make it four and a half."

"Five apiece for any half-dozen."

"Five and a half for the two in the corner."

"Those are mine. I'm offering six for them."

Iolo sold his cattle in ten minutes for an average of six and half guineas. As the last two were led away, Cadwal darted to and fro with short bewildered howls, trying to warn Iolo they were getting lost.

"Yes, they're gone, Cadwal," he said as she tugged at his breeches. Iolo went on counting out the golden coins on the stable-yard flagstones. He lost track of what it all came to. It was too much to keep in his head at once but one thing was obvious: he was a wealthy man. Wealthy beyond most people's dreams. He sat in silence and stared at the pile of gold till he became aware of six equally silent faces staring with him.

"Here," he said to Michael, tossing him another guinea. "Split this between you." Iolo wondered whether to give them more. But wealth made him cautious. He mustn't be extravagant. The six boys sidled away, casting backward glances at his hoard. Iolo rapidly scraped it together. He couldn't carry it!

How could he guard it? He'd be robbed. He stripped the shirt off his back, tied knots in the arms and collar and poured the gold in.

"Good sale, sir?" the innkeeper asked breezily, as Iolo slunk past.

"Yes." Iolo tried to linger and appear casual. "Quite good." He raced up to his room and shot the bolts behind him. He'd never get away alive. He couldn't entrust the money to anyone and he couldn't possibly carry it around like this. Iolo nearly wept to be so rich and so helpless. Gradually a solution came to him.

He cautiously shot back the bolts and opened the door a crack. "Host!" The innkeeper arrived at once. "I'm feeling indisposed." Iolo imitated Sir George Cobham's nasal drawl. "But I wish to do some business with the tradespeople of the town. You will send me a tailor, a bootmaker and an armourer—the best of course." The innkeeper bowed low, glanced under the bed at the gold and left. The tradesmen arrived half an hour later. While the tailor measured him for a pair of corduroy breeches, a silk shirt and a scarlet riding coat, Iolo selected two finely-tooled Spanish pistols and a sturdy poniard. The bootmaker he kept till last.

"I want a leather waistcoat with inside pockets—large ones—all round it, back and front. How soon can I have it?" The bootmaker pondered.

"I have one ready-made which would fit you. I could add the pockets in, say, two or three hours?"

While he was waiting, Iolo practised with his short sword against the bedpost and aimed his pistols at the coat of arms above the bolsters. Unfortunately he forgot that the armourer had shown him how to load them and left the shot in: the coat of arms came crashing down, bringing the bed-curtains with it.

"I'll pay, of course," he said to the innkeeper, blowing smoke from the barrel.

"Please feel at home, sir." The innkeeper raised an eyebrow as the coat of arms was carried away in pieces.

In his new clothes, with his fortune safely stored inside his waist-coat, the two pistols tucked into a silk sash and his scabbard jangling proudly against his knee, Iolo strutted out into the streets of Hereford.

A horse. He couldn't be without a horse. So he bought one—a magnificent chestnut mare of sixteen hands—an embossed saddle, a bridge and a silver-handled riding crop. A gold watch caught his eye in a shop window. A hat with peacock feathers in it took his fancy . . .

Iolo was riding back to the market-place when he passed an open gate. He turned his head for a second and saw a man wearing a blood-stained, striped apron, with a black hairy mole just beside his chin, raise a pole-axe and sink it up to the hilt between the eyes of one of Iolo's bullocks. He died without a murmur, his glassy eyes turned toward Iolo saying, "Farewell, comrade." Iolo leaned forward onto the mane of his chestnut mare. This was where he had led them. This was what they had followed him for, shared his trials for, trusted him for. He had dragged them hundreds of miles to their death so the English could gorge on their flesh and he, Iolo, their perfidious leader, could wear a feather in his hat. He rode back to the gate.

"Stop!" The pole-axe was poised above the last placid forehead. "How much for that cow?" The butcher surveyed the young gentleman curiously.

"She's not for sale, sir." He made to strike.

"Six guineas for her." The butcher leaned insolently on his axe.

"Why do you want her?"

"What's that to you?"

"Well, I paid nine for her," he said, sensing a windfall.

"Twelve."

"Fifteen."

Iolo threw him the money without further argument, took Betsi—for it was Betsi—on the end of a halter and led her through the market-place. She would have followed him anywhere. She'd recognized him at once.

"Found an old friend, sir?" the innkeeper asked jauntily.

"Make sure she's fed." Iolo scowled and ordered his dinner. The great hall of the King George was already packed for the evening's entertainment, which was to start with a fist fight. Iolo pushed his way through groups of drovers discussing the day's business, assessed the two combatants, who were already stripped to the waist and eyeing each other across the floor, and casually placed five guineas on the obviously weaker man. Iolo didn't give a cuss which of them won. It suited him to watch two of his fellow men knock each other senseless for money. He held the world and himself in contempt. A little savagery would do him good. Iolo downed his first tankard at one draught, held it out for more and did the same with the second.

"Some French brandy, to help it down, sir?" asked the tapster. Iolo helped himself to the brandy bottle and shouted himself hoarse with the rest of the crowd. His scraggly champion seemed to have lost an eye, but persisted in getting up off the floor to be knocked down again.

Iolo was so engrossed he scarcely noticed what he was eating. The brandy had taken its effect by the time the innkeeper removed his plate saying: "A steak from one of your own runts, sir. I procured it specially for you. A nice touch, don't you think?" Iolo wearily complimented him on the cooking. It made no difference now. He watched with satisfaction as the challenger was carried away half-dead and his five guineas vanished into someone's pocket.

"Filthy money," he muttered, burying himself in a corner with his bottle of brandy and another quart of ale. Occasionally one of the women of the town flounced up to him, but a grunt was enough to dissuade her. Nor did he think much of the next act: a flea-bitten, nearly bald monkey who danced to a fife and drum and then jumped over everyone in sight.

"Gentlemen!" cried a grizzled dwarf scarcely three foot tall, in a silver and gold brocade uniform, who was being held at arm's length in the hand of an impassive negro giant. "Need I introduce him to you? The strongest man in the world! From the lost tribe of Israel, recently come to light in blackest Ethiopia, I present to you Solomon the Mighty!" Solomon tossed the dwarf over his head and caught him in the other hand to resounding applause, and then lifted anything he was asked to. At the same time, a clown with a chalk-white face, red nose and blue eyes, dressed in silk harlequin pantaloons of parti-coloured diamonds, made the crowd laugh by hopelessly apeing everything Solomon did. High above them in the rafters of the hall a blonde girl in a dazzling white costume stepped off the gallery onto an invisible wire and floated like an angel through the firmament.

Iolo leaned back, watching her. His addled mind soared to meet her, leaving the noise and smoke behind. She belonged with him somewhere. Whether he had dreamed of her, or knew her before, he couldn't tell.

"Now who shall we choose to assist Dr Faustus, our incomparable magician?" the dwarf said. Several burly drovers stepped forward.

"A gentleman, please. We must have a gentleman!" The drovers sat down, embarrassed. The dwarf looked through the audience, then pushed his way to the back and caught hold of Iolo's sleeve. "You, sir! Would you be so gracious as to assist Dr Faustus?" Iolo looked into his stubbly face, with its close-set eyes and fixed professional smile. Somewhere beneath his drunken stupor a memory stirred. The dwarf dragged him out onto the floor, crying, "Applause for the gentleman, please!" There was raucous laughter and clapping. The gentry were always popular as scapegoats.

"Please, sir," said Dr Faustus, who wore a black gown, skull-cap and a false white beard, "Would you kindly hold these two pink balls up so the audience can see them?" Iolo held them up. There was nothing in his hands. Iolo opened and closed his fingers, bewildered. He looked down to see the magician whisk the balls away from his crotch and display them to his audience. Iolo grinned foolishly as they shouted ribaldries at him, wild, contorted faces screaming, leering, gloating. For another two tricks Iolo played along with the crowd, trying to control the panic rising in him. The magician lowered at him out of a childhood nightmare. Any moment he would pull out a red-hot stake. This time no Gruffydd.

Separate memories were hopelessly confused. He was somewhere else. Numbly his mind fought its way out of a beer-drenched cloud. Dwarf and negro, harlequin and dancer squatting around him. Their faces leapt up at him one by one, then receded. It seemed he knew them all, wanted to stop them, catch them, call out to them . . .

"Just hold this stick for a second," Dr Faustus was saying to him. A blue, red and white striped barber's pole.

Where had he seen that before? His brain struggled like a runner through sand. Suddenly it burst on him. Time, place, people—he knew them all. Sheet lightning laid bare a landscape whose existence he'd forgotten, clearing the darkness and the mist that enveloped him.

"No," he said distinctly. "You hold it." Expectant silence. The magician sighed indulgently and held up the barber's pole. His hands were empty. Before a confounded and delighted audience the pole reappeared in Iolo's hands, whisked between the conjurer's legs.

"How did you know how . . . ?" Dr Faustus stammered.

Could they still not see?

"You should know," Iolo said. "You taught me." The magician looked blank and shrugged apologetically to the audience. The other performers turned away embarrassed. The act was ruined.

"Do you still not know who I am? Have you no eyes?" Iolo raised his hand to his face as if to say, Who else could possibly look like this? Very slowly the dwarf got to his feet and walked over. He stared up at Iolo and a puzzled frown, then a dubious smile of wonderment, passed across his elfin face.

"This gentleman," he said to his colleagues. "I think this gentleman is Iolo, Gruffydd's son." They whispered together. To some it meant nothing, but others crowded round amazed. The dwarf was already three feet off the ground, wrapped in Iolo's arms in an impulsive bear-hug.

"I'm Iolo, I'm Iolo," he said over and over again, embracing them all in turn, even the ones he didn't know. "I'm back." He was home again. The circus might have changed. There were new acts, new people, but all his old friends were there too. "Your name is Amaranth," he said, as the trapeze girl took both his hands, smiling. She had a high forehead and perfectly straight sun-coloured hair parted in the centre. "I always admired you. You used to roast chestnuts for me over the campfire."

"No. I'm Phoebe. Amaranth was my mother. She died a year ago."

"Oh. I'm sorry . . . You look just like her. Just as beautiful."

"Remember? I was the one you used to fight for the chestnuts. You bit my arm once. I still have a scar, here." She lifted her gauze sleeve. "It's all right. I loved you just the same. You were always my little brother."

Much later, when the show was over and the drovers had left or were in bed, the whole circus fraternity lay around the fire that blazed in the cavernous stone hearth, and exchanged memories. They were propped up on bundles of luggage or dozed with their animals—a monkey or performing dog. The innkeeper had long since gone to bed, leaving an open barrel of ale for them on Iolo's account. Some had drunk themselves unconscious. The others gladly listened to him talk as they drank the night away. Iolo nestled his head farther into Phoebe's lap.

"Do you remember the time the big tent blew away in that gale, with us all carried along on the guy ropes?"

"Ay," said the dwarf, whose name was Adam, smiling sadly. "We held on to it that time. But it blew away for good five years ago, over the cliffs near Penzance. Things haven't been so good since."

"How's that?"

"We can't afford the canvas for a new one, so we have to rely on inns like this or play in the open. There's no money in it, you see."

"How much would a new one cost?"

"About fifteen guineas. Perhaps twenty." Iolo held up his mug to be refilled.

"But tell us about yourself, Iolo," said Dr Faustus, a smooth-faced twenty-five without his beard and skull-cap. Iolo had known him as a day-wage wagon-driver who shared with him all the new tricks he learnt.

"How's that old rogue Gruffydd?" said wart-faced Barnabas affectionately, his skin blotchy and ravaged without his harlequin cosmetics. "Who is he hoodwinking now? By God, he could spin a yarn." Barnabas scratched his warts with his little finger. "You know, Iolo, he once told me that your mother was an immortal lady who

237

lived beneath a lake, in the water, I mean." Phoebe felt Iolo's body tense against her legs. She ran her hands gently over his chest.

"But he always owned up to his lies when you got him drunk," Hugh the lion-tamer muttered out of his half-sleep.

"Ay," agreed Barnabas, lost in his own story. "One night he confessed to me the girl was just a miner's daughter who lived next to the lake."

"What else did he tell you, Barnabas?" Iolo kept his voice as steady as he could.

"Let me think . . . That's right now. When his father, that's your grandfather, was thrown out of the house they lived in, the girl wouldn't leave her home with Gruffydd, so he took the baby—that's you, Iolo—without asking her."

"Did he never tell you that, Iolo?" the dwarf asked curiously.

"Yes. Yes, of course." Iolo had to lie. He couldn't admit to them that Gruffydd had taken him in for seven years with that story of an other-worldly mother. Even at his most sceptical, in his worst moments of resentment, Iolo had never quite disbelieved Gruffydd. All those days he had spent watching Llyn Isaf, believing his mother would rise from the water. God, what a fool he was. Gruffydd had lied, he was lying all the time. Those crosses behind the hut . . . his mother was dead, he knew she was. She died because Gruffydd deserted her and Iolo had never known her. He wept silently, trying to stop his chest from heaving. They mustn't see. The darkness of the great hall protected him. Only Phoebe noticed that her fingers were wet when she touched his face.

"Anyway," Barnabas said, "you've outgrown him by a long chalk. You've become quite a gentleman. How did you make your fortune, Iolo?"

Iolo wished he were miles away. "The cattle trade."

"What are your plans now?" the dwarf asked, cleaning his long, pointed fingernails with one of Phoebe's hairpins.

"Nothing much," Iolo said truthfully.

"Well," Adam held up his hand to the firelight. "With a new big tent we could be an attractive proposition for an investor. We have a lot of talent. You and I could make this circus greater than ever."

"Thank you, but there are people expecting me."

"Let them wait." Adam smiled as he gently stuck the pin back into Phoebe's hair. "We have other attractions." Phoebe slipped her hand lightly over Iolo's groin, as if by mistake.

"You belong with us, Iolo," Barnabas said sentimentally. "You're one of us." They all agreed. Phoebe took Iolo's hand and led him to the staircase.

"Let him sleep on it. He needs to rest."

The main oak door at the end of the hall flew open and a band of armed men entered at a run. There was bedlam as the circus people fled or clutched at their belongings and an officer of the watch shouted: "No one is to leave, by order of the sheriff."

"What does this mean?" asked the dwarf grandly.

"We're looking for an Abel Johnstown. A Welsh cattle drover. We know he's in this house." All eyes turned to Iolo. No one uttered a word.

"What has he done?" Adam's face was a mask of composure.

"He's one of a gang that's been pillaging this country for years. He's a murderer and a cattle thief."

Iolo's heart sank. He was going to be hanged for Abel's crimes. Mari had known this would happen. The last thread that tied him to Wales snapped. One by one the circus hands were questioned, Iolo last of all. Because of his clothes, the officer showed him some respect.

"My name," Iolo said in his best English accent, "is Griffiths. I was here tonight to inspect this circus. I'm happy to say I've just bought it." Stunned silence.

"Surely you have heard of Griffiths' circuses?" Adam asked the officer. "It's an honour to have Mr Griffiths with us."

"His room is empty, sir," said one of the constables from the landing. "We found a few old clothes with his licence in it, no trace of him otherwise."

"Missed him again," said the officer furiously. "All right, let's go."

The circus left Hereford at dawn. The last caravan was followed at a little distance by a solitary Welsh runt driven along by a shaggy black and white mongrel bitch.

December 1752

CHAPTER SEVENTEEN

I

GRUFFYDD'S HANDS WERE bruised and bleeding. Layers of skin had come away where he had carried a frost-covered stone too far. The balls of his fingers were swollen with chilblains—they had ached for so long he had ceased to be aware of them. He worked with unthinking, reckless intensity, lifting rocks his own weight onto his flattened back and crawling step by step to the huge oval mound that was rising from the very peak of Black Rock. He never paused for breath. As soon as one stone was in place he went in search of the next, hunting farther afield as the bright, icy day wore on. He had sworn to be finished by sunset. The end was almost in sight. Under an outcrop of grey slate he found his top-stone, a broad-based, pointed chunk of quartz. He tore it away from the heather and saw a sling wedged into a moss-covered crack.

Only one person had ever herded up here, he thought, firing a pebble at a passing raven, which flew away croaking. At the top of the cairn Gruffydd held the sling to his forehead, glad to have some possession of Iolo's to represent him, then wedged it between two stones and slid the smoky-brown quartz on top. The last rays of the sun, eclipsed by Grogwynion four miles away down the valley, shone through the quartz and made it live, suggesting a dusky half-world stirring within the stone.

"Wherever you lie," Gruffydd said, facing the eastern mountains already lost in night, "you lie here also. Your memory will live as long as these stones and the earth itself." Sweat poured off his exhausted limbs—as strong but not as supple as they had been—and rose into the frosty air like the soul departing the body. He had lost a son and was tired. Gruffydd stretched himself face downwards on his cairn, arms and legs spread-eagled, head resting against the quartz.

He saw Iolo tying up his tattered boots on top of Grogwynion. You were in no hurry to get here. No wonder. I thought I was bringing you home, but I've sacrificed you to this place. Long-forgotten events shuffled through Gruffydd's mind: crossing a river, Iolo in his arms, the ferryman sneering "nursemaid"—the next moment the ferryman was in the river; Iolo learning to walk on the deck of a rolling ship, the sailors calling him bandy-legs; that terrible night, near York, when Gruffydd had been escaping from constables and had dropped Iolo at a full gallop, and when he had picked him up his face was smashed and there was almost no life in him—Gruffydd felt a pang of remorse even now; the companionship of innumerable cold nights and fruitless journeys; Iolo saving him from hanging at Stafford Fair; then the circus, where Iolo would invariably defend Gruffydd against mockery . . .

He had never sided with an enemy. Not even here. Not even when they were estranged and Iolo defenceless in a foreign world. He had seen through Gruffydd, though. He had known from the start. Gruffydd vividly recaptured that awkwardness between them, slight at first, then intolerable, whenever there was talk of conjuring.

"You *are* a conjurer, aren't you?" he heard Iolo, a young boy, asking over and over again, till he must have despaired of a straight answer and drawn his own conclusions.

Gruffydd had let it destroy their friendship. But did Iolo understand what he was trying to do here? More than ever Gruffydd needed Iolo's approval. He'd never have it, now.

"Forgive me," he said, placing his hands on top of the quartz in propitiation of his dead son's spirit. A vision of Iolo's mother standing by the lakeside rose to accuse him. He opened his eyes to avoid her. "Some other time I will appease you."

In the darkness, flames leapt skyward all around him and faces stared at him in silence, waiting. Thomas Jenkins stepped out of the circle.

"They're waiting for you to speak," he whispered. "You asked me to call them here at nightfall." They were the villagers of Cwmystwyth, assembled here at his request. Gruffydd suddenly remembered why he had built the cairn. He wanted to tell them of the gipsy's message. The news of Iolo's death, of his sacrifice for them, would swing them behind him again.

"It's a blessing in disguise," Madlen had said, when the gypsy finished his story of how Iolo had been murdered for his money in the hour of his triumph. "None of them believe he's coming back, anyway. If you play it right you'll win them to you again."

But grief took Gruffydd unawares and he couldn't remember a word of his carefully rehearsed speech. He struggled to his feet on the pile of stones. His legs were numb. They swayed under him. The people gazed at him, hungry and sullen. He had halved, then quartered their rations with the promise of Iolo's return.

"Friends," Gruffydd said. "Last night a Romany came to the Round House with news of my son." They all started talking at once and Gruffydd realized with horror that they still thought Iolo would be back. He had told them as much countless times and they'd believed him. How could he possibly disappoint them? They had obeyed him faithfully all this time and he couldn't now tell them it had been for nothing. They would flay him alive. He thought of lying to gain time, but the rumour would be out by morning—others might have talked to the Romany as well. He needed a gesture. It came. He threw back his head, flung his arms wide and, with only a fragment of the grief he really felt, cried: "My son is dead!"

The babble of voices stopped and a hush descended on Black Rock like a blanket falling on a candle flame. An owl hooted from an elm nearby. Then a murmur spread through the crowd and grew to a terrifying roar of frustration and rage. They closed in around him, shaking their fists and shouting curses. He retreated to the top of his cairn and called for silence, but they were past listening to him. If he didn't control them soon, they would kill him. He was shaking with fear, searching desperately for a way out. He had to find a scapegoat, anything to appease them.

"The English killed him!" he yelled with all the breath in his lungs. "Iolo would be here now if it weren't for them. The English have robbed us of our cattle as they have always done." It made little impression, but the power of his voice alone seemed to give him some protection, so he went on screaming as loud as he could. "Iolo reached England all right. Not even the Water Horse or the dragon of Towy Forest could stop him. But on leaving Hereford he was cut down by an English knife for the money that was ours." Gruffydd worked himself into a frenzy. His face went purple and his eyes bulged in their sockets. He raved and ranted with no idea of what he was saying, and very slowly he pushed them back. If they were helpless with fury, he was more furious than any. In his convulsing body they saw their own feelings enlarged and they forgot that he alone was responsible for their misery. He was one of them again and spoke for them all.

"There are English surveyors camped on Cefn Coch," shouted a voice from the back. Gruffydd seized his chance. They had to have some victim.

"They're planning new enclosures," he said, filled with righteous indignation. "You'd better stop them, or the English will steal your land as well!"

245

"We'll show them!"

"Let's get them!"

"To Cefn Coch!" the cry went round and the crowd streamed away, brandishing sticks, skinning knives and torches. Gruffydd followed, shouting louder than them all, till he could slip away unnoticed into the woods.

He was horrified at himself. What had he done? The surveyors were John Ffowlke's and Ffowlke was losing patience already. One spark of trouble and the militia would be sent in and that would be the end. After three months Maude showed no signs of pregnancy. How long till Ffowlke caught on? Even Madlen seemed to have her doubts. Ffowlke would call in his rents and how would they pay him? It was past thinking about. Gruffydd paused for a moment by Hafod pool. The stone basin was frozen over, the water solid as the stone itself. Not a splash. Not a ripple. The silence scared him. He thought of the surveyors. What was happening to them now? He suddenly saw the old, demented conjurer holding a red-hot stake over Iolo's heart and realized that he had just done the same with those surveyors. To save himself in an awkward moment he had sacrificed innocent victims. His own survival sickened him. He should have let his people take their revenge on him. He headed for the abandoned hunting lodge that stood in the clearing between two woods, a furlong above the river. He pushed the solid oak door. It swung open and he stepped into the room. Somewhere upstairs a chair fell over and rattled on the floorboards.

"Are you here?" he asked his great-great-grandfather. Gruffydd's voice was swallowed by the rotting timbers. "I let you out of that bottle. Now it's your turn to help me." He sat down by the cracked marble mantelpiece, which smelled of stale meat. The wind whistled in the chimney, chilling his spine. "You were a conjurer, weren't you? What would you do in my place?" A mouse crept out from the skirting-board and inspected him. Gruffydd tensed. "Well? What have I done wrong?" The mouse fled. The ceiling creaked. Heavy footsteps, as of someone deep in contemplation. A sigh. Weeping. Gruffydd climbed up the heavy-timbered staircase. A step gave way beneath him and crashed to the floor. He leapt to the landing and tore open the bedroom door. A chair lay on its side in a ray of moonlight. Downstairs the front door slammed. Through the window Gruffydd saw a shadow flitting away toward Hafod pool.

"He has deserted me! My ancestors are deserting me!" Gruffydd raced out of the house and up the mountainside. He needed comfort, from the living or from the dead. The hermit's hut slipped past. The mines fell away to his right, the barren scree slope of Frongoch gleaming a moist, shiny green in the icy moonlight.

Llyn Isaf was not far now. His first love. Long careless days sauntering arm in arm on the hills or lying naked beneath the trees counting the clouds. He had promised her an empire. Gruffydd could hear her laugh at his boasting, then she'd suddenly turn serious and say, "Don't scare me, cariad." He had boasted so long he finally had no choice but to go out and conquer. She was an empire in herself—if only he'd understood that then. Or if only, now that he had conquered his kingdom, he had the same blind confidence of those days. Gruffydd ran up the pebbly bank of Llyn Isaf and stopped in his tracks.

He was going mad. This wasn't the lake. There was no lake. He'd followed the usual path, the woods hadn't changed but the lake was gone. No water. Before him stretched a nightmare crater of black, fissured mud frozen into motionless ripples in which branches were stuck like prehistoric skeletons. The wooden shack was gone. Its timber and slate were scattered over hundreds of yards together with metal pots and tattered blankets as though some passing giant had idly practised black-ball. Gruffydd picked his way through the wreckage, dazed. Something trailed on his foot. He picked it up and stared at the shreds of Iolo's hanging cradle. "God help me," he whispered. "I've sinned most terribly." He tied the cradle tightly around his neck, as farmers tie a dead chicken to the dog that killed it, heaped the debris on his head and stayed there, prostrate, until the moon had set. Then he dragged himself back through the darkness to the Round House.

Sera sat by the Round House hearthstone. Owain had woken her with his crying and was now guzzling her milk. "Are you teething, then?" she asked him. She wasn't sure. Her own baby had died after four days, so she didn't know when to expect Owain's teeth. She touched his gums cautiously with her little finger. Nothing there.

"Hush, my baby, don't you cry. Your mother is a lady and your father . . ." she crooned tunelessly, trying to fill the silence of the sombre stone house. It scared her to be left alone here with this baby. She daren't confess it. She needed the job. Her uncle, Thomas Jenkins, had sworn she was an experienced nurse. "Your father . . ." She couldn't find the right rhyme. Owain was asleep. She put him back in the rocking cradle and pressed the treadle with her foot while she braided her thick, marigold hair. What word would she use for the conjurer?

247

Gruffydd was standing in the doorway, filthy and bedraggled, a maddened look in his eye.

"Go on," he said with an evil grin. "Your father is . . . *What* am I?" Sera quickly hid her ankles under her long night-gown.

"I was going to say 'prince'. But it doesn't rhyme."

"What with?"

"'Cry.'" Sera watched him lurch towards the cradle.

"Have you been crying?" Gruffydd drawled, tapping his forefinger on Owain's chin.

"Don't disturb him. He needs to sleep." The conjurer straightened up. His eyes narrowed.

"Don't tell me how to treat my son," he said. She winced as he clamped an arm around her shoulder and pointed with the other at the cot. "Do you realize," he whispered heavily in her ear, "that you are entrusted with the last hope of the house of Rhys?"

"Yes, sir." She didn't know what he was talking about.

"Look." Gruffydd pulled a dirty parchment from a cranny near the hearthstone. "This cross at the bottom is Iolo. He's gone. Dead." Gruffydd scratched out the mark convulsively with his thumb-nail. "And this one is Owain, here in the corner. He's the last." He rolled it up, watching her suspiciously.

"Do you like it here?"

"Of course, sir," she stammered.

"Good. I want some hot water." Sera took the cauldron off the pot-crane and helped him wash the dirt off his face and arms. "Now take your clothes off."

She stared at him as if she hadn't heard right.

"Do you wish to keep your job?" he said quietly. "Then I must have your body, now. There are things on my mind which I choose to forget. You must help me." His upper lip curled back over white, wolf-like teeth.

"What of my mistress, sir?" Sera said, backing away. She knew what happened to Gruffydd's other women and she lived in dread of Madlen.

She didn't want any trouble, but a serving-girl didn't refuse the conjurer. Frightened, she slipped off her black-and-red-striped flannel gown and pulled the shawl from around her neck. Her breasts were swollen with milk.

"Go on," he said. She fumbled with the ribbon around her waist that held up her petticoats. It had broken yesterday and was too short for a bow. The knot was tight. Her finger-nails weren't long enough to unpick it.

"I'm sorry," she said, blushing from her waist up. Gruffydd cut the ribbon with a flick of his hunting-knife. Her petticoats dropped to the floor. He lifted her in his arms and put her down by the fire, then explored her body with a distant sadness, as though he'd known her countless times before. She found herself caressing his long, shaggy hair without knowing why. When he came inside her she didn't hate him. Several times she felt a spasm run through him. He choked it back, trying to prolong his oblivion to eternity. Then suddenly he swore. Owain was crying. Gruffydd kicked the cradle. The wood creaked. The crying stopped. But Gruffydd's concentration was gone. Then Owain bawled again. A second, harder kick had no effect. Gruffydd picked himself off the girl and paced furiously around the room. Sera slipped on her gown and lifted the baby into her arms.

"There. It's all right."

"Don't accuse me," Gruffydd said, infuriated to see her so tender over the child.

"I wasn't." Sera had misunderstood him. "You were very gentle." He laughed, full of self-loathing. Owain was screaming louder— short, convulsive shrieks, not the usual demand for attention. They were cries of pure agony. His eyes dilated with shock a split second before each scream. His face was drained of blood. Gruffydd reached for Mihangel's medicine chest.

"They usually go red when they holler. Where is Mihangel?"

"He's been out all night."

"A woman?" She shook her head. "What, then?"

"Don't know. I've never seen him interested in a woman."

Gruffydd crushed some alder bark in the stone mortar. What would Mihangel prescribe now? A syrup of black cherry. He used it with children—they always liked the taste. Gruffydd mixed it in with the alder powder at random. Owain's tiny mouth was clamped shut from pain.

"Hold his jaw open," he snapped at Sera and tried to pour the liquid in. It unnerved him to see Owain's nurse so scared. The syrup came straight back up and ran down Owain's chin. The screams continued, ear-splitting, at irregular intervals. Sera started to cry.

"If you want something to do, you can run down to Brithgoed and fetch your mistress." Sera shook her head wildly. "Madlen won't eat you. Go on." He slammed the door behind her.

Gruffydd lifted his son out of the cradle with trembling hands. "It's all right, little boy. I'm here. Nothing can harm you." He rocked Owain to and fro in the flat of his palms, as though he might break.

"How can you make so much noise? You scarcely stretch from thumb to thumb. I'm sorry I kicked your cradle. Don't hate me for it. Please don't cry." He hummed an old tune. It brought back Iolo. Iolo had never bawled like this. Owain's face was livid, his eyes unlike anything Gruffydd had seen. The screams were unearthly. "Who's doing this to you? Has somebody been hurting you?" Gruffydd took the sprig of mountain ash hanging from the lintel and waved it several times above the baby's head muttering: "Leave this place. Let my child be. I command you to leave this place." But Owain screamed on, his tiny outraged eyes unable to tell his secret.

Rhiannon hugged Hannah closer to her. The nightmares had got worse since Iolo left them. Hannah had no companion now, with Rachel gone. She was too young to understand the meaning of death, but she knew that Iolo would never come back. She had just dreamt of him lying at the bottom of a deep pit, unable to climb out.

"Go back to sleep. It's all right," Rhiannon whispered. "Iolo is happier where he is now." Hannah moaned and fell asleep, her head nestled against her mother's breast. Rhiannon hadn't closed her eyes all night.

Iolo couldn't be dead. What were they going to live on? The potatoes would be gone in a week and what would they eat then? She forced back the tide of panic. There was not a penny in the house, so they couldn't buy anything, and they had nothing worth selling. Nobody would help them. The whole valley was going hungry and Gruffydd had nothing left to give to anyone. Why had she sent Iolo off with everything they owned? Why did she let him go at all?

"Hywel!" Rhiannon cried. Hannah shifted uneasily beside her. "If you knew how we suffered, could you live with yourself? Is this just? Whatever my fault, can you let us starve?" She buried her face in the straw-filled sack that passed for a pillow and clasped her hands under her chin. "O God, I have believed in You," she said quietly, as if scolding a very small child. "I believed in You all these years, as Hywel would have wished. Send him back to us. Please, God, send him back to us before I begin to doubt You're listening." She fell into a fitful sleep, never quite unconscious of the hollow ache in her stomach.

Someone knocked at the door.

"Is it Iolo?" Hannah asked.

"Shush," Rhiannon whispered, scared. "Keep still and they'll go away." The banging went on. Rhiannon reached for Hywel's old musket.

"In God's name, open," came a deep, ringing voice. Rhiannon listened in disbelief.

It couldn't be! She was imagining it—but who else called upon God so fervently? Who else could move the heart like that? She couldn't mistake his voice, even after all this time. She scrambled down the ladder, still holding the musket.

"Who is it?" Rhiannon's hand was already turning the key.

"It's me. Let me in." Rhiannon shot back the bolts and swung the door wide.

In the faint moonlight a massive figure stood blocking the door. Rhiannon saw only the outline of a full beard, wild hair streaming over hunched shoulders. How could she have mistaken that voice?

"He's dying," Gruffydd said and held out a bundle swathed in his cloak. "For God's sake take him. Please help me." Rhiannon quickly put down the musket and took the baby. He seemed to be sleeping peacefully.

"Come in." She closed the door and bolted it, tucked the baby under her bosom and went over to the hearth, where she lifted the turf covering off the embers and lit a rush taper. A pale glow spread through the room.

Hannah slipped down the ladder, staring wide-eyed at Gruffydd. So this was Iolo's father, the one Rachel told stories about. He didn't look very fierce. He had slumped down by the door with his head in his hands like a tired old dog. She felt sorry for him—he must be cold. She kindled the fire with twigs from the pile that they kept beside the hearthstone, while Rhiannon put Owain down on a blanket and unwrapped the filthy cloak. His linen was soaking, but he seemed unhurt. There were no burns or cuts anywhere.

"What's wrong with him?" Gruffydd muttered something inaudible and Rhiannon for a moment thought Iolo's death had unhinged his mind and he imagined the baby was Iolo.

"He was screaming," Gruffydd said at last.

"Babies do cry at night, you know. He probably had wind or he may be teething early." Gruffydd shook his head despondently. "Where's Madlen?"

"In Brithgoed."

"Doing what?"

"Looking after Ffowlke's wife." Rhiannon pursed her lips but said nothing. How Madlen could entrust her first-born to a wet-nurse she didn't know, especially with Gruffydd half-demented over Iolo's death. She changed Owain's swaddling bands as gently as she could so as not to wake him. The baby did look a bit pale, but no more than

251

she'd expect from his being carried half a mile through the cold night air. It would be a miracle if he weren't ill after such a buffeting. She had no idea why Gruffydd should come to her. It gave her no pleasure to see him humbled and she felt no desire to gloat. He had brought this wretchedness upon himself and must be in torment. She took his hand and helped him up, led him to the three-legged chair by the hearth and heated for him the last beaker of potato soup which she'd been keeping for Hannah's breakfast. Gruffydd refused it. Nobody in the valley could afford to give away food and he didn't deserve it.

"You think I'm possessed," he said. "But I swear to you he was screaming as you have never heard a human child scream."

"Why did you come to me, then?"

Gruffydd closed his eyes. The loneliness of the Round House had terrified him and Rhiannon was the only person in Cwmystwyth he could talk to. She might be harsh with him—and that was welcome—but she wouldn't turn him away. She was indebted to him, as she said herself. Now was the time to repay him. He gazed at Hannah, who was sitting by the fire opposite him with his son on her knees. It was all his doing that she'd grown into such a fine girl.

"Seven years ago," he said slowly, "I saved this child of yours. I thought you might be willing to save mine."

"How could I? I haven't got your skill!" Rhiannon was moved to hear him speak of that first meeting and glad that Hannah had seen him at last, but if Owain was indeed ill, then Gruffydd would know better than she how to cure him. For a conjurer it shouldn't be difficult. "Of course I will do all I can. But how do you imagine I can help him?"

Gruffydd looked away from her. He couldn't tell her now. With Owain sleeping soundly his despair seemed fanciful, even ridiculous. When he'd tried every medicine and every charm he could think of, there'd been only one way left for him to turn. If Rhiannon would assist him, he was willing to invoke the God of the Calvinists—anything to save his son Owain. But he wouldn't admit this to her now. She would lose what little respect she had for him.

"I thought you might have some honey . . . It might be good for him." Rhiannon could tell he was lying. Any family in the valley would have long since eaten the honey they had left over from summer. Gruffydd got up and collected his cloak, then lifted Owain gently off Hannah's knee. "I'll take him home now."

"No," Rhiannon said. "He's to stay here till the morning when his nurse can come for him." But Gruffydd refused to listen. His mood had suddenly changed and he brushed past her with hardly a word of thanks as if he wished he hadn't come. As he opened the door, Owain woke and screamed. Rhiannon jerked round, shocked. It was an unbelievable, unbearable sound. Gruffydd seemed about to collapse. She ran to take the baby from him and reached for a syrup that she'd used with Hannah, but Owain spewed it up.

"Please. I'll do anything. Just save him," Gruffydd said.

"But why me? What can I do?"

"You have a God, haven't you? Can't he manage something for me?" Rhiannon was stunned. He was asking her for faith and she hadn't any left herself.

"I can pray for Owain, and for you."

"Is that the best you can offer?"

"What else do you want?"

"I need some cure!" In her panic Rhiannon remembered a relic that her father had once spoken of.

"Listen. In the abbey at Strata Florida there's a cup. My father called it the Healing Cup. Joseph of Arimathea brought it to this country. Our Lord Jesus drank from it while He hung on the cross. My father told me it will cure anyone with faith in his heart who drinks from it."

"But how can Owain have faith?"

"You must believe for him." Rhiannon grasped his huge, coarse hands and pressed them between hers. "I can fetch the Cup, but you must put your trust in God."

Owain screamed, a cry of betrayal and despair. Gruffydd lifted Rhiannon's fingers to his lips and whispered: "Make me believe."

II

John Ffowlke slapped two kings and an ace onto the table. "Can you match that?" Madlen woke with a jolt and scrutinized her hand through half-closed lids as though she'd been mulling over her next move. Three aces. Oh, dear.

"Well?" Ffowlke insisted. Her lazy smile was tantalizing.

"You've cleaned me out." Madlen threw down eight, jack, queen. Surely he'd let her go to bed now?

"Ha! You'd never make a gambler."

"Not against you, sir," Madlen sighed. "Tell me, is it skill or luck?"

"Both." Ffowlke raked in her pile of coins. "Here, I'll give you another chance." He tossed a couple of sovereigns back to her. Madlen groaned to herself. Wasn't it all his money anyway?

"I ought to see if my lady is comfortable."

"One more game. Just one more," Ffowlke pleaded. He reached for the new bottle warming in the grate. Madlen caught his wrist.

"You promised me. Only one bottle a day."

"Don't tell me what to do," Ffowlke said furiously, but her look of reproach was irresistible. "Oh, all right. I drink too much. The gout hasn't been quite so bad since you've been here. I'm very grateful." Madlen locked the bottle in the inlaid cabinet.

"It's not just that. You forget there's no way of tasting it." The last canary had died that afternoon of alcohol poisoning. Ffowlke was convinced it was Talbot. She didn't argue.

Ffowlke's hands shook as he struggled out of his leather-covered armchair. "I'll get him one day. I'll invite him to a reconciliation dinner and offer him his own bottle."

"He can't touch you," Madlen soothed him and massaged his shrunken, drooping shoulders.

Ffowlke fell back in the chair again, exhausted. He watched her reach for the candle on the mantelpiece. "You know, my dear, it's a pity you weren't born a lady."

She knew this old man's ploy. When she'd had her way for too long he'd put her in her place with some carping reminder of her low birth. It infuriated her, because he usually treated her like a lady and she had come to think of herself as being one.

"Yes, it's a shame. You wear that dress far better than Maude ever did." So he'd turned it into a compliment after all—a clumsy compliment, perhaps, but genuine nevertheless, for she could hear the admiration in his voice. She was pleased. It was a low-cut, tight-waisted court dress. She looked ravishing in it, she knew.

"Thank you, Lord Kirkland." She curtsied to him, displaying her elegant white forearms, as she touched the scarlet silk shot with silver. She wished she had a more appealing audience. Ffowlke tapped his hands together in genteel admiration and eyed her cleavage, envying Gruffydd from the bottom of his heart.

"I shall miss you, my dear, when my son is born."

The door opened and Mihangel came in unannounced.

"Haven't you learnt to knock?" Ffowlke said drily. Madlen rose from her curtsy.

"What do you want, Mihangel?" she said. He stared at her tongue-tied. Through the study window he had seen Ffowlke playing cards with his wife. Now Madlen stood there more dazzling than ever, the last person Mihangel wished to run into here.

"Answer the lady, boy." John Ffowlke motioned Madlen to sit. A spasm of jealousy crossed Mihangel's face as she curtsied to Ffowlke again with a knowing smile.

Madlen was trying to work it out. How long had Mihangel been a visitor here? How could he have got past her? He'd been cheating them after all. Spying for Ffowlke, who obviously wasn't as helpless as he made out. What agreement did the two of them have? How much did Ffowlke know about Gruffydd?

"I had important news," Mihangel said with an arrogant turn toward the door. "But it can wait."

"You will leave when I tell you," Ffowlke roared. "Now say what you came to say."

"Your two surveyors on Cefn Coch have been murdered." Madlen swore under her breath. Ffowlke looked dangerously composed.

"By whom?"

"A riot from Cwmystwyth."

"Where's Gruffydd?"

"With your tenants. He drove them on to it."

"He's lying," Madlen flared. "Don't trust him, my lord. He's deceived us all this while and he's surely deceiving you too." Mihangel shook his head calmly. He had scarcely changed in manner, yet suddenly his malice was transparent, his long-nurtured treachery blindingly obvious. How could she have missed it? He knew everything about her. What if he had told it all to Ffowlke . . .

Ffowlke tried to penetrate Mihangel's murky eyes. He remembered Reuben. Subordinates were always envious. Maybe he was lying about Gruffydd, but probably he was not. Mihangel had been an invaluable spy. Always accurate. He'd never breathed a word against Gruffydd before, though he reported faithfully each week on the conjurer's activities. If he was ambitious, he'd had the sense to hide it.

Mihangel bowed sardonically to Madlen. "Go and find out for yourself."

"I will." She rose, wishing she could kill him there and then. "May I take Venus, sir?"

"I think perhaps you should." Ffowlke weighed his words. "I've been patient over many things. In return, Gruffydd promised me a quiet time." He caught Madlen's hand as she swept past. "You do understand, my dear, don't you? If there's any trouble, Talbot can send the militia onto my land. That's just what he wants."

The long winter night was at its blackest. Dawn still hours away. Half a mile out of Brithgoed, Madlen was forced from a canter to a trot; half a mile farther, to a walk.

"Come on," she growled, kicking Venus in the ribs for all she was worth. "It's only a shadow." Why hadn't she risked the short cut over the hills? It could take forever along the river.

Gruffydd couldn't have caused a riot, she kept telling herself. He had nothing to gain from it, unless Iolo's death had driven him mad. Mihangel would be telling Ffowlke all about Iolo right now. Why hadn't she crushed him when she could? Madlen felt sick. The relentless jogging had gone to her stomach. She leaned to one side to puke without stopping Venus. Not again. Not so soon. She was three weeks overdue and there was so much to be done. It couldn't have come at a worse moment.

The Round House meadows and paddocks were dotted with fires, the villagers of Cwmystwyth huddled around them like an army silently awaiting the morning's battle. What were they all doing there? Madlen pulled the horse to a halt. What in God's name was Gruffydd playing at?

She tied Venus to a fallen birch tree, wrapped her cloak around her head and picked her way through the fires, thankful to have changed back into her village dress. No one gave her a second look. Half a dozen men were sleeping against the Round House door, Thomas Jenkins among them.

"Why are they here?" she whispered, putting a hand over his mouth to stop him squawking.

"Thank God you're back. They won't move till Gruffydd tells them what to do. They're terrified of Ffowlke after what they did to the surveyors."

So it was true. She'd only half-believed it. "Who was it?"

"I . . . I didn't see."

"If you want to save your own neck, tell me."

"Huw Lloyd . . . and half a dozen others."

"Was Gruffydd there?"

"Not at the end. But . . ."

"Well?"

"It w-was Gruffydd's idea," Thomas stuttered.

"I'd forget that if I were you." Madlen knocked firmly on the door.

"Leave me in peace!" cried an anguished voice she scarcely recognized.

"It's me. Let me in."

"I'm sorry about your son," said Thomas, anxious to make it up with her.

"What do you mean?" Madlen grabbed his hair and shook him. "What about my son?"

"I thought you knew. He's dying."

The door opened. Madlen caught her breath. Gruffydd looked shrunken, drained of blood. His whole body sagged. His wide-eyed, sleepless face was yellowish, like crumbling plaster, with the luminous serenity of a death-mask. He took her arm, moving and speaking in a trance.

"Come in. Did Sera tell you?"

"Sera?"

"No matter. You're here now."

"It's not true, is it? Where's Owain? He isn't dying!" He led her silently to the rocking cradle hidden in a far corner, a semi-circle scratched around it on the flagstones. Above it hung whole bunches of mountain ash in a canopy and curious stones, animal bones and metal charms dangled almost to the cradle. Owain was breathing in short intermittent gasps. Occasionally he would whimper slightly. He didn't cry. His white face was wrinkled like a very old woman's.

"Oh, my poor baby!" Madlen was too horrified and scared to weep. She had spent so little time with him, scarcely suckled him or played with him, her first-born, the fruit of seven years' labour. He couldn't die now. She reached out to hold him but Gruffydd held her back.

"Leave him. You'll break the charm." Madlen shivered. His hands were clammy.

"Who is it? Who is doing this to us? Why?"

"I don't know." Gruffydd put his hands on her shoulders. He had to tell her now, had to warn her not to expect any miracles from him. She must understand. He needed her more now than ever before.

"But you can save him, can't you?" she said as he turned her face towards him. "You can lift the spell?" The same look as seven years ago when she first came to him for help in the Ystwyth meadows. He saw her kneeling at his feet, saying. "Only you can help now." The same irresistible, unquestioning eyes as called him to Rhiannon's bedside. Why couldn't he simply say again, "He won't die. That's why I'm here"?

Madlen watched his clouded face as though Owain's horoscope were written across it. "In God's name, say something. Tell me you can save him." She pressed her fists against his chest and he flinched. Through the fold in his cloak she saw deep gashes. The flesh was raw, between the flaps of skin. His belly was covered with bloodstains.

"What happened? Who did it?"

"I did."

"Why?" He scared her. "Why?"

"I thought that I could take on Owain's suffering, draw the evil spirits onto myself. They refused me. They torture me in a different way." He shuddered and fell forward against the hearthstone, head in his hands, back arched in exhaustion. For an age not a muscle in his body stirred. Was he concentrating? Or was he just absent? Owain whimpered. Madlen couldn't bear the silence. Couldn't she do anything? Owain might be dead by the time Gruffydd pulled himself together.

"What about the cure you used for—"

"I've tried every charm and every potion I've ever heard of." Gruffydd didn't even raise his head. "I've sung myself hoarse with threats and promises. The spirits won't move."

"He's your son!" Madlen screamed in his ear. "If you can't save him, what can you do?"

Nothing, Gruffydd thought. He had drunk to the dregs the same rage and contempt she felt now. Fate had chosen him as its fool and tossed him about like the pig's bladder in the Ystwyth black-ball match. It had given him a gift he hadn't asked for, then taken it away when he most needed it. Pointless crying "unfair." Bladders were for kicking, not complaining. Anyway, it was horribly just, in one sense. At first he'd known perfectly well that his power was only on loan, that he'd have to render it up one day, but gradually he'd forgotten. He'd been a conjurer for so long he had come to think his powers were permanent and had forgotten that he was one thing and his position quite another. No use pleading: "But look what I've done with what you gave me." Fate wasn't interested in good deeds. It had a purpose of its own.

"You can't give in," Madlen whispered more gently, caressing his head. "You must go on trying."

"Don't disturb me. There's one thing I haven't tried." Gruffydd pressed his forehead into the hearthstone.

"I've never believed in you," he prayed truculently to the God of the Calvinists. "What do you expect? Look what you've done for Rhiannon. She threw away her life for you and you spewed on her for it. We'll let bygones be bygones. If you bring Rhiannon back in time with the Healing Cup, and if it works . . . I'll build you a church in Cwmystwyth and take holy orders."

Owain rallied just before dawn. Gruffydd was pacing around the room, muttering to himself. Madlen took it for a magic formula.

"You've saved him!" Owain's face was a healthy pink. He was breathing quietly and occasionally gurgled to be fed. "Can I hold him, or should we leave him?" Gruffydd gazed in wonder.

"Thy kingdom come," he murmured. His prayers had worked. Madlen lifted Owain out of the cradle and gave him her nipple, though her milk had long since run dry from not feeding him herself. He sucked nonetheless, his tiny hands waving to and fro. Madlen wept with joy and relief.

"How can you forgive me for doubting you?" Gruffydd was alarmed. It was too easy. Fate wasn't impressed with last-minute repentance. He still didn't, couldn't, believe in Rhiannon's Calvinist God. He hadn't the faith she spoke of, not even with the Cup—so what hope was there without it? He couldn't trick a God in whom he didn't believe into saving his son. They shouldn't have taken him out of the circle. Gruffydd wished he'd kept to his own charms.

Half an hour later Owain fell asleep peacefully at his mother's breast. He didn't wake up. They couldn't tell precisely when he stopped breathing, because nothing in his face changed. Death seemed most terrible in someone so unfinished. It left no mark and no sign of understanding.

Madlen rocked her baby to and fro as if to comfort him. Gruffydd kissed the cold lips and blew to breathe life back into him. He had a vision of saving Owain, grown to a young man, from drowning in the Ystwyth: a quite distinct person whom Gruffydd had never seen before yet knew was Owain, as though the tiny form in his hands carried in it the image of a life that could never come about. Gruffydd plunged into the river after him. Owain was already sucked under. Gruffydd's breath rattled in the empty lungs and left them.

"My son is dead," Gruffydd cried for the second time in one day. He'd thought himself prepared, but now he crumbled like a beaver dam in the autumn flood. His line was extinct. He had nothing more to hope for. He howled and threw himself against his hearthstone and tore at it with his bare hands, trying to uproot it. After all his offerings and prayers, the spirits of this place had deserted him. Now he would destroy them and all his ancestral relics.

Madlen put her cheek against Owain's head. Cold as any stone. She shivered and put the tiny corpse back in the cradle, overcome with sudden fear. The evil spirits would be leaving Owain's body now their work was done. They would be looking for a new home. She heaped blankets over him and turned away. She had no son. An ache tore through her from her heart to the pit of her stomach. Her first-born was dead. It were better her womb had never spawned. She had treated that miracle too lightly and had not given her long-awaited baby all the love he deserved. Why hadn't she been with him more? She yearned to hold her own, living child in her arms again. Owain had been alive just now—it might be an eternity ago. "I would give Brithgoed and the whole of Ceredigion to have you back again," she said. "I would live in the poorest shack on the barest hill, if you would come back." She looked at the pile of blankets as if it might move. The time for tender care was gone. She had neglected her beloved child; now it was too late. She sat beside the rocking cradle staring at a red and white bonnet she had knitted for Owain long before he was born.

Gruffydd had collapsed beside his hearthstone. It was stronger than he and would long survive his vengeance and his despair. Neither of them spoke. They were too deep in their separate griefs, their separate guilt. Madlen looked across at Gruffydd and tried to find words. They wouldn't come. He was a stranger to her. He had failed—deliberately, it almost seemed—when he was needed most. Surely he could have saved the baby if he had willed it strongly enough? What secret jealousy had made him sever the blood-bond between them and destroy the creature that made them more than just lovers? "I don't understand," she wanted to cry out. She wanted to hold him. She couldn't. He had cut himself off.

An hour passed, maybe two. Outside, the villagers were stirring. She could hear them pouring milk for their breakfast. Soon they'd be knocking at the door again, demanding to see Gruffydd. How could he explain away yet another failure? If they thought he had outlived his own powers they were quite capable of despatching him to avoid bad luck and her with him for good measure. They'd always hated her. In a way she was glad of the danger. It forced her mind off Owain and dulled the pain of his death.

"What shall we do?" she said.

"What is there to do?" Gruffydd's voice was like an echo from a dungeon.

"We can't stay in here for ever. What are you going to say to them?"

Gruffydd took a deep breath, straightened his spine against the hearthstone and stared up into the rafters.

"I shall tell them a story."

"They don't want a story," Madlen said impatiently. "They want to be given orders."

"Listen, my love. It's for you, too. I knew a man once, he came upon a fairy dance one night on a mountain near his home. They asked him to join in. Their music was so sweet and the dance so wild that his feet were moving before he could stop them. He danced all night. When the morning came, the fairy chief said to him, 'Please accept this chest of gold as a pledge of friendship.' The chest was full of sea shells. 'Thank you,' he said, not wishing to offend them, and carried it home to tell everyone of his adventure. When he reached the valley, he found that his one night with the fair people had been twelve years of mortal time. His wife had died of grief for him. People spoke of him as long since dead. They made the stranger more than welcome because he brought with him a chest crammed with gold pieces. He was wealthy beyond men's dreams . . . What was he to do? There were many old friends he wanted to help, many old enemies he couldn't resist harming. Above all, if his gold would bring happiness and prosperity, what right had he to tell them it was nothing but worthless sea shells? He kept quiet." Gruffydd sighed. "He told them nothing about who he was or where his wealth came from. Gradually he came to think of sea shells as valuable currency."

"So what changed?"

"What changed? Well, one day real gold was needed. Someone he loved fell very ill and all that could cure him was a potion of gold-dust, so my friend ground the sea shells to powder. It wasn't the same. It didn't work."

"Perhaps because he didn't believe in it enough." Gruffydd looked at her perplexed. Hadn't she understood?

"No. He knew it wasn't gold."

"Everyone else thought it was," Madlen said desperately. "How can you be sure they weren't right?"

"Don't you see?" Gruffydd said, taking her hands. "I've never been what you thought I was. I can no more charm away evil spirits than you or Thomas Jenkins, or anyone."

"You can!" Madlen's face was flushed with anxiety. "You have done, often. You mustn't give in just because this once they were stronger than you." Gruffydd smiled sadly. Her faith warmed him, but it couldn't convince him. "And if you pretended just for their sake"—Madlen pointed through the wall at the waking villagers expecting some word of guidance—"how can you desert them now? They need you more than ever." Gruffydd spread his arms, grappling with doubts he had no words for.

"As long as it was for good I had to pretend. As a conjurer I could help them, but not if I was one of them. Now it's different. I first felt it in Tregaron—they wouldn't follow me to England with the cattle because they didn't trust my power that far. If they didn't, how could I? Since then I've tried too hard to make up for it. I've made mistakes, trapped myself. I can't get out. If I stay here I'll make worse mistakes and in the end I'd destroy everything I've built. I'd ruin you all. It's time to stand down."

Madlen flung open a hatch-window. "Look at them! How long will they last without you? They're lost. They need you. If you desert them now, they'll sink back into the mud you dragged them out of. How are they going to sell their cattle? How are they going to pay their rents? How do they explain the two surveyors? You've brought them this far, you must see it through."

"You don't understand—"

"You missed out the end of the story. Your friend decides to tell everyone how he came by his fortune. That very moment all the gold turns back into sea shells. What happens then? They tear him and each other to pieces. Is that what you want?"

"If that must be. I'm ready."

"What about me?" Madlen screamed. "I've given everything for you. Am I to be sacrificed too? What do you think that mob out there will do to me? I've given everything for you and you didn't even love me enough to trust me. Why didn't you tell me? I wouldn't have given you away. I'm nothing without you. I have nothing left of my own. I've held nothing back from you . . ."

"I didn't mean to deceive you," Gruffydd said helplessly, hugging her as she wept, his huge arms locked together behind her. "Of course I trusted you. Our lives are one—they always will be. Only this I couldn't share. I needed your faith in me. From the moment you called me to Rhiannon I couldn't do without it. Perhaps that's one reason I can't go on now."

"I still believe in you!" But she was lying. She could never believe in him as before. The balance of her life had swung irrevocably. Why had she left Rhiannon and Hywel, braved the whole valley, running it as though she were a born monarch, and played such a dangerous game with Ffowlke if not because she had a conjurer for a husband who would send the very elements to her rescue if one hair on her head was threatened? "Tell me one thing. Is Maude pregnant?"

"She has as much hope of spawning as I do." Madlen hid her face in her hands.

"Oh, God. What are we going to do?"

"Leave here," Gruffydd said, kneeling beside her. "Leave here with me. We'll take what we can and move on."

"How will you keep me, Gruffydd? Where will my clothes come from? What shall we eat?"

Gruffydd longed for the freedom of the uplands on a clear night. "You can find shelter anywhere in this world. The stars never flatter and they ask no lies of you . . ." Madlen shook her head. Seven years ago his words might have led her round the world in penury. Too much had been won since then to be thrown away without a struggle. She gripped him by the shoulders.

"You must fight. You've cut out a kingdom for yourself, now you must fight for it!"

"Why?" He looked at her balefully. "When it will die with me?" He went to the cradle and picked up the tiny corpse swathed in blankets. Then he went to the door. "I don't want to fight. Too many people would be hurt. I don't want their blood on my conscience."

"Stop," Madlen shouted. "There'll be more children. You'll soon have another heir . . ." The door had slammed. Gruffydd was already surrounded by his shouting, pleading people.

Madlen sank onto a stool by the fire. Why hadn't she thought of it sooner? Why hadn't she told him she was pregnant?

"He's burnt out," said a soft voice behind her. Madlen leapt up.

"How did you get in?"

"You always leave your bedroom door open," Mihangel said, amused. "For your spies. Have you forgotten?"

"You were listening?"

"Yes. But don't worry. I heard nothing I didn't know already."

Outside, Gruffydd's voice rang out. "Owain is dead. The magic was too strong for me." Madlen ran to the window. Gruffydd was standing on the rabbit hutch in the middle of the meadow.

"We don't believe it," Old Isaac shouted from the back. Gruffydd pulled away the blankets and held out the tiny, linen-wrapped corpse. One by one they filed past to see for themselves.

"Anyway," Mihangel said, "I was only waiting to speak to you."

"What about?" Madlen was oblivious to him. She was watching Gruffydd throw away everything they'd ever fought for.

"It came as a shock, didn't it?" Mihangel gloated. "I've known for years that Gruffydd was no conjurer."

"How?" For an instant she looked back at him.

"Because I am one."

"No. No. No," the crowd was chanting and Gruffydd was thundering above it. "I can do nothing more for you. Let me go in peace."

"They should take his advice," Mihangel said. "I'll do a far better job for them." Outside, quite near the window, a distraught woman wailed: "Who has done this to our conjurer?"

Who *had* done this to Gruffydd? Madlen thought. Who had destroyed him? The answer was standing behind her, leaning over her, watching with her. All the potions Mihangel had given her . . . Owain refusing her milk . . . She stole a glimpse at his triumphant face and knew for certain. He had murdered Owain. He had poisoned the milk in her breast. To destroy Gruffydd he had killed her baby, and every time she had held Owain in her arms she had been slowly poisoning him.

Mihangel's face was close to hers and she could feel the warmth of his breath on her cheek. His black eyes glowed like coals in hell. "You'll keep everything that's yours. You'll always be the conjurer's wife." He kissed her forehead. His lips scalded her. "Just as long as you leave Gruffydd immediately to the fate he obviously desires and help me instead. Only I can protect you." Madlen turned desperately towards the door. The crowd had swept away down the hill shouting, she couldn't make out what. There was no sign of Gruffydd. Why didn't he come back?

"Otherwise I shall have to tell Lord Kirkland that you tricked him about Maude's pregnancy. You've been cheating him all along." Mihangel put his arm around her waist and pulled her hips in to him. "You owe me a kiss, do you remember? In return for three of Gruffydd's hairs. I swore I'd get that kiss." Madlen was scarcely conscious of his mouth closing upon hers. She had to get away as fast as she could. Perhaps it was not too late to save Gruffydd despite himself. She had to try, if only for the child they'd lost, and the child that she was now carrying. She had to get to Brithgoed before Mihangel.

God knows if it will work, she thought.

CHAPTER EIGHTEEN

I

THE RAIN-BARREL was frozen over. Beneath the ice the water was murky black. Rhiannon saw the icicles hanging from the eaves just above her head and shivered in the early morning breeze.

"Perhaps I won't wash today." She had stayed in bed too long thinking about the conjurer's visit and her body was warm and drowsy. So difficult to get up when there was nothing to eat. It only made the stomach feel emptier. "Why should I bother when there's no one to see me? My cheeks are so hollow, does it matter if they're dirty?"

Rhiannon smashed the ice with a stone and washed, as she had done every morning for ten years. Not because she heard Hywel saying, "Cleanliness is the beginning of all virtue." She had forgotten most of his sayings. The few she remembered sounded odd to her now, like a lesson recited parrot-fashion by a class of children. Even Hywel's face was blurred. She saw a broad forehead and curly black hair, and called it Hywel to reassure herself. She couldn't really remember his face. She had been too scared of it. Rhiannon went on washing herself just as she went on praying: not because of anything Hywel had said, nor because she believed in it herself, but simply out of habit. She had washed and prayed for too long, and to give it up now would be to give in.

She caught her breath as the water stung her face and trickled over her shoulders. There were ice splinters in it that cut like steel. Then she lowered her head and scrubbed behind her neck. The hair-line was warm from the pillow. She shuddered and her breasts trembled slightly. They were still beautiful. She fought off the sadness it caused her. Still firm, like a girl's. Her hair might be more white than blonde, her face so worn she couldn't bear to use a mirror and felt for her parting with a forefinger and comb, but her body was a young woman's, a bride's. Her thighs were sleek and well-rounded, not like the sinewy legs of Cwmystwyth women who strutted around with skirts hitched up to the waist; her belly wasn't bloated like theirs, despite hunger. Perhaps because she had been spared their continuous childbirth. She watched the blood race beneath her pearly skin. Childbirth! What chance had she had to bear children? No man had been near her since Hannah was born, and who cared if her thighs were fine? Who even knew? Rhiannon tried to remember Hywel as a lover—so restrained, he never really abandoned himself to her. Perhaps he'd been afraid of his dissolute youth. She wished she had known him then. She was startled to have admitted it, for she usually never allowed herself to think of men, even Hywel, in that way. She was always too busy. Another day to get through, another year. She could have made some man happy—Hywel, perhaps, if he'd known how to love her. She tied her petticoats around her waist with short, convulsive tugs at the ribbon. Then she pushed her hair defiantly out of her face, threw the towel around her shoulders and went in, slamming the back door behind her. The room was dark, the fire still low after the night. Her black dress was hanging from a pot-crane. It wouldn't be warm yet. Someone coughed. A man was sitting on the three-legged chair in the darkened window recess, his body hunched, his head resting on his knees. Her heart leapt. She knew it was Gruffydd. Just as she was reaching for her dress, he raised his head.

"Couldn't you get it?" He seemed oblivious to her nakedness.

"Get what?"

"The Healing Cup. I was praying you might get back with it in time."

In time? Rhiannon thought, and said: "How's Owain this morning?"

"He died around dawn." Rhiannon steadied herself against the pot-crane. It swung slightly, creaking. The towel fell off her shoulder, leaving a breast uncovered. She scarcely noticed. "I prayed all night. Only the Cup could have saved him, I think. Wouldn't they let you have it?"

"I . . ." Rhiannon faltered. "I didn't go." For a moment he didn't seem to understand, then his face broke into a thousand fragments.

"Why not?"

"I got half-way but then I turned back. I didn't believe he was dying," she stammered.

"But I told you!"

"I thought you'd save him. You'd have to. You're a conjurer." She saw him kneeling by her bed, saying, "Lady, have no fear." He couldn't have failed! Not with his own son.

"I told you I couldn't help him," Gruffydd said wildly. "Why didn't you take me at my word?"

"I don't know! I don't know! Please leave me alone."

"You told me my charms wouldn't work. You told me only the Cup would save him. I believed you. You robbed me of my strength. Murdered my son."

Rhiannon screamed as he raised his hand to strike her. "Don't you understand? I never believed in the Cup. I've never believed in Hywel's God. I've only ever believed in you." Gruffydd stepped back as if she'd scorched him. For seconds they stared at each other, equally shocked.

"Oh, God," Rhiannon whispered. "What have I said?" He'd dragged her child out of her a second time. She'd never known it was there. It wasn't Hywel she'd been waiting for. It wasn't Hywel she'd cried for through so many lonely nights—Hywel who had never loved her as she deserved, whom she'd married only to provide a home for Madlen. Why did she love Hannah with such wounded, tortured passion, if not because of her miraculous birth and other-worldly deliverer, and why had she loved Iolo as her son, if not because he had been the image of his father? Why had she so jealously secluded the boy, if not out of revenge for Gruffydd's indifference, the masterly arrogance with which he'd raped her soul with an oyster-shell lamp and discarded her for a worthless sister? The only reason she had sought to convert him was to reverse that supremacy, for her own faith had been buried after six weeks of Hywel's absence, and the only cause she'd had to hate Gruffydd with such fervour, quaking at his very name, was that she'd loved him to the point of madness, preferring to waste as a widow than to take any other man.

"Don't despise me," she said hoarsely, utterly at his mercy now. One unkind word would destroy her. "I never knew . . ."

"Please," Gruffydd said gently, taking her hand. He guessed only a fraction of what she was feeling and would never comprehend what chaos he'd unleashed in her by merely answering a chance call to assist her labour. He saw only a long-hoarded pain greater than his own, the end of a masquerade more bewildering even than his. Both of them had dropped their guard. "How could I despise you? . . ." Rhiannon's arms were round his neck, pulling his mouth down to hers.

A voice rang out inside her, a trumpet calling the dead to new life. The lid flew off her tomb and she stared up into the crystal-blue sky at the back of his eyes. He tasted sweet; the rich smell of his body— smoke and sweat and semen—rose in her nostrils, drugging her. She put her hands to his face and forced her tongue between his teeth, obliterated herself against him and felt him alive to her touch, strength spreading through every limb she touched, pulsating back into her. His lips closed around her breasts, sucking avidly like a hungry child, his beard was soft. She remembered it brushing against her cheek as she lay in bed swollen with child.

"I'm not what you think I am," Gruffydd whispered in her ear. She turned her head slowly and looked into his eyes. So gentle and so blue.

"Forgive me for not understanding sooner," she murmured, caressing the dark hair streaked with white that waved around his temples. "Whatever you are, whoever you are I love you. I've waited for you so long." Gruffydd's grief melted in her tenderness. They had suffered the same sorrows—many of hers caused by him, Gruffydd knew—and they could share the same solace without having to explain. He couldn't begin to understand, yet surely her need sprang from the same well as his own.

"Are you sure?" he asked, fearful of injuring her.

"Whatever happens to us."

It wasn't easy. Rhiannon was scared because she was older than the women he was used to. She didn't understand he revelled in every warm, pain-filled line on her face, worshipped her white hair and the vulnerable, fumbling apology with which her ageing hands unbuttoned her skirts. He understood every uncertainty, sensed the cause of every scar. She was so anxious to please him, to be everything she imagined a woman should be to a man, that she ended by rushing him, feigning the passionate abandon which she genuinely felt.

"Slow down," Gruffydd smiled and caressed her smooth white belly, firm and rounded like a coracle. "Enjoy yourself."

"Hywel never taught me how to. He just told me to lie still." A stab of guilt crossed her face. Neither of them needed reminding of Hywel. He was present in the stone and clay around them.

"You don't have to convince me of anything," he said gently, lifting her into his arms. "You're a beautiful woman." She had a warmth and a dignity he had never found in Madlen. And sadness. How important that was, he thought. Understanding never came without it and perhaps passion always left with it.

"Show me," Rhiannon said. He could never hurt her more than he had already. It reassured her. She knew him by the pain he'd caused her. "Make me enjoy myself." She lay back against his mountainous chest and listened to all the new sensations he awoke in her. Wrists and arms, which had only ever ached from carrying too much, became a pleasure to possess. He discovered parts of her she scarcely knew existed. When he finally came inside her it caused her none of the discomfort she'd known with Hywel. Every inch of her rose to greet him.

"Aren't you cold?" asked a voice from the loft, as they lay resting by the fire.

"How long have you been there, Hannah?" Rhiannon asked, stretching luxuriously on Gruffydd's cloak. "Have you been watching us?"

"Yes. It looked like hard work. Why did you make all that noise?" Rhiannon laughed.

"Because I was enjoying myself. Come down here." Hannah climbed down the ladder looking solemn.

"What was it all for?" Rhiannon pulled her down between them.

"All for love. Look at Gruffydd, Hannah. I want you to love him, always. He saved both our lives once and now he's saved mine again." Gruffydd lifted Hannah onto his knee and kissed her on the forehead, brushing a lock of curly black hair out of her face.

"Why have you got all this?" Hannah tugged at Gruffydd's beard exactly as Iolo used to. It filled him with a terrible yearning, mixed with wonder. He'd lost one family today, only to discover another.

"You're her real father," Rhiannon said. "You know that, don't you?" Gruffydd nodded. He cupped his hand under Rhiannon's chin and drew her mouth gently up to his, then he pulled her closer to him and they fell asleep with Hannah between them.

None of them heard the tap at the door. The handle turned noiselessly, missing the latch that usually held it shut—only someone who knew it well could work it. The door opened a crack, just as far as it would go before the hinge creaked. Madlen squeezed in through the gap.

It was like creeping home at daybreak to avoid Hywel, and she remembered the night the Round House was built. She threw a last glance towards the forest. Someone had followed her back from Brithgoed, she was sure. She needed a place to hide. Rhiannon wouldn't give her away, whatever their differences, and there was no one else in Cwmystwyth who would offer her shelter. She couldn't go back to the Round House. That was the first place anyone would look. Venus neighed gently from the barn, where Madlen had tethered her. She shouldn't have kept her, but she was reluctant to lose her one means of escape. If only Venus kept quiet . . . There was a sudden movement in the half-light at the edge of the forest. Maybe only a fox, but Madlen was scared. She lifted the door silently back onto the latch and padded along the flagstones, feeling her way along the beams that held up the loft. By the ladder she stopped.

"God help me!" Rhiannon cried. Madlen was two yards away, as pale as death, with a hectic rash across her forehead like a cattle brand . . . She lunged. Her knee pressed down on Rhiannon's belly, hands around her neck, squeezing with demented strength. Rhiannon clawed at Madlen's face, thrashed out with her legs, bit deep into her arm. She was nearly throttled before Gruffydd could separate them. Then Madlen turned on him.

"Do you know what I've done for you?" she screamed again and again. "Do you know what I've done for you?" She shook her head hysterically while Gruffydd held her at arm's length. A white froth trickled down her chin. Gruffydd hit her hard across the face, back-handed against the right cheek, palm against the left. She gazed at him, stunned. He had never struck her before.

"Now get out of here," he said. She couldn't believe he was being so cruel to her. Why was he treating her like this? How could he desert her just when she needed him most, when she was grieving for Owain and longed to be comforted, when she had just risked her life to help him? Had it been any other woman she could maybe have shrugged it off. But to come to Rhiannon, her own sister, the one woman in Cwmystwyth whom Madlen could fear as a rival and who might take him away from her! Rhiannon had waited for seven years to get Gruffydd. She would never give him up again. How cleverly they'd deceived her. She'd thought she knew everything that went on in the valley, yet none of her spies had told her of this. Madlen was suddenly overwhelmed by the futility of her life and of what she'd just done.

"You can stay here now," she said helplessly. "You and your slut. You're quite safe. Maude's dead." Gruffydd let go of her.

"What?"

"I thought you'd be pleased. Ffowlke will never know she wasn't pregnant. I've just poisoned her for you."

"You're mad."

"Oh, don't worry. They'll never know it was me. Nobody saw me. The phial will be found in one of Talbot's handkerchiefs under her window."

"Talbot?"

"Clever, isn't it? Ffowlke will trust me more than ever." Gruffydd was horrified and fascinated. She'd killed for him. Killed an old woman just to protect him, to possess him. But it was none of his doing. He hadn't asked for it.

"You don't imagine that I'm going to feel grateful, do you?"

"Feel what you like, but don't try to leave here. You belong to me. If you try to escape with that bitch"—she spat at Rhiannon, huddled in the hearth corner, pulling her black dress over her knees—"I'll set your friends onto you. They've already sacked the tannery and your new mill. Mihangel would love to have a go at you too, if he knew where you were."

"Mihangel?"

"When will you learn? He's been double-crossing you all along. Where were you when he tried to rape me over your dead son's cradle?" Gruffydd's lips tautened. "Don't worry. I kept him off. Do you know why? I'm carrying your child."

"You're not!" he blurted.

Madlen took Gruffydd's hand and placed it on her belly. "Your heir is in there. I can feel him already."

"So soon?" She was telling the truth. He could tell.

"You know I've been feeling sick," Madlen said impatiently. "I'm three weeks overdue. In nine months you could have everything you've ever dreamed of. Maude's dead and Ffowlke wants an heir. He's going to marry again for sure . . ." A wicked, amused glint crossed her eyes. "Your son could own all this valley. You could be the most powerful man in Ceredigion. All you'd have to do is marry me to John Ffowlke."

"You're mad," Gruffydd said again, swallowing heavily.

"It's not just a good idea, it's our only chance. You've lost the whole valley with your antics, Ffowlke's all you've got left."

"Works out fine for you, doesn't it?" Gruffydd drawled. "Lady Kirkland. Very pretty."

"Stop it," Madlen yelled at him. "Can't you see? Do you think I want to be married to him? To have to lie with that rotting carcass of a man? I don't want it for myself—I want to make life safe for you and for our child. What more do I have to do for you, to make you love me?" She screamed still more angrily to hide the desperate tears overtaking her. "What do you want me to be? Mihangel's whore? Is that how you want your son to grow up?"

"Wait." Gruffydd tried to hold her. She was gone, slamming the door behind her. A horse cantered away down the hill.

"Poor Madlen," Rhiannon said cautiously, leaning her cheek against his shoulder.

"Yes."

"You won't leave me, will you?" Rhiannon whispered. "Dear God, please don't leave me now."

Iolo lay awake in the narrow bed of his caravan and listened to the thud of wooden mallets on wooden tent-pegs. He remembered dimly how reassuringly that sound had woken him every day when he was a child, but now each stroke meant trouble. The big tent was drawing no custom. Who would leave the safety of their city limits in mid-winter just for a circus? Iolo was tempted to cut his losses, sell the tent and go back to playing in taverns and market squares, but they'd never accept it. He knew that before he'd even considered it. He could never pay them the same wages. He cursed his very first mistake of putting them all on a wage instead of a cut from the take. While people paid to see them, a wage was fine. "But you can't pay yourself what you don't earn," he tried to explain, without success. They thought his treasure trove was bottomless. It wasn't. It already gave off a hollow echo.

What a crew. Iolo laughed cynically at his one-time illusions of a happy devoted family. They had fleeced him for all he was worth. He was past hating them for it. They robbed him without disguise or apology. For his part, he showed he knew quite well what was happening.

"We helped you out of quite a fix, Iolo," Adam would say wryly.

"And ever since then you've helped yourselves."

"You're safer with us." The blackmail was quite explicit. Iolo even found it amusing. He had no more self-respect to lose. Adam had knocked that out of him within the first week. Iolo had learnt every cheat, every swindle, every trick to attract an unwilling audience and suck the last penny out of them.

He watched steam rise from his nostrils into the icy morning air. He ought to get up and try and draw some custom from Shrewsbury. This might be their last chance to pull through. He hauled himself onto the pillow and fell back, sickened. His night-shirt and sheets were soaking for the second night running with the same repulsive discharge.

"Slut," he said beneath his breath to the woman asleep beside him. Her tangled yellow hair fell enticingly around her face—a young, beautiful face, unmarked except for two deep lines around the mouth. No one who saw her now would guess she was a whore. Angel he had called her and she still looked like one, but see where she'd brought him. He daubed his hand in the rank, milky liquid and smeared it across her face. Phoebe moaned, squirmed and turned over. God, he had been green! The first few weeks had been so happy. When Phoebe started getting back late after the show he'd scarcely noticed and certainly hadn't enquired. It turned out she was running a show of her own. Every night, in whatever town, she'd stay behind with men from the audience and take them one after another, all together or whatever they suggested. "It's all part of circus life," she'd explained innocently when Iolo found out. "It was Adam who suggested it. We sometimes do a double act." Of course she had sworn to stop it and Iolo forgave her because she had no idea it was wrong. Adam was found one night with a bullet in his head. "It's all part of circus life," Iolo had said to the troupe and found another master of ceremonies, but Phoebe hadn't changed. Iolo was so infatuated he'd chosen to remain in ignorance as long as he could. Whore or not, she was his one consolation, but he couldn't ignore the rot that was gnawing at his loins.

"Oh, God," he groaned, shifting to try and ease the pain. "What have I come to? Where have You let me wander?" He was sick of his life and frequently thought of putting an end to it with his Spanish pistols. He was sick of his assumed cynicism. He knew how many people he'd betrayed, however hard he tried to dismiss them as part of a separate life for which he was somehow not answerable.

He tried to reason that he hadn't wanted to go to Cwmystwyth in the first place, so why should he be accountable for what happened there? He had been too inexperienced to understand what he was undertaking with his drove and Gruffydd shouldn't have let him go so unprepared, especially after neglecting him for seven years. Besides, Gruffydd had sinned unforgivably in deserting Iolo's mother and deserved no better . . . but as soon as he reached this point, Iolo realized that his treatment of Rhiannon was no better and that sitting in judgement on his father in no way excused his own behaviour. Far from exorcising Gruffydd from his life, the more Iolo accused him the more he understood that they shared the same frailties, and came to love and miss him more than ever. Cwmystwyth haunted him. It was his only real home, even if not of his choosing. He tried to erase it from his mind but his guilt only tormented him more. Then he would summon all his courage and force himself to go back, confess, be judged, submit to any punishment as long as he could be rid of his self-loathing and despair, but before he could even mount his horse, the thought of Rhiannon starving, emaciated and maybe dying struck him cold with remorse and he knew he could never face her again. He had sunk too far and was too ashamed to repent. Sooner or later, when even depravity had lost its last consolations, he would put an end to himself, probably on some quite trivial impulse and without much further thought.

Outside, the thud of mallets stopped, a chorus of ribald jeering went round and an imposing clerical voice started declaiming immediately below Iolo's window.

"This place is a brothel!"

"Too true," Iolo muttered, managing a laugh.

"I will ask you only one question: Are you happy with your lives? . . . You say that you are, but you have not answered my question. Let me ask you again: If you look at yourselves and examine your lives, are you happy with what you see?" It was a resonant, well-placed voice devoid of bombast, ringing with urgency and goodwill, with a slight Welsh flavour in it. Iolo ached for home. "I ask you only because I have myself passed through Sodom once or twice and I know what it smells like." There was a grudging laugh or two, which the voice picked up instantly. "It smells of fear. Not of pleasure and not of luxury but of fear. The fear of death."

That was true, Iolo thought. He could taste it on his own tongue.

"That is the smell that reeks in my nostrils when I pass through your camp."

"Leave over," came a few disgruntled cries. The noise of hammering resumed.

"You can turn your back on me, but not on your own fear."

"One more word," Iolo heard Hugh the lion-tamer say, "and I will teach you the meaning of that word 'fear.'"

"Me you can silence, but the fear of death inside yourself, never." Hugh roared like one of his own lions. A gurgling noise followed.

"I'll have Hugh put down if he does this again!" Iolo swore and leapt out of bed. In the door of the caravan he fired his pistol over Hugh's head. The lion-tamer jumped back, leaving the preacher half-throttled, kneeling on the ground.

"The next one won't miss, Hugh," Iolo said, blowing smoke from the barrel.

"What is it?" Phoebe asked drowsily, sitting up in bed.

"Hugh, as usual." Iolo helped the preacher to his feet. He was a short, powerfully built man of forty-five or so, with a square jaw and heavy eyebrows. His hair was grizzled white with age.

"Thank you," he said, looking Iolo in the eye. "I believe you saved me from a cudgelling once before." Iolo's heart missed three beats. It was Hywel Bevan.

CHAPTER NINETEEN

I

IT WAS AN hour since Gruffydd had finished his story, and neither he nor Rhiannon had moved. Gruffydd sat cross-legged by the smouldering peat fire, as he had done all night, chin cupped in his hands, fingers spreading upwards across his mouth as though it had already said too much. Rhiannon sat on the kitchen chair where he'd placed her, looking down on him. She'd wanted to be closer to him, but he wouldn't have it. "Don't try and make it easier for me," he'd said. "I need your judgement, not your sympathy." She'd felt hurt then, but as the night wore on she'd become grateful for that knobbly kitchen chair. At least it was solid.

"Well?" Gruffydd muttered, without moving his fingers. Why didn't she speak? All the relief of having at last spoken, rising elation as his story got stranger and more wonderful, triumph as layer after layer of deception was stripped away and he finally dared to reveal his origins, his struggle, his weaknesses and his guilt—even the warmth of having at last a friend he could confide in—had all seeped away in those minutes of silence while her verdict hung above him, a sword dangling from a horsehair. One word and the sword would cleave him utterly. "Well?" he repeated.

"What?" Rhiannon was startled. Had he said something? Her back was aching.

"What do you think?"

"I think . . ." What could she think? She could scarcely understand what she'd heard, let alone believe it. Gruffydd sat before her transformed, claiming that nothing of what she'd seen in him was true. He might have turned himself into a dragon or a spider and she'd have been less surprised, but the spiritual metamorphosis he had just performed before her eyes, the dwindling of his magical stature to the cheapscape charlatanry of a circus trickster—how could she ever accept this? This wasn't the man she had hated and worshipped. Years she had spent brooding over his power, pondering the intimacy of that one moment when the other world burst into her life, illuminating it as Hywel's pale promises had never done, and now

275

Gruffydd was telling her it was mere sleight of hand, a brazen gamble in a fit of inebriated confidence. She refused to accept it. He was deluded now rather than then. Grief had unbalanced him and guilt for Iolo had driven him to self-destruction.

What if he had grown up here and knew everyone's names when he returned? That still did not explain how he had cured the cattle plague, or how he had saved her life and delivered Hannah when everyone else had given them up for lost. Those eyes which had stared at her from the oyster-shell lamp had been there in the oil, a physical presence and not some fancy of hers. They had been too vivid, too real, to stem from her own mind. She should know best, because she had seen those eyes and he had not. The more she considered it, the more she feared for Gruffydd's sanity, but it was pointless to argue with him now. She had to humour and comfort him and get him away from Cwmystwyth as fast as possible, because he'd recover his right mind only in quiet and seclusion, somewhere far from here where she could nurse him back to health and strength. She had heard her father talk of a brother in Llanidloes. Surely they would find shelter with him if they went there? She left her chair and went to Gruffydd, where he sat watching her, waiting for her judgement. She knelt beside him and took both his hands in hers.

"I'm glad you told me. I think you were right to act as you did, from that first day onwards, and I will never forget what you did for me and Hannah. You saved us, and nothing changes that." He smiled and his body straightened, as if an immense burden had been lifted from his shoulders, and he leaned forward to kiss her lightly on the mouth with gratitude in his eyes. If she could accept what he had told her that night, nothing more she discovered about him could possibly destroy the trust between them. "But let's not talk any more now. It's not safe for us to stay here. Come away with me and Hannah, anywhere else, we'll make a new life."

"Yes, we'll go," he said. Pure joy bubbled across her face like a mineral spring from under a stone. She threw her arms round his neck and hugged him fiercely. He'd never seen a woman made more beautiful by anything he'd said, as though a faded daffodil had defied nature and flowered twice.

"I'll wake Hannah. We must get ready."

"There's time. I have some farewells to make first."

"You can't. No one must see you." Gruffydd smiled sadly.

"No one living."

"Please don't. Don't leave me alone, even for a minute. Anything could happen. Let's go now, before it's too late."

"Before what's too late?"

"I don't know!" Rhiannon clutched at his arm, suddenly terrified. He freed himself and raced off towards the valley shouting: "Only half an hour."

Gruffydd kept to the woods, his feet swimming weightless over the leafy floor. He felt supple, light-headed, young again for the first time in seven years. He could levitate for sheer exuberance. Soon he'd be free of this place. It peeled away from him as he ran. He saw the ransacked mill, its meadow frosted with flour, torn sacks strewn for hundreds of yards around; the cattle sheds where a charred carcass smouldered on charcoal while the tethered herds bellowed for attention; the tannery, awash with dyes trickling from the upturned vats, staining the Ystwyth purple. They were all deserted, the work of years demolished in one fit of rage. Would they always need a conjurer to scare them and to stop them burning and killing? They hadn't changed. However long he had stayed, they wouldn't have changed. Better they come to terms with themselves now than have Gruffydd carry on lying to them. He climbed the wooded slopes beneath Grogwynion and saw the villagers gathering below on the pebbly banks of the Ystwyth, armed with pitchforks and torches. The occasional shout rose above the sighing of the trees and the river. Someone was haranguing them, as Gruffydd had often done himself. He was too far away to see who it was, but he knew anyway. It was Mihangel.

Gruffydd plunged through the undergrowth, along the familiar paths. He found his waterfall at last. He hadn't been there for months and had a score to settle.

"You led me a fine dance," he said waiting for his spirit to start singing.

"Will the stream ever dry up?" Iolo had asked him once. The stream still flowed but the lady behind it was silent. He knew why. She was not there and never had been. Gruffydd leaned forward till his face grazed the waterfall. He put out a hand letting the water cascade around it. Then he thrust his fist through it. His knuckles hit a rock. He searched every corner with his fingers. Still the same: a flat, smooth, hard expanse of stone.

"No more lies. You were the last of them." His head was clear at last, clear and hollow like a dead tree-trunk that the wind whistles through. With a heart too heavy to be borne Gruffydd turned to go, when he heard, just behind him, the sound of a young woman singing with the even measure of a cradle rocking on wooden hinges. It was a lullaby for his child who was sleeping in Madlen's womb. He stopped. He listened.

II

Madlen reined Venus in to catch her breath. She'd trotted over the mountain track hardly able to see three paces ahead of her, but now the wind had swung to the west and the mist had lifted. Brithgoed lay beneath her shimmering in an unearthly late-afternoon light. The sun sat like a halo on the hills towards the sea, its horizontal rays grazing the uplands, turning the lush green valley—broader here than in Cwmystwyth—to a luminous emerald shot with scarlet. Madlen lost herself for one blissful second, her white haunted face softened and restored to life by the sunlight.

She stretched her aching body towards the sky. It was nicer here and she would be living in this place soon. A slight queasiness reminded her what she was carrying. This time there would be no mistake. Owain was alive again inside her. This time he would get the inheritance he deserved.

The pointed Tudor gables of Brithgoed bristled up at her, a serried rank of pikes. Somehow she had to brave them. She had to carry her plan through to the end, with or without Gruffydd. The courtyard was deserted and the wrought-iron gate hung listlessly ajar. The carefully sculpted French gardens were long since overgrown, their geometric precision lost in a tangle of shrubbery. One of the willows by the Ystwyth had been felled by lightning and left to rot, its trunk gaping hollow.

With a crew of twenty, the grounds could be put to rights in a fortnight. Madlen made a mental note of the best men to employ. The house needed new timber, new slate, new everything. She could see the gaps in the roof from here. Perhaps it would be better to pull it down and start again. Light and modern. With columns in front . . . Madlen saw a palace rising out of the Ystwyth, broad and tall, with a triangular pediment on a marble colonnade, a hundred clear-glazed windows blazing with a thousand candles while an orchestra played. She knew how the gentry should live. She'd seen the mansion Thomas Powell had built at Nanteos when his father died, and heard the tales of balls lasting two nights in a row. And who was Powell? A modest squire. Brithgoed was the heart of the county and Madlen had decided to set it beating again. Her son would receive their guests in an ante-room, at the top of a majestic staircase, while she sat on a dais in the ballroom and looked down on them all. The

278

ailing Lord Kirkland would be confined to his bed and occasionally Dr Madog, well rewarded for his services, would allow him a few visitors. And Gruffydd . . . she couldn't bear to think of Gruffydd. This palace was to have been for him, returned to him by right like any stolen property, shared with him as they had shared everything. Now she discovered he was not worth it and didn't remotely deserve it. He'd betrayed her countless times over. Not so much with Rhiannon. Madlen had almost laughed that off by now—prim, faithful Rhiannon throwing herself at Gruffydd after all these years. She'd get her fingers burned like all the others, and she'd kill him with boredom within a fortnight. No. If Gruffydd could find any comfort with her sad-eyed sister, Madlen would not deprive him. It hurt, but it wasn't the main point, and nor was Gruffydd's sudden, insensate renunciation of everything he'd ever fought for—the pain or Owain's death was enough to explain that. She could understand his despair and she shared it, though her pregnancy was a miraculous consolation and gave her hope for the future. What really galled her, what she would never forgive Gruffydd for, was his deceit. For years he had suspected he was no conjurer, yet he'd never told her. She'd shared his life, but not his mind. She'd known nothing about him. Gruffydd had taken advantage of a girlish fantasy and had kept her enthralled to it so he could feed off her. Madlen had long outgrown it, she understood that now. Faith in his magical powers had been a protective chrysalis, nothing more. Now she could shed it in the fullness of her own confidence. She didn't give a cuss if Gruffydd was a real conjurer or not, because she'd learnt from her own experience that man controls his own destiny: success in this world is not in the gift of spirits—you must fight for it with every means in your power, fair or foul, and the winner is the one who wants it most. She realized now, of course, that nothing but her own foresight had sustained Gruffydd this long and that if he'd only been straight with her she could have done better. He could have had an ally, if only he'd trusted her. Now it was too late. He'd ruined himself and nearly ruined her. She would save him if she could, because she still loved him—more than ever in some ways—and all his insecurity and waywardness, which had seemed demeaning in a conjurer, were understandable in this ordinary mortal who was struggling with such a lonely secret. Beneath her bitterness stirred an unwilling admiration for his resourcefulness, his powers of invention and his ability to inspire and control the minds of men. Why had he been reluctant to admit to himself and to her that these gifts were native? If only he had had the courage to use them to the full, for his own ends, he would have been invincible, but he'd allowed petty doubts and a misconceived idea of duty to distract him. It infuriated her, because their present misfortune was so unnecessary. They could have blamed both Owain's death and Iolo's on Mihangel and disposed of him while saving themselves. But she wouldn't let Gruffydd drag her down. There were too many good things in life that she'd only just started to enjoy. With Maude dead, the field was open.

A single candle flickered into life in the diamond-paned window of Maude's room. Madlen was suddenly alert. Maude was lying in there. They must have found her hours ago. There was still no movement anywhere around Brithgoed, no one rushing about giving orders, no hammering, no mournful peal from the chapel bells, no rumble of hearse wheels. Madlen wanted to shout from the hillside: "Don't you all know she's dead?"

But perhaps she was not. Had Madlen used the wrong bottle? Maude might not have died for hours, and could then have told Ffowlke who did it. Why was there only one light in the whole house? A childhood memory leapt to her mind with terrifying clarity. She was standing in a shift at the bedroom window watching the full moon. Rhiannon was asleep. As she stood there a pale bluish light, two feet off the ground, came through the closed door of Job the Carpenter's cottage, across the Ystwyth. It crossed the bridge, travelling faster than a man can walk, and passed beneath the vicarage window. No one was carrying it. It hovered for a few seconds above an elder bush in the graveyard, then it vanished. The next morning Job was found dead in his bed. The elder bush was torn up to make room for him. "That was the corpse-candle you saw," Madlen's father had said gravely. "Others have seen it before you. Now forget about it." She couldn't think of her father now, or of herself as that girl in the shift watching the full moon.

The corpse-candle had come to visit Maude now. She would be carried to the graveyard soon, to lie in the ground. Madlen stared at Maude's window till night had spread from the valley bottom to the tip of Pen Dinas on the western skyline by Aberystwyth, and the dew rose frostily through her thin leather boots. Then she pulled her shawl tighter around her neck and nudged Venus forward at a walk. Whatever had happened, she couldn't run away from it now. She made her way down the rocky track, looking behind her every twenty yards. The fields on either side were deserted. Ffowlke's cattle had been taken in for the winter or sold off to the drovers. She tethered Venus to one of the willows dangling forlornly into the Ystwyth. The wrought-iron gates creaked gently. She passed the gap in the hedge which she'd squeezed through only that morning and felt nervously for the rip in her sleeve. Of course it wouldn't give her away. It could have happened anywhere. Madlen had to stop herself from creeping under the windows again.

You're going to betray yourself, she thought, horrified. You've no idea she's dead. You've just come to find out how she is. It's your job. You're meant to be here. She threw back her head and walked firmly up the cracked steps, past the lopsided stone cannon-balls on the balustrades. As she pushed the door open she glanced at the flower-bed beneath Maude's window. The phial of poison and Talbot's handkerchief were gone. They must know she was dead, then. Would anyone really believe Talbot had done it?

Through the gloom of the panelled entrance hall she felt her way to Ffowlke's study. It smelled of tobacco. Not a glimmer from the hearth. Her foot hit something metallic. It fell over, clattering on the stone floor.

"Is anyone here?" she shouted, far too loud. Her voice echoed from the cellars to the ceiling. Madlen climbed the stairs, feeling for each step with her toe, clinging to the smooth wooden banister. As she reached the top her hand met someone else's. Madlen screamed in pure terror.

III

Gruffydd had been gone all day. Rhiannon had packed up as much as they'd be able to carry in horsehair blankets. The blankets would keep them alive at night. Many of her own belongings—the spinning wheel, the cradle, baking dishes, pots and clothes—would have to be left behind. She'd taken nothing of Hywel's. Rachel would find the house in perfect order when she returned from Ystrad Meurig. Rhiannon had nailed a note for Thomas Jenkins on the door, instructing him to send for Rachel to take possession of her property. She wondered what Rachel would do with the house. Sell it? Or use it to entice one of the more eligible young men in the valley? There were plenty who would take her, though God help the poor lad she accepted.

Hannah was swinging on the trapeze that Iolo had hung from the rafters of the new barn. It worried Rhiannon to see her running about and playing. They had to leave for good soon. She called her and tucked her under her cloak, and they waited together on the blankets in front of the door as though Gruffydd would only pass once and they must be ready to follow him that second. Hannah dozed off.

Would she be all right? She was so young, so small. Was Rhiannon right to take her away from her home? It would be a terrible journey. There'd be snow on the top and they mightn't find shelter, or firewood. She'd managed to provide enough scraps for a day or two. It should be enough. Llanidloes was only twenty miles away, so she'd heard. Her father had often spoken of his brother who lived there, a weaver with a business of his own. Pray God he was still alive. Surely he would help them if he had only half of his brother's charity. Llanidloes lay to the north-east. They'd find the way somehow.

"It's dangerous," she whispered in Hannah's ear. "But we have to do it."

Where was Gruffydd? The woods were ominously still. There was no sound from the nearest cottages and not a murmur from the valley. She couldn't get used to the silence of the farm: no cows bellowing, not a dog barking—all of Iolo's had long since been eaten. The nests in the barn-eaves were deserted and soon not even Rhiannon would be here. Another hour went by, perhaps two. Time might have stopped, leaving them frozen by this door. The cold crept through Rhiannon's wooden clogs and thick woollen stockings, but she couldn't go back in. She would never come out again.

"Please, dear God, send Gruffydd to me now!"

From far beyond Black Rock a distant thud broke the icy stillness. A crow flew squawking from the beech by the new barn and the forest moaned gently. She heard it again. Connected this time, carried on the wind or, rather, driving a wind ahead of it. Horses' hoofs. Quite distinct. Coming over Black Rock. Two of them by the sound of it and getting closer. Had Gruffydd stolen horses for them? They'd be in Llanidloes tomorrow! But maybe he was being followed. Maybe they'd both be thrown in gaol.

The horses hit the valley like a clap of thunder. Hoofs echoing from the mines, through the woods, off Black Rock. Suddenly it sounded as if they were converging from all sides. It might be a whole squadron of cavalry.

It was the militia! Of course—the militia. Gruffydd had said they'd be out. They were chasing him. Who else would they go for? She dropped the bundle and swung Hannah, still bleary-eyed, onto her hip, ready to leap into the saddle behind Gruffydd.

Two horses burst from the woods at a gallop. Two horses with two riders.

It wasn't Gruffydd. Nor the militia. They weren't in uniform. Two men in black coats, covered in mud. Rhiannon settled down for another long wait. The men must have ridden a long way. They were slouched forward, exhausted. One of them waved to her, shouting something, and she waved back disconsolately. They wheeled about just opposite the gate and one of the riders tried to jump the fence but the horse shied. He leapt off and vaulted the fence, then ran towards her on shaky legs, arms outstretched. A young man, wild-looking, with a tousled beard. He carried a dagger and pistols in his belt. Rhiannon backed away. He resembled Gruffydd. The likeness was uncanny and scared her worse than his weapons. Then she screamed in sheer terror. It was Iolo. Ashen-faced and winded from the headlong ride, he fell to his knees ten feet away from her and crawled through the frozen, cratered mud to her feet. Rhiannon squeezed herself flat against the door.

"Are you flesh and blood? Or have you come from hell to torment me?" Iolo lifted his hand. "Don't touch me," she shrieked. He seized the hem of her dress and pressed it to his lips.

"Forgive me. Please forgive me," he said again and again, in a voice hoarse with tears. He fumbled in his breast pocket with the other hand and pulled out a leather pouch.

"For the cows. Not enough, but it's all that's left." Rhiannon was too dazed to speak. "Don't accuse me, please," Iolo begged her, seeing only the rejection he expected. "I know what I've done to you. Take it, for God's sake." She slowly put out her hand. Iolo pressed the pouch into it. She could feel the ridge of coins beneath the leather, hear the chink of metal. His fingers were cold, but they were solid.

"You're alive! You've come home! My son is alive." She threw her arms round his neck.

Iolo pressed his cheek against hers and wept uncontrollably.

"I never meant to desert you. I didn't want to harm you. I wanted to help . . ."

"Shush," Rhiannon said gently, caressing his mud-splattered hair. "There's time to explain."

"I always meant to come back. You must believe me."

"I do," she said, smiling. He was older and more rugged, but he hadn't changed. "Your father was told you were dead."

"My father?"

"You'll see him soon." Surely Iolo would come with them now? What else tied him to Cwmystwyth besides herself and Gruffydd? "But who is your friend? We mustn't leave him outside." The other rider was leaning against the fence, turned away from them, recovering his breath. He'd cast a furtive glance or two in their direction, but he seemed anxious not to disturb them. He was much older than Iolo, with grizzled white hair cropped close to the skull; solidly built, but hardly able to stand after the ride. "He looks very tired. Who is he?"

"Don't you recognize him?"

"Should I?"

"Of course you should. It's Hywel." Rhiannon turned pale, swaying slightly.

"No. It can't be. He looks nothing like Hywel." Iolo put an arm round her waist to support her.

"I may have lost a lot of your money, but at least I brought Hywel home to you." He was so anxious to please her, so desperate to be forgiven.

"Oh God, Iolo. What have you done?" Her eyes were dry, she was past weeping. Her new life with Gruffydd, every hope of happiness, was snuffed out like a candle by a slammed door. Fate had patiently waited through seven years of renunciation to play this monstrous joke on her. "One day sooner and you'd have saved me, my honour, my faith in God, everything. Now I'd be better off dead." Iolo stared aghast at her hostile, stunned eyes. He understood only that he'd made a disastrous mistake. Why did everything always turn out wrong? Hywel had seemed a heaven-sent redeemer, rescuing him from the pit of self-loathing, dragging him out of a mire of contemptuous indifference . . . and in his very person offering the means of atoning to Rhiannon.

"I thought if I brought him back with me, you might forgive me. If it weren't for him I wouldn't have dared show my face. Please don't say we shouldn't have come back!" Rhiannon scarcely seemed to hear him. Her eyes were fixed on some point far behind him.

"How terrible Thou art, O Lord," she muttered quietly. "Thy judgement lies heavy upon sinners." Iolo clasped both her hands in his.

"Hywel's waiting for you. Please go and talk to him." A sudden spasm of rage crossed her face.

"No!" she said savagely. "Tell him he's too late. Does he think he can just walk in here after what he's done to me?"

"Hannah!" she called, swinging their bundle over her shoulder. "We're leaving." She was going with or without Gruffydd. She would not lie to Hywel, nor would she beg his forgiveness. He could plead for hers first. She had climbed too far to return to wifely obedience, and might as well be damned for a happy sinner as a wretched one. Hannah came running from behind the new barn. She was flushed and excited.

"Gruffydd's in the barn," she whispered in Rhiannon's ear. Hannah hesitated a second, mouthing her message to make sure she'd got it right. "He says: 'I am ready to go this minute, if you will come with me.'" Rhiannon's heart leapt. They could still be happy. This meeting with Hywel was nothing but a final reckoning, a glorious revenge. She would walk away from under his nose with his greatest enemy.

"Please," Iolo said, following her gaze to the barn. "Go and speak to Hywel. Just a few words. You owe it to him."

"I owe him nothing," Rhiannon snapped. She seemed to be a different woman, strident, harsher.

"Perhaps not, but the least you can do is hear him, after he's come all this way." He tried to take the bundle from her. Rhiannon pushed his hand aside.

Hywel turned his head towards her and looked away again when he saw her watching him. His face was heavily lined, an old man's. What could he have to say for himself? He couldn't hurt her. They'd both changed and what could there possibly be between them now? Rhiannon nodded her head deliberately three times towards the barn and raised her hand. Then she walked across the farmyard.

Hywel stood with his hands side by side, palms down, gripping the fence. He stared at her. Not unpleasantly. He was charting her face, comparing it to a map unrolled somewhere in his head, a mariner exploring a long-forgotten coast. It unnerved her. He was unshaven. His cheeks were slack and his stubbly beard was quite white. The old, dark, threatening countenance was gone. Only the forehead was the same, heavy, brooding as before, strangely unlined. His dark eyes were veiled by an opaque, whitish film. He screwed up his eyelids as though he had trouble seeing. Rhiannon found him distasteful. His fresh, mud-spattered travel scars hid a deeper grime. He hadn't washed for days. His clothes were not so much old as uncared for. An odour of moral decay rose with the stale sweat of his armpits.

"God bless you!" His voice was as powerful as ever, a bass rumble, its old authority intact behind his disreputable appearance. Rhiannon shuddered. She had just recognized her husband. "I've come to ask your pardon." His voice was defiant, conscious of its own effect. Hywel lowered himself painfully onto one knee. "Then you must choose what's to become of me."

"Get up, please." Rhiannon was embarrassed. She wanted nothing to do with his guilt.

"I won't," he said doggedly, prepared to kneel all night. "I've done you a great wrong. I won't move till you've heard me."

"Well?" Simplest to let him speak. Had Hywel discovered humility at last?

"Iolo's told me what your life's been like. He's a good boy, Iolo. I wouldn't be here if it weren't for him. Whatever you think of me, don't be hard on him."

"Iolo doesn't need you to plead for him. Say what you want to say."

Hywel tried to pull his thoughts together. They wouldn't come. He had to confess and didn't know where to start. He'd heard too many confessions from others and resented being made to change roles before a woman. Not even regret came naturally to him.

"I . . . I was wrong. I should never have left you." Rhiannon almost laughed. Did he imagine this was enough?

"Why did you?"

"Because I . . . damn it . . ." The first time she'd heard him swear. "You hurt me. You lied to me. You made a fool of me." His head was lowered behind the fence but she could feel the scowl on his face. Even now he was angry with her. He had not forgiven her yet. He hadn't changed.

"Why do you think I lied to you?"

"Because I bullied you." Hywel took the words out of her mouth. "I treated you like a child. You were scared of me." Rhiannon nodded, surprised. "I've been through it countless times. I brought it on myself. You weren't to blame. I left in anger and that's no way to leave anyone, let alone a wife. I knew at once I was wrong."

"Then why didn't you come back?" How fruitless his self-knowledge was now.

"Pride," Hywel whispered with a strange gnashing sound. "Pride made me leave, because you'd made such a fool of me that night that I couldn't bear to look at a soul in this valley again for fear they'd laugh in my face. Pride kept me away, because I couldn't admit I'd been wrong in the first place." He thumped his clenched fist against his forehead as if to dislodge some terrible growth inside. Rhiannon felt sick. Seven years wasted for a man's wounded vanity. Every second that she'd believed he was justly punishing her, Hywel had merely been too scared for his own dignity. Anything else she could have forgiven him, but not this, not such rank cowardice. "So to cover up for myself, I swore that I'd be the greatest preacher in Wales, just to prove myself in the right. By God, I did it! You should have seen them, flocking to me in their thousands. 'Hywel the Baptist,' they called me. 'He gave up everything he had, left his land and his family behind, just to preach God's Word.'" Hywel laughed bitterly, his passionate voice mocking its own power, contemptuous of its own emptiness. Rhiannon had never heard such a terrible sound uttered by a human soul. "Oh, there's a terrible pride in poverty! Renunciation's not so hard if you have the right reasons. Little did they know, those legions that I dragged by the scruff of the neck to salvation, that I was half-way down the road to hell myself because I'd sold my dearest for the glory of being Wales's best preacher. And it's not gone yet." Hywel shielded his head as though winged demons were clawing at it. "That's the worst of it. I can't speak, can't even think without it creeping up on me. It'll never leave me. I'll be fighting it till I die." He threw this at her almost as a threat. A challenge, perhaps.

Rhiannon stared at him through the slatted fence as if through the grille of a confessional or the bars of a prison. She was shut out again. Like that day in Aberystwyth gaol, like every day of their life together, he had let her in as far as he wished her to see, no further. She had never met such merciless, unflinching self-criticism. Not a trace of self-pity. No room for compassion or companionship either. She was overwhelmed by the futility of his story. Hywel was set on contemplating the dreary wastes of his own soul and nobody could distract him or make it easier for him. She couldn't then, and certainly couldn't now.

"Please don't imagine that I ever forgot you," Hywel said anxiously, guessing near enough what she must be thinking. "I tried to, but I never came near it. I carried your face with me at every step, tormenting myself with it . . . Oh, God, I've missed you!" His mouth trembled violently. Without warning tears gushed from his eyes. "Oh, God! Have pity on me, Rhiannon. Give me some rest. To my soul at least, if not to my body."

Rhiannon was shocked. She had never seen him cry. Why couldn't he have cried before? Seven years ago she could have comforted him. She tried to summon her old, thwarted tenderness for him. It wouldn't come. Any affection she once had was dead.

"Why are you crying?" said a voice at Rhiannon's shoulder.

"Run along, Hannah," Rhiannon scolded her. Too late. Hywel put his hand through the fence, fumbling over the girl's face.

"Are you Hannah?" he asked, in wonderment, his hardened features breaking into life.

"Yes. Who are you?"

Hywel leaned over the fence and swept Hannah into his arms. Rhiannon was panic-stricken. She'd listened too long. How could she get Hannah away from him? How could they leave now?

"Wait," she said. "You don't understand. There are other men." Perhaps if she exaggerated, she'd put him off. Hywel's forehead tensed.

"The blame is mine." This was his punishment. He had no right to judge her. "It was a long time."

"You don't know," she blurted, trying to say "Gruffydd"—nothing else would put him off. She couldn't get the name across her lips. Hywel's presence had taken possession of her again.

"Are you my father?" Hannah asked curiously.

"Yes, Hannah." Hywel smiled for the first time in years. "May we go indoors? The child is cold." She had to say no, this instant. Once Hannah was in the house she'd never get her out again. But what hope had she now of taking Hywel's daughter from him? He'd never allow it and by law he could claim her as his own however long he'd neglected her. If they escaped he would only follow them and then he might forbid her to see Hannah at all. She couldn't risk that. She couldn't abandon her only child to such a father. Whatever happiness of her own was at stake, she had a duty to Hannah. She prayed that Gruffydd would understand. She loved him more than her own soul, but not more than the child he'd brought into the world. It tortured her to think of him alone, believing perhaps that she hadn't cared for him or that she'd betrayed his trust. But she had no choice. How could he love her if she deserted Hannah?

Rhiannon opened the farmyard gate and watched Hannah run to join Iolo by the door of the house, with Hywel chasing after her. Then very slowly she followed them, averting her eyes from the new barn. She didn't look back and she made no sign as she closed the door.

A few minutes later, Hannah came out again and ran across to the gate. Making sure she couldn't be seen from the house, she doubled back to the new barn. Gruffydd was sitting in the dark on a cart-wheel, the same as an hour ago.

"My father's come home," she said excitedly. Gruffydd lifted her onto his knee.

"I know."

"I don't like him," Hannah prattled. "He's too old. And so sad."

"Be quiet and listen. I want you to remember what I tell you now, always. Will you?" Hannah nodded silently, impressed, her lips tightly pursed. "You must never mention me to your father. Never tell him I was here while he was away. Have you got that?"

"Why not?"

"It doesn't matter. If you love your mother—you do, don't you?" Hannah nodded again, frowning, very serious. "Then never talk about me, to anyone. I want you to remember me. Remember that I love your mother and you—"

"I'm sorry we can't go away together," Hannah interrupted. She knew why he was unhappy.

"—And if either of you ever need me, you must come and get me. Will you do that? Because I have something that belongs to you. You were born in it. It's very lucky."

"What is it?"

"Just remember to ask me for it. Now, where are you going?"

"To ask Thomas Jenkins to send for Rachel in Ystrad Meurig. Iolo's going to marry her."

IV

The hand gently folded around Madlen's and a man's voice laughed in the darkness. Madlen leapt back and tripped down several steps. Her ankles buckled under her and she fell on her knees on the next landing. Two heavy thuds followed her. He was coming down four steps at a time. She scrambled up and tried to flee. An iron grip caught her wrist, swung her round. Massive hands lifted her off the ground, pushed her back up the stairs, forced her at a run down the corridor. They were going towards Maude's room. The door was open. He shoved her and she tumbled through it and fell on the floor. Maude was propped up on a pillow facing her, eyes open, smiling cryptically.

"It's all right. She's thoroughly dead." Madlen swung round. Talbot. He was leaning with his back against the door, both hands clasped on the handle behind him, lowering like a bull about to charge.

"What do you mean? What do you mean, 'all right'?" She went to the bed and touched Maude's forehead in mock concern. Stone cold. Already smelling slightly. Probably twelve hours gone.

"You poisoned her."

"Poisoned?" Madlen exaggerated her surprise.

"With this." He pulled Mihangel's phial out of his scarlet military coat, watching her closely.

"I've never even seen it before. I have to speak to Lord Kirkland." Talbot grabbed her shoulder and pushed her back against the bed. Madlen sat down abruptly on Maude's feet.

"Do you know what I found with it?"

"I've no idea."

"I found this handkerchief. It's mine." He held it up to within an inch of her face. Madlen looked down her nose at it.

"What's that to me?"

"You put it there," Talbot raged, infuriated by her composure.

"To implicate me. To blacken my name still farther with my brother."

"God forbid that I should come between brothers." Talbot hit her across the jaw. She keeled over onto the floor nearly unconscious.

"She told me," Talbot said, pointing his finger at Maude's amused face. "She told me herself." Through the blinding pain in her head Madlen was somehow conscious he was bluffing. The voice was hollow, the wave of the finger too rhetorical. Pass out, she told herself. It's your best defence. She remained stubbornly conscious. Talbot hauled her up by the shoulders and shook her, shouting in her face. Then he pulled off the silver-buckled belt that he wore around his waist and raised his arm.

"You're mad. I was only her nurse. Why should I kill her?"

"I don't know. But I intend to find out." Madlen backed away. He swung the belt at her. It caught the bedpost. She ran for the partition door into Ffowlke's bedroom. He cut her off, slashing at her face. She lifted her hands just in time. The leather bit deep into her wrists. She was trapped in a corner. Talbot loomed over her, blocking any escape. He was going to maim her. Madlen screamed. For a second he hesitated and looked round. Long enough. Madlen's hand reached out for the candle—the corpse-candle—and with one thrust she stabbed the flame and the boiling wax into his eye. Talbot squealed in a sudden darkness like a stuck pig. It felt as if his head had been split open. He reached for the water jug and knocked it over. Then his rage got the better of him. He thrashed around the room, throwing the furniture over, kicking and flailing in every corner to find her.

"I'll kill you," he bellowed. "I'll murder you for this." Madlen crawled into the bed beside Maude and pulled the bedclothes over her head. Talbot swung his fists above the bed but he never felt inside it.

"Have you finally taken leave of your senses?" John Ffowlke stood in the door holding an oil-lamp. Talbot looked around, dazed, fumbling at his eye. He saw nothing through it. The room was utterly destroyed. Only Maude's benign smile remained the same. Madlen slipped out of the bed and sobbed pathetically on the floor.

"He tried to kill me," she wailed. "I only came to help her ladyship and he accuses me of murdering her."

"You have dishonoured our family, and insulted my wife," Ffowlke said, holding on to the bedpost and trying to conquer the alarm he felt in Talbot's presence. "You have finally revealed yourself for what you are. I must ask you never to enter this house while I live." Talbot wiped his mouth on his sleeve and made to speak. "Get out. Get out. Get out."

"I'll see you hang," Talbot spat at Madlen and left.

"My poor girl," Ffowlke said, helping her up and hugging her to his chest.

"Oh, thank you for rescuing me," Madlen bleated, huddled against him. "You were so brave. He might have turned on you. I had no idea her ladyship had passed on. What a terrible blow for you . . ." She looked up at him tenderly, tears in her eyes. "Just as she was carrying your child." Ffowlke's eyes met hers. She squeezed closer to him and his decrepit body trembled.

"There may be another chance." Madlen hardly dared to breathe.

"You mean . . . you might remarry?" Her head was turned up, inviting. His mouth quivered and he made to kiss her and put his arms behind her waist, then a spasm of terror crossed his face and he broke away.

"Where's Gruffydd?" he said, suddenly furious. "Why were my surveyors murdered? Where was he when my wife died? I want him here, now." He stamped like a petulant child, wild at not daring to take what he wanted. Madlen closed her eyes wearily. His lust alone was not enough. He was too scared of Gruffydd to risk offending him, even with his rents unpaid and the valley in turmoil. She needed Gruffydd's consent. She'd have to persuade him somehow. "I won't give in to Talbot. I'll father an heir despite him. I want Gruffydd to find me a bride. A local girl, proven child-bearer. Any wench will do."

Madlen set out on foot for Cwmystwyth. The undertakers had arrived and had commandeered Venus for Maude's funeral.

CHAPTER TWENTY

I

GRUFFYDD SAT FOR hours in Rhiannon's barn, gazing up into the darkened rafters where a colony of bats, which he'd disturbed in its hibernation, was flitting restlessly to and fro with sharp, indignant squeaks.

"I won't trouble you long," he said quietly. "Just give me a few more minutes." An hour later he was still there. Voices drifted over from the farmhouse, sporadic bursts of laughter, Hywel's deep voice ringing with some prayer or other. Gruffydd listened for Rhiannon. He never heard her. Her voice wouldn't carry, he told himself, and wondered if she was talking and laughing too. He couldn't believe he'd lost her. No woman had ever turned him away. She couldn't go back to Hywel, not after what had passed between them. She would come out any minute.

Gruffydd carried on an imaginary conversation with Hannah, to pass the time. "Where shall we live? Where would you like me to take you?"

"To see the painted Indians," Hannah said. "The ones that sailors talk about in Aberystwyth." Gruffydd commandeered a boat and they set sail for America, the three of them, where he built them a log cabin by the side of a broad, lazy river . . . The bats began to swoop at him, their leathery wings grazing his hair. Gruffydd pulled an old oilcloth over him and stubbornly continued his day-dream. He'd often thought about America. It was one of the few places he'd never been. Acres of free land. He tried to imagine the inland prairie a French soldier from Quebec had told him of. No one to interfere. No magistrates. No gentry. No redcoats. They would have done well there.

Would have. He knew he was pretending. She had left him. Why couldn't he face up to it? The bats chased him as far as the door. It was snowing. Strips of yellow candlelight fell across the farmyard from chinks in the hatch-windows, catching each snowflake for one brilliant moment before it was sucked on into the darkness by the wind.

Gruffydd's feet crunched softly. The snow settled at once on his beard and in his long tangled hair, turning him into the Grey King whom mothers whisper of to scare their children.

He stared at the cracks of light, oblivious to the snow and the wind. Why had he waited so long by the waterfall? He'd proved for certain there was no real creature living there, spirit or human, yet the lady continued to fascinate him despite his apparent logic, an unbroken spell cast around the valley holding him in, more secure than hoops of iron around a barrel.

"You've ruined me," he murmured, shivering with a sudden presentiment of his end. "I'll never leave here now. You knew that, didn't you?"

From the farmhouse came the strains of a Calvinist hymn. Gruffydd swore under his breath to think their moonshine could have taken him in for one minute. Hywel's booming bass drove the other two irresistibly along. Rhiannon's tremolo sometimes drowned altogether, Iolo enthusiastically out of tune. Gruffydd huddled under the eaves and squinted through one of the cracks in the shutters. At first he saw only the fire, as if at the end of a long tunnel, but when he put his head sideways and looked with his left eye he could see the three of them clearly, framed in an oval with the fire behind them, a cameo in silhouette. Hywel's head was thrown back, his mouth agape like a gargoyle spouting rain-water.

". . . Chastise my erring flesh . . ." they were singing. Gruffydd hadn't heard a Calvinist hymn in the valley for seven years. The resonant, congratulatory tones of self-abasement made him sick with anger.

How could she? How could she go through with this lie? Gruffydd lifted his fist to beat on the hatch-window. Rhiannon turned away from the other two, lifting her hand to her face as if she had something in her eye, and came to the window barely a yard away from Gruffydd. Her face was an agony of lines, eyes screwed up, lips curled under her teeth. From the way the light hit her cheeks he could see they were soaking. Hywel gazed at her crumpled back with a benign smile. When he'd sung the hymn to the last mellow note, he went and held her heaving shoulders, saying: "Your tears of joy will wash away our sorrows." Rhiannon nodded vigorously and put her hand on his, then she turned abruptly and buried her face in his chest.

A cold sweat broke out on Gruffydd's palms. She was glad Hywel was back. Any minute she'd fall on her knees and beg his pardon, confess that the wicked conjurer seduced her with his magic, that she never loved him. No, of course she hadn't loved him. She would promise Hywel that, and he needn't worry. It was true. She had abandoned him with the greatest of ease. Gruffydd dug his fingernails into his hands. He needed physical pain to distract him. Rhiannon had tricked him. She'd only wanted him because she couldn't manage alone. She had been thinking of Hywel all the time. He'd thrown away everything on her. He stared at his hands and didn't recognize them. "What have I done?" he said aloud. His voice thudded dull and metallic inside his head. "Deserted Madlen. Abandoned the valley. Betrayed my ancestors and my offspring. And what for?" His infatuation with Rhiannon crumbled like ancient clay exposed to fresh air. It was a child's fantasy, a senile dream of renewed first love. Gwenllian's face leapt to his mind, fair and frail, suggesting a mysterious inner life. Rhiannon even looked like her. Why hadn't he realized? He was trying to appease Gwenllian through Iolo's foster-mother. He couldn't make amends to her through Rhiannon! Rhiannon couldn't shrive him. You can never atone for the dead. You can never relive the past.

Gruffydd was running out of excuses for himself and began to wonder if he hadn't just got cold feet. Rhiannon had just been an easy way out of trouble. He hadn't been able to face staying here, so he'd latched on to Rhiannon and left Madlen to clear up the mess he'd caused. All his doubts, all his qualms and his conscience—just cowardice. He was a coward. He sat under Rhiannon's window and considered this, throwing pebbles into the frozen rain-barrel.

Iolo's muted voice came from inside the house, telling the story of his drove. Gruffydd couldn't bring himself to listen. Iolo had betrayed him. He had run off when he was needed and come back when he wasn't. He should have stayed dead.

"Thank God Hywel found me," Iolo said, his voice ripe with religious fervour. Gruffydd turned his head to the crack in the window in time to see Iolo, flushed and elated, seize Hywel's hand and lift it to his lips, saying, "My spiritual father."

"We have work to do, you and I," Hywel said. "God's word has spread to every part of Wales. Only this valley remains in ignorance. Our own home! There are chapels and schools to be built. Congregations will spring up like—"

Gruffydd brought a rock down on the rain-barrel, shattering the ice.

"What was that?"

"Nothing," Rhiannon said nervously.

"Of course it was something. Someone's out there."

"I'll go." Iolo took the musket from its rack. Rhiannon caught his hand.

"No, leave it."

"He might need it," Hywel snapped.

Iolo made his way round the house, musket at the ready.

"Don't move," he said fiercely, raising it to his shoulder. A man was leaning against the rain-barrel, a huge shadow against the snow. "Who are you?" The man walked slowly towards him. "I said don't move. I'll shoot."

"Why don't you? Finish off what you've begun."

"Father!" Iolo dropped the musket and ran towards him. Gruffydd's fist landed on Iolo's nose and he collapsed in the snow, blood streaming from his nostrils. "Please. Let me explain!"

A horse-drawn sledge, carrying a single oil-lamp, trundled out of the woods.

"Your bride, I think," Gruffydd said. "Shouldn't you get up to greet her?"

"Iolo!" Hywel called from the door.

"You don't understand," Iolo said, struggling to his feet. "You've never understood." Hywel came round the side of the house brandishing a pickaxe. Gruffydd pulled his cloak over his head and plunged into the forest.

"Stop," Iolo shouted, firing the musket in the air.

"Who was it?" Hywel asked.

"No idea." Iolo wiped his nose on his sleeve. "Never seen him before in my life."

II

"Gruffydd is back," Madlen cried aloud, limping round the last promontory of Black Rock. The Round House was ablaze with rush torches, a Catherine wheel spinning against the dark granite of the cliff behind it. Madlen raised a hand.

"Dear God," she murmured, sitting gingerly on the nearest stone. She felt dizzy and sick. "Not a miscarriage, please. Not after all this. If Gruffydd is sane again we might have a chance still."

Her jaw ached where Talbot had hit her and she was covered with scratches and bruises. "If you survive this," she said to the child inside her, "you'll survive anything." Heavy, brooding snow-clouds sat immovable on the hilltops, disgorging their load with a quiet vengeance. Madlen had scarcely felt it. She saw now that steam was rising from her bodice. Her torn skirt was soaking to the knees. Not far

295

now. She dragged herself to her feet and walked the last few yards. The torches burned warm and welcoming. Half a dozen villagers were working around the house. A good sign. Gruffydd had won back a few friends. She smiled bravely at Huw Lloyd, who was carrying sacks from a horse-sledge to the kitchen door. He glanced at her from under his load and passed by without a word. The heavy oak front door, carved with scenes from Gruffydd's arrival, was guarded by two burly labourers with pitchforks. She'd never seen them before.

"No entry," they said barring the way.

"What do you mean?"

"The conjurer's not to be disturbed."

"Do you know who I am?"

They shook their heads impassively.

"I'm his wife. Go and tell him I'm here." They conferred in whispers and one of them went in. He reappeared almost immediately.

"The conjurer says you can go in." Madlen pushed past them. Mihangel was sitting cross-legged by the fire, his back to her.

"Where's Gruffydd?"

"Gone."

"Gone?"

"No one can find him. Just as well for him." Huw Lloyd came in from the kitchen.

"I've left the barley in there, master," he said, avoiding Madlen's eyes.

"Good," Mihangel waved him out. "And don't forget the six cows." Madlen felt as if she had strayed into a different world.

"What's happening?"

Mihangel held his hands up to the fire.

"It's my payment. I'm the conjurer now."

III

Gruffydd stood on the great rock Grogwynion and stared at his homeland.

He forgot to brush the snow out of his hair and cloak, forgot that this was the last time he would see it. The snowstorm that had hounded him through Cwmystwyth and up the mountainside had rolled eastward, leaving the night air crisp and rarefied like beaten silver. Ridges and valleys stretched at his feet towards every point of the compass, lit not by the pale full moon behind the clouds that still floundered on the distant hills, nor by the myriad stars so bright he could almost pluck them from the ether with his hand, but by a magical bluish light that pulsated within the snow itself and gave the world a second daytime.

No, not daytime, Gruffydd thought, his anger dissolving in wonder. Daylight always brought noise with it. The country beneath him lay smothered in silence. Not a sound rose through the snow. Only ten miles away there might be thunder, but nothing reached his ears. It was how he imagined the underworld—sunless and soundless. Some of the landscape's radiant peacefulness seeped through him, filling him with a terrible longing to stay, to be accepted back in the community he'd grown up in.

"I only ask to live here," he said to the spirits of the valley whom he suspected to be listening still, despite his profane unbelief. "Just as an ordinary man, like my neighbours. I don't want anything special. I don't lay any claim to any power any more." He pulled out the parchment strapped around his shoulder and slowly tore it up, watching the pieces float one by one into the darkness and down to the Ystwyth. It had been an empty dream. His dynasty had been cut off before it began, snuffed out by the early death of one son and the Calvinist treachery of another. He thought briefly of his unborn child in Madlen's womb, saw himself prostrate in front of her, begging her to take him back. Impossible. He couldn't do it. How could he go crawling to Mihangel begging to be left in peace, confess everything to John Ffowlke, or worse still go on lying to him? He didn't want to see Iolo grow into a black Calvinist scab and he refused to be drummed into church on Sundays with a servile, hypocritical congregation whispering behind their fingers, "That's Gruffydd. Pretended he was a conjurer. Seven years. Of course, I never believed him. Ungodly superstition." No, he wouldn't stay. He was angry with himself for considering it.

He hadn't meant to come to Grogwynion at all. The place always had a power to hold him. Gruffydd shook off his weakness and swung away from the valley. Five steps through the snow and the bleak, uninhabited slopes of Pumlumon's five peaks faced him on the northern skyline. He shivered. It was just as before. Just like that other parting twenty years ago, only then he'd had a father and a son to go with him. His father had died in those hills, in weather no worse than this, younger than Gruffydd was now. What were his chances? Two, three days? No one was going to spare him food in midwinter. What would he do—put a spell on them? Kill them? He was too old, too old. He'd never thought of it before. He'd had other things to worry about. He was nearly forty—most men of his age expected to live another five years if they were lucky. He'd always assumed he'd go on for ever. How long would he last away from Madlen's bed and a warm roof? And if he made it through the snow, what then? America? A gust of wind whispered mockingly through a hollow tunnel in the rock.

He couldn't afford to think of Madlen, but her face kept intruding. "I gave you all I had," she said to him. "I believed in you, I trusted you, I killed for you. You betrayed me."

He had. For a few scruples and the memory of a boy's infatuation he had deserted her and he would never find another like her. What was the point in crossing the world? He would still be himself, and the thought of her would still accuse him, however far he went. Gruffydd howled into the night like a wounded wolf or a dog for its dead master. Anything to drown the lilt of Madlen's voice in his head. Already she haunted him and she would always. His cries rang across the valley and were drowned without echo in the snow. Four miles away in the Round House Mihangel broke off what he was saying to Madlen and cocked his head to one side. A strange smile crossed his face. Madlen didn't understand it. She heard nothing.

Gruffydd felt with his foot for the edge of the rock and stood suspended over the abyss. The Ystwyth rustled gently up at him out of the darkness, soothing and inviting. No point in running away from her. She'd nearly had him once before, when Dan Rowlands pulled him out of Hafod pool, and she wouldn't be cheated of him now. Gruffydd suddenly saw his mother, quite distinctly, washing red flannel clothes in a natural stone basin by the Ystwyth bridge. He recognized the place. She smiled at him, brushing a wisp of fair hair off her face, beckoning him into the water. She was going to teach him to swim. He hadn't remembered her face in all his adult life. She'd died when he was four.

She was calling to him. It would be best this way. Madlen would understand and forgive him in time. She could say Mihangel had killed him if it suited her, or make her peace with the boy. It was all one now. He turned his face up towards the stars and closed his eyes. His body seemed weightless, seemed to float upwards rather than falling. There was something in the palm of his hand. He squeezed it. It cut his skin, dragging him back with massive force from his flight. He tried to drop it but his hand wouldn't open. The skin was hot and wet. Gruffydd's feet touched rock. He opened his eyes. The moon had risen above the clouds and silver light poured from the east the whole length of the valley, picking out every jagged crag and bristling wood, turning the river below to a thin streak of muddy silver in a dreary waste of pebbles. His mind was brilliantly alive, lucid with pain. He stepped back from the edge, prising his fingers apart with the other hand. Blood gushed out, black against his white skin. He felt in the wound and delicately pulled out a narrow, pointed piece of metal, scarcely the length of a finger joint. He held it up to the moon. An arrowhead. Man-made. Nothing in nature had such a point. Gruffydd had no idea how it had found its way into his hand. On the shallow side of Grogwynion, the circular ridges cast deep shadows into the snow-filled ditches behind them.

"Our ancestors fought off the Romans here fifteen hundred years ago," Gruffydd heard his father say. Perhaps this arrow had killed one of them. Or one of us. The slopes around him suddenly swarmed with the tumult of battle and the untrodden snow rang with the clash of swords, war-cries in his own tongue and another which he couldn't identify. He saw a hard-pressed garrison of long-haired, unarmoured warriors, bodies painted in wild greens and reds, retreat from one palisade to the next before the inexorable onslaught of iron-clad men yoked together in a solid phalanx, retreat from each ridge, scores lying dead, to the very peak of Grogwynion where their womenfolk waited patiently beside the precipice. As each warrior fell, a woman would seize his spear and fight beside the men until she fell. Gruffydd closed his eyes and put his hands over his ears. He knew the end. Not one of that tribe chose to throw themselves off the precipice before the enemy sword cut them down. They fought until they were killed or thrown off.

"You have always taken the easy way out," they accused him. "What have you ever seen through to the end?"

It was true. Whether with women or war, a part of him was always held in reserve ready for a quick flight. He'd never committed himself irretrievably to anything but now he was caught out. He'd lost through his own faint-heartedness in giving in so easily and all his escape routes were blocked.

". . . We can build a nation, here on the Ystwyth, stronger than anything our forefathers achieved," he had said. His own words rang hollow in his ears.

All the fine speeches he'd made, the enraptured faces of captive audiences, thunderous applause . . . He was always good at talking but who did the man's work? Gruffydd suddenly remembered himself with Adam's circus in the days just before his return to Cwmystwyth. They were rehearsing a play, a history of Edward III. Gruffydd was given the part of the King because of his height and his Welsh voice. "Something different. It'll bring them in," he could hear the dwarf

Adam saying. All these memories had vanished when he became a conjurer. The first performance was a revelation to Gruffydd: spell-bound spectators cheering him on to the battlefield, the crown placed on his head in the moment of victory. For that instant he, Gruffydd, was in every way the King he impersonated.

And he'd believed ever since that the crown made him a King. All he wanted was to hear the roar of the crowd adoring him. He needed them to love him, and as long as it was a play, they did. But in the real world you can't expect to be loved. If you fight a war you expect to get killed, and you fight it with all the cunning and all the stealth you can muster. He'd been given a weapon to fight with, but at the first sound of battle he'd thrown it away and fled.

Gruffydd stared up the valley to the slate roofs of Cwmystwyth, angular black shadows against white snow in the moonlight. What did it matter to those people down there if he could conjure spirits from the earth? He had helped them and that was all that mattered. What did they care and what did the tribe that died here care about his doubts? Gruffydd knew that the arrowhead would strike him down, too, sooner or later. He sensed that the black tide of Hywel's Calvinism would eventually sweep away the exuberant old beliefs he had grown up with, as the Roman phalanx swept his ancestors over Grogwynion. But like them he would fight until the arrow struck.

His own people might despatch him themselves. He'd deliberately destroyed their belief in him and now it was their turn to destroy him, if they chose. Better to submit to them than to the snow, or the cliff. They must judge him. No one else could.

IV

Iolo lay back on the oak linen-chest with his head in Rhiannon's lap. His nosebleed wouldn't stop. Every so often she would gently wipe his lip with a damp cloth and stroke his hair with her hand. She was pensive and seemed glad of an excuse to leave Hywel and Rachel on their own by the fire.

"Ouch," Iolo said as she brushed against the tip of his nose. "I think it's broken." He laughed grimly to himself. The only bit of his face left intact, Gruffydd had to go and break. Rhiannon leaned forward, pretending to examine it.

"It was Gruffydd," she whispered, "wasn't it?" Iolo looked up startled. She deftly put a finger on his lips.

"How did you know?" he breathed. She smiled, secretive. Iolo had never felt so close to her—she was a mother to him—and yet she had changed. She struck him for the first time as a woman, warm and mysterious. It's because Hywel is back, he told himself. And after all, I've learnt more about women. But it didn't concern Hywel. It went far deeper. In a strange way—which aroused him but which he could scarcely admit to himself—it was directed at him, Iolo. "How did you know?" he said again, with a thrill of intimacy.

"Perhaps your father will tell you, one day." Iolo looked so like him, something about the faint lines around his eyes. "Don't hate Gruffydd. It's my fault. He's going to need you now, very badly."

Iolo couldn't believe his ears. Rhiannon had always frowned at the slightest mention of Gruffydd. She was making him party to a conspiracy against Hywel. Something Hywel couldn't be told, wasn't to know. Iolo tried to sit up. They might be overheard. Rhiannon put her arm on his chest and pressed him firmly down.

"Are you sure she's right for you?" Rhiannon picked out Rachel with a flick of her eyes. "Do you think you can settle down with her, be faithful to her after all that's happened to you?" Iolo looked at the young woman by the fire sitting on a three-legged chair, her back tirelessly straight, even a little concave at the base of the spine, her hands firmly locked in her lap. Her light-brown hair was pulled back tight off her forehead and gathered behind her head, leaving her long neck bare above the unadorned collar of the grey flannel dress. Rachel had a fine profile, with a long straight nose and small mouth, but she wasn't beautiful. She was severe, with scrubbed, polished skin and a low, even voice that betrayed no emotion. Iolo couldn't make out what she was saying.

She was what he needed. She was honest and upright and would make a good wife and mother, and above all she was a virgin. She was clean. Iolo shuddered to think of the disease that Phoebe had left him with. It was only just leaving him. The ride had been sheer agony.

"Don't tell them you're going," Hywel had warned him, as they sat in the cramped caravan conspiring together. "Or you'll never get away." The big tent, the flashy clothes, he'd abandoned them all.

"What about Cadwal and Betsi? How can I leave them?"

"A dog and a cow, against your salvation?"

"I promised to revisit Mari," Iolo had said. They were leading two geldings from the paddock during the grand finale, exactly as Gruffydd and Iolo had escaped seven years earlier.

"She's a whore! Didn't she first lead you into adultery? And that stone fetish you left with her was nothing but a pagan idol."

He was right, Iolo thought, watching Hywel and Rachel in earnest conversation together. He owed Hywel his life.

"The best safeguard against sin," Hywel had shouted at him across the wind, as they galloped over the mountains side by side, "is marriage. Take my word for it. I'd sunk even lower than you before I met Rachel's mother."

"Why not Rachel?" Hywel had said ten miles later, overtaking him.

"She'll never have me."

"You've been very good to her. She'll do as I say." The idea had grown on Iolo as the sun came up through the mist behind them. Rachel had always fascinated him. She was pure and inaccessible, unlike any other woman he'd met.

Surely she would keep him from falling again. She was everything a woman should be. Iolo desperately needed to believe in womankind. There must be women in the world who resembled his mother, the fair-haired lady of the lake whom Iolo imagined as radiant and other-worldly as before, despite his better knowledge. He'd been deceived so often. Rachel was the nearest approximation he could find.

"Iolo!" Rhiannon shook him gently. He'd dozed off. "I'm only thinking of your happiness." Iolo woke with a start and looked round alarmed.

"Thank God," he said and fell back on Rhiannon's lap. "It's not the circus. Thank God I'm back with you."

"Iolo, please think carefully." Iolo nodded absently. Hywel and Rachel were coming over to them.

"Rachel has been telling me about her work at the Grammar School in Ystrad Meurig," Hywel said proudly. "She's going to help us start a school here to dispel the clouds of superstition that smother our valley." He broke off abruptly. "Haven't you something to ask Rachel, Iolo?" Iolo struggled to his feet.

"I . . . I . . ." he stammered, unable to look at her.

"His sins are great. But they have been forgiven him. Will you take him, Rachel?"

She gazed straight back into her father's eyes and said: "God's will be done."

"I suggest Christmas Day," Hywel said with a broad smile and joined their hands.

Rhiannon was appalled. Another Christmas wedding! Had he no memory? Within hours of his return Hywel had slipped serenely into his old mould, taking charge of his household as if it had never for a second escaped his tender supervision, instructing Rhiannon on how to run the farm, making arrangements without the least consultation.

Of course, his manner had changed. He behaved towards her with the greatest deference. He had sinned against her and would never let her forget it. He took it as a licence to redeem himself by whatever course his salvation dictated. Before he had punished her, now he pampered her. Either way, Hywel did what he pleased. His repentance was absolutely sincere, she knew that. Hywel had never been and never would be a hypocrite because his self-deception was too profound, but his regeneration was a purely personal affair. It didn't begin to affect his understanding of her.

Rhiannon tried desperately not to regret her baffling renunciation in throwing over Gruffydd, and the only moment of happiness she had ever known, for a man who would never grasp the meaning of love however often he spoke of it. The only consolation was that she was not bound to Hywel. It would be more difficult if he had really changed. A breath of freedom had blown through her life and she had no intention of crawling back to the musty cellars of marital servitude.

"Oh, yes," Hywel said, as Rachel whispered urgently in his ear. "I nearly forgot. There is one condition, Iolo."

"Yes?" Iolo raised one eyebrow.

"You must promise to stay here with us. Give up droving. It's an ungodly business. Besides, we shall need you here for the farm."

"Gladly," Iolo said and clutched at Rhiannon. His nose was bleeding again.

v

Madlen swayed slightly on her feet. Her head was a hundred miles from the floor. She hadn't eaten for eighteen hours at least, but she was too proud to sit down. She gazed round the room. No wonder she felt like a stranger here. Every trace of her life was gone. The rocking cradle, Owain's toys, her spinning-wheel had vanished—even the wall tapestries. The room was no longer lived in. It smelled of damp, naked stone and medicine. The walls were lined with bottles and jars she'd never seen before. So Gruffydd had deserted her. He'd left Cwmystwyth as he'd said he would, taking Rhiannon with him, in all likelihood. She hadn't believed he could do it.

"So you're the conjurer, are you? Since when?"

Mihangel swung round lithely on his haunches and flashed her a tolerant smile, which only just betrayed the honeyed taste of victory on his lips.

"Since this morning. By the acclaim of the whole valley."

Madlen watched him give new orders to the guards at the door. He was so young and arrogant. Hardly a full-grown man. He'd played a clever game.

"Aren't you afraid Gruffydd will come back?" She scolded him like a little boy, her eyes wide with mockery. Mihangel struggled for a witty answer. None came. He turned away furious, his face suddenly taut with anger.

"You can't treat me like a child now, you know. If Gruffydd comes back here they'll tear him apart. I won't stop them." He shook his finger at the villagers sleeping quietly in their beds up and down the valley. It was the same gesture that Gruffydd had used. A lonely gesture, frightened even. Who could know what they were dreaming? Madlen was struck by the futility of Mihangel's treachery. Would he ever sleep peacefully again?

"Listen. I'm a conjurer—do you understand that? Gruffydd was a charlatan. He fooled everyone for years, even me. He was using me all the time and I never realized it. He had nothing of his own. Nothing. He lived off me . . ." Mihangel ground his fist into the palm of his other hand and talked on, his fair skin turning white, then blushing violently as he spilled out years of malice. "Very, very gradually I began to understand what he was doing to me. Every time we predicted the weather, he got it from me. Every time the miners hit a new vein, they'd been guided by me. Every time he cured a lame goat or a barren cow or a bedridden old hag, the cure always came from me! Well, now it's my turn." He jumped up and paced restlessly around the room. "Conjuring is an art, and Gruffydd shat on it. Look." He pulled down two leather-bound volumes from a row of books. "That's Latin. I taught myself to read so I could learn the secrets in here. I sat up with a candle until dawn while you two were grunting in there like rutting dogs." His voice trembled. He turned away abruptly, slamming the book shut. "Gruffydd knew nothing of Latin. He wasn't interested in the real mysteries of conjuring. He used his position just to get his own way. Did anybody here ever ask him to build a tannery and a new mill and change the way we've lived for centuries?"

"No. But many are glad he did."

"They're not. They were just scared of him. And of you . . ." For a moment their eyes met and he seemed uncertain whether to go on, suddenly wary of her. Then he lifted his hand and touched her cheek. "That's a bad bruise, I'll put something on it. You must be hungry. Sit down." Madlen was too tired to resist. If he wasn't going to evict her she'd stay at the Round House for a day or two, for there was nowhere else she could go. With Gruffydd gone, many of her enemies would be out to settle a score or two. She had to accept help from any

304

quarter. She had no choice. What was the point in being high-handed with Mihangel for betraying Gruffydd? Hadn't Gruffydd just betrayed her in turn, and with her own sister? None of them was blameless and it was all one now. She had to get by somehow.

Mihangel put a pot of fish soup on the fire to heat and poured the broth into the usual wooden bowls. He had always done most of the cooking because, of the three of them, he'd been the best at it. Gruffydd had been too busy and Madlen lacked the patience. Watching him now, she had a strange sensation that nothing had changed. It might be any other evening over the last few years except that Gruffydd wasn't there, but there was nothing very unusual in that as he'd been out at night more often than not. They ate in silence and Mihangel watched her intently over the rim of his bowl. Then he collected the scraps of barley bread, put them away in the dresser and took down an odd-shaped jar from the top shelf. With one hand he brushed the hair off her face and cradled her head against his shoulder, and with the other he very gently rubbed a cool, fragrant unguent over the bruises on her cheek. His body shivered as it touched hers. He had never been with a woman before, she was sure. How long had he desired her like this? Why hadn't she realized before? No wonder he hadn't thrown her out with Gruffydd.

"I need you," he murmued nervously, as he smoothed out the lines of tension under her eyes with his thumb. "I need you to help me as a conjurer. I'll treat you far better than Gruffydd ever did. He slept with every whore in the valley." His puritan disapproval amused her—it coupled grotesquely with the ruthlessness of his actions—but his hands were smooth, infinitely beguiling and she relaxed to his touch. She didn't care if he was corrupt. So was she. Any human warmth was reassuring after the last two days. What if he was a murderer? So was she. Nothing she did now could be worse than what she'd done already. Mihangel pleased her and made her feel alive again. All her passion had gone into ensnaring Gruffydd and having his child, and she had never been loved by a young man before. She relished the idea of giving herself to Gruffydd's rival and only regretted that he would never hear of it. She had wasted her youth on him—why shouldn't she enjoy herself at last?

Mihangel's face was hot, flushed with excitement as his fingers ran over her neck and shoulders. She liked watching the effect her body had on him. She was still capable of attracting a handsome young man even if Gruffydd did prefer her faded sister. Mihangel would be useful to her until she could persuade Ffowlke that Gruffydd was no longer a threat. She knew already what she'd say to him: "He's deserted us both," and Ffowlke would take pity on her and more especially on himself, and they'd console one another. But for now Mihangel's protection was necessary because nowhere in the valley was safe for her. There would be time to avenge Owain's death later. She let Mihangel roll her over and massage her ankle, swollen from her fall at Brithgoed. Her calves were aching from the long walk back; his clever, uncalloused palms eased the flesh, unknotted the muscles, travelled upwards. She mustn't let him think he was doing her a favour. She sat up.

"Thank you. That was very nice."

Mihangel's whole body shook. "I haven't finished."

"Oh? What do you want, then?"

"Don't you understand?" Mihangel cried. "I want you to . . ." How could he say "love me"? With all the power he'd ever dreamt of—with a stranglehold on Madlen's future, her very life, Mihangel suddenly realized he'd failed. "Don't you see why I've done all this?" He jerked his thumb over his shoulder at the naked, desecrated room. "Not because I hated Gruffydd. He was good to me. I had no quarrel with him. I did it because of you. I had to make you need me." He laughed bitterly. "You've taken me for granted, just as Gruffydd did. Quiet, faithful Mihangel, always does what he's told. I did the most terrible things for you and then you offered to pay me. Pay me! As if my services could be bought, like some whore. What did you take me for? I loved you and you never even guessed it. More than anything in the world I wanted to possess you."

Madlen closed her eyes and shook her head. He was right, she'd never given it a moment's thought. Mihangel had just always been there. His devotion had amused her, flattered her vaguely. He was so self-effacing, she'd never felt any need to reciprocate. She'd deliberately kept him enslaved and now her own power had undermined her. Her blindness had destroyed them all—Mihangel, Gruffydd, Owain and herself. She put out her hand and gently stroked his smooth, pale cheek.

"I've wanted you so much, I . . ." Mihangel was a boy again, stammering, incoherent. She paralysed him. No more could he now take what was his than claim his rightful kiss seven years ago. "I'll make you rich," he said passionately. "We'll run the valley together. We'll be equals."

"Hush." Madlen put a finger over his mouth. "Time enough to talk of that later."

His adolescent fervour took her back to her girlhood, so far away now, which she'd squandered on petty intrigue and the heady delusion of power. This was where it all ended up, in the oblivious, idolatrous embraces of a boy she'd ignored. Had she been wrong all along? she wondered, as his cool, fragrant body floated above her like a dream.

VI

Ffowlke put his ear to the front door but kept it bolted. The latest batch of servants had deserted him like their predecessors and he didn't trust night-visitors.

"Who is it?"

"Me," came a weary voice. "Gruffydd." Ffowlke opened the door and held up a letter. His face was tense with anger. He wasn't drunk.

"Take it," Ffowlke snapped with a jerk of the wrist. "Read it." Gruffydd stood in the freezing night air and held the scroll up to Ffowlke's oil-lamp.

"From the Lord Lieutenant." Gruffydd pointed to the seal, unable to admit he couldn't read a word. "Militia?"

"Militia." Ffowlke snatched the letter back and read it aloud with ironic relish. "'Owing to the growing unrest in the Ystwyth Valley, which you, My Lord, appear unable or unwilling to restrain, I feel it my duty to His Majesty and to other landowners of the shire to order a detachment of the County Militia, under the command of Colonel Thomas Johnes, to enter the valley at midday on 24th December, 1752. They will encamp at Brithgoed. You will kindly furnish them with all possible aid and sustenance.' It arrived an hour ago, together with this"—Ffowlke displayed a similar scroll—"by the same messenger. From Talbot. He accuses me of disgracing the family name, mismanaging the estates, squandering my patrimony, and calls me before the High Court to hand over control of all Kirkland lands to him, as I am clearly incompetent and not in my right mind."

Ffowlke crushed the two letters in either hand. "And he'll win because of you. Don't attempt to deny it. You promised to control them. Our bargain. You betrayed me. You've used me for your own ends and now you've ruined me." Ffowlke's voice suddenly dropped to a hiss, his eyes mere slits in his puffy, inflamed face. "Leave. Get out of here. If the militia catch you, I hate to think how you'll end up. I won't stop them. I couldn't if I wanted to. You've seen to that."

The door slammed in Gruffydd's face. He'd just lost his last ally.

CHAPTER TWENTY-ONE

THE FIRST RAYS of the sun brushed the soft, powdery snow off the Cwmystwyth scree slopes and fell through the open hatch-window of the Round House bedroom onto Mihangel's blissful, sleeping face. Madlen woke and stared at the ceiling. She hadn't surfaced once all night. Strange, to feel Mihangel's soft, restful body beside her—comforting, like Rhiannon's, when they shared a bed as girls—instead of Gruffydd's massive frame tossing and heaving sleeplessly, pushing her into the farthest cranny of the bed. Mihangel lay flat on his back, legs fully stretched, his head turned slightly towards her on the pillow and one hand to his smiling mouth, like a child. His face glowed roseate in the sudden sunlight, far gentler, more relaxed than she'd ever seen him awake. Madlen leaned over and kissed his full red lips, still swollen from their love-making. A novice he might be, but he'd pleased her, last night. Perhaps she should feel disgusted with herself for sleeping with the murderer of her child, but she didn't. She had enjoyed it. For the first time in her life she had accepted sexual pleasure for its own sake with no thoughts of love or responsibility. She didn't care if it was unforgivable—she felt rejuvenated and ready to face life again. Mihangel's hairless body no longer repelled her. She was hypnotized by its sleek, elusive contours, well muscled, but with none of the hardness or the abrasive, hirsute touch of the one man she'd known in her life and always thought of as the model for all men. Mihangel was all air and water, hovering over her with the delicate caress of a rain-cloud on a parched summer's day, refreshing all her senses and lifting her out of herself. Gruffydd, compounded of earth and fire, had crushed and consumed her. She realized now that Gruffydd hadn't fulfilled her sexually for many a month—whether through worry or sheer habit, their bed had grown stale. Madlen ran the tips of her fingers over Mihangel's rounded chest, down his flat silky belly, and twisted them gently through his warm, curling hair. He moaned softly and his whole body stretched then suddenly relaxed again. He didn't wake. Madlen was tempted to shake him. She wanted him again, but he must be exhausted.

They hadn't finally extinguished the flickering rush taper in its wall bracket until hours past midnight. Madlen stepped out of bed. The flagstones were cold beneath her flushed, moist feet. She pulled the velvet cover up around Mihangel's neck almost to his mouth, and stood watching him for a minute, wishing he'd wake. Reluctantly she turned to her dressing-table, to prepare for the day. The whole valley would arrive in a few hours to greet Mihangel and confirm his position and Madlen was determined to make the right impression. A few minutes later she sensed that he was watching her as so often before and turned. Mihangel was propped up on his elbows, staring at her, enraptured, over the end of the bed.

"You're beautiful," he said.

"How long have you been watching me?"

"Not long enough. Why didn't you wake me?" He leapt out of bed and ran over to her, his agile feet noiseless on the stone flags, threw his arms around her and kissed her hungrily on the neck. She could feel his warmth through her dress. He lifted the hem, running his hand up the inside of her thigh. She trembled and pushed him gently away.

"You must get ready," she whispered. "They'll be here before long."

Mihangel's mood changed abruptly, as if his private emotions were no longer of any concern to him. Madlen watched fascinated as he swiftly pulled on a full black gown and crowned himself with a black skull-cap. She'd never seen him dressed as a conjurer before. With his hair completely covered, his face looked even younger than before, asexual, impersonal, utterly indeterminate yet somehow stamped with a sombre authority, knowledge of a different world. He scarcely acknowledged her as he seized his wand and strode into the main chamber of the Round House where his helpers were waiting to receive his orders. With the briefest of directives, spoken in a low, impressive monotone, he sent each about his business, then opened a leather-bound book on a lectern and sat reading, totally absorbed, for an hour, not noticing the queue of patients forming around him. None of them dared to disturb him.

"Yes, Gwilym?" Mihangel said quietly, closing the book when he'd finished taking the horoscope for the day. There were elements in it he didn't understand, others that worried him. Mars was almost at the zenith, exerting a baleful influence. Whenever he could, Mihangel avoided open conflict. Everything he had read suggested a sudden reversal, probably the one which had just occurred in his favour.

"My sheep have the colic, master. Can you do anything for them?"

"I'll come this afternoon." Nothing in Mihangel's manner suggested the uncertainty in his mind. "Here, take this powder and spread it over their pasturage. This should help for the time being." At the last moment his fingers switched from one of the countless bottles in his medicine chest to the next. Madlen smiled at him from the bedroom door, unseen by the visitors, and twirled a hand through a stray wisp of hair in the nape of her long, slender neck, her hips thrust to one side, inviting. Mihangel shuddered and closed his eyes as a fire in his loins leapt out to her.

"Master?" The conjurer had slipped back into his trance, the medicine bottle clasped in his fingers. Gwilym gingerly reached out to take it.

Mihangel came round with a start. "Here. Who's next?" One by one he dealt with their requests, consulting his books whenever he was in doubt, giving all his advice in the same relaxed, familiar voice devoid of both ribaldry and bombast, confident of its own authority without needing to assert it. Mihangel deliberately styled himself on everything Gruffydd was not. He was cautious, retiring, undramatic, constantly soothing. In his many private conversations with villagers—over a consultation or a chance meeting, with no fear of disturbance—Mihangel had learnt for certain what he'd always suspected: they were sick of Gruffydd's showmanship; tired of constant excitement, relentless change; exhausted by the demands he made on their labour; and terrified by the way he let the other world constantly intrude in their lives, apparently revelling in it, instead of keeping it firmly at bay, which had always been the sole function of his position.

"We don't pay him to conjure up spirits," Siân Evans had grumbled. "We pay him to lay them."

"A conjurer never used to do so much," Old Isaac had explained to Mihangel. "In the old days he never used to be seen much. Too busy conjuring."

"If he's out working all day, what time has he got for his magic?"

"No wonder things are going badly."

The verdict was unanimous: Gruffydd had abused his trust, and appropriated powers never envisaged for a conjurer. None of them had seemed to think he'd last. He had perverted his art and brought it into disrepute. Mihangel was determined, first and foremost, to redefine the limits of his office and cleanse its reputation. He had no regrets about purging Gruffydd, however close friends they had been. Gruffydd had been an evil force in the community. His excision had been imperative for the good of all.

"Headaches," Simeon groaned.

"Right." Mihangel reached out for several bottles and started mixing ingredients in his stone mortar. Madlen stared up at him out of the swirling, churning mixture. Her naked, inebriating body. Her legs opened to him again. Had he dreamt it? Last night was vividly, intolerably alive inside him. Nothing else mattered. His body, so submissive before, was a mere vehicle for wild sensations he'd never even imagined. He had to test them again, now, at once. Were they real? Was he possessed? Mihangel remembered the horoscope with a start. Why was his brain so sluggish? He could usually predict the exact configuration of the zodiac and interpret its effect on human affairs before he'd opened his lexicon. Now he couldn't even recall the constellations on a page he'd been staring at less than half an hour ago. He dragged his thoughts together just as Simeon was saying, "Isn't it ready yet?"

"Yes. Of course." Mihangel poured the liquid into a bottle, spilling a few drops. He'd never spilt anything before. As he wiped the bottle with his sleeve, he dropped the cork. Simeon picked it up for him. Mihangel pretended he hadn't noticed.

Iago One-Leg's raspy fiddle screeched up through the woods, a faint murmur of approaching voices behind it.

He must go out to greet them, Mihangel told himself. He mustn't look concerned. He got up and went to the door, leaving his petitioners waiting on the benches around the chamber. By the door he looked up. Madlen was still there, smiling. He longed to be alone with her.

"Go now," she breathed to him, her lips moving silently, tantalizing.

Outside the snow lay ankle-deep, painfully bright. The sun bounced off it straight through his head like a branding iron; its image raced across his closed eyelids from temple to temple. Very slowly he peered from behind two fingers. The sky was cloudless, a deep, royal blue verging on black at the meridian, a plush, oppressive velvet. The whole valley was stripped naked, the deep forests dirty green stains, the cottages shabby smudges of grey adorned here and there with multicoloured washing lines, red flannel dresses flapping maddeningly in the breeze. Behind him Black Rock was as black as its name, a monolithic slab of slate without contour or relief. The slag-heaps of the lead mines up-valley protruded from the snow like mammoth sheep's droppings. Nowhere was a trace of the subtle greens, the soothing mists that blurred the outlines of this harsh country and made it bearable.

The laughter and shouting came closer. Siôn Edmunds was bellowing a bawdy song, twice as loud as the rest. Up the path from the valley they came. The first heads bobbed up and down behind the hill, Iago higher than anyone else on Siôn's shoulders. Young girls darted around them, throwing snowballs at Iago. Some of them had brought sledges with them, knocked together from driftwood or old planks.

Mihangel pulled his hand away from his eyes and forced himself to look out into the white fastnesses. He'd never realized the Round House meadow was so vast. The empty space closed in on him, exposing the chaos in his own head. The crowd burst into the clearing, bright, cheerful explosions of colour scattering in all directions, kicking up snow-spray behind them, rolling and snowballing. They dashed at him from all sides, welcoming faces, arms stretched out to him holding gifts. Then they were around him. Mihangel suddenly relaxed. His tongue was loosened. Nothing could happen. He was among friends.

"Thank you, all of you," he said simply, just loud enough for everyone to hear without having to strain. His words came freely. "You're all welcome here. With your goodwill I hope to serve you for many years. I shall be honoured if you will accept my hospitality." He pointed to the kitchen garden, where the snow had been cleared for a fire. One of the bullocks they had given him in payment had been slaughtered and was being trimmed for the spit. They cheered loudly, appreciating his generous gesture. "But first I would like to present the lady who has agreed to be my companion." A few jocular whistles. Mihangel was a boy and they liked him for his unworldly innocence. There was something radiant, divine almost, in his youthful, androgynous features. No one had ever thought of his taking a wife. He had as much woman as man in him on his own.

The Round House door opened and Madlen walked towards them, eyes lowered, unassuming. They didn't understand at first. They saw only the old conjurer's hated mistress. Madlen put out a hand to Mihangel. He drew her in to him, arm around her waist. The crowd fell back five paces.

"Mind what you're doing, boy," said Old Isaac. "She's destroyed one man before you."

"Witch! Witch" they chanted, stamping in the snow. Madlen didn't look up. Mihangel squeezed her hand tightly.

"Listen!" he shouted. "Do any of you remember Madlen, the daughter of our last minister? Is this that girl? For seven years she has not been herself. The whole valley has been enslaved by one man. How much more is that true of Madlen? He wove a web of enchantment around her but now she is free. Madlen is herself again!"

"Is this true?" said old Isaac.

"It is," Madlen whispered, her face purged of all pride, empty, vulnerable, as if she'd just awoken from a deep sleep. One day she would have them all under her thumb, but for now she must appease them. "Mihangel saved me. Take me back. I am one of you."

They were no longer listening. The crowd had swung outwards, staring up at the woods below Black Rock. A solitary, ragged figure stepped out of the forest, watched them turn to face him and slowly walked down the hillside towards them, lifting his feet with difficulty above the snow-drifts. His hair was frozen into fantastic shapes, as if he'd slept in the open and the snow had turned to ice and stuck to him. His beard was mangy, cleft at his chin into two forks as though some starving field-mouse had breakfasted on it. He limped on one leg, and his limbs protruded through his shredded cloak like scarecrow poles through old sacking. No one needed to ask who he was. Only two days ago he'd lived in this place. Now it seemed his fly-blown ghost was returning to haunt it.

Mihangel remembered Mars at the zenith. Why had Gruffydd come back? Was he trying to kill himself? He could gain nothing by fighting. He looked round at Madlen and she squeezed his hand. She had no idea what Gruffydd was doing but she wished he'd stayed away. It was madness to be seen here. She couldn't possibly help him now.

"Friends!" Gruffydd's voice rebounded off Black Rock, the echo tinged with mockery. His arms were spread in the old embracing gesture.

"Friends!" The crowd took up the word and threw it back and forth in derisive mirth, their faces distorted in taunting imitation of his once-imposing expressions. Gruffydd put one hand to his ear, trying to make out what they were saying. They roared with laughter, bending double and slapping each other on the back, copying his gesture. Even Mihangel couldn't resist smiling. Suddenly a dozen or so of the men broke away and ran towards Gruffydd. Mihangel watched them anxiously. What were they up to? No one could defect to Gruffydd after such a resounding humiliation, but the less they had to do with him the better.

"Friends!" Gruffydd called again, staggering down the hill, arms flung wide to greet them. A snowball landed by his foot. He laughed like a child and lobbed it back. Then he stooped to make more, pelting them as fast as he could. One by one the men raced into his range, threw their heavy ice-packed snowballs and escaped again. He side-stepped. Most of them missed. Then the party fanned out around him, came from all sides, like dogs baiting a circus bear. Snowballs thudded against his neck and spine. Another two caught his ear and knocked him to his knees. They were all shouting, Mihangel couldn't make out what. The whole crowd had rushed off to watch. Rolo Blacksmith charged forward and stabbed his head into Gruffydd's back. They went down in a pile, a dozen more on top of them, with Gruffydd on the bottom, face down in the snow.

"Shouldn't you stop them?" Madlen murmured to Mihangel. "No good for you if they kill him. Ffowlke wouldn't like it."

"Off" he shouted. They scattered like hounds from the kill at the huntsman's horn. Rolo and Thomas Jenkins lifted Gruffydd under his armpits and dragged him down the hill. His head hung heavily between his jutting shoulder-blades. Mihangel drew a tankard of ale from the barrel and put it to Gruffydd's lips. They were blue and scarcely moved.

"Why didn't you leave me?" Gruffydd muttered as the ale coursed through him. "You should have left me. It would have been better for everyone."

"Why did you come back?" Mihangel said gently, looking round for Madlen. She'd gone. He could understand why.

"To find out what I've just found out."

"That they hate you?"

"To submit to whatever they had in store for me." Gruffydd could stand on his own now. He looked at the hostile faces gathered round them.

"Well now you know," Mihangel said wryly. "So what else do you want?"

"I ask only one thing. Just to be allowed to stay here."

"No," muttered the villagers. "Don't let him. He'll bring bad luck on us all."

"You must leave," Mihangel said firmly. "They won't let you stay here. For your own safety, please go."

"For my safety?" Gruffydd exploded, blood rising in his cheeks again. "Where do you expect me to go? I'd rather die here. If you can't learn to live with me, you must get rid of me. I won't do your dirty work for you."

"Why should we let him leave anyway?" Morgan roared above the din. "He's got to repay all the sacks of barley, all the cows and the pigs we gave him. Let's make him work for us."

Gruffydd spat contemptuously at Morgan's feet. "I'd rather work in John Ffowlke's pigsties. The pittance you gave me was no more than my due as conjurer."

"You a conjurer! You've ruined us all with your conjuring."

"Ay." They edged in, skinning-knives levelled at him. Mihangel tried to cool the anger on both sides, but control was slipping from his grasp. Gruffydd was deliberately provoking the villagers into murdering him.

"I am a conjurer," Gruffydd thundered. "You were the first to say so, Morgan, the day I cured the cattle plague. Have you all forgotten that day? Have you forgotten everything I've done for you since then?"

"We didn't want your crazy ideas," screeched Mali Fishpond from the back.

"We didn't need a new mill." Flour fell off Simeon as he shook his fist.

"You didn't, Simeon. Everyone else did."

"And what about the cattle?" said Dic Richards, haggard with worry. "We can't pay the rent, all because of you and your plans."

"If you had obeyed me, the herds would have been in England three months ago and you'd have enough money to pay your rents five times over."

Nobody listened except Iolo high above them on Black Rock. He had no idea of what had happened in Cwmystwyth since he'd been gone. As far as he knew, Gruffydd was still firmly established in the Round House. He'd come to Black Rock to brood about last night's rebuff, maybe to catch a glimpse of his father without losing face. He was too proud to ask Gruffydd's pardon now. The scales were just about even, he reckoned. But this spectacle below, every detail clear to him from this height, brought home to him exactly what his absence had meant to Gruffydd, to the whole of the valley. He'd been thinking only of his own salvation while they were depending on him for their lives.

"Leave, Gruffydd, *now*!" Mihangel whispered. "Or I'll destroy you. You're leaving me no choice."

"Go ahead, you've been working at it long enough."

"So be it." Mihangel raised his hands to the crowd. "He claims to be a conjurer again." Loud jeers. "Only two days ago he crawled at your feet confessing he wasn't one."

Gruffydd noticed Madlen standing in the doorway, her eyes fixed on Mihangel. "And why did I say that? Because this man had blinded me, destroyed my reason. His black art gnawed away at me from within, leaving no trace on the outside. How can you trust such a man? He's stolen my wife and if the truth were known, he murdered my son."

A murmur of excitement ran through the crowd. Mihangel struggled for ideas. If Gruffydd went on any longer they would start believing him. He was more dangerous than ever. Madlen's presence lamed him—he could think of nothing but her warm body enfolding him once this trial was over. This whole event seemed unreal. It couldn't be happening. Gruffydd had given up, renounced everything. He couldn't be asking for it back now.

"All right, Gruffydd," Mihangel said. "If you're a conjurer, give us a sign."

The villagers slowly pushed forward, prodding the bedraggled ageing man onto his knees with their sticks.

"Give us a sign! Show us what you can do."

"What miracle can you perform, Gruffydd?" Mihangel taunted, his beautiful mouth curled in triumph. "Surely you must have some trick up your sleeve?"

Gruffydd stared up at the boy's overweening, arrogant black eyes.

"Damn you," he said hoarsely. "I'll see you in hell and we can fight it out again there." He lowered his head as the crowd closed in on all sides, waiting for the first blow.

Who would strike first? Siôn? Morgan? Or someone who had never held any malice towards him in his life? Perhaps a friend, if only he struck fast and hard.

"In God's name stop them," Madlen begged Mihangel, but he took her hand and tried to lead her to the house. She wouldn't move. Her eyes were fixed on Gruffydd till the end, her face set in a terrible, impenetrable mask.

"Strike, damn you!" Gruffydd roared. Rolo raised his pole-axe. Madlen's mouth opened in a silent scream.

"Leave him!" A voice rang out from the forest below Black Rock. A bullet whistled past Rolo's head. The crowd howled in terror and fell back. Gruffydd's familiar had returned from hell to save him. Gruffydd raised his head and looked into the belligerent, protective eyes of his son.

Gruffydd's wits were suddenly alive again.

"A sign! You asked for a sign and I give you one. I have brought my own son back from the dead to chastise you." Gruffydd seized the second pistol from Iolo's startled hand and fired it in Mihangel's direction. Iolo looked round aghast. Of course—they all thought he was dead. "If you repent now, and throw out that viper Mihangel, perhaps we will have pity on you. My son will sell your cattle for you. Can Mihangel do as much?"

Iolo felt the old trap closing round him. His vow to give up droving had just been broken for him. Gruffydd had set him up again, only this time Iolo was not going to have his decisions made for him.

"Don't let him fool you," Mihangel told the wavering crowd. "Iolo was never dead. He's flesh and blood, isn't he? Since when have spirits needed to carry pistols?"

He watched the crowd split almost evenly between their old master and their new. The time for reason was past and no amount of talking would win them back. The longer he waited, the more would go over to Gruffydd. Mars in the ascendant. Mihangel had to face up to him or go under. Madlen smiled at him reassuringly, urging him on. Mihangel strode out between the lines, his black cloak billowing behind him. "It seems you have two conjurers." He took in both sides with a majestic sweep, suddenly confident, indomitable. Gruffydd had played his last trick and was spent. At last Mihangel understood the true sense of his horoscope. "Which would you prefer, the stronger or the weaker?"

"The stronger," both sides yelled back.

"So be it. To save bloodshed between friends and family, Gruffydd and I will decide between us." He stripped off his cloak and stood waiting, his sinewy arms bare to the shoulder, lithe and graceful as a cat. Gruffydd's heart sank. He was exhausted, his legs shook with weakness. He hadn't slept for two nights. His stomach was empty to the point of nausea.

"I stand here for my father," Iolo said fiercely. Gruffydd leaned heavily on his shoulder to catch his breath.

"I must face him. If he kills me, look after Rhiannon."

"What do you mean?" Iolo shouted after him, but Gruffydd was gone, lumbering through the snow, sizing up his enemy. Mihangel was twenty years younger than he, and no stripling either. There was a lot of muscle in there despite his womanish face. In happier days they'd had friendly trials of strength over the kitchen table. Mihangel wasn't easy game. Gruffydd turned to the crowd, appealing for a delay, but they shouted him down. The two opposing ranks swung round into two crescents whose horns almost met. Iolo struggled to stay near the front, but they held him back and pushed Gruffydd out into the middle.

He stopped ten paces from Mihangel and dropped his cloak into the snow. He shivered in the morning wind, his linen shirt wet from snow and sweat. His flesh wasn't as firm as it used to be. His chest sagged slightly. Blue veins protruded on his legs.

"This is not what I wanted," he said.

"Then why did you come back?"

"Because you'd betrayed me."

"I never betrayed you. No one wants you here, can't you understand that?"

"Enough talking."

"Whether you kill me, or I kill you, I want you to remember one thing always: Madlen loves me now. We made love in your bed last night."

Gruffydd howled with rage and flung himself at Mihangel. Mihangel side-stepped, kicked him in the knee and slashed at the back of his neck with his fist. Gruffydd slumped to the ground. Mihangel dragged up a stone from beneath the snow and hurled it at his head. Gruffydd rolled. It grazed against his ear, stunning him. A high-pitched whine ran through his skull. Gruffydd charged again, clutching at Mihangel's shirt, his hair. The boy slipped out of reach just when Gruffydd thought he had him and sent Gruffydd floundering in the snow, then pursued him with swift, lethal kicks at his head and scrambled to safety when he tried to get to closer quarters. Gruffydd was losing. A high kick to the midriff winded him. His legs lurched and collapsed beneath him.

Mihangel edged near. No movement from Gruffydd. A deep gash along his hair-line spilled blood into the snow. A victory cry burst from Mihangel's lungs. He threw himself on the inert body. Gruffydd sprang to life. He clamped one arm around Mihangel's throat, the other under his shoulder, and his legs closed around Mihangel's waist as a pincer. They rolled over and over in the snow locked together. Gruffydd tightened his grip. Mihangel clawed at Gruffydd's hair and face, scratched with his long, pointed finger-nails and bit into Gruffydd's forearm with the manic ferocity of a dying man. Gruffydd felt the teeth sink through the skin and the flesh beneath. He forced himself to hold on through excruciating pain. Just a minute longer. Mihangel's teeth reached a nerve, maybe a bone. Gruffydd shrieked and passed out. When he came to a few seconds later, he was slumped over Mihangel, who was writhing and gasping for air, his eyes bulging out of their sockets. They both knew they had no reserves left. Mihangel put an arm over Gruffydd's chest and they lay together heaving. The crowd pressed closer.

"Fight. Fight. Fight." They were determined to see one of them dead. Gruffydd and Mihangel edged away from them through the snow, no longer scared of each other. At the back there was a sudden commotion.

The solid wall of faces parted. Through the gap, carried by two hefty labourers, came Madlen. Her arms were pinioned behind her. A third man held her hair to stop her from biting. Her eyes were wild with terror. They put her down in front of the two men.

"You've known them both," one of them said. "Which one is the better conjurer?" The mob surged forward, mauling her and shouting: "You decide. Which is the real conjurer? Which one shall we keep?" Gruffydd rolled over onto his side and hid his face in the snow. He had no desire to outlive this day. Seven years' work had achieved nothing. The valley had slipped into a worse savagery than he'd ever known.

"No," Madlen screamed, as they shoved her forward. "It's not my choice. Why should I choose?" They pulled her skirts up. She could feel cold clammy hands on her legs. Men were pressing forward on her, pushing and shoving from all sides. Calloused fingers prised her buttocks apart. Hard flesh battered her from behind, pushing into her. A coarse hand seized her cheeks and a reeking mouth pressed to hers. Madlen bit on the scaly lips as hard as she could.

"Gruffydd is the conjurer!" she shrieked. They dropped her.

In the stunned silence she gazed for an instant into Mihangel's horrified eyes. The next second they fell on him. Madlen curled up in the snow as they trampled over her to get at him and she bayed like a wolf-bitch in revenge for her poisoned baby and in lament for her murdered lover.

"Leave him! Leave him!" Gruffydd struggled to reach Mihangel. They didn't hear him, paid no attention, couldn't care. Iolo tried to reload his pistols. They were snatched out of his hands. Someone pushed him to the ground. He lay still in the snow, arm hugging his head. For one minute, no more, the work of destruction raged about them. There was the sickening, ominous silence of savage concentration, disturbed only by the occasional grunt or gasp for breath. Then, as if at a signal, they withdrew, sated and fulfilled, and retreated into the forest faceless, indistinguishable one from the other.

Gruffydd, Madlen and Iolo stood alone in the Round House clearing. Mihangel's dismembered body lay scattered around them, a leg here, an arm there. His head was attached to the torso by a single filament of tissue. His mouth and eyes were open. Slowly the red stain in the snow spread outward, engulfing the three of them like ink on blotting paper.

"No," Madlen screamed, her lungs at last released in a cry that rang through the woods as far as Rhiannon's house and down the valley to the gates of Brithgoed. "I didn't mean it. I loved you. Why didn't you tell me that you loved me sooner?" She crawled to

Mihangel's severed head and pressed her lips to his, tearing at his hair as though she expected him to return her kiss.

Gruffydd leaned on one elbow and puked into the snow. Iolo collected his pistols and walked home.

CHAPTER TWENTY-TWO

COLONEL JOHNES'S TROOP of Cardiganshire militia gleamed resplendent as it trotted over the narrow mountain pass that leads from the high plateau of Elan to the Ystwyth valley and Brithgoed. Occasionally Colonel Johnes, a florid-faced gentleman with whiskers the colour of his newly-tailored scarlet redingote, would look over his shoulder to ensure that his squadron was in proper formation, and especially to admire their uniforms—blue jackets with white facings and brass buttons—which he had paid for out of his own pocket, not to mention the sixpence each man received for the expedition.

It was a costly business and he was gratified to think it would make no impression on his fortune whatsoever. That fortune had been made in English steel, but not by him. He merely married into it. His father-in-law had done the work and Johnes provided the ancient, if impoverished pedigree. Now he was returning to his native Cardiganshire to make his mark and to further his electoral ambitions. "The seat will shortly fall vacant," Sir Lewis Pryse had assured him. "Your candidacy would be most favourably considered."

Thomas Johnes, M.P. The initials rolled seductively off his tongue, but Colonel Johnes was not entirely happy. The Honourable Talbot Ffowlke, a lowering, taciturn gentleman, who rode beside him together with the urbane Sir Lewis, had explained that the purpose of the expedition was to provide a display of punitive ferocity for the benefit of his brother, Lord Kirkland, who had recently turned feeble-minded and was proving unable to maintain order on his own lands. Johnes was not averse to quelling a riot, especially if the rioters carried no firearms. An action of this sort would reflect most favourably on him in the eyes of the county's electors and was much to be desired. But meddling in a family feud—and he was not so anglicized as to forget what these feuds could be like in Wales—and interfering in the personal affairs of a peer of the realm, however deranged—this was a very different matter. Talbot Ffowlke had assured him that he would not even meet his lordship, but Johnes had his doubts. His two companions were too cordial to him by far.

"We are approaching Cwmystwyth, the source of the unrest," said Sir Lewis, his pallid, aquiline face smiling blandly. "I would advise you to order sabres at the ready."

"We had intelligence of bloody murderings here only yesterday," Talbot added. "They're quite capable of an ambush."

"Of course." Johnes was indignant at being lectured on his tactics. True, the Honourable Talbot was an officer in the regular army and Johnes had never led any men into action before. "Draw sabres," he ordered hurriedly, scanning the black deserted mines, a barren wilderland of scree and rubble riddled with holes in which a legion of men could lurk undetected. The jangle of sabres in their scabbards suddenly ceased. The silence was oppressive. So was the narrow, overhanging valley. Johnes had never seen such uninviting country. Blotches of half-thawed snow on the colourless hillsides only added to its dreariness.

"There's one fellow in particular you must be sure to apprehend, Colonel," Talbot said, loading a brace of pistols while effortlessly controlling his horse, despite the black patch which he wore over one eye. "He's a head higher than anyone else here. Possibly even taller than me. You can't miss him."

"What is his offence?"

"He's the ringleader, a violent brigand." Sir Lewis's gravity alone conveyed the terrible crimes involved.

"And he has an unfortunate ascendancy over my brother." Talbot whistled down the pistol barrels. Sir Lewis frowned and Johnes shifted uneasily in the saddle.

"You understand, Colonel," Sir Lewis said with a pointed glance at Talbot, "we hold no personal animosity towards Lord Kirkland. But his indulgence towards this fellow has come to threaten all right-thinking people." Sir Lewis sometimes wished that Talbot were less pliable and more intelligent. He was scaring the poor colonel to death. Talbot was a dubious ally but with him established in Brithgoed the whole Whig opposition would collapse. Sir Lewis would have the whole county in his grasp, as well as the highly profitable mines that Talbot had offered in return for his support.

They reached the stone bridge across the Ystwyth, but there was no sign of any inhabitants, belligerent or law-abiding.

"Where are they all?" Johnes asked, nervously. "Sergeant, take ten men up that hill. Corporal, ten up there. Knock at every door." Johnes was anxious to make his presence felt.

"Does one usually disperse one's men, Colonel?" Sir Lewis enquired tactfully, as though uninformed in military matters.

"Oh, they'll be back soon." Johnes ran his finger through his whiskers. Talbot grunted and fired a pistol at a passing sparrow. It fell like lead.

"Should . . . should you have done that?" Johnes said, as the echo died away.

"I thought you wanted to attract attention?"

"Ah! Quite. Quite." The two platoons returned with nothing to report except empty houses. Johnes moved on towards Brithgoed, trembling in his boots. As they rode beneath Grogwynion he had visions of a hundred men toppling that massive, precariously-poised rock down onto them. For five miles along the river they saw not a soul. Then, half a mile from Brithgoed, they heard bells. Talbot called a halt, much to Johnes's annoyance.

"Listen. A treble peal, that's an alarm call."

Johnes was beginning to wish he'd stayed in England and forgotten about Parliament. "What shall we do?"

"Attack. What else?" They trotted on until they heard the low drone of countless voices in harmony. Talbot swore under his breath. "They're expecting us. They have to sing to keep their courage up, the scum."

"Perhaps we should reconnoitre?" Johnes suggested, out of his depth.

"Nonsense," Talbot barked. "Charge in strength. They won't know what's hit them." Sir Lewis questioned this course but Talbot had taken over. The men sensed a shift in the command and followed him without regard to their paymaster. "Advance, at the gallop!"

The squadron shot like a bolt from a crossbow, carrying the wretched Johnes before it abreast of Talbot. Sir Lewis neatly sidestepped and brought up the rear. They swept round the walls of Brithgoed, sabres raised.

Before the wrought-iron gates stood a huge crowd facing inwards around some black object on a raised platform. The squadron broke and parted around them, horses plunged and reared, oaths and battle-cries rang from the eager recruits. The crowd held tight. Not a face turned to the intruders. Not a hand was lifted in resistance. As the neighing and the clank of steel died away and the squadron came to a frustrated standstill, Johnes realized that the black object was a coffin. The dirge that had sounded so bellicose half a mile away was a funeral hymn conducted by a reverend gentleman in a white surplice, and beside him on the dias stood Lord Kirkland dressed in black silk and adorned with all the decorations of a peer of the realm. His lordship raised his hand. The singing of his respectful, grief-stricken tenants died away. Ffowlke addressed the unfortunate Colonel Johnes.

"Do I take it, sir, that you command this"—he paused to scrutinize the bewildered soldiers—"this rout?"

Johnes turned from scarlet to beetroot. He was sweating copiously. His collar was impossibly tight and prickly. His mount wouldn't stay still. "Yes, I do."

"And would you be so kind as to tell me what you are doing here?" Ffowlke was magnificent. His drunken senility had vanished. He was erect and impeccably, witheringly polite.

Johnes realized in a flush of utter horror that he'd been set up. Instead of the infirm and wayward bedlamite he'd been warned of, he saw a venerable, imposing patriarch basking in the respect of his people. Johnes cleared his throat and did his best to sound military.

"There were reports of trouble, My Lord . . ."

"Do you see any?"

"No, My Lord." Talbot had just succeeded in steering his horse out of the Ystwyth and back to the house after his impetuous gallop. Sir Lewis Pryse was just arriving at a trot. They were too late.

"Then if you will excuse me, Colonel, my wife is waiting."

"Certainly. Of course. My condolences. And, er, my apologies." Colonel Johnes turned tail and cantered back towards his English steel foundries and was never seen again in Cardiganshire. His confused squadron fell in behind him. Neither Sir Lewis's blandishments nor Talbot's threats could stop them. Colonel Johnes sold their uniforms a month later to a Jewish firm in Cheapside.

Lord Kirkland allowed his visiting chaplain to finish the funeral service for form's sake, then turned to his tenants, with whom, for the first time in his life, he was delighted.

"Loyal tenants and fellow Welshmen," he began. "My dear wife, Maude, was an angel from heaven and she will be sorely missed by us all." Everyone murmured agreement, though most of them had never set eyes on her. "At this very moment I hear her voice calling to me from beyond the grave. 'Let not my good work go to waste,' she says. She reminds me of my duty to this great house, to my ancestors and to you all. She says to me, 'Find me a successor. A woman worthy to step into my shoes.' She tells me to remarry." A ripple of excitement spread through the crowd. Madlen's heart pounded uncontrollably. She steadied herself against the iron railings of the gate, just two yards from where Ffowlke stood beaming, enjoying his newly-discovered role of friend, confidant and protector of the people. He hadn't looked at her once throughout the ceremony.

He has found an heiress, she thought and cursed Gruffydd for deceiving her. Ffowlke continued: "Many of you will be asking yourself: 'What great lady will we see as mistress of Brithgoed?' I have a surprise for you. The bride I have chosen will be found in no register of this land's peerage. She has no title, no fortune, no rank." A tide of triumph surged through Madlen like waves crashing onto the beach at Aberystwyth. She would be Lady Kirkland. She heard nothing of the rest of Ffowlke's speech. She was waiting for that sweet, inebriating moment when he would stretch out his hand and raise her to the peerage, far above the common horde she had so long despised and yearned to leave behind. ". . . a lady of virtue," Ffowlke was saying, "who tended to the needs of my dear departed wife in her last days among us and smoothed her path to eternity." He turned, just as Madlen had known he would, and with the very smile she had foreseen, benign and lecherous together, invited Madlen onto the dais beside him. She curtsied and kissed his hand, as she had rehearsed it countless times in her imagination. He raised her up and kissed her cheek. Then they both turned towards the crowd, hands joined. The villagers were stunned, and started muttering angrily, but at that moment the great bell in the chapel of Brithgoed pealed in mighty celebration. Thomas Jenkins, stationed at the back and bursting with the secret he'd somehow held on to all day, shouted at the top of his voice: "God bless Lord and Lady Kirkland!"

The cry spread, sweeping the doubters along in democratic enthusiasm. Madlen waved back, looking over their heads.

Inside the chapel tower, straining at the end of the bell-rope and listening with huge satisfaction to the acclamation, was Gruffydd. He'd kept his side of the bargain—to get rid of the militia as soon as they arrived—and John Ffowlke, reluctantly trusting Gruffydd, who had turned up that morning with every tenant in the valley to offer his support, had kept his promise too: namely, to marry Madlen, "your faithful and humble servant" as Gruffydd had called her with heroic renunciation, finally convincing Ffowlke of his devotion to the house of Kirkland.

The lady of the waterfall had been right after all. Gruffydd had won his lands back and the heirs of Brithgoed would be his heirs. And in six months no one would remember Mihangel ever existed, except Madlen. It would be many years before the memory of these last few days lost their bitterness and maybe the bond between them would never be restored in full. This marriage to Ffowlke was a blessing in many ways—it would take Madlen's mind off the past. Gruffydd accepted that he would see little of her at first and it was best that way, because they found it hard to be with each other. The thought of Owain pained them both and they hadn't dared talk of Rhiannon or Mihangel at all. But Madlen had sworn a solemn oath on her father's grave, before Gruffydd agreed to betroth her to Ffowlke, that she would bring up his unborn child as he wished and allow him all reasonable access. In return Gruffydd had promised never to threaten the Ffowlke's interests or embarrass her in her new role as Lady Kirkland. It was a workable arrangement. A reconciliation would take longer.

CHAPTER TWENTY-THREE

HYWEL LAID OUT the sacramental wafer for the wedding communion and looked at Iolo gravely.

"We are disappointed in you, Iolo. There's no point in disguising it. Breaking your vow and so soon after making it." He shook his grizzled head in anticipation of dire consequences.

"But I haven't broken my vow," Iolo said, trying to hide his irritation. "And I have no intention of doing so. I've only asked you to release me from it." It was as clear as daylight to Iolo, but Hywel regarded the very discussion of Iolo's ever droving again as apostasy. They had stayed up till the early hours bickering and then resumed at dawn, when they began to prepare the cottage for the wedding ceremony.

Iolo wished passionately that the wedding were over. The women were staying with friends of Rachel in Ystrad Meurig because Hywel had deemed it unseemly for bride and groom to sleep under the same roof on the eve of their nuptials. "Not conducive to holy thoughts," he had said. "Marriage, like death, is a reflection of eternity." This hadn't helped to boost Iolo's morale. Hywel's friend and colleague Morys Williams, an ordained minister of the Church who was to perform the ceremony, had set off on an inspection tour of Cwmystwyth. Iolo hoped he'd be back soon. Williams seemed more open to reason than Hywel.

"You see, Iolo," Hywel said, polishing the silver engraved goblet that the Reverend Williams had brought with him. "A vow is indissoluble in the eyes of God. I cannot release you from it. Only death can." He raised his eyebrows in a kind of innocent apology, which irked Iolo. Hywel just didn't want him to drove. God didn't enter into it.

"But isn't service to one's fellow man of equal importance?" Iolo protested, waving the bottle of communion wine in a manner that shocked Hywel. "What will happen to the valley if I don't take the herds? Isn't it my duty to love my neighbour?" Hywel removed the wine bottle.

"Your own salvation is your first and foremost duty. All other considerations are secondary." Hywel frowned and his black eyes burned like fiery coal. "Be certain of your own grace before you concern yourself with others." Hywel was worried about Iolo. The lightning conversion was over. Now followed the long drudgery of consolidation, which could break a man, Hywel knew.

"But how secure can my salvation be if I'm afraid to face the temptations that ruined me before?"

"Temptation comes soon enough, without looking for it." Hywel banged the wine bottle onto the white table-cloth with a look of doom. "Enough argument. Learn to obey."

Iolo was outraged. It was a question of his duty to the valley, not of what he wanted for himself—though perhaps this was not quite true. Since he had come back to Cwmystwyth the business of droving hadn't seemed quite so unappetizing. He longed to escape again from Cwmystwyth's brooding violence. Mihangel's death surpassed any of the horrors he'd encountered on his drove or with the circus, and he realized with appalling clarity that he was, in a way, responsible for the savagery of the villagers. They had expected their salvation from him. Gruffydd had overplayed the importance of Iolo's drove in every way, but their frustration and fears had grown with every day he'd stayed away. Iolo owed it to them and to his own hard-won experience to drove for the Ystwyth valley. It was his calling, a vocation that existed in him independently of his desires or vows, as natural and necessary to him as any organ of his body.

Iolo was a little peeved that his own sense of right coincided exactly with what his father had in mind for him, because he had returned determined not to take any orders from Gruffydd at all. He'd allowed himself to be pushed around far too much in the past, and Gruffydd's welcome, a punch in the nose and scarcely a word of thanks for Iolo's saving his life, had done nothing to make Iolo feel indebted to him. But he did feel anxious for his father, because Gruffydd had only just escaped with his life and was obviously depending on Iolo even now. So the sensible marriage that Iolo had decided on at least in part to free himself from Gruffydd was now threatening to succeed in this more than he wished, for Iolo feared that at some point very soon he would have to choose between deceiving Hywel or deserting Gruffydd. He wished he felt happier about this marriage, but there was nothing he could do about it.

The Reverend Morys Williams returned from his walk full of enthusiasm for Cwmystwyth and the evangelical challenge it offered. He was a tall, elderly gentleman with a shock of white hair, pink translucent skin and apparently boundless energy. He carried a stick, but twirled it more often than he leaned on it. He wrote hymns, which he intoned with no warning as the fancy took him. Iolo liked him.

"Well, Hywel," Morys Williams boomed, livening the heavy atmosphere, "your garden is choked with weeds of sin. The dank smell of corruption greeted me wherever I went." Williams liked to patronize Hywel a little because he was ordained, which Hywel, to his chagrin, was not, though he had applied to the Bishop often enough and Williams had introduced Hywel to the other leading preachers of the Awakening at their Association five years earlier. It was Williams's suggestion that they should adopt the title Calvinistic Methodists to distinguish themselves from the suspect English Wesleyans.

"Your own fervour, your very presence will soon change that," Williams said with expansive goodwill. "You can count on all our support. I will have one of our circulating schools visit you for a few months every year to teach these young heathen ragamuffins how to read their Bible. I have found an excellent site for your new chapel already . . ." As the two men discussed their plans, Iolo swept out the dust from between the flagstones with a switch broom and listened. They spoke with confidence of a world utterly different from the Cwmystwyth Iolo knew, as if the conversion of a whole community would take a matter of months and was a foregone conclusion. They talked familiarly of people with grand titles whose assistance could be counted upon and who had already pledged themselves to the cause with resounding success in other parts of Wales. The more they reasoned, the more Iolo saw his homeland as some misshapen embryo that had slept in its dark womb long past its time and was now to be dragged screaming into the light by the iron determination of its midwives and plunged into icy baptismal waters.

"I passed a curious house on the hillside up there," the Reverend Morys Williams mentioned in passing. "Conical in shape. Certainly not a Christian dwelling."

"Paganism is rife here." Hywel sighed. He had half hoped that Gruffydd's spiritual tyranny over the valley would have reaped its own harsh rewards long before now without any need for an open reckoning. The Antichrist's dominion had proved tenacious and subtly persuasive. Hywel foresaw a protracted struggle before the Archangel Michael hoisted his standard in triumph over Black Rock. He did not relish that struggle. Gruffydd was a cunning opponent. Something about him dislocated the very roots of Hywel's self-confidence and disarmed him. Hywel feared no mortal weapon except laughter.

"Paganism will be stamped out," Williams said, with no more reflection than it would take to swat a fly. "I noticed that the snow was stained with blood. Some primitive sacrifice, no doubt? A sheep or goat?" Hywel looked enquiringly at Iolo, who shrugged in ignorance.

"Something of that nature, no doubt," Hywel said, pouring the holy wine into the silver chalice.

The ceremony began, when Rhiannon, Rachel and Hannah had arrived from Ystrad Meurig, with the six of them singing one of Morys Williams's hymns, *When travelling through this weary land*. Williams himself was too tall for the low room and stood with his head on one side. This gave his voice a curious throttled quality but diminished none of his enthusiasm. Rachel stood next to Iolo. Her singing voice was a penetrating soprano. It gave him a headache.

"And bring us peace at last," they were singing, when Rhiannon heard the noise she'd been dreading all morning. A large, raucous crowd was coming up the path from the river. The two older men were singing too loud to notice. Iolo had heard it. He saw the sudden look of terror on Rhiannon's face and took her hand without anyone noticing. She was trembling. Gruffydd was coming. She had known he would. He had come for revenge and was going to betray her to Hywel. The shouting came closer. There was noisy laughter and the rattling of wheels. Hywel and Rachel stopped singing simultaneously, leaving Morys Williams alone in the middle of a line, looking offended. Hywel turned immediately on Iolo.

"Who is it?"

"I've no idea." He had, but he wasn't going to let Hywel think he was involved.

"What is the matter?" Morys Williams asked drily, when he'd sung the last note.

"Uninvited wedding guests." Hywel strode to the door. This time none of them would enter his house.

At the head of the long, ebullient procession of villagers coming into the farmyard was a horse-drawn open carriage covered with white silk streamers. On the red velvet seats sat a man whom Hywel had last seen seven years ago in a crowded courtroom and was not pleased to see now, especially in the company he kept.

Madlen tucked the plaid rug more firmly around her new husband's knees. "You wait here. I won't be long. Hywel!" she cried, jumping down from the carriage as if she had found a childhood friend. "How are you? You're looking wonderful! Where's Rhiannon? Where are the bride and groom?" She kissed his startled, seedy face on both cheeks. Rhiannon looked nervously through the crowd for Gruffydd.

"We mustn't keep you."

"Nonsense." Madlen embraced Rachel and remembered every sour glance, every envious calumny this prude had ever inflicted on her. "What a beautiful bride she makes. You're such a lucky man, Iolo." She turned to Hywel, her pearl-grey eyes wide with innocence. "You don't mind us dropping in, do you? We've just been married ourselves, you see, so we thought it would be nice to congratulate the other couple."

"We're not married yet." Iolo was shattered. He'd heard nothing of this other marriage and didn't care to be associated with it.

"Oh?" Madlen said gaily. "Second thoughts?" She swept Hannah into her arms. "You must be Hannah! Would you like to ride in a carriage?"

"No," Hywel said abruptly. His authority and self-control had vanished. Madlen was the very spirit of discord, harbinger of disaster. This marriage of hers couldn't augur worse for Hywel's mission.

"Oh?" Madlen's voice hardened with aristocratic insistence. From now on, nobody crossed her. "Lord Kirkland will be so disappointed. He was looking forward to it. You must come and meet him." Hywel stammered an excuse, unsure whether to treat her as a peeress or as the Abishag that she was. Lord Kirkland waved his silver-topped cane in welcome. He was in excellent humour. His wedding had gone off without a hitch. Just the two of them, with Gruffydd and the same visiting chaplain who had buried Maude as witnesses. The time and place had been so well hidden that Talbot, who had sworn to prevent the match, had turned up long after the bit about holding your peace, at which Ffowlke had laughed vulgarly. Anyway, Gruffydd had had some friends stationed outside the country chapel, who had dispersed Talbot's hired bullies with a good number of cracked skulls. Ffowlke breathed in the fresh air and his tenants' applause, confident he'd live for another century.

"I know your face," Ffowlke tapped Hywel on the chest with his cane. "I can't think where from . . ." Hywel flushed and made way for Morys Williams, who bowed obsequiously. "Ah, my late wife thought highly of your hymns. Though alas she did not understand them."

"She was too kind." The Reverend was flattered.

"We have heard a great deal about both of you. My cherished Lady

Kirkland"—he patted Madlen's hand—"has praised your work. You must come and see us in Brithgoed." Hywel looked at Madlen in shocked disbelief. She raised an eyebrow at him and smiled faintly. She would have her own uses for Hywel. He would be a steadying influence in the valley and could teach excitable tenants to think more about heaven and less about riots. "And this is the hero of the hour." Ffowlke inspected Iolo through a pair of old opera-glasses from his London days. "The one who will make us all rich with his cattle-droving."

"Of course. Of course," Hywel said and Ffowlke seized Iolo's hand.

"Congratulations, my boy. It's a fine life." He turned to the crowd and led a round of applause for this odd-looking, bashful young man, on whom apparently all his hopes of ever recouping his lost rents depended.

Iolo watched the hopeful, respectful faces of the villagers, the same ones that wouldn't have come near him six months ago. He had always thought they might need him one day. He'd been right to come back. He'd found his place. He had already made a note of the young men he hoped to recruit for the next drove.

"Now." Ffowlke took charge. "Bring everything out here. You can marry them outside, can't you, Reverend?"

"Certainly," Williams said with alacrity, delighted to be offered such a huge congregation for so little effort.

The heavy oak table was carried out into the farmyard by Siôn Edmunds and Rolo Blacksmith, both grunting under its weight and swearing foully when it had to be turned on its side to get through the door, until Hywel rebuked them for profaning such a solemn occasion. Morys Williams processed in front of the bridal couple with the silver chalice while Hywel carried the wafer. They bowed to Lord and Lady Kirkland, sitting to the right of the altar in their carriage with Rhiannon beside them, and then Morys Williams spread his arms to take in the crowd standing far up the hillside.

"Dearly beloved brethren, we are gathered here today to join in holy matrimony . . ."

Iolo shivered slightly. Rachel's hand was icy on the back of his. She stared straight ahead, a statue, ignoring him totally. An unbroken circle of faces pressed in on him twenty deep.

"Do you, Iolo, take this woman . . ." The silver chalice in Williams's hands flashed in the sunlight like a conjurer's staff above Iolo's head. He looked pleadingly at Rachel. Her stern gaze never faltered. ". . . to be thy lawful wedded wife?" Iolo couldn't make his lips move. A terrible numbness spread from Rachel's fingertips through his whole body into his brain. He only knew he was caught in a bitter mistake far too complicated to put right. ". . . to be thy lawful wedded wife?" Morys Williams repeated. Hywel coughed. Rachel didn't budge.

"I . . ." Iolo's voice broke as he swallowed heavily. He cleared his throat and was about to try again, when round the corner of the Bevans' cottage—in full view of the whole crowd, except Hywel and Morys Williams who stood behind the altar—appeared two glaring, brassy eyes on an inquisitive horse-like snout. The head lolled cross-eyed from side to side, inspecting the scene, then a floppy bundle of old sackcloth flounced out into the clearing. A ripple of laughter spread irresistibly over the hillside and hilarious whispers passed through the crowd like a breeze in long grass.

"The Mari Lwyd! The Mari Lwyd!"

"Silence," Hywel said indignantly. The Mari Lwyd quietly danced a jig behind his back.

"Answer," Hywel roared at Iolo, imagining the ribaldry was due to his hesitation. Iolo couldn't say a word. Rachel's palm had broken out in a cold sweat on his hand but she continued to stare straight ahead, speechless, like Lot's wife turned to a pillar of salt on seeing the flames of Sodom.

"What is this?" asked Lord Kirkland. Madlen's face was pale with fury. Gruffydd was breaking their agreement already.

"An old custom of the people. They always perform it at marriage ceremonies." Rhiannon tried to get up but Madlen grasped her wrist and muttered. "Let it take its course. Interfering will make it worse."

"Do you, Iolo . . ." Williams shouted, his hand raised in dire warning and his pink face throbbing like a cow's udder. The Mari Lwyd shambled forward, stuck her head across the altar between Williams and Hywel and neighed: ". . . take the old grey mare to be thy lawful wedded wife?"

Williams staggered away terrified. Hywel snatched up the silver cross in exorcism. The Mari Lwyd reared in mock terror, then she stuck her head greedily into the silver chalice and emerged with a drunken red-stained leer. The crowd applauded wildly and John Ffowlke leaned back against the velvet cushions and laughed louder than any. Madlen tapped him on the arm and stood up in the carriage.

"Enough!"

The Mari Lwyd eyed her balefully in the sudden silence, then loped to the carriage and fawned at Lord Kirkland's feet, lilting in high falsetto amazement: "Hast thou, John Ffowlke, Viscount Kirkland, Lord of all the World, taken this woman to be thy lawful wedded wife?"

"He has," Madlen hissed.

"Oh!" The Mari Lwyd rolled her head in awe.

"My Lord, may we continue?" Hywel said with dignity.

". . . lawful wedded husband?" the Mari Lwyd asked Rhiannon in passing, head cocked on one side. She nuzzled her snout affectionately against Rhiannon's knee.

"Let me be," she said, but a hand reached out from under the sacking and pulled hers in. She felt a small bundle of linen pressed into her palm. "Keep this for Hannah," came a whisper. "She was born in it. While she carries it, nothing can harm her." The Mari Llwyd moved on, neighing softly, "Remember the old grey mare." She pranced back to the young couple, scaring Lord Kirkland's horses, who stamped nervously in their harness. "Wilt thou, Iolo . . ."

What choice have you ever left me? Iolo thought, staring at the grey mare's arrogant brass eyes.

"I take thee, Rachel," he said in a clear determined voice that rang around the hillside, "to be my lawful wedded wife." The Mari Lwyd heaved a heart-broken sigh, rolled over onto the ground, kicked feebly once or twice and expired amidst wild applause from the crowd.

Gruffydd struggled out of a mountain of sackcloth in clouds of hemp dust.

"You can have him," he said cheerfully to Hywel. "He can't be of my blood. They just about deserve each other." He winked at Rachel, whose gaunt face suddenly came alive with outrage.

"You are an abomination," Hywel thundered. "You are Lucifer incarnate."

"And you're out of breath. Don't take it so badly. It was only my wedding present to the bride and groom." Hywel would have hit him with the silver cross if Lord Kirkland hadn't arrived, pushing through the crowds that swarmed around them. He clapped Gruffydd on the back and wiped tears of laughter from his eyes.

"Gruffydd, you're a rogue. I haven't enjoyed myself so much for years. You mustn't be angry with him." He tapped Hywel on the chest with his cane. "He's done me many a good service. Come, give him your hand." Gruffydd extended his hand with an apologetic smile and a dangerous glint in his eye.

"Never!" Hywel lowered behind his bushy eyebrows.

"Take it. Or by God I'll throw you back in prison." Hywel started guiltily. For a second the old martyr's urge stirred within him and he yearned for the consoling darkness of Aberystwyth gaol. Then he thought of Kirkland patronage and decided he owed it to the valley's salvation. He would compromise with the fiend for now, the better to destroy him later. Hywel stretched out his hand.

"Welcome home, brother," Gruffydd said with a grin and squeezed until Hywel's joints cracked.

CHAPTER TWENTY-FOUR

I

MADLEN STROLLED WITH a single candle-flame through the darkened halls and long corridors of Brithgoed, pulling dusty sheets off long-forgotten velvet-covered furniture, making a mental inventory of everything she now owned. The house was quiet as the grave but she was not in the least nervous. This place had been destined for her. Nothing could harm her now. Tomorrow she would change it all, she decided, choosing her own bedroom and the shade of pink brocade in which it should be papered. New staff would be engaged. County society had to be invited. Her silk night-gown—so recently Maude's—billowed behind her, caressing her skin like a warm evening breeze.

Lord Kirkland's frustrated voice thudded through the walls. He was calling her. He had drunk and talked too much over dinner; now he would expect her wifely attentions. She hurried to his room. What would it be like? She found him repulsive, but sharing his bed was the price she had to pay. It was vital that she should. He was expecting an heir from her.

Ffowlke was sprawled against the four-poster, soiled breeches around his ankles and his arm half out of his gold-embroidered wedding coat. His bald bullet head was apoplectic from struggling with the laces of his whalebone corsets, below which empty folds of nether-belly spilled out over his privates, hiding them completely. He looked like some ferocious eunuch.

"Don't stand gaping," he snapped. "You've seen a naked man before, haven't you?"

Madlen helped him with the stays and pulled the breeches off over his silver-buckled shoes. His body was a sallow, dirty white. Grime was embedded in the folds of his stomach. A stench of stale sweat and wine, mixed with snuff and strong perfumes, stuck in her throat. Her stomach was heaving as Ffowlke leered at her breasts. Unconsciously she pulled her night-gown together. As she pulled off his last garter and stocking, he lunged at her, tearing the delicate fabric immediately, his hands like meat-hooks clawing at her flesh with jagged, unfiled finger-nails. He asked no permission and showed no respect, going straight for her thighs like a drover prodding a promising heifer. He pushed her onto the bed and clambered up between her legs with huge heaves on the bed-post. His massive weight suffocated her, shoved her down into the feather quilt until she gasped for breath. He was oblivious to her as he fumbled desperately with his flaccid pizzle against her inert body.

"Help me, for God's sake," he exploded. "Hasn't Gruffydd taught you anything? Don't you know any tricks?"

She'd no idea it would be like this. Gentry were meant to behave differently. She lay rigid beneath Ffowlke's heaving body and tried to think of anything other than what was happening to her. She tried to imagine her son who would grow up as the future lord of this house and all its great estates, but he had no face that she could see. He was less real to her than a dream. Would he be any consolation to her when he was born? Was it worth going through this torment just to dress in silk and eat off silver? Gruffydd shouldn't have let her do it. He should have taken her to China or the New World sooner than let her go through this humiliation. Where was he now—with what new woman? She watched the moonshine falling onto the drapes of the four-poster and Mihangel's black eyes stared back at her balefully from behind the diamond-paned windows. They always would.

II

Rachel unbuttoned her white bridal gown while Iolo was looking the other way. "I shall never forgive you for breaking your vow to me."

"I had to," Iolo protested in an unhappy whisper. "Your father insisted. Lord Kirkland asked especially." Hywel and Rhiannon were sleeping beside the fire, leaving the loft to the young couple for their wedding night. Iolo was crippled with embarrassment at having them so close, within earshot. He'd offered to go into the barn. Hywel had been shocked.

"A Christian marriage must be consummated in a Christian bed," he'd said, "not amidst the filth of animals." Iolo hadn't mentioned the Nativity. He hadn't given their wedding night a moment's thought until then. Of course, Rachel would expect him to be a husband to her. He'd imagined their marriage as a series of prayers and Bible-readings. He stared into the oyster-shell lamp and wondered if Mari was thinking of him now, then he turned back to Rachel as if he'd committed adultery in his heart already. She'd let her hair down. Her dress was open over her white, bony chest. Her pale face looked terrified.

"What do you want me to do, Iolo? I'm your wife now." She was so scared and he hadn't even noticed. She knew she had a duty to fulfil this night, and any other night Iolo chose. Hywel had indicated that much. She knew what that duty was. She'd seen cows and horses breeding often enough, though she never understood how God could have condemned His highest creation to the same indignity. She was determined not to fail in this trial but she had no idea how to go about it. Iolo just sat on the end of the bed, brooding. "Please help me, Iolo." Her voice was hoarse with anxiety.

"I'm sorry," he said guiltily. "Let's sleep, shall we?"

"No." Rachel was near tears. "I know what I have to do, but you don't want me, do you?"

"That's not true." He was lying and ashamed of it. He held her clumsily by her arms. "You're very attractive." It sounded preposterous, so he kissed her hastily before she could answer.

Rhiannon couldn't sleep. She found it hard to associate Rachel in any way with the noises that were coming from the loft. They disturbed her, in every way. Her thighs were damp with thinking of Gruffydd, imagining his powerful, tender arms holding up her buttocks to him. She'd never feel them again, would never see that warm, amused smile on his face. Perhaps she'd never know any man again. Hywel had shown little interest in her body since his return, whether he was too old or too absorbed in the business of salvation she couldn't make out. Not that she wanted him. She found his religious fervour repellent now. It was childish, unmanly, and it concerned no one but himself. How soundly he slept. His loud snoring had settled into deep, measured breathing, punctuated by an occasional sigh. His flushed face, in the fading firelight, wore the pouting, beatific smile of a baby. His lips were moist. Rhiannon stared up at the shadows dancing in wild patterns across the raftered ceiling. At least she had loved. It didn't last long. But she had loved him, and he had loved her. She was sure of that. Gruffydd loved her. If only she had been braver . . .

Hywel sat bolt upright without warning. "In God's name, leave this place!" Rhiannon shook him by the shoulder. Hywel woke with a dazed expression, looked round and groaned.

"I was dreaming of the conjurer."

"Curious. So was I."

"What's that noise?" It sounded like rats.

"What do you think?" Rhiannon said, exasperated. He'd managed to sleep through it all.

"Oh." Hywel frowned and glanced at the loft. "Have they been at it long?"

"How should I know?" Rhiannon snapped. "I've been asleep." She could feel Hywel lying awake beside her, listening. After half an hour he gingerly put a hand on her waist and moved it downwards.

"I'm asleep," she grumbled, pretending she hadn't understood. She preferred to dream of Gruffydd than be satisfied by Hywel.

"Of course. Of course." Hywel was embarrassed. "I just thought . . ." He sighed. Within a few seconds the contented snoring resumed.

III

Morgan's Inn at Pendre had blazed all night with the flames of a hundred rush tapers shining high above the Ystwyth like the light-house on the cliffs of Llanrhystud. Two hours before dawn Llewelyn Tapster was still fending off impatient cries for more ale with a cheerful "The sooner you get it, the sooner you'll piss it out again." He could scarcely move for all the bodies strewn around the floor in various stages of sleep and inebriation. The far end of the low, oak-beamed room was shrouded in a haze of ale fumes, smoke from the log-fire and steam from several score of sweating, shouting, laughing customers. No different from any other winter night. Morgan's Inn was the warmest place in the valley, more comfortable by far than the dark hovels that most of the villagers lived in. As soon as the snows came, Gwilym the swarthy crofter had brought his wife, baby son and two sheep down from the top and hadn't moved for a week, except to empty his bladder.

"Make way!" Llewelyn shouted, carrying half a dozen frothing mugs above his head.

"Nowhere to move to," Rolo Blacksmith grunted, one arm sprawled around his old enemy Siôn Edmunds, the other round Dic Richards' daughter Rhonwen, whom he was thinking of marrying if the cold killed his present wife, as expected. Llewelyn put one foot between Rolo's beefy legs and then tripped on the way to the next vacant patch of floor, landing somewhere around the groin of paunchy Joshua Cae Glas. He teetered on through the maze of limbs till he reached Gruffydd, propped up against Thomas Jenkins in the place of honour to the right of the fire.

339

"Sorry," Llewelyn said with his fatuous grin. The mugs were half-empty.

"No matter," Gruffydd said drowsily. He'd had too much already. As far as he could remember he'd talked for two hours, sometime around midnight, about bringing Iolo back from the dead and then persuaded one or two villagers to help Iolo on the next drove, but he couldn't recall who they were. Nor would anyone else tomorrow. He desperately wanted to sleep. The day had gone on too long. Too much had happened, too fast. His head was churning with conflicting impressions, triumph curdled with bitter regrets. Faces he half-recognized pushed forward, thrust themselves into his with questions, congratulations and requests that he couldn't hear, let alone understand. Thomas Jenkins babbled unceasingly at his side, not noticing when Gruffydd dozed off on his shoulder. Gruffydd never slept for long. As soon as his eyes closed he saw Madlen lying between silk sheets with John Ffowlke on top of her. He woke with a shudder, calling for more beer. But it wasn't Ffowlke that Gruffydd was jealous of. Ffowlke was obscenely alive and Madlen hated him with a vengeance. No, Ffowlke was in their grasp. He could never seriously come between Gruffydd and Madlen, in business or in love. It was Mihangel whom Gruffydd would envy for the rest of his life. Mihangel, whom Madlen had loved, if only for a night, and would go on loving year after year. Mihangel, who was dead and happy in the knowledge that he'd been loved, leaving Gruffydd tortured by never-ending doubts.

His son would own this valley, he reminded himself, but it didn't scare away the nightmare galloping through his head. Another time he saw Rhiannon, her face distorted, larger than life, standing on top of a Calvinist chapel with a silver cross held in both hands across her breast. The chapel was built out of the bodies of Cwmystwyth men, all lying face up, Iolo on top of them all.

"Come down," he screamed at her. She shook her head. Then she froze like a Church Madonna. He knew he'd never be able to touch her again and an aching sense of loss woke him.

"Oh, Thomas," he groaned. Thomas Jenkins broke off his story about the three-legged billy-goat. "I've had this terrible dream . . ." Gruffydd stopped, realizing there was no one here, or anywhere, to whom he could tell his dreams. He had lost or sold all his closest friends. The people here distracted him for a while: he couldn't bear to be alone. But he didn't love them any more, and he certainly didn't trust them.

He tried to match his murderers with the jovial men drinking with him now. Many of them had been there, pushing him down into the snow. They wouldn't hesitate to try and kill him again. They might have torn him apart instead of Mihangel. Why should that surprise him? He'd known from birth that they would turn to burning and killing if things went wrong. They had murdered his father and drowned dozens of old women as witches when harvests failed. Why should he expect them to have changed?

Because of seven years' prosperity, he might have thought, seven years of working together for the common good. All his achievement had been destroyed in a few weeks. The dragon had broken loose just when he'd thought it tamed. He would pick up the shreds of his work now, rebuild the mill, restore the tannery, put up new sheds for the herds . . . But it would be different this time. Gruffydd's old beliefs were bled dry, old hopes crushed out of him. The drudgery was to come. He would need Ffowlke's authority, through Madlen, constantly behind him to bludgeon opponents into acquiescence. Common consent was too much to expect now. He'd spoken every speech and pleaded every appeal he could think of. His words had drifted through their heads like foam on the tide. Enthusiasm was not enough.

It would be easy to blame Mihangel for everything, but it wasn't his fault. He had only released what was there all along. It was Gruffydd who let it build to a head. He missed Mihangel as if he'd been a son. He remembered vividly their first meeting, the black-eyed boy saying, "May I be your apprentice?" Something had gone terribly wrong. They had worked so closely, for so long . . . Gruffydd had no idea what was going on inside him. Why hadn't Mihangel told him? He wouldn't have minded him setting up on his own. . . . But was that true? He had depended on Mihangel and hadn't given him the credit he deserved. What was he going to do without him? In his deepest conscience Gruffydd couldn't lay to rest a suspicion that the wrong man had died three days ago in the snow. Mihangel was more a conjurer than Gruffydd was or would ever be. Why had he led them on till they killed him? But the more Gruffydd thought of that day, the less either of them seemed responsible for its outcome. What he remembered most clearly were the faces in the crowd. Not any one in particular—he couldn't distinguish them then and he couldn't now. Those faces were identical, each filled with the same expectation, the same demand that blood be spilled to placate some spirit of misfortune that had settled over the valley. Which of them died—Gruffydd or Mihangel—was immaterial. One had to be sacrificed.

Gruffydd lurched through the morass of sleeping bodies to get some fresh air. Whatever he did they would still need a victim, and the longer it was denied them the more violent they would become. It would be Gruffydd's turn next. It seemed to him now that he'd always known this. He'd escaped three times: on leaving, on returning and on trying to leave again, but he was not invulnerable. Whatever spirits he conjured would one day break his spell and devour him. If he wielded power it would consume him. If he swam with the Leviathan he must expect to become its prey. Curiously this didn't alarm or depress him. Gambling with the inevitable appealed to him.

Gruffydd stared through the inevitable mists of daybreak at the huge, black outline of Grogwynion above him. So that's what you meant, he thought. That's what you meant when you gave me the stone amulet up there, as we were leaving.

He heard his old, exhausted father's voice and felt his crooked fingers press the stone amulet into the palm of his hand. "As long as you wear this, you will not die until you have stood here again."

"Why didn't I understand?" Gruffydd said aloud, as though his father's spirit were listening from the craggy rock. "That wasn't just a blessing. You gave me no choice but to return. I couldn't die until I'd done so, and once I'd returned, the amulet lost its power. You knew I'd never leave here again. I would die here unprotected. Did you foresee all this?" Gruffydd shivered and pulled his cloak tighter around him. A freezing wind blew up the Ystwyth, sending the mist swirling skyward, laying bare the valley at one stroke from the mines to Hafod, beneath a crystal-blue sky.

The words of an old song drifted over from Morgan's Inn to where he stood on a snow-covered knoll. First carried by one voice only— Old Isaac's, Gruffydd guessed, by its cracked, faltering falsetto—then swelled by dozens more as the small, half-timbered cottage came alive to the morning.

> *Will you come to the woods? said Dibin to Dobin,*
> *Will you come to the woods? said Richard to Robin . . .*

Then the chorus rang out like the baying of hounds:

> *What shall we do there?*
> *Hunt the little wren!*

The door of the tavern opened and the villagers came out one by one. Some already carried staves and wood-bills. One or two brandished a rusty pistol or musket. Others ransacked Morgan's farmyard for pitch-forks, cudgels, anything they could lay their hands on.

Gruffydd suddenly remembered—it was the day after Christmas, the day of the wren-hunt. The wren was believed to be the King of Birds, despite its diminutive size and drab brown plumage, perhaps because it had such a resonant, clear song and made itself heard above larger birds even when it couldn't be seen. At all other times of the year the wren was protected by its own royalty. To harm it was sacrilege. It could bring nothing but bad luck. But on this one day the wren captured by stealth the previous day had to be carried in procession throughout the valley for all to jeer at it. Hunting the wren, they called it.

On a pole slung between their shoulders, Huw Lloyd and Rolo brought out a tiny house in which the wren was imprisoned, a wooden replica of any Welsh cottage with hatch-windows and a door, coloured garlands draped over the roof like thatch. It could easily have been carried in one hand, yet Huw and Rolo were bending under its weight as if bowed with grief and unable to bear such a massive burden as the King of Birds. Gruffydd had seen his own father do exactly the same.

"Come and lead us on, Gruffydd," Rolo called up to him. "We must hunt the wren today."

"Ay, ay," Old Isaac said. "Blood must be shed today if it's not to flow in the New Year. The King must be killed to save us all."

Gruffydd shivered with a chilly sense of foreknowledge. If it weren't the wren, it would be him. He ran down and led the hunt forward to the beat of drums and the clanging of iron. Occasionally he looked over his shoulder. The stalker could so easily become the quarry. Gruffydd could never again forget it.

September 1753

CHAPTER TWENTY-FIVE

I

GRUFFYDD PEERED THROUGH the lattice window of the clerestory down into Lord Kirkland's private chapel where the congregation was already assembling. He had a perfect view and settled down in the hidden chamber to watch. He'd often noticed the narrow passage that led to it—a mere cranny at floor level—as he climbed the spiral stone staircase of the Brithgoed bell-tower. He came this way practically every night, as there was a secret door into Madlen's bedroom near the top. No one would disturb him here. He had a clear view of the black marble altar, dominated by a painting of Christ in Jordan so grimy that only the white dove descending stood out clearly; of the carved, double-panelled doors that led to the heart of the mansion, from where the procession would appear; and—most important—of the weather-beaten, granite font in which his son was about to be baptized as heir of Brithgoed and of all the Kirkland titles, lands and revenues in the realms of England, Wales and Scotland.

His ancestors had come into their own at last. He wished he could shout it out loud to all the dignitaries of Church and State, gathered below in their ecclesiastical purples and military scarlets, their golden croziers and silver decorations glinting in the warm autumn sunlight that filtered through the stained-glass Gothic window in narrow shafts which brimmed with tiny particles of dust kicked up by polished boots and jewelled slippers. The Lord Rhys had returned to reclaim the Ystwyth, and all had come to pay him homage. Gruffydd preferred to look down on them. He despised them all and had no desire to rub shoulders with such riff-raff.

"Upstarts, the lot of you," he muttered, listening to the babble of insidious English, which he hadn't heard for years. "If any of you were ever Welsh, you've forgotten it. My son will weed you out. He'll scatter the chaff to the four winds . . ."

It would have been most unwise for Gruffydd to have been seen in Brithgoed today. The last few months had not been easy. Talbot had questioned the child's paternity and fought his brother from the county courts to the House of Lords. Madlen had kept to her bed for the last twelve weeks and managed to prolong her pregnancy by a fortnight, making such a fuss at her delivery that the midwives swore she must be in labour before her time. Gruffydd had helped with constipants that he found in Mihangel's medicine chest. In the end all their efforts made little difference. Their lordships reasoned that any peer should be the judge of his own wife's honour. If Lord Kirkland was satisfied, so were they. Talbot's case was thrown out. He'd paid Madlen several visits since then, ostensibly to make his peace. Madlen never let the baby out of her sight, on Gruffydd's advice. If Owain had been neglected, her second son would be smothered with every possible attention.

Gruffydd growled to himself as Talbot entered the chapel flanked by Sir Lewis Pryse, who moved away from the loser at the first opportunity, and Thomas Powell, whose debauched and prematurely ravaged face was powdered and pomaded beyond recognition. Gruffydd was tempted to lean more heavily on the stone cornice at his elbow and despatch all three of them at once. The sound of footsteps echoed up the spiral staircase and Gruffydd squeezed farther out of sight. Two heavy, mud-stained boots dashed by just above his head, then returned slowly step by step. I know those boots, Gruffydd thought. But he's only been gone a month. He should be in England still. As the boots passed again Gruffydd leaned out and tapped them with his forefinger. Iolo looked down, saw nothing. Gruffydd tapped again. Iolo fell on one knee and peered into the hidden recess.

"There you are!"

"You're back," Gruffydd cried as loud as he dared, pulling Iolo down beside him through the narrow stone conduit. "How did you get on? What are you doing here? Who told you how to find me?"

"Madlen." Iolo grinned. "She said you'd be here." He was sunburnt, more open and more relaxed than Gruffydd had ever seen him. He was bursting to tell his news.

"How did you get to see Madlen?"

"Delivering Ffowlke his dues. I made his day." Gruffydd watched him eagerly. This was the second drove on which Iolo had taken the whole valley's herds. The last one, eight months ago, had raised just enough money to pay off Ffowlke's overdue rents, with nothing to spare. This drove, the second, was crucial. All Gruffydd's plans for the valley depended on it.

"Well?" Gruffydd exploded. Iolo was deliberately tormenting him with a long, dejected expression. "How much have you brought back?" Iolo pulled his hands out of the pockets of his leather jerkin and tossed Gruffydd two huge leather pouches.

348

"Eight hundred guineas." He watched Gruffydd's incredulous expression with huge amusement. He'd been trying to imagine it all the way back from Hereford. "After the rents."

"How did you do it?" Gruffydd was almost angry with pride. His poor opinion of Iolo had taken a buffeting this year. He couldn't get used to the idea of lack-lustre Iolo as the most successful, most respected businessman of the valley. Now this was the last straw. Iolo had just handed him a fortune. Everything Gruffydd had ever dreamt of building could now be built without driving the community to the verge of starvation to achieve it. "Don't just stand there, tell me how you did it, you cocky bastard."

"Shouldn't use that word on a day like this." Iolo glanced down into the chapel where his baby brother was about to make his debut. Gruffydd suddenly relaxed. He was glad Iolo knew. They had no secrets from each other now. The awkwardness of these years in Cwmystwyth, the mistrust and animosity, had vanished. They were equals again, for the first time since Iolo's childhood.

"I hear you're making me a grandfather," Gruffydd said as they sat side by side in the alcove. It was rumoured Rachel was pregnant.

"I have already." Iolo blushed and pretended to examine the congregation below.

"What do you mean?"

"Here." Iolo pressed something into Gruffydd's hand. "For God's sake don't let Rachel see it." Gruffydd looked down—it was the stone amulet his father had given him, the leather thong still dangling through the hole in one end. So Iolo had visited Mari again. Gruffydd couldn't help laughing. Iolo was following his father's wicked example, despite Hywel's pieties.

"Boy or a girl?"

"Girl. Mari called her Elen."

"Good name. Sure she's yours?"

"As sure as any man can be." Iolo had misjudged Mari. Among all the people he'd trusted and who had betrayed him, she stood out as the one who had helped him without any thought of gain, only to be betrayed by him. She had haunted him across the countryside on his first big drove. Only the vision of Hywel breathing hell-fire had stopped him from visiting her. His route passed three miles north of her farm. By the autumn she had become an obsession. Surely Hywel had been wrong to stop him fulfilling his promise to her? How could Hywel call her a whore without ever seeing her? Iolo had pondered this on his next drove, the wind-swept grassy uplands exposing to his mind the narrowness of Hywel's philosophy that rejected so much of the good in this world in the name of salvation. Iolo had felt responsible for Mari and it was not right to discard her. As he approached Erwood on the home run, well-mounted and with his profits jangling at his belt, he could resist his own instinct no longer. If it damned him eternally, he would see Mari. Just see her. Nothing more.

Mari had leaned on her shovel, in the potato-patch that Iolo had dug for her, and smiled ruefully, without reproach.

"I knew you'd be back."

"How? How did you know?" Without any further greeting she'd taken him to the cowshed. Next to Pedr, the runt he'd left with Mari, nestled Betsi, whom Iolo had rescued from the butcher in Hereford and abandoned when he fled the circus with Hywel. Beside her was sleeping his black and white shaggy mongrel bitch, Cadwal.

"Lord knows how they found their way here," Mari had said, "but whatever idea brought them back to me was sure to bring you too; sooner or later." Then she'd taken Iolo to the cot by the fire where his next surprise was waiting. He'd stayed for one night only, enough to make him never want to leave. He would be back, twice yearly, he knew that, and he refused to feel guilty. After all, he had been married to Mari before Rachel, in a way . . .

Gruffydd rattled the gold in the leather pouches.

"You'll need some of this, now you're a family man."

"Not much." Iolo wasn't interested in the money, as long as he could go on droving. "There's one condition, though."

"Oh?"

"I want enough of that money for Hywel to build a chapel."

"No," Gruffydd said flatly.

"We'll talk about it." No point in arguing now. Gruffydd had no choice. Iolo was well aware of his new power and he wouldn't be afraid to use it as he saw fit.

"There he is, the black beetle," Gruffydd pointed at the altar where Hywel was in earnest conversation with a bishop wearing a mitre and jewel-studded vestments. "Crawling to his superiors. What does he want?"

"To be ordained, I think."

The bishop brushed Hywel aside with his pastoral staff and Gruffydd laughed.

"Well, he's not getting far."

"That's because he's Welsh," Iolo said with cold sarcasm. "And he wasn't educated at an English college." Gruffydd fell silent, the first time he'd felt any sympathy for Hywel. The preacher retreated to a corner behind the font, head stubbornly thrown back and lips pursed in anger, muttering something out of the corner of his mouth. Gruffydd craned his neck, trying to see who he was speaking to. Rhiannon. He hadn't seen her since Iolo's wedding. His heart turned in excitement, then it practically stopped altogether.

"She's pregnant," he said.

"Who? Rhiannon?" Iolo watched his father curiously, remembering the odd way Rhiannon had talked of Gruffydd and he of her. "Yes. Very near her time, I should think. I'm surprised Hywel let her come out." Gruffydd stared at the protuberance in Rhiannon's belly and made some rapid calculations. How would he ever know? It could be his. But how could he allow a child of his to be fostered by Hywel Bevan?

"Why shouldn't she be pregnant?" Iolo asked, guessing at least half the truth.

"Hush. They're coming." This one secret Gruffydd couldn't share even with Iolo, for Rhiannon's sake.

The great double doors swung wide. The procession advanced, led by Lord Kirkland, wearing the ermine mantle and carrying the full regalia of a peer of the realm. Beside him Madlen glittered in a silver brocade gown. Her hair was piled high in minute ringlets that had taken hours to set, held up with jewelled pins and topped by the simple gold coronet of a viscountess. Her startling aristocratic pallor—from her long confinement and ample white powder—was charmingly set off by a black beauty spot on her left cheek-bone. She looked neither to left nor to right, her dignified, unsmiling expression revealed none of the wild elation she felt. Her breasts heaved against the low, ribbed bodice which barely held them in. A murmur of appreciation ran round the chapel as she entered.

"Wouldn't they love to be where we are?" Gruffydd muttered, gazing straight down the frontage of her dress. Lord and Lady Kirkland came to a halt opposite their guests. Innumerable respects and courtesies were exchanged. One by one the gentry of Cardiganshire and beyond came forward to greet and congratulate the new, mysterious and radiantly beautiful Lady Kirkland, about whom so much interesting scandal had been spread before she had been introduced into society. Without her ever having been presented there, her name was now well known in Westminster and at the Court of St James's, where most of those here present could never hope to be seen, let alone talked about.

Madlen thought her legs would give way beneath her. Etiquette required a deep curtsy for many of the guests—she had memorized exactly which ones during long, tedious, bedridden weeks—after which she had to lift not only herself, but five layers of petticoats, side-hoops of bent wood and whalebone, and sixty feet of pleated French brocade. She'd been offered two maids to assist her, but indignantly refused. Her main worry now was that the black dye on her eyelashes would run. She was sweating copiously.

The procession advanced to the font and peeled away to each side of it. Last of all, almost as an oversight, a buxom, white-dressed wet-nurse waddled in with the baby. He was screaming for all he was worth.

"Good for you," Gruffydd said delighted. "I'd do just the same if I were down there." Madlen looked less pleased. So did the Bishop of St David's, who held the infant throughout a rambling address, of which Gruffydd caught nothing. He did notice, however, that at one point during the service, Madlen's and Rhiannon's eyes met and Rhiannon, with a strange, quiet smile of victory, ran her hand over her belly. Madlen turned away abruptly and never looked at her sister again.

At the climax of the ceremony the baby suddenly fell silent, as if listening. Gruffydd heard the old, drooping bishop pronounce, in a crisp voice that belied his years:

"I baptize you John Talbot Caversham Ffowlke."